DEUS EX
BL△CK LIGHT™

ALSO AVAILABLE FROM TITAN BOOKS

Deus Ex: Icarus Effect
by James Swallow

The Art of Deus Ex Universe
by Paul Davies, Jonathan Jacques-Belletête,
and Martin Dubeau

Deus Ex Universe: Children's Crusade
graphic novel by Alex Irvine and John Aggs

DEUS EX
BLACK LIGHT™

James Swallow

TITAN BOOKS

Deus Ex: Black Light
Print edition ISBN: 9781785651205
E-book edition ISBN: 9781785651212

Published by Titan Books
A division of Titan Publishing Group Ltd
144 Southwark St, London SE1 0UP

First edition: August 2016
10 9 8 7 6 5 4 3 2 1

A CIP catalogue record for this title is available from the British Library.

Printed and bound by CPI Group (UK) Ltd, Croydon, CR0 4YY

SQUARE ENIX

ONE

"How much do you remember?"

It was a woman's voice, careful and steady, metered with just the right balance of maternal concern and authoritative firmness.

He opened his mouth to speak, but all that came out was a dry, papery rasp. It was difficult, as if the act of using his voice had become foreign to him. He gave up on the attempt and tried something else. He tried to focus on the woman's words, to find her in the room.

"Take your time," she told him – then an order, to someone else. "Give him some water."

An infinite white space surrounded everything, blurred bright but without dazzling his eyes, and if not for the warmth and the stillness of the air he could have believed he was on some expanse of frozen tundra, stretching away to an unseen horizon. At the edges of his vision, trains of golden icons trickled down, vanishing one after another. He half-raised his hand to wipe them away, as if they were raindrops

7

caught on his eyelashes, before remembering that they were being projected directly into his synthetic retinas.

The hand and the arm it belonged to ghosted up before him. Black as a shadow, the fingers moving, twitching. It fell away again, and he understood that he was lying in a bed, the pull of gravity holding him down. The tundra was a ceiling high above, out of reach, and by degrees he felt himself shifting upwards as a mechanism behind the mattress raised his torso to a shallow incline.

Other ghosts came into sight. The sketches of human figures.

He flinched at the sight of strangers, the echo of a fight-or-flight reaction triggered by something he didn't immediately recollect. It was the dying ember of another memory, gone before he could grasp it. It left him unsettled and wary.

A robotic manipulator drifted closer, proffering a squeeze bottle of clear liquid, and he leaned forward to meet it, letting a nozzle hook his lip. Cool, fresh water whispered into his arid mouth, a faint medicinal taste washing over his tongue. It was like he hadn't taken a drink in centuries, and for a long moment he just let himself enjoy the simple pleasure of it.

But then the flow of the fluid touched a different fragment of recall. Suddenly he was drowning in icy salt water, the cold filling his throat and his lungs, the impossible force crushing him like the fingers of a giant hand. He choked and spat out the liquid, gasping and retching, shock throwing him forward. Wires hanging from sensor disks on his throat and his chest pulled taut, others tearing away, sending contradictory signals to the monitoring devices crowded at the head of the bed.

A tidal wave of absolute panic crashed over him, the brutal and unstoppable force ripping away all his defenses, crushing his will in an instant. He knew that this was death pressing in on him, knew it without question because he had been through it before, *more than once*.

The first time, it had been a cauldron of razors and fire, ripping pieces of him away within and without, changing once and for all what he would be. He had survived that. *Barely*.

The second time, it was cold and pressure threatening to crush him into oblivion and leave nothing behind.

He remembered some of it now. Not a distinct chronology of events, not second by second, but flashes of action disconnected from one another. A random pattern of blinding, painful moments held together like pearls on a string.

The shrieking of tortured metal under the impact of a colossal volume of polar ocean. The wild screams of the mad and the dying. The thunder of his fading heartbeat. Lances of light through glassy, shifting waters. And a terrible knowing, a certainty that he would die out there and *nothing* would stop that from happening.

I should be dead. The thought grew, sharp and diamond-hard.

His artificial eyes adjusted steadily, the color tone of the room shifting as it gained greater definition. Digging deep, he reached past the fear and found the steel that had never left him. Took it, held on to it.

The next breath was rough, but it was controlled. By force of will, he moderated his ragged breathing and concentrated on calming his racing pulse. In the corner of his vision, a softly blinking warning icon faded to nothing as the hammering of his heart subsided. Sweat beaded on his flesh, and he swallowed hard.

"I remember the sea." They were the first words he had spoken in months. "The cold."

"You're very lucky to be alive," said another voice. A man, this one, the accent behind it a firm northwestern burr while the woman had sounded more like a southerner. Those facts emerged in his thoughts automatically, some ingrained means in his mind immediately sifting their words for data, for *clues*.

He blinked again and now he could see them better. The woman, of average height with a dark face framed by a white headscarf; the man pale and fatigued. Both of them wore doctor's coats and cradled digital pads in their hands. At their shoulders, a small monitor drone the size of a softball floated on a cluster of whispering impellers, patiently framing everything in the room with a blue-tinted lens.

The woman tried on a practiced smile. "You were clinically deceased when they plucked you out of the ocean. But a combination of the chill and the actions of your Sentinel implant kept you from going beyond our reach. They were able to pull you back."

"A lot of other people weren't so fortunate," said the male doctor, and there was an edge of reproach to the words.

He settled back against the mattress, pushing the squeeze bottle away, uncertain how to respond. His thoughts were still churning and disordered, and when he closed his eyes all he saw was a torrent of jumbled recollections that had no sense of order or narrative. He looked down again at his hands, his arms. Both of them were identical, carbon-black synthetic constructs that terminated at his shoulder joints. Once they had been smooth and polished, but now they were scarred and pitted with surface damage. He tried to remember the time before he'd had them, but for now there was a blank space where any memory of meat and bone might have once existed.

Touching his bare chest, he found healed scars but again, nothing to connect them to. The part of him that was flesh felt almost as artificial as the metal and plastic.

"Is there anything else?" said the woman. "Anything more you remember?"

"*Darrow*." Unbidden, the name floated up to the surface of his consciousness and drifted there.

The two doctors exchanged a look, a silent communication passing between them. "Do you know who that is?" she asked.

"He died up there." Past the pair of them, the wall came into sharper focus and it was suddenly clear that he was looking out of a window on to a snow-covered landscape. The near-absence of color in the surroundings, the room, the people before him, it knocked loose another shard of recall and he remembered being in a different white room. Someone there had been important to him. The memory brought with it a bitter sting of emotions that he could not parse. He shook his head, forcing the moment away.

"Can you tell us?"

"My name is Adam Jensen," he said, cutting down the question as his impatience flared. "I remember who I am. But not where the hell *this* is."

Within a day, the two doctors – the woman was named Rafiq and the man McFadden – decided he was lucid enough to leave the recovery room and move to the facility proper. They described it as a place to heal, but it wasn't like any hospital Jensen had ever spent time in.

Rafiq told Jensen he had been a police officer once, and he recalled pieces of that life, more and more of it as the days passed by.

This place reminded him of the secure wards where, as a cop, he had sent psychologically unstable criminals – not quite a prison, more like an asylum. What that said about how he was seen by his doctors made him uncomfortable.

When Jensen asked them if there was a next-of-kin he could talk to, they told him they had no records of anyone – but he was free to place a vu-phone call to anywhere he wanted. An instinctive reaction that came out of nowhere made him lie; Jensen told them he didn't recall any contacts, but that wasn't true. He just didn't want them listening in on any communications he made. As for his infolink implant, that stayed resolutely offline, doubtless disabled along with anything else that might have made him troublesome.

Facility 451 was a collection of prefabricated modules that had been assembled into an unlovely pile of blocky shapes, and parked out in the sparse landscape of the Kenai Peninsula. Two decades of unrestricted corporate exploitation and rampant pollution had turned this part of Alaska from carpet of forest into a bleak shadow of its former self, a naked space of half-dead scrubland coated with gray, polluted snow. Remote and thinly populated, the World Health Organization had chosen it as one of a dozen sites for places like 451. They called them 'processing clinics', but as Jensen walked the limits of its corridors and high fences, he found himself thinking of other, less palatable ways to describe it.

There were people here from all ethnicities, all walks of life, and a broad spectrum of ages and backgrounds. There was only one common denominator: everybody had an augmentation of some kind, from replacement limbs to cyberoptics or neural implants.

The character of the clinic's residents was the kind of forced-together, beaten-down community he had seen in skid row districts and shantytowns, or the enviro-refugee camps in the Kansas dustbowl and the flood zones down in Florida. At first, the other 'processees' – no-one ever called them *patients* or *inmates* – kept their distance from him, leaving Jensen to eat alone in the cavernous cafeteria or walk in silence around the yard during the hours of weak daylight.

And that was okay. He needed the space and the time to get his head straight. To put everything that he could remember into some semblance of order. It came slowly for the most part, now and then in jagged fits and starts. Reminiscence was strange that way. Fragment by fragment, Jensen reassembled himself. McFadden told him blankly that he had been in a comatose state for months, and he personally had never expected Jensen to recover. *A man doesn't cheat death twice*, said the doctor.

"Beg to differ," Jensen said aloud, answering the memory. His breath made a puff of white vapor that escaped into the air.

"What's that?"

He turned as someone came walking his way, deck shoes that were way too light for this chill climate crunching on frost-covered asphalt. Jensen saw a stout man with a round face and the kind of deep, leathery tan you only get from a lifetime of working outside. He had the fuzz of an ill-kept beard and a bald, slightly uneven head. Jensen stood taller than the new arrival, and as he met his gaze, he saw the man had natural eyes. Curiosity was clear there, but caution too.

"Nothing important," Jensen told him. "Just thinking out loud."

"Right on." The man wandered to the fence line and placed both his hands on it. Like Jensen, his body was mechanical from shoulders to fingertips. But where Jensen's cybernetic arms were athletic and sleek in design, this guy's augmentations were heavy sleeves of battered metal that resembled parts of a construction vehicle scaled down to human size. Thick hands with an additional thumb each side made claws and held on to the chain links of the fence. The metal barrier creaked audibly under his grip. "Some view," he added.

"Better without the fence," Jensen replied.

"I heard that," the man replied with feeling, then turned and offered him a handshake, as if his reply had been the right answer to some unspoken question. "Folks call me Stacks. You're Jensen, right?"

He accepted the gesture. "You know me?"

Stacks nodded toward the clinic, where two orderlies in heavy parkas had gathered to watch the pair of them, another monitor drone circling lazily over their heads. "Heard them say your name."

Jensen studied the orderlies. He'd seen the stunner truncheons they carried and the Buzzkill tasers in their quick-draw holsters. Why the WHO needed armed guards in a place for healing people was a question that nobody had a good answer for. But then again, none of the orderlies had visible enhancements of any kind. Being around so many augmented people had to make them nervous. He looked away. "West Coast, right? Where you're from?"

The other man broke into a brief grin. "You got it. Tell that from how I talk?" He didn't wait for Jensen to reply. "Yeah, from Seattle. Lived there my whole life, until…" A shadow passed over his face. "Well, y'know. I was a steeplejack. Building towers and alla that. What about you?"

"I used to be a cop."

Stacks nodded again. "I figured. You got the look." He paused, clearly framing his next words. "People are wonderin'. They ain't seen you before, then here you are. Questions getting asked."

"Let me guess, you drew the short straw. *Go talk to the new guy.*"

He chuckled. "Something like that." He went on: "Most of us have been here a while. Tends to be that folks get rotated out, if they're lucky… But not a lot of fresh faces come in, know what I mean?"

"I really don't," Jensen said, watching him carefully. "New here, like I said."

Stacks eyed him. "Well, not exactly. I mean, you been here a while too, but on ice, yeah? There's a bunch of folks like that, in the coma ward. Never woke up. Not like you. Sleeping beauties, we call 'em."

"McFadden told me I was lucky." A gust of cold wind whipped around Jensen's shoulders. The clinic had provided a thin, military-surplus jacket, and he pulled it close. "I'm not really feeling it."

When Stacks spoke again, his tone shifted. "There's talk about you and the other sleepers. Say you were out there, in the middle of it all when it happened. Right at the heart of the action, up in the Arctic. That so?"

Icy salt water and crushing pressure. He tensed at the memory. "Panchaea." Jensen said the name without thinking. It was as if uttering it opened another floodgate in his memory. He was assailed by a rush of confused images, all of them dominated by a vision of a hole in the ocean, an endless black well into nothingness. He shook off the moment. "Yeah. I was there."

Stacks's face hardened. "Were you *part* of it?"

"No." The answer was as much a lie as it was the truth. Jensen held up his machine hand. "We were *all* part of it, right?"

"Yeah. True enough." The grim cast in the other man's eyes faded. "I... I lost my wife and my daughter that day."

"I'm sorry."

Stacks gave a hollow sigh that seemed to come from miles distant. "So am I."

Jensen changed tack. "How long have you been here?"

"Since it happened." Stacks let go of the fence and stepped away. Jensen saw the orderlies visibly relax. "I lost a lot. Up here." He tapped his temple with a thick metal finger. "Gettin' right takes time, I know that. But I thought I'd be done by now." He shot a look at the two guards and gave them a humorless smile. "They're scared I'm gonna do somethin' crazy. Rip a hole in this here fence and make a run for it."

"Are they right?" Jensen glanced up as the first drops of a dirty rain began to fall.

When Stacks replied, it sounded like he had the weight of the world on his shoulders. "Might just be, one of these days." He started walking. "C'mon. Too damn cold out here, man."

But as Jensen turned to follow him inside, he saw that a third guard had joined the other two. A severe-looking man wearing a data monocle, he scanned the yard and found Jensen. "You," he called out, his voice carrying. "Got a visitor."

Jensen's jaw stiffened. *Who knows I'm here?*

"Don't get your hopes up." He found Stacks looking at him glumly. "Trust me, ain't what you want it to be," he said, reading the question in his gaze. "Not by a long shot."

They took Jensen to a part of the clinic that he had never seen before, a lower level where daylight didn't reach and the sickly glow of florescent lamps made everything look like it was coated in a layer of grimy transparent plastic.

The guard opened a door and Jensen entered a chamber that could only be described as an interrogation room. A cluster of monitoring devices looked down from behind an armored glass bowl set in the middle of ceiling, above a metal table bolted to the tiled floor. On his side of the table, a metal chair. On the other, the same but occupied by a rail-thin woman of average height in a characterless black jacket and trousers. She didn't look up as he walked in, engrossed in the glowing display of a digital pad. The cold color of the screen reflected off a milk-pale face, framed by short, shock-red hair. He spotted the telltale dermal markers of neural implants, and saw that her right hand – delicate and long-fingered like its organic twin – was made of brushed steel. Her manner and her outfit screamed *government agent* to Jensen's ingrained cop instincts.

He dropped into the empty chair without waiting to be asked and rubbed the unkempt stubble on his chin. The woman's gaze flicked up to study him, then back to the digital pad. The quiet between them stretched, and Jensen's lip curled. The silent treatment was one of the first questioning techniques they taught police officers in the academy, that the mere act of saying nothing would sometimes compel a suspect to fill the void with words and maybe incriminate themselves along the way.

But this was amateur hour, and he wasn't in the mood for it. Jensen leaned forward across the table and fixed the woman with a hard eye. "If you're gonna make me wait," he began, "I could use a cup of coffee."

Was that the ghost of a smirk on her face? It was gone before he could be sure, and she flicked one of those long fingers over the surface of the pad. Jensen caught the sound of a high-pitched buzz from beneath the surface of the table, and without warning his right arm slammed down and locked firmly against it, pinned there as if it had been pressed into place by an invisible hand.

There was a thick steel bracelet around his arm; it had been there when he woke up in the recovery room, and Dr. Rafiq had promised him that it was just a medical monitoring unit to keep tabs on his wellbeing. Jensen hadn't bought that for a second, not after he'd seen the same thing on Stacks and all the other residents of 451, but he hadn't figured it would work like an *actual* restraint. Buried in the table, there had to be an electromagnetic generator that was keeping his arm in place. The woman, he noticed, was sitting exactly far enough away to be out of reach of his one free hand.

"All your offensive aug systems were inhibited after your initial recovery," she said, confirming his earlier suspicions. Her accent was mid-American but deliberately colorless. She put the digital pad on the table and produced a wallet from her pocket, unfolding it to present him with a badge and identity card. In the process, Jensen caught a glimpse of the butt of a matte black pistol protruding from an underarm holster. "I'm Agent Jenna Thorne, with Homeland Security."

"Federal Protective Service…" He read the information off the digital ID card. "Thought you guys were just security guards."

The wallet went back into her pocket. "Our mandate has been greatly expanded in the last couple of years."

"Right…" He nodded at the bracelet. "You expecting trouble from me, Agent Thorne?"

"That's part of the job." She glanced up at the monitor cluster, and Jensen saw it rotate to present a different camera head to peer down at him.

He made himself very still. If this woman wanted to play head games, that was fine. She had information that he wanted to know as much as the reverse was true.

"You know why you're here?"

"People tell me it's because I'm lucky."

Thorne went on as if he hadn't spoken. "Facility four-five-one is part of a network of medical clinics set up to help the victims of the Aug Incident reintegrate into society."

Despite himself, Jensen's eyes narrowed. "Is that what they're calling it? An *'incident'*?"

"You name a thing and you rob it of its power, Mr. Jensen," offered Thorne. "Nine-Eleven. The Vilama Superquake. The Cat Fives. The Incident. Give it a name and you can put it in a box, contain it. It's an important coping mechanism. It helps people to rebuild."

"In my experience, it takes a lot more than that."

She nodded. "And you *do* have experience, don't you? More than enough human disasters in your personal narrative. The situation in Mexicantown when you were with Detroit SWAT, the terrorist attack on Sarif Industries—"

"They weren't terrorists," he corrected, then halted. He'd given her an opening, and he retreated from it, trying another approach. "You act like you know a lot about me. Maybe you could help me with something." He tapped a finger on his brow. "Like where I've been for the last year."

Thorne spread her hands. "Here, Mr. Jensen. You've been here, as I understand it, slowly climbing your way back out of the coma you were in when they found you in the Arctic Ocean." She leaned in. "What I'm interested in is where you were *before* you took a swim. What you were doing at the Panchaea facility and what part you played in its collapse."

"I don't recall." But that wasn't true, and they both knew it.

Built as part of an experimental weather modification program, the keystone in a process that would attempt to reverse the creeping trends of global warming, Panchaea was a vast complex rising up from the sea bed, layers of complex systems using current control, iron seeding and dozens of other methods to turn back the clock on the thawing of the polar icepack.

All of it a false front, of course. Jensen didn't doubt that the reasons for building Panchaea, and the people who had the vision to make it happen, were genuine. But others had taken that ideal and used it as a cover for something sinister.

His personal crusade to learn the truth about the attack on Sarif – the attack that had almost killed him – came full circle in the closing months of 2027, as Jensen had journeyed to that hole in the ocean and learned what *really* lurked down there. Thinking machines that used kidnapped human beings as component parts, devices turned to the work of a callous, secretive power group that had been lurking in the shadows of human civilization for centuries.

And with all of that, the fruits of a plan originated by one bitter genius who had been rejected by his greatest discovery. A Frankenstein out to kill his monster. A Daedalus intent on tearing away his wings.

"Were you present when Hugh Darrow died?" Thorne's question was a scalpel, bright and cutting.

"I don't recall," he repeated. But he did. Because he had been there, and he had seen what Darrow had wrought, firsthand.

The man the world had once called the father of human augmentation technology, forever prevented from experiencing his creation himself thanks to a rare genetic disorder, Darrow had devised a scheme that was breathtaking in its scope and its sheer horror. The scientist had engineered a way to reach almost every augmented person on the planet at once, via secretly implanted biochips that triggered a catastrophic neurochemical imbalance – an artificially induced psychotic break. Their fight-or-flight reflexes stimulated beyond all rationality, those affected sank into a haze of temporary madness. In their wake, there was death and destruction that burned cities, shattered lives and tore a ragged wound in society. Darrow wanted to show the world that his creation was a dangerous mistake, to make people fear it – but beneath that, it was his buried spite at being left behind that made him lash out... and millions were still paying the price.

Jensen had been spared, for reasons he still wasn't fully certain of, but people like Stacks, the others in Facility 451 and elsewhere had been forced to endure the plague of madness. Darrow's scheme was cut short, but they were still suffering.

Worse still, the people behind Darrow, the ones who wanted to use his mechanism to *control* rather than *destroy* the augmented… They were still out there.

"After the incident, after all the damage done, it was inevitable that Panchaea would be wrecked… But there is evidence that you were in the core of that facility, just prior to the final collapse of its structural protection systems." Thorne cocked her head, studying him with her blank, doll-like cyberoptic eyes. "What did you see in there? How did you get out when the flood controls went offline?"

"I don't—"

"Recall, yes, so you keep saying," Thorne spoke over him. "Darrow was insane. He got what he deserved. No-one on Earth will question that, not after what happened. But the loss of Panchaea… There's a lot of unresolved issues surrounding that. A lot of blame that until now has been unassigned. Do you follow me?"

"I went there to stop him." The moment the words slipped from his mouth, Jensen regretted the admission. "And I nearly died because of it. That's all I have to tell you."

"Really?" Thorne raised an eyebrow. "So, with Darrow at the bottom of the sea somewhere, we should all just move on? Is that what you think?"

He shifted in his chair, frowning as his arm remained firmly set in place on the table. "You're the one who talked about coping. Rebuilding."

"For that, we need to know who gave Darrow the means to do what he did. The man might have been a billionaire but his resources weren't limitless."

Jensen concentrated on maintaining a neutral

poker face, but it wasn't easy. Pieces of memory kept rising out of the depths of his thoughts when he least expected them, sometimes triggered by a word, a sound or a smell. When Thorne talked about Panchaea, things he might rather have forgotten pressed into his consciousness, fully formed and real.

At first, Jensen had felt a directionless kind of anger burning away inside him. A fury directed at ghosts he couldn't name, couldn't see. But with each passing day, each hour, more and more of it was coming into sharp focus.

Illuminati. The word was ancient, heavy with contradictory meanings, double-speak and fantasy. It was a catch-all term; it conjured up images of cabals stocked with old men intent on running the world, of self-selected elites ruling the lesser masses by guile and force. Decades of sensationalist fiction and half-truths made it seem more legend than reality. Just a scare story, a lunatic conspiracy theory for the credulous.

But the *fiction* was the *fact*. Jensen had learned that through bloody example, in the aftermath of the attack on Sarif Industries and then in the days that followed. While Hugh Darrow's part in the Illuminati's complex web of schemes had ultimately been stopped, the puppeteers holding the man's strings had faded back into the shadows, untouched and unpunished.

"He must have had help," Thorne was saying. "Dangerous allies. People who need to be brought to justice."

They have operatives everywhere. A warning voice sounded in the back of Jensen's thoughts. "Guess you got your work cut out for you, then," he said, after a moment.

The truth was, trust and raw gut instinct were what

had kept Adam Jensen alive in those days after the SI attack. Those instincts were telling him now that Jenna Thorne was not someone he could confide in.

"Tell me what you know." Thorne enunciated each word, coldly and firmly. "Otherwise, I'm going to think you have something to hide, Mr. Jensen. And those issues of blame will need to be considered."

He sensed something odd in the air of the room, a sudden feeling that made the flesh on the back of his neck prickle. Thorne was trying to play him; those cybernetic eyes of hers weren't the only body-mods she had working to read his intentions. Jensen was willing to bet that the agent was also augmented with a social interaction enhancer, an insidious piece of tech that allowed the user to get real-time data from a conversation subject and manipulate them with it, even coerce them with a controlled pheromone release. He wasn't going to fall for that.

"You can think whatever you damn well want," he said, his patience running thin. "But right now, if you're not helping me piece together the blanks in my memory, or walking me out of this place, why the hell should I keep talking?" Jensen leaned back. "I reckon I'm done here."

Thorne seemed like she was about to shoot off some kind of sharp retort, but then she caught herself and reeled it back in. "For now," she told him, and tapped the digital pad again.

The buzzing from beneath the table ceased abruptly and Jensen's arm jerked as it was released. He grimaced, flexing the artificial muscles.

"We're done *for now*," she repeated, and left the room.

* * *

He told himself he was doing it just to keep his mind sharp, to try and conjure up a little of his old skill set, but after another day or two of walking the perimeter of 451, Jensen had the beginnings of an escape plan. It wouldn't be simple, though. There were whole areas of the facility that were off-limits to the processees, and for now he only had rough estimates of guard numbers and security systems.

And then there was the bracelet. He looked down at it as he walked, fingering the surface of the device. Jensen had no doubt it was broadcasting his exact location right that second, and unless he could find a way to spoof its signal or remove the thing entirely, any attempt to leave Facility 451 would be a wasted effort.

No-one here was being told they were a prisoner, but the lack of open doors and the bleak remoteness of the location put the lie to that. Dr. McFadden had said something about the clinic's isolation being for purposes of 'safety', and Jensen had to wonder exactly *whose* safety he was referring to. It didn't take a lot to assume that anyone out beyond the fence line in the wider world, the ones who were not augmented, feared those who were. The 'Incident' had made sure of that.

Jensen scowled at the thought and turned back toward the complex. He caught a glimpse of himself in a window as he passed, the black commas of his eye shield implants framing an angular face and haunted eyes. His beard was unkempt and too long for his liking, and the electric razor they had given him just wasn't enough to tame it. In the end, he let it go, that and hair that had grown shaggy. He imagined that few who knew the Adam Jensen who left Detroit in 2027 would recognize the man he saw in the dull glass. He wasn't really certain if *he* did. Looking himself in the eye, Jensen felt an odd sense of disconnection that didn't sit well with him.

Then he caught the sound of Stacks's voice on the breeze and the moment faded.

He found the other man in a shaded corner of the open quad, with three more of the clinic's residents clustered around him in a threatening half-circle. The biggest of them was a broad, thickset woman with lank brown hair and a bodybuilder's silhouette. She had worn, gunmetal cybernetic legs covered in swirling etched detail, and he pegged her as a former panzer-girl from the disbanded aug mixed martial arts leagues. At her side were two guys in the same nondescript jacket that Jensen wore. One of them had a mono-vision band across his face, turning his eyes into one seamless digital sensor grid, and the other had tech-tattoos that suggested he was packing neural implants of some kind.

"You know how it goes," the woman was saying, a sing-song lilt to her words. She prodded Stacks in the chest. "I mean, it's us and them, am I right? Augs in here, natches out there. And natches ain't gonna stick up for us. Augs gotta look out for augs, is what I'm saying."

"Yuh." Mono-Eye bobbed his head in agreement, while his tattooed buddy stood by silently. Despite the content of the conversation, Jensen knew a shakedown when he saw one. The panzer-girl's next words confirmed it.

"That's what we do. We look out. And it's not much to ask that people give some consideration for that in return, Stacks. You get me?"

"I just go my own way, Belle." Stacks managed a weak smile. "Okay?"

"No." The woman prodded him again, harder this time. "Not okay."

Stacks caught sight of Jensen approaching at the same moment the guy with the tattoos did. The thug touched Belle on the arm and she turned to face Jensen. Her jaw hardened. "Well. New guy. You wake up now, sleeping beauty?"

He ignored her. "Stacks. You got a minute? Need to ask you something."

Stacks took a cautious step past Mono-Eye, grateful for the out but wary about making it into something more. "Hey, Jensen, we're all cool here."

"Jensen," echoed the tattooed man. "The floater." He laughed at his own joke, a quick nasal chuckle.

Belle looked Jensen up and down with an expression that was somewhere between a sneer and a leer. She pointed at his hands. "What you got there? Sarif tech, right? I know the hardware. Top drawer." She shrugged and ran a hand down her thigh. "Not my kind of metal, gotta say. I go TYM, all the way."

He didn't look away. "What are those legs, Aries-model heavy mods? How's that forty percent fail rate working for you?"

Belle's expression hardened and he knew he'd struck a nerve. Tai Yong Medical, the constant rival of Sarif Industries in the augmentation business, may have had a bigger market share but they lacked the finesse and reliability of Sarif's high-spec engineering. She shrugged. "I'm good. Kicked a man's head clean off one time. You wanna see me do it again?"

"I'll pass." He beckoned to Stacks. "I need a coffee. Let's get inside."

"See you around, Jensen," Belle called out as they walked away, her words carrying after them.

* * *

Thorne stood by the window on the upper floor, and anyone who passed her by might have thought she was in some kind of fugue state. She stared down at the quad, her eyes losing focus as Jensen and the other processee moved beyond her field of vision. It would have been easy for her to run a wireless remote intrusion into the clinic's security grid and keep following him via 451's network of monitors, but there was no need. She'd programmed Adam Jensen's tracer bracelet icon into her infolink's head-up display and now she watched it drift away below her, a black diamond edged in gold moving through the corridors toward the cafeteria.

Someone watching Thorne closely would have seen her blank eyes flicker and then lose focus. They would have seen the movement in her lips as she began a subvocalized conversation on her infolink, filtered via a portable sat-com encryption device she carried in a pocket. The words she spoke never fully formed in her mouth, they were never uttered aloud – but her handler on the far end of the transmission heard them as clearly as if they had been in the same room together.

Thorne's report was, as always, terse and to the point. She wasted no time with preamble, sticking to the facts, pausing only when her handler responded with new directives. For long moments, she stood motionless, processing her next orders.

Finally she acknowledged them with a single spoken word. "Complying."

The ghost signal to her infolink cut and she became animated once more. Thorne watched the black diamond, and began considering how Adam Jensen would be dealt with.

TWO

She raised the heavy crystal lighter to the tip of the cocktail cigarette, and set it burning, savoring the taste as she drew it in through bright lips the color of blood. Exhaling, she turned across the glass table and blew a thin line of smoke out over the balcony.

The man seated across from her laughed gently, amused by the act. As the sun had set and cast its fading light over the Gulf of Naples, they shared a bottle of that agreeable Conterno Monfortino, here in the hotel's presidential suite. Now, amid the cool evening air, they basked in the afterglow of the potent wine.

"I do like the silence," she said, and with a sweep of her hand she took in the room. "Tonight, this belongs only to us."

He smiled. "My dearest Beth, *everything* belongs to us."

She drew on the cigarette again. Aside from this suite, the entirety of the Hotel Imperioli was unoccupied. The only other humans in the grounds were their security detachments and a skeleton staff of serviles. The former groups were amusingly bullish toward each other, each squad of personal bodyguards sizing up the other like competing packs of wolves stalking the same territory.

The actual cost of such extravagance would never have crossed her mind. Elizabeth DuClare lived in a world where what she wanted was what happened. It was like a force of nature, as ingrained in her existence as the rising and setting of the sun. To even consider a reality where the world did not bend to her will would have been anathema to her. Born into great affluence as a daughter of one of the richest dynasties on Earth, it was her birthright. And as such, being a woman of great means and intellect and ambition, it was inevitable that she would fall into the Illuminati's orbit.

They hadn't *recruited* Elizabeth, like talent scouts spotting an aspiring athlete. It simply didn't work like that. No, in a way she had always been one of them, groomed from birth to take a place on the Council of Five. It was meant to be, and there had never been an impulse in her to question it. DuClare was a queen of the world… Why would she ever have wished otherwise?

Her dinner companion leaned in and patted her on the hand, his smile widening. She wondered if it might be a hint of interest in her that ran beyond the professional. "You do look lovely this evening, my dear," he noted.

"Lucius," she said, with mild reproach. "Flattery will get you nowhere."

He grinned at her. "You can't blame an old man for trying."

Although his actual age was his most closely guarded secret, Lucius DeBeers carried himself with the thoughtful gravitas of an elder statesman. Much of that stemmed from the cutting-edge biotechnology she herself had put his way. Her role as the de facto head of the World Health Organization gave DuClare unprecedented access to experimental medical systems that the common people of the globe would never be aware of. She helped DeBeers fight off the ravages of time and illness, and in that a special bond had been born between them.

But despite knowing those truths, she enjoyed him. His fatherly manner could be comforting, and while she would never be so foolish as to talk of childish things like *love*, she possessed a unique kind of affection for Lucius that she could not deny.

Is it a fondness for him, or for his power? DuClare had asked herself that question many times, and never examined the answer in too great detail. It didn't matter. DeBeers was, as he liked to call himself, the *Prima Illuminatus*, the leader of the council. To be the woman he considered his peer and occasionally, his confidante, was a very good place to inhabit.

"Do you think the others talk about us?" she said. "Your protégé? Or Stanton and that damned climber Page?"

"Morgan, Dowd and all the rest..." DeBeers chuckled and looked away. "They know you and I have our private conversations. But does it matter what sordid motives they might ascribe to us?"

"They'll think it makes us weak."

He gave a nod. "Good. Wrong thinking emboldens foolish choices, and I'd rather I knew sooner than later if one of them is going to strike at me... At us." He poured out more wine for them. "Page, perhaps, if the day ever comes that he can find his courage. Dowd will never make a move. He likes his domains too much the way they are."

DuClare made a sour face. "Dowd's Templar minions are the reason I stay away from Paris these days. I smell them on everything when I go back to the chateau. They act like they own the city."

"Well, they do. But we own *them*." DeBeers handed her a glass. "Pay it no mind, my dear. Besides, the climate in Geneva agrees with you. You're positively radiant."

She gave him a kittenish smile, and gestured around, the red tip of the lit cigarette dancing like a firefly. "But it is so desperately *dull* there. I leapt at a chance to come to Italy."

He nodded, crossing the balcony to the balustrade. "One might almost think it was a pleasurable experience to share my company," said DeBeers, in a mock-sad tone.

"Lucius, don't be melodramatic." Her voice switched back to her more usual manner; a colder, harder tone that she used on her inferiors. DuClare stubbed out the cigarette as she sensed a shift in the tenor of the conversation. The real reason for their meeting was about to emerge.

"Our latest adversary…" he began, his back to her. "Who do you think it is?"

"My answer is the same as it was before. Janus hides his or her identity better than anyone we've ever come across. We won't find them easily, not unless a mistake is made. And given previous form, that doesn't seem likely."

"Janus…" DeBeers sounded out the name. "The Romans and their minor god, seeing past and future all at once." He snorted with derision. "Two faces on one head. What a trite choice for a double-agent's sobriquet." He shot her an irritated look, and in that instant he looked like the old man that he really was. "There have been too many interdictions of our work, Elizabeth. Events too precise and too perfectly pitched to be the deeds of some random troublemaker. Janus is an uncommon foe."

DuClare had to admit he made a strong point. Failures like the botched assassination of William Taggart, once the leader of the now-splintered pro-humanist Humanity Front, or the damning leak of the secrets held in the black site prison at Rifleman Bank could not have been chance events. There was a guiding hand at work, one in clear opposition to the Illuminati's grand, complex design.

DeBeers's mood was shifting, turning irritable. "I told Morgan that Janus and his ridiculous little band of hackers were dealt with. But it seems I declared victory too soon. The so-called Juggernaut Collective is not as dead as I would wish it to be. Like roaches. Hard to stamp them out in one go." He glared at her, all warmth suddenly gone. "Who do they think they *are*?" he demanded, affronted by the temerity of an enemy that dared to antagonize him. "I have not sacrificed my years, I have not made our plans my life's work, just to be derailed by a pack of activist children sniping at us from the cover of cyberspace!"

"We'll deal with them," she told him. "Of course we will deal with them. Our group has always weathered such attacks, from the very first days of Weishaupt and the founding. We have never veered from our course." DuClare allowed a careful measure of warmth into her voice. "I remember something you once said. *The burden of governance, the stewardship upon us is great.*

Perhaps at this moment in history greater than any of our group have ever had to shoulder."

"The responsibility falls to us..." he said. "Yes. I recall that day."

"History is how we transcribe it. We are the ones with courage, the insight and the moral right. We lead, Lucius. That's what we are destined to do. The acts of some faceless coward cannot prevent that."

He fell silent for a long moment. "You're right, of course." His smile returned briefly. "You center me, dear Beth. Thank you." DeBeers put down his glass and took her hand. His grip was firm, more so than she found comfortable. "But I don't need a reminder of our mandate. I want a way to cut off Janus's head – whomever he or she may be – and terminate these irritants once and for all. Mankind is at a critical societal juncture, it is divided and fracturing. There is too much at stake to become distracted!"

"I promised you I would formulate a plan of action," she told him. "And I have. I've utilized certain resources in our possession. Pawns across the board are in motion." He released his grip and gestured for her to carry on. "We will need to play a subtle and lengthy game, Lucius. Janus will make it hard for us to get close, but I believe I have found a way."

"I want Janus's true face, dear girl," he said, his voice dropping to a whisper. "I want to know it and expose it. Then we'll erase these upstarts from the world. Every moment of their lives, every iota of their identities, every mark they ever made will be gone forever. I'll make it so they never existed."

DuClare felt an icy, familiar thrill run through her. *The exercise of real power, more potent than any drug.* "We have already begun," she told him.

FACILITY 451 – ALASKA –
UNITED STATES OF AMERICA

If there had been more time, he might have been able to do something that was better than just *reacting*. Later, he would ask himself if it had all been part of a plan working against him, a way to force his hand before he could tackle the situation on his own terms.

In the end, it didn't matter. The situation was what it was, and he had to respond to it. In Adam Jensen's experience, the world liked to take that kind of choice away from a man, and make him deal with it in the moment. Succeed or fail. No second chances.

He knew it was a trap when he entered the day room and saw Stacks in the far corner, nursing a bloody nose. He knew it in the way that Belle and her playmates were standing around, wound tight with nervous, pre-fight energy. He knew it from the small crowd that had gathered, all of whom looked at him with hooded, wary gazes. And he knew it because he hadn't seen a single micro-drone or orderly in the corridor along the way.

"Now we'll get some answers," Belle began, without preamble. "Stacks here don't seem to have none."

The crowd parted to let Jensen come closer, and he eyed them. Other residents he'd seen during the past few days, who up until now had all seemed disinterested in him, looked on as if they bore a grudge. What had changed?

"Jensen—" Stacks tried to step forward, but Mono-Eye let an electro-prod truncheon slip out of his sleeve and he menaced the other man with it. Even though the ex-steeplejack had size over the skinnier guy, he was cowed by the humming halo around the head of the baton.

"Stay there, big man," said the thug, "and shut up."

Belle's other lieutenant shrugged out of his jacket to show off his glowing tattoos, and Jensen saw the distinctive rough skin on his bare chest that indicated dermal armor implants beneath the flesh. He shifted on the balls of his feet, licking his lips. The first attack would come from him; it couldn't have been more telegraphed if he'd been wearing a neon sign over his head.

"There a problem here?" Jensen ignored both the thugs and kept his attention on Belle.

"You're damn right there is, and I'm looking at it." She bared her teeth when she spoke. There were a few grumbles and angry murmurs of support from the other residents. She pointed with both hands. "I got a vibe off you from the start, Jensen. And I didn't listen to my gut." Belle shook her head. "My mistake."

"I don't have time to play games." He let his arms drop to his sides. "You got something to say to me, spit it out. Or else, get your toy boys out of my way."

Belle spread her arms in a gesture that took in everyone around them. "See these people, Jensen? We all got something in common. We all lost things in the incident. Lovers and families. Homes. Money. Our goddamned lives, we lost." There were more growled assents, and a cold, creeping realization dawned on Jensen as the woman went on. "And now those natches blame us for everything. We're prisoners here, man. All because *somebody* fucked us." She pointed right at him.

His breath caught in his throat as another unbidden memory came to vivid life in his mind's eye. Another woman's voice – the silken, almost childlike tones of Eliza Cassan – laying out a series of brutal, final choices before him, each one more unpalatable than the last.

"You were there, in that place that sunk into the sea," Belle snarled, her voice rising. "Did you do it, Jensen?" Her words became pure fury, and he guessed that despite her brutish manner, Belle had been as much a victim of Darrow's terrible attack as anyone else. "Answer me!"

He pushed his reaction aside. "Who told you that?"

"It doesn't matter what I was told," Belle shot back. "I don't hear you denying it." She advanced on him. "Look around, you son of a bitch. Look what you did. To people just like you!"

He could see them all, drawing on the anger and the pain that had been festering beneath the surface for those long months. They desperately *needed* someone to blame, someone who was here and real and in front of them, not a ghost like Hugh Darrow, his body crushed beneath thousands of tons of steel in the Arctic Ocean. They wanted a scapegoat, and somebody had decided it was going to be *him*.

Jensen lost focus for a moment as that thought echoed through his head, and it was enough for someone behind him in the crowd to shove him forward, spitting and jeering. He stumbled, and the tattooed man hurtled toward him, snarling. He had kitchen knives in both hands.

Reflexively, Jensen cocked back his cyberlimb and triggered the nerve impulse that would have deployed the blunt-tipped nanoblades concealed beneath the forearm – but there was nothing but a hollow click and he recalled too late that the augmentations had been disengaged. Instead, he went into a clumsy block that set the knives cutting across the polycarbonate shell of his arm.

Jensen turned the inelegant move into a counterattack, dropping low and throwing a punch into the tattooed man's gut. He took it with a grunt but little else, the shear-thickening gel in the dermal armor absorbing most of the force of impact.

The crowd were shouting at him, baying for his blood. It wouldn't matter what he said to them. He was the outsider, the new and the unknown, and even if she was their tormentor, Belle was still one of them. It wouldn't have been hard to manipulate people like this, to pour all their hate into one single target. They didn't care about the truth. Jensen had been on Panchaea, that was a fact, and it was like they smelled the scent of that place – and what was done there – still on him.

The knives fell toward the exposed flesh of Jensen's throat, but his attacker was inexpert with them and held the makeshift weapons too close together. Jensen's free hand snapped up and grabbed the closest blade, hearing the metal crunch against the surface of his cyberarm's synthetic palm. He pulled the tattooed man toward him, forcing him to overbalance. Then, as he fell, Jensen struck with his other arm and caught the man hard across the face. His assailant's nose broke with an ugly cracking sound and blood jetted. He fell, howling in pain, losing the knives along the way. Jensen kicked them away as Belle and Mono-Eye came at him together. The bigger woman was powerful, but she wasn't agile, and her heavy augmented leg failed to hook Jensen's and bring him down.

Instead, he slipped back, grabbing a folding chair. Jensen swung around and beat the other thug across the shoulders with it. Mono-Eye jabbed at him with the electro-prod, arcs of blue-white fire sparkling. He missed, but the aura of the weapon was so close as it passed Jensen's temple that his right-side optic implant briefly became blurred by the electromagnetic field.

Where are the orderlies? Jensen wondered. *Why are they letting this happen?* But then he was fully back in the fight a heartbeat later.

Mono-Eye's limbs were organic, and that made him vulnerable. Jensen grabbed the wrist beneath the hand holding the prod and broke it cleanly, using the servos in his cyberarm to twist it to a degree off true that no human bones could bear. The thug screamed and Jensen plucked the prod from his nerveless fingers, slamming a point-blank punch into the mono-band over his eyes. Plastic fragmented and splintered, and the second of Belle's men went down to the floor.

But Belle herself had not waited for the outcome, and she put a trip-hammer kick into the back of Jensen's legs. He buckled at the knees and crashed into a table, collapsing it underneath him. He lost the weapon and twisted, rolling away as Belle stamped down with the force of a wrecking ball. Her steel foot crumpled the table and smashed the prod into pieces.

Jensen scrambled, trying to get back up, but the crowd were following the example he had set and threw chairs at him, along with anything else they could lay their hands on. He saw Stacks coming to his aid, but a savage blow from Belle knocked him aside and the other man stumbled against a wall.

Belle crossed the short distance toward Jensen in two heavy pneumatic strides. She spat at him and went for the killer blow, her leg coming down to crush his chest and stop his heart.

He was fast enough to block the fall with his hand, and for long seconds it became a contest of hardware –

the exacting, precise mechanism of Jensen's Sarif-built cyberarm versus the brute-force power of Belle's Tai Yong-made augmetic leg.

In her eyes there was nothing but raw hate. "You'll pay!" Belle cried. But Jensen would never learn what personal cost the woman was trying to balance.

There was motion in the corner of his eye and suddenly Stacks was there, his face bloodied, swinging a fire extinguisher like a club. The unit connected with the side of Belle's head and she was knocked away. Stacks's dual-thumbed hand came down and grabbed Jensen's, hauling him up.

Belle rolled and rose on one knee as the rest of the angry crowd closed ranks behind her, but before they could react Jensen snatched the extinguisher from Stacks and aimed the nozzle at them. He thumbed the trigger and sprayed an arc of freezing, choking CO_2 gas at them, stopping any new attack in its tracks. "Enough!" he snarled.

The day room's doors crashed open and a dozen orderlies came rushing in with electro-prods drawn, shouting out orders and making threats. Thorne followed them, scanning the room with a measuring gaze. Jensen let the extinguisher drop and raised his hands as the rest of the processees reluctantly did the same. He saw Belle give Thorne a questioning look that the federal agent completely ignored, and Jensen knew immediately that she had been the one who revealed the circumstances of his recovery from Panchaea.

"You have a knack for getting yourself into difficulty, Mr. Jensen." Thorne looked him up and down, sparing Stacks a brief glance.

"It happens." He wiped a trickle of blood from his lip. "Why are you still here?"

"I told you, we are not done. And it seems I was right to take a closer interest in you."

Jensen's lip curled. "Bullshit. You made this happen. Trying to soften me up?"

Thorne's gaze drifted back to Stacks. "Things can go wrong during incarceration. It brings out the worst in people."

"Thought this was a clinic, not a prison," Stacks muttered. "More fool me."

She paid no attention to the other man's comment. "I think it would be best to isolate you from the general population for the moment, Mr. Jensen. Until we can resolve things." Thorne beckoned over three of the orderlies. "Take him across to the segregation block and hold him there."

Jensen knew the place she meant. He'd seen it on his walks of the facility's perimeter, a prefabricated blockhouse set off on its own. It was supposed to be there to house any processee suffering from an infectious illness, but Jensen imagined that function was as much a smokescreen as the main complex's stated purpose. One of the orderlies gave him a shove, but he resisted. "What about *him*?" He nodded toward Stacks.

"What about him?" Thorne repeated. "He'll go back to his bunk. He's not my concern."

Jensen saw the shadow of denied vengeance on the faces of Belle and the other residents, and he knew that if they couldn't get to him, they would take it out on Stacks. The man would be punished for being kind enough to show Jensen some friendship. "No. It's not safe for him here."

"I'll be okay, brother," Stacks said quietly, unable to mask his fear. "Don't worry none…"

"Always the policeman, aren't you, Adam?" Thorne sniffed. "Protect and serve? And here with a man you hardly even know. If you'd read Harrison Stacker's file, you might think differently."

Jensen let that pass without comment. "You leave him here, he'll wind up with a shiv in his ribs."

Thorne folded her arms, silently evaluating them both. Then she nodded. "Of course. You're right." She gestured to the orderlies. "Take Mr. Stacker as well. We'll keep him out of harm's way… for as long as we can."

The orderly shoved Jensen again and this time he moved, falling into step with Stacks as the guards drew in around them. Jeers from Belle followed them out into the corridor.

"I'm sorry," Jensen said quietly. "Thorne's got an axe to grind with me and you took some of the blowback."

Stacks eyed him. "Just tell me that Belle was wrong. You and that bastard Darrow—"

"Hugh Darrow is dead because of me," Jensen said, cutting him off. "Believe that."

They walked on in silence through 451's narrow corridors, and Jensen's mind sifted through the rapidly collapsing series of options before him.

Thorne's bit of theater back in the day room had all been calculated to push him off-balance, and Jensen knew that his gut-check distrust of the agent had been right on the money. She had put Stacks in danger to draw him in, set up the rest of the facility's residents against Jensen so he had no support, all of it to give him nowhere to go but back to her. Sending him to isolation would give her full control over what happened next, and on the surface, asking for Stacks to be pulled out of the communal bunks seemed like he had handed her another tool to use against him.

He played it out in his head. Thorne would threaten to send Stacks back into the general population and Belle's tender mercies, unless Jensen gave her what she wanted. She'd lean on his innate instinct to stick up for the defenseless. It was more textbook interrogation technique.

Jensen studied Stacks out of the corner of his eye, wondering. Was the other detainee part of Thorne's elaborate game? The agent had manipulated Belle, had she done the same to Stacks? *Can I trust him?*

Stacks saw him looking and frowned. "What Thorne said, 'bout my file… she's right. I did some bad things… I didn't have a choice…"

Jensen nodded. "I know how that goes." He listened to his instincts, and all of them were telling him this man was being played as much as he was. *Guess I'll find out for sure.*

The orderlies led them outside and they trudged through a cold, sleeting rain falling from the relentlessly gray sky.

"How long have you been here?" Jensen said, addressing the question to Stacks but looking straight ahead.

"You asked me that already," said the other man. "I told you. Since the incident."

"When were you supposed to rotate out?"

"They said six months," Stacks sighed. "But then Doc Rafiq, she said it would take longer. And so it goes."

"I've been here six days." Jensen flexed his hands and tensed. "And that's long enough."

The plan he had was half-formed, just pieces that didn't come together in any way that could be certain of working. But what Jensen *was* certain of was that Agent Thorne had no plans to ease up on him now. If she was capable of risking the life of an innocent man just to get Jensen where she wanted, there would be no way to evade her reach inside Facility 451. His time was about to run out.

The inhibitor bracelet on Jensen's arm dialed down a lot of the key functions of his augmentations, but the neuromuscular facilitator implant in his torso was too broadly distributed to be so easily impeded. It didn't exactly allow him to dodge bullets, but in a combat situation the NMF aug made his reflexes fire much faster than baseline human norms. He triggered the 'Quicksilver' and without warning his hand snapped out like a striking cobra, grabbing the wrist of the nearest orderly.

The man had an electro-prod in his grip, the activator switch in the *on* position. Before the guard could react, Jensen made the first of a series of gambles and yanked him close, jamming the prod's emitter tip into the frame of the metallic inhibitor.

A searing electric shock crackled over his cyberarm, making the artificial myomer muscles jerk and twitch – but the risk paid off as the string of indicator lights ringing the bracelet winked out.

The orderly shouted a warning, and the other two guards turned on Jensen and Stacks.

Stacks brought up his big industrial cyberarms and blocked the other guards while Jensen dealt with the first. The man caught on quick, he noted.

With the inhibitor dead, Jensen felt a surge of energy as the rest of his augs reactivated in quick succession.

Indicator glyphs blinked in the corner of his vision. But he didn't have a lot of power to spare, so each choice he made would have to count.

Swinging around, Jensen struck the struggling orderly across the face with the heel of his hand, intentionally pulling the blow for a knockout rather than a fatal hit. The guard went down into the slushy snow and lay there, groaning in pain. Jensen ripped off the dead inhibitor and threw it away, still clutching the electro-prod.

Stacks shouted wordlessly as the other guards swiped at him with their own weapons. The ex-steeplejack snatched a fistful of one orderly's jacket and tossed him toward Jensen, at the same time swinging his heavy-duty arm back and forth toward the third man.

Jensen met his next opponent by jamming the prod into his stomach. The weapon discharged with a low, buzzing hum and the orderly's cry of pain was cut short as he was shocked unconscious.

"Code Red! Code Red!" shouted the last guard, yelling into a handheld radio he plucked from his belt. "We got a—"

"Shut your mouth!" Stacks yelled, and closed the big, talon-like fingers of his cyberlimb around the orderly's hand. The guard screamed as Stacks crushed flesh, bone and plastic into a broken mess. Then, with a brutal shove, he propelled the last man away and to the ground. He rounded on Jensen. "Shit, man! You could have warned me you were gonna go for it!"

"Didn't know myself until just now." He jogged across to the high fence, scanning the buildings on the far side, picking out the shapes of snow-dusted trucks and jeeps. "Vehicle park just over there... We need to—"

"I got this." Stacks pushed him aside and flexed his artificial arms.

"Let me help you with that." Jensen found the inhibitor he wore and pressed the prod to its surface. "This is gonna hurt." He didn't wait for Stacks to reply, and fired a crackling surge of voltage into the device.

Stacks cried out in pain, and Jensen caught the acrid stink of burning plastic. Then suddenly the other man was at the fence line, clawed fingers tearing into the metal links. Sparks flew in showers of orange as he ripped open a ragged tear in the enclosure, and belatedly sirens began to sound across the length of the compound.

Above the sirens, Jensen heard a high-pitched whine and glimpsed an insect-like shape rising off the roof of the main building, angling toward them. "Drone incoming! We gotta move!"

Discarding his burnt-out inhibitor, Stacks shouldered his way through the inner fence and repeated his destructive actions at the outer line. Jensen followed him through and out. For what seemed like the first time in forever, both men were beyond the walls of the complex that had confined them – but they were far from being free.

Guards emerged from the isolation block and the main building, hooded figures seen through the rain as it came down harder. Jensen's optics picked out weapons in their hands. Not stunners this time, but short-frame bullpup flechette rifles.

"Your show now, man!" said Stacks. "What do we do?"

"You know how to hotwire a truck?" Jensen jabbed a finger toward a pick-up parked a few meters away, the flatbed piled high with maintenance gear and spares. It was an older, gasoline-powered model from the 2010s, more reliable in the colder Alaskan temperatures than modern hybrids or e-cars.

"Hotwire?" Stack repeated. "What, they never teach you that in cop school?"

Jensen's reply died in his throat as something fast whistled past his head, dropping to skitter away across the wet tarmac. He whirled around just in time to see a second object strike Stacks harmlessly on the ironclad shoulder of his aug arm. A tranquilizer dart.

"Start it up!" he shouted, catching sight of the drone again as the airborne robot pivoted in mid-air. The bigger cousin to the little monitors that buzzed about the corridors of 451, this unit was the size of a soccer ball, held between four spinning rotors, with a chin turret of sensors surrounding the black barrel of a tranq gun.

The drone took aim, but as it fired again Jensen dashed toward it, shortening the distance so the dart shot went wide and hit nothing. Sweeping down into a low turn, he scooped up a wad of dirty slush from the ground and threw it at the hovering drone. The makeshift snowball struck its camera eye with a wet smack and the drone's rotors shrilled in complaint as the unit momentarily lost its target.

Behind him, Jensen heard Stacks grunt with effort and then the crunching grind of tearing metal. He turned to see that the other man had ripped off the door to the pick-up and now stood hunched over the steering wheel, yanking at wires. Jensen sprinted back to the vehicle, pulling down the tailgate, looking for anything to use as a weapon.

"Ha-ha!" Stacks let out a cry of victory as the truck's motor turned over and caught. "We're rollin' now!"

"Not yet…" Jensen snatched at a length of metal rebar and dragged it out of the flatbed as the drone shook off his distraction and came diving at them. For a moment, he held it like an over-long sword, wondering if he could swat the robot out of the air before it pegged him with another dart. But then something better occurred to him, and he let the targeting augmentation keyed to his cyberoptics go active. Jensen turned the rod in his hand until he held it like a javelin, and at the last second he threw it into the air. The blunt tip of the rebar struck the drone with enough force to dislocate one of its rotors, and it plummeted into a crash spiral.

More shots cracked at Jensen's heels – lethal flechette rounds now – as the guards came through their improvised exit. Stacks was already pulling away, the pick-up's wheels spitting ice and rainwater as he slewed it around toward the highway.

"Come on!" he bellowed. "Run, damn it!"

Jensen broke into a sprint and leapt the last half-meter to the tailgate, scrambling aboard as other loose items spilled out on to the road. "Gun it!" he shouted back, as a round cracked against the bodywork.

"Oh yeah," Stacks called back, stepping on the gas pedal and aiming the truck into the wall of rain. "Let's make those bastards work for it!"

The service track from Facility 451 joined a road that crossed the peninsula, and from Stacks's reading of the pick-up's sat-nav screen, it connected up to a bigger interstate freeway a few miles further on.

Jensen slipped into the cab alongside him and confirmed what he already suspected. The pick-up had only local tags, and no clearance for interstate travel, which meant the moment they took to the freeway, police drones would be scrambled to intercept them.

"That's gonna happen no matter what," said Stacks. "Odds are, our pals back at the ranch are calling the State Troopers right now with a description of these wheels."

Jensen shook his head. "I don't think so. I know how these people work. Thorne's gonna use her own assets to come after us first. Locals will be a last resort."

Stacks shot him a look. "*These people*?" he echoed. "Ain't that the World Health Organization you're talking about? You make 'em sound like the, what, the CIA."

"You just spent eighteen months being held prisoner by them," Jensen shot back. "You tell me."

"Fair point…" Stacks conceded. "Shit. This is all fucked up."

"No argument here." Jensen leaned over the sat-nav screen, scrolling around the map. "Look, there's an automated service station where the roads link up. Head there. We'll ditch this thing, find another vehicle."

Stacks scowled. "Hate to break it to you, brother, but if you and me ain't the only humans within fifty miles of that, I'd owe you a buck. Nothing but them goddamn big-ass robo-trucks run up and down this stretch of road, from Anchorage down to the border or back to the oil wells. Alla that acid rain and everything, Alaska don't get tourists no more. Towns round here are dead and gone."

"I know," said Jensen. "And I got a way we can use that. We get on board one of those automated rigs, we can ride it down to Juneau, get a connection back to the States. Put as much distance as we can between us and Facility four-five-one."

"I hear you," Stacks said, with feeling. "But you forgetting, those mechs have killer security, yeah? Don't take no hitch-hikers."

"Yeah." Jensen ran a hand over the hexagonal plate above his right eye, bringing another of his augmentations back to life. "I know a guy who can help us with that."

SOLDOTNA STATION – ALASKA – UNITED STATES OF AMERICA

As Stacks predicted, the auto-station was utterly devoid of human life, and likely had been for a long time. A few faceless tanker trucks emblazoned with corporate logos, their prows bristling with antennae and sensor palps, filled machine-controlled refueling bays where spidery crane arms fed power umbilicals into waiting slots on their flanks. Jensen watched one of them finish topping up the charge in its massive batteries, and detach itself with a surge of movement. The robotic vehicle cruised past him toward the freeway on-ramp, infrared running lights flicking on. A shocker turret mounted on the side of the tanker turned to track him as he stood there, a mute warning to stay away. The simple artificial intelligences that drove these trucks had only a cursory interest in humans, as either obstacles to be avoided or potential hijackers to be terminated. The price of real fossil fuel made the theft of such transporters from the vast Alaskan fracking fields an ongoing problem, so the machines were programmed to automatically distrust anything organic that approached them.

Jensen watched it go, accelerating to over a hundred miles per hour in a skirl of tire noise. He frowned and looked away, considering his next move. They didn't have a lot of time, maybe a twenty-minute lead on their pursuers at best. He would need to work quickly.

The auto-station had some cursory shelter, an afterthought built into the place on the off-chance that someone flesh-and-blood might be unfortunate enough to find themselves stranded out here. Behind a thick, windproof door with failing seals, chairs and tables made out of a kind of extruded polymer were lined up across from a fetid chemical toilet, an emergency phone, a broken wall-screen and a pair of vending machines that were out of order. The latter hadn't stopped Stacks from using his augmented strength to peel open their shells and help himself to what was still inside. Jensen eyed the bloated cans of expired Nuke Cola, the crumbling packs of Soy, and grimaced.

"That junk'll poison you," he told the other man. "It's gotta be old enough to have kids."

Stacks offered him a stale Proenergy bar. "Don't get to be picky. So. What about your guy?"

Jensen reluctantly took the packet. "Any second now…"

"Let me know how it goes." Opening a salvaged pack of caffeine sticks, Stacks lit one with a shaky hand and wandered outside.

Within a day of being there, Jensen had realized that Facility 451 was surrounded by a masking field that smothered any kind of long-range cellular signals. While he was inside, his implanted infolink was dead metal, unable to transmit or receive, blocked from even the most basic tracking signal. But now he was a few miles clear of 451, and with nothing to interrupt the feed, the infolink was rebooting itself. The start sequence concluded, and for anyone who knew the implant's covert contact protocols, Adam Jensen was effectively back on the grid.

Two minutes later, a familiar voice echoed through the transceiver implant in Jensen's mastoid bone. *"Who is this?"* The demand was brusque and distrustful.

"Hello, Francis."

On the other end of the line, Jensen heard a sharp intake of breath. *"Identify yourself. Or I cut this transmission right now and scrub the contact."*

"I don't have time for games, Pritchard. It's me. I figured you'd still be monitoring this comm-code."

"After a year of silence?" Frank Pritchard's tone rose, becoming terse and sneering. *"Maybe I should—"* He stopped, catching himself, and his manner changed. *"Adam Jensen was listed as missing presumed dead after the destruction of the Panchaea complex. I have no reason to believe that fact isn't true. If you're Jensen, prove it."*

"Your middle name is Wendell. Your hacker handle is Nuclearsnake. With a number 3. Good enough?"

"Any competent investigator could dig up that data."

"You're also a prick."

There was a long pause. *"Well,"* said Pritchard at length. *"If you're not Jensen, you're a very convincing emulation of him."* He paused again. *"Locator ping is showing you in… Alaska? Perhaps you could provide some kind of explanation as to why—"*

"No time," Jensen cut him off. "If you got the location, you know exactly where I am. I need a ride, Pritchard, and I need it now."

"Is that all? You contact me out of the blue because you need a favor?"

"Pretty much, yeah. Can you do it?"

"Of course I can do it," the hacker snorted. *"Where do you need to go?"*

The door banged open and Stacks rushed in. "Jensen! I seen a chopper, off out to the west, lights scanning the road. Coming this way." He shook his head. "We got about five minutes before they're here, no more."

He nodded to the other man and looked away. "Detroit," he told Pritchard. "It's time I came home."

THREE

It was cramped and uncomfortable in the automated truck's maintenance compartment, barely big enough for the two men to share it without stepping on top of one another. But somehow they managed the journey in companionable silence for the most part, Stacks gently snoring his way through it and Jensen hovering on the edge of the same, but never quite allowing himself to slip fully away into sleep.

With nothing but a small glass porthole in the hatchway, there was no view to speak of, and so Jensen gave up on marking the passage of time as the vehicle headed eastward through the day and into the night. It was early evening when he felt the truck start to slow down from the constant pace it had kept up since Alaska, and he nudged Stacks with his boot.

"I'm awake," grumbled the other man. "We there yet?"

"Looks like." The truck rocked and he felt it shifting lanes, until finally it came to a halt. The hatch hissed open on hydraulics and a gust of cold, damp air blew in. Jensen climbed out, grimacing at the aches in his back as his boots hit the road.

Stacks was a step behind him, taking a deep, grateful breath. "Man, that whole rig stinks of oil. I almost forgot what fresh air tastes like." He coughed and spat. "Well, not that this air is so fresh, neither…"

They were barely out of the compartment before the hatch hissed shut and the truck rumbled away, leaving them behind on the shoulder of the freeway. Jensen glanced around, finding a road sign telling him they were on an elevated section of I-94 – the Detroit Industrial Expressway, just past Dearborn. As he got his bearings, he turned around and found the dark band of the river to the east, beyond the ill-lit streets of Mexicantown. And further to the north, the city of Detroit itself, a cluster of skyscrapers that glowed faintly through the low cloud. A fire was burning steadily out there, and the flames reflected off the bottom of the cloudbank, giving it a sullen glow. Jensen picked out the Renaissance Center toward the riverfront and used that as a reference mark to search for the twin pillars of the Sarif Industries building.

For a jarring moment, it seemed as if the towers had been erased from the skyline. He was used to seeing the glass and steel spars lit from within by soft golden light for miles around. His optics adjusted for the distance, and he realized what was wrong.

The Sarif towers were still there, but they were pitch dark against the night sky, no illumination visible in them except for the pinpricks of crimson aircraft warning lights at the very highest levels.

Stacks made a show of looking around. "Nice place here. Now I'm wishing I'd got your buddy Pritchard to detour us to Seattle instead."

"He'll get you there, if that's what you want."

"Maybe..." Stacks winced and shifted his arm stiffly. "Don't know if I'm ready to go back," he went on, almost to himself.

Jensen crossed to the guard rail, casting a wary look over his shoulder at the traffic streaming past behind him on the freeway. He pressed a fingertip to his mastoid bone, bringing his infolink out of sleep mode. "Pritchard. You there?"

The response took a moment. *"Welcome home, Jensen. A pity it's not under better circumstances."* Was that sarcasm, or a note of real regret in the other man's voice? It was hard to tell with someone like Frank Pritchard. *"There's a metro station to your northeast. Get there, head into the ticket hall."*

"Copy," he nodded, beckoning Stacks to follow him.

"Watch your step," Pritchard added, *"and try not to draw any attention. This city's not how it was when you were last here."*

The two of them slipped over the rail and made their way down a steep embankment, emerging in what used to be the grounds of a public park. Once there had been a line of trees to screen off the area from the noise of the freeway, but all of them had been cut down for firewood, with lines of ragged stumps protruding from the yellowing, piebald grass.

The park was choked with people, hundreds of the homeless packed into a makeshift campground built out of discarded packing materials, the shells of stripped vehicles and ragged sails of plastic sheeting. Groups of them clustered around oil drum fires, while others stayed concealed in the deep shadows that fell in the gloom. There were no working streetlights, many of them cut down like the trees and others torn open at the root so power-snatchers could tap into the city's electrical grid.

Wary faces caught sight of Jensen and Stacks, some seeing strangers and electing to turn away, others measuring them with rapacious, threatening gazes.

"Didn't we just leave this party?" muttered Stacks.

"No guards here, though," Jensen said quietly.

"Wanna bet?" The other man nodded toward the gates of the park, where a police cruiser slowly rode past, a cop in the passenger seat using a handheld spotlight to cast a beam over the faces of the dispossessed and desperate.

"Hey," said a voice, and Jensen felt a tug on the hem of his jacket. He looked down and saw an emaciated young woman with an athlete's recurved cyberlegs splayed out beside her. The legs were Kusanagi models, he noted – a high-grade brand, not that it seemed to matter here. The woman held up a crumpled disposable cup, gesturing with a stub where her other arm should have been. It ended at the elbow joint in a cluster of bare metal connectors and trailing wires. "You help a sister out? Spare some change or a little nu-poz, yeah?"

Jensen's lips thinned. "I can't do anything for you."

The woman turned her attention on Stacks. "How about it?"

Stacks hesitated, his expression tightening. "I... I don't have any pozy on me, girl. I'm real sorry about that."

"Then fuck off," she snapped, her expression turning spiteful.

"Look, I—" Stacks started to say something else, but Jensen pulled him away.

"You heard the lady. Come on. Keep walking."

"Yeah, you better!" shouted the woman, rising unsteadily to her feet. "Don't come down here and pretend you're better than us! Goddamn wrench!" She hissed, flinching in pain with each step she took after them, finally tottering to a halt.

Jensen had seen the effects of neuropozyne withdrawal before, and it was always an ugly, sorrowful sight. Part of the forced bargain anyone with human augmentations had to make, synthetic anti-rejection drugs like neuropozyne were a necessary evil. Anyone who had an implant or a cybernetic limb was subject to a condition known as DDS – Darrow Deficiency Syndrome – where glial tissue would slowly build up around the interface between the augmentation's electrode pick-ups and the implantee's nerves. Neuropozyne kept those connections working, but without regular doses, augmentations would start to misfire and cause severe pain, seizures, and in the worst cases, systemic nerve damage. The drug's availability had always been controlled, and it had always been costly, but in the wake of the incident Jensen had to wonder how much harder it had become to get hold of it. There were few alternatives, with poisonous 'street' versions cooked up by criminal gangs and hazardous untested variants like riezene taking more lives than they saved.

Stacks was asking himself the same questions. "Everyone here," he began quietly, "Jensen, they're all augs like us. A damn mech ghetto, is what it is. All these poor bastards, every one of them has to be hurtin'…"

"We need to keep moving," Jensen insisted, pushing Stacks in the direction of the park gates. Across the street was the metro station Pritchard had mentioned, above it the curves of two monorail lines threading in and out of the building. Less than thirty seconds away.

But the woman was on the move again, coming after them once more. "You seen enough, huh?" she shrieked. "You boys go back downtown to your natch master and be good little wrenches, get your nu-poz while the rest of us choke!"

Some of the other augs were taking notice, and Jensen felt the tension in the air building an edge.

"You gotta have something!" cried the woman, her anger finally crumbling into a desperate sob.

But Jensen hadn't lied before. He'd never needed neuropozyne to keep his augmentations operable; he didn't understand all the medical jargon behind it, but there was something different about his genetic structure. His ex-lover Megan Reed had once told him he was a 'super-compatible', a rare human anomaly who could accept augs without the yoke of the anti-rejection drug to keep him whole. Jensen was still undecided if that was a gift or a curse, and he couldn't stop himself from wondering if this unique quality was some loose thread left behind by other unanswered questions from his past. Questions that for now, he had to push away, along with other troubling memories that Megan's name brought up.

He had more immediate problems. The woman's tirade attracted the interest of other augs, none of whom seemed to consider Jensen and Stacks as anything other than unwanted intruders. He looked around and saw the police cruiser swinging back around. The situation was slipping toward an explosion of violence with each second that passed.

But then Stacks was holding up his hands in a gesture of surrender. "Look, just stop! You're right, I'm sorry!" He dug in the pocket of his jacket and pulled out a plastic packet containing a single drug capsule. "Here. This is all I've got." Stacks handed it to the woman. His voice caught as he spoke again, "You just... you take it. Reckon you need it way more than I do. Okay?"

"Thank you..." The woman reached into the pack with trembling fingers and dry-swallowed the neuropozyne. The moment of tension eased, but didn't fade entirely. They were still unwelcome here.

"Stacks, come on!" Jensen didn't wait around to see if the other dispossessed augs would change their minds about them, and he hustled the other man to the gates and across the street. The light from the police car swept over them and kept on going.

"That girl, she..." Stacks swallowed hard. "Kinda reminded me of my daughter, you know?"

Jensen nodded. "I get it. But you gotta focus. We're fugitives. We have to stay anonymous."

"You probably reckon Ol' Stacks, he's a soft touch, yeah?" Stacks gave a rueful chuckle as they entered the ticket hall. The place was dimly lit and covered with graffiti and gang tags, and in one corner a line of automated vendor screens glowed with dull yellow light.

"I've got no quarrel with someone putting more good into the world," Jensen told him. "But just be careful, okay?" He took a breath and activated the infolink again. "Pritchard, we're here."

"I know."

The voice came, not from his implanted cellular comm, but from the gloom beside the metal staircase leading to the platforms. A thin figure in a dark brown jacket over a shapeless hoodie emerged from behind the cover of an illuminated map display. Hands reached up to roll back the hood and Jensen saw Pritchard's face there. The hacker looked drawn and weary, his tapered features appearing gaunt and hollow in the waxy half-light. He cocked his head, studying Jensen carefully, one hand firmly held inside a jacket pocket.

Jensen eyed the bulge in his coat. "You gonna shoot me, Pritchard? I know we've never exactly been best buds, but I thought we'd parted on better terms than that."

The hacker's manner eased a little, and he looked around, peering into the corners of the hall. "Can't be too careful." He leaned closer – and then suddenly Pritchard reached out and snatched a trailing hair from Jensen's head. He backed away, producing a small handheld device, and stuffed the hair into a sample tray.

"A DNA check?" Jensen's eyes narrowed. "You still think I'm not who I say I am?"

Pritchard didn't answer, eyes flicking back and forth between Jensen and the device's readout. After a moment, it gave a low chime, and the hacker relaxed slightly. "You could have been a surgically altered double, for all I know… Gene scan matches the samples from the company files, so now I believe you." He looked Jensen over. "You seem well for a dead man."

"Thank Sarif for that. Sentinel implants kept me alive in the water."

"Yes, of course." Pritchard nodded. His tone was mordant. "You've made survival against the odds your *raison d'être*. I suppose it shouldn't come as a shock to me. I might have known you'd shake off drowning just like everything else."

Stacks nudged Jensen in the ribs. "Man don't seem happy to see you," he said guardedly.

"Pritchard's never happy," Jensen noted.

"What did you expect?" snapped the hacker. "*A hug*? Wherever you go, trouble follows!"

"What's he mean?" said Stacks.

Jensen raised a hand. "Not the time, *Francis*." He put acid emphasis on the other man's name. "Do you have what I asked you for?"

An older man in a heavy coat walked into the ticket hall and faltered on the steps, seeing the three of them and immediately suspecting something illegal going on – which in fact, was true. Irritably, Pritchard beckoned Stacks and Jensen over to a shadowed corner and the passer-by did his best to pretend he'd seen nothing, almost at a run as he went up the steps.

Pritchard produced two pocket secretaries and handed them to Jensen. "Snap covers," he explained. "Identity passes encoded on there, nothing special, plus a faked credit account with Bank of Detroit. It won't last long, though. There's enough for a couple of meals and a bus ticket."

"I don't plan on leaving here any time soon," Jensen shot back. "I came back to Detroit for a reason."

Pritchard scowled at him. "I knew talking to you was a mistake. I should have scrubbed that infolink code after they said you were dead." He shook his head. "Jensen, things are different now. If you thought it was bad before the incident, you have no idea. This city is the *last* place you should be. Your face is known here. And I'm risking my own safety just being in the same place as you."

"Yeah." Jensen nodded. "Gotta admit, seeing you out in the field is a new wrinkle. Since when did you get out from behind your desk?"

"I don't even *have* a desk anymore!" he said hotly. Then his tone shifted, becoming sullen. "Let's just say, I don't have the reach that I once did."

From above them, there was a low, throaty rumble as a 'people mover' train approached the platform, and Jensen heard an automated announcer calling off destinations. "I need to take a look," he told Pritchard, unsure of where the impulse had really come from. "I have to see the city with my own eyes."

"You'll regret it," Pritchard relented, and he turned toward the stairs. "I already do."

"So we going with?" asked Stacks, with a shrug.

"We're going," Jensen told him, and followed the hacker up.

There were only a few travelers waiting for the train, and when they spotted Jensen and Stacks emerging on to the platform, they immediately put distance between them.

Jensen's lips thinned. He'd experienced anti-aug sentiment directed at him more than once, from subtle prejudice like people crossing the street to stay away from him, to outright bigotry with cries of 'hanzer' and threats of physical violence – but now there was a new hostility he sensed in the people around him, a mix of fear and anger bubbling away just beneath the surface.

The train slid to a frictionless halt and the doors automatically hissed open. Jensen took a step toward the closest carriage, and heard Pritchard call out his name to make him wait, but it was too late. He had one foot off the platform when he found himself face-to-face with a pair of police patrolmen in black and orange body armor. They blocked his way on to the people mover, the mirrored visors across their faces making them look robotic and inhuman. "Where d'you think you're going?" said one of them.

The other cop jerked a thumb at a decal on the window of the carriage, right next to the NO SMOKING/ NO FIREARMS sign. The decal showed the simple stick-figure icon of a male and a female against a black background with a green border. Jensen had never seen it before, and there were a dozen of them, plastered on to the windows of five of the six carriages of the people mover. "Know what that means?"

"Enlighten me," said Jensen.

"It means *naturals only*," said the first cop, and he shoved Jensen back a step with the heel of his hand, his other dropping to the grip of a nightstick hanging from his hip. He nodded in the direction of the rear of the train. "Get back there."

Jensen was tired and it was making him short-tempered. He hesitated on the brink of giving the two patrolmen some choice words, but reeled back the urge, remembering his own advice to Stacks.

The rearmost carriage of the monorail bore a different symbol on the doors, the same man-woman icons but this time bordered in red. He noticed that both of the abstract figures had an arm or a leg colored crimson to indicate the presence of an artificial limb.

"You're kidding me," said Stacks.

"The segregation rules came in a while after the incident," Pritchard told him. "Augmented humans are second-class citizens these days."

Jensen followed them aboard, and glanced down at the homeless encampment in the park as the people mover sped away from the station. "And everyone just let it happen?"

Pritchard eyed him. "Do you really think that people gave a moment's thought to the rights of the augmented after seventy percent of them went on a psychotic rampage? Things moved fast, Jensen. Anyone who didn't accept the decommissioning of their cyberware had to sign up for registration, stringent controls, enforced licensing... compulsory confinement and hardware removal for the non-compliant ones. These days, if you're an aug and you're not eking out a life on expensive, insufficient nu-poz allocations, you're either rich or you're indentured to someone who is." He spread his hands. "It's a brave new slave economy."

The bleak tone in the other man's words was something Jensen had never heard from Frank Pritchard before. Beneath his usually waspish and arrogant exterior, something had changed. Like everything else, it seemed, Pritchard had gone through a lot during Jensen's missing time.

"I saw the towers," said Jensen, nodding toward the city skyline. "What happened to Sarif?"

"The man or the company?" Pritchard gave a humorless chuckle.

"Both."

Stacks stood at the window, watching the buildings flash by, while Pritchard took a seat across from Jensen and leaned close, lowering his voice. "Around here, David Sarif isn't a name you want people hearing you say. Remember all his bold plans about making Detroit 'a beacon city', about bringing back technology, prosperity and jobs?" He shook his head. "All gone, crumbled to dust. That golden future he talked about? Turns out it was toxic."

The last time Jensen had seen David Sarif, his employer was at the Panchaea complex, having arrived there as part of a political gambit only to become caught up in Hugh Darrow's apocalyptic plans. He remembered Sarif imploring him to confront Darrow and make the right choice for the greater good, but after the collapse of the facility, Jensen had not known if the man had made it out alive.

He listened intently as Pritchard laid out the whole sorry story. Jensen wasn't surprised to learn that Sarif had got away aboard a private mini-sub, but as the hacker explained, it wasn't without cost. "His submersible was damaged getting to the surface, and by the time the UN rescue ships got him on board, he was suffering from severe nitrogen narcosis. He was in a coma, you see? And so he slept through most of everything that came after."

A coma. Jensen felt a strange flicker of recognition. *Sarif and me both, dead to the world while everything we knew unraveled.*

Pritchard went on. "In the weeks that followed, people were desperate for someone, anyone, to hold responsible for the incident. There were attacks on every augmentation manufacturer worldwide, on tech labs and research centers... They burned down the LIMB clinics."

Jensen nodded grimly. Liberty in Mind and Body International, also known as LIMB, were the world's largest network of cyberware clinics, and for many they were the modern face of human augmentation. They would have been the most immediate, most visible targets for any angry retaliation. There was a kind of horrible irony in that, as it had been covert agents working through LIMB who laid the groundwork for the incident's night of chaos, by implanting biochip controls during a mass firmware upgrade that let Darrow's signal do its work.

"One by one, all the major human enhancement corporations have gone under. Isolay was the first to declare bankruptcy, then Kusanagi, Caidin Global..." Pritchard trailed off. "A couple of the little fish are still swimming, but they won't last beyond the end of the year. The only one of the majors that is holding together is Tai Yong Medical."

Jensen scowled. "Figures. They just roll right on, like nothing has happened." Both men knew that Tai Yong was backed not just by the Chinese government, but also by the powerbase of the Illuminati. With such forces behind them, TYM was the one corporation that would be able to weather the storm.

"When the stocks of every other augmentation company crashed, Tai Yong was there to swallow them up," said Pritchard. "And with Sarif on ice, the board of directors at SI folded." He pointed toward the darkened towers of the distant office building. "So now, everything that matters has either been bought by the Chinese or burned out by people who wanted some revenge..." He looked away and sighed. "I was one of the last to leave. I was there on the day they formally shut the place down and boarded it up." A note of helpless anger entered his voice. "I don't know, I thought I could do something... try to keep things going! But when Sarif woke up, when he finally came back... I think it broke something inside him, to see his dream torn apart like that. He couldn't stay and watch it die by inches."

Jensen nodded. "I can believe that. I never figured David Sarif for the kind of man who handles failure well."

"I don't know where he is now," Pritchard concluded. "I reached out to him through some back channels, but so far... nothing."

"Maybe that's for the best."

The other man scowled. "Easy for you to say. While you dropped off the face of the Earth, I've been hanging on by my fingertips." He looked away. "In order to keep my head above water, I've had to... go back to using some of my older skill sets, if you catch my meaning."

Jensen could imagine what that meant. Prior to his gainful employment as head of digital security at Sarif Industries, Frank Pritchard had moonlighted as a black-hat hacker. The poacher had turned gamekeeper – and now back to poacher again, if Jensen understood correctly. "We do what we have to."

"You don't *have* to be here." Pritchard gestured toward the window of the carriage, as the monorail curved around the side of a tall, crumbling brownstone and into the downtown sector. "The world already thinks Adam Jensen is a corpse. Why not let it stay that way? Go off the grid and don't come back..." He sighed. "I'm thinking about it myself."

"No." Jensen shook his head, a cold surge of righteous anger tightening in his chest. "I've had enough of being one step behind *them*." He caught himself before he said *the Illuminati*. Pritchard knew full well who he meant. "They broke open my life. They destroyed everything that mattered to me. I lost all choice about who or what I was..." The black polycarbonate fingers of his hand closed into a fist. "I've got a year-long gap in my memories. So I'm done letting them take from me, or anyone else."

Despite himself, Pritchard let out a derisive snort.

"What do you think you're going to do, Jensen? Take the fight to them?"

He met the other man's gaze. "You know me well enough to know the answer to that question."

"You're deluded."

"No." Jensen looked away as the people mover slowed to a halt. "I just don't have anything left to lose."

"Cold here," said Stacks, as they walked down the stalled escalators from the station and out on to the windblown street.

Jensen nodded absently as he looked around. They had emerged near Derelict Row, a sprawling construction site that in 2027 had been the beginning of a planned redevelopment initiative. Now it was a colossal heap of wreckage resembling the remnants of a war zone. What walls were still standing were covered with a layer of fly-posters bearing strident anti-aug slogans – PROTECT OUR FUTURE, KEEP OUR STREETS HUMAN, ARE YOUR CHILDREN SAFE?

More of the dispossessed congregated around the ruins in a ragged shantytown, and from it Jensen caught the odor of greasy, cooked meat on the breeze.

"I'm gonna go get me something…" Stacks went on, catching the same scent.

"That's rat they're barbequing over there," Pritchard told him. "Just so you know."

"I ain't choosy. Just hungry." The other man jogged across the street and started a negotiation with a vendor.

Pritchard watched him go. "Do you trust that person?"

"He saved my life, helped me escape the WHO clinic where we were being held. I owe him for that."

The hacker eyed him. "You didn't answer my question."

"He hasn't given me a reason not to trust him," said Jensen. "And right now I need as many allies as I can get."

Stacks came back with a stringy hunk of meat on a skewer, attacking it like he was starving. He walked with difficulty, limping with each off-step. "Y'all wuh-want a bite?"

"I'll pass," said Jensen. "You okay?"

"Stiff," he said, by way of explanation. "Where now?"

"This way." Pritchard started walking.

Every other building was dark and unlit. Those that hadn't been covered with metallic safety panels to lock them off from potential squatters were skeletal frames that had been denuded of everything. Blank, dark voids where windows had once been looked back at them like the eye sockets of a skull, and everywhere there were piles of debris.

"After the incident, a lot of these places were just left to rot," said Pritchard. "No-one had a reason to come back and rebuild."

They turned a corner and Jensen saw a familiar sight – the Chiron Building, the apartment complex where he had lived during his time working for Sarif. The Chiron looked different now; there were heavy poured-concrete jersey barriers blocking off the main entrance, the kind that one would see on a military base. Outside, an automated security bot rolled back and forth on an endless patrol, its scanners projecting a fan of amber laser light across its path.

On the wall of the apartment, Jensen saw the same 'naturals only' symbol that had been on the side of the train carriages. The robot spotted him and turned in Jensen's direction, rising up on its wheels to point a gun barrel toward him as a warning. He ignored it, and fell back into step with Stacks and Pritchard.

"Just how much of this segregation crap is there?" he demanded.

"It's everywhere," Pritchard told him. "I've heard talk on the net about so-called 'safe harbor' cities outside the US but I don't know how true that is."

"This isn't what I wanted…" Jensen said to himself.

Stacks made a negative noise. "You and me both, brother."

"Down here." Pritchard cut through a trash-choked alleyway, emerging behind a squat, slab-sided building with a partly collapsed roof. "This is it."

"The Rialto…" Jensen peered up at the darkened movie theater. "I thought this place had been bulldozed." Faded billboards showing weather-stained posters for decade-old feature films hung on the façade of the cinema, and toward the front where the ticket booth had been there was only a portcullis of metal security fencing.

"That was the plan," said Pritchard. "But like everything else around here, the incident got in the way of that. It's isolated, it has a power train good enough for my needs, and most importantly no-one bothers me." They circled around to the back of the building. "Of course, it's not exactly the Hilton-Fujikawa, but as I'm extending you the hospitality, you're in no position to complain."

Jensen had been quietly taking note of the gang tags spray-painted on the walls since they had got off the monorail, his old cop instincts coming to the fore. When he had lived in the city, a street gang called the Derelict Row Ballers considered this area of Detroit as the buffer zone to their turf – but the DRB's red diamond symbol wasn't anywhere to be seen. Instead, Jensen picked out multiple instances of three yellow letters – MCB, the initials of the Motor City Bangers, the sworn enemies of the DRBs – scrawled in prominent locations.

He glanced at Pritchard. "Since when has this part of downtown been Banger territory?"

The hacker blanched. "Let's just say they expanded their reach after the incident. With no serious police presence in the aftermath, the MCBs made their move. Their competitors are either dead or they fled."

"Yo, Snakey!" shouted a rough voice, and Jensen saw a figure climbing out of a car parked beside an overturned dumpster. The man was wearing gang colors and sported a pair of skeletal cyberarms. "You talking trash about us, man?"

Three more gangers in MCB yellow got out and stood with him. They'd been staking out the rear entrance of the Rialto, and Jensen chided himself for not catching sight of them before they got too close.

"Oh, crap." The sudden shift in Pritchard's body language spoke volumes. He clearly knew these men.

"Friends of yours?" said Stacks.

"Oh, we good buddies," said the ganger with the aug arms, before Pritchard could answer. As he came closer, Jensen saw that he was missing an ear, the lobe replaced by the grille of a surplus military aural augmentation. He had to have been listening in on their conversation as they walked down the street. "Ain't that right, Snakey?"

The other MCB members sported at least one

cyberlimb, mostly low-grade Tai Yong athletic models, and they all carried pistols in their waistbands. Jensen felt underdressed without a weapon of his own.

"What do you want, Cali?" Pritchard feigned annoyance, but Jensen could tell he was worried. "I'm paid up with you people. We don't have any more business."

"Oh, issat so?" The one he called Cali shared a snarling chuckle with his friends. "No, man, that ain't the way it goes." He advanced, and his gang mates came swaggering along with him. "See, Bangers run things here now. So you live on our turf, you a..." He paused, fishing for the right word. "A *tenant*."

Pritchard folded his arms. "I made a trade with Magnet," he insisted. "Burned the police jackets on a bunch of those augs you're wearing so the cops can't trace them. In return, I get my place and I stay out of your way."

Cali shook his head, running a hand over his goatee beard and grinning. "Nah, nah. See, Snakey, you too *useful*, is what it is. Mag, he the boss and he got other jobs you can do."

"I'm not interested." Pritchard shook his head.

"Ain't about what yo' skinny white ass want, geek," snarled one of the other gangers. "Do what yo' told. Maybe you and your ladies here get to keep breathin'."

Cali gave a shrug and cocked his head. "So, that's how it is. See, Mag's real busy right now with a big deal, but he's gonna come around here when he's done—"

Jensen decided that things had gone on long enough. He stepped forward. "Maybe you don't hear so well with that aug after all." He put himself between Cali and Pritchard. "Frank doesn't want to play ball.

So why don't you be on your way?"

Cali fingered his beard again and giggled. "Well, look at this slick son-of-a-bitch! What are you, his manager?"

The thug who had shot his mouth off pulled a snub-nose Copperhead .40 revolver from his belt and let it dangle at the end of his arm. Cali saw and smirked.

"Just a work colleague," Jensen corrected. He flexed his arms, feeling the mechanisms within shift under the impulses from his nerves. With the inhibitor cuff long gone, he was free to deploy his augmentations at full offensive capability. There was a sudden snap-click of spinning micro-gears, and a pair of meter-long blades extended out of hidden slots in Jensen's wrists. Black alloy with fractal monomolecular edges, the weapons were capable of slicing through most materials like butter. The smirk on Cali's face froze and his eyes widened to saucers as Jensen put one of the blades right under his chin. "Careful there," he told the gangbanger. "Don't make any sudden moves, unless you want a real close shave."

The thug with the revolver hesitated, and Stacks took the opportunity to take a menacing step forward, bringing up his heavy duty arms. He opened his dual-thumbed claw hands wide and let them rotate slowly around his wrist joints. "Uh-uh, Youngblood," he told the other ganger. "Take a muh-moment there."

Cali swallowed – slowly and very carefully – then raised a hand to wave off his comrade. "Hey, be cool. Just giving Snakey a message, right?" He backed away from the blade edge and Jensen let him go. "Mag, he be coming around, is all." Cali retreated toward the car, trying to gather up a little of his earlier bravado. "You better be ready to put in some work. And make your boys here be civil."

The thug with the pistol finally holstered it and, pausing to spit on the ground, he joined the others in the car. Jensen retracted the nanoblades as the vehicle revved and drove away.

When the car was out of sight, Pritchard rounded on him. "Same old Jensen! You have to interfere with everything!" He prodded him in the chest. "I was going to handle that!"

"Oh yeah?" Stacks stifled a cough and raised his eyebrow. "How so?"

"I live here now," Pritchard went on. "That means there are certain realities I have to accept. I don't need you upsetting the status quo any more than you already have!"

"You're welcome," Jensen retorted.

Pritchard gave an exasperated snort and went to the Rialto's rear entrance, punching a code into a hidden keypad. A heavy metal fire door clunked open and he went inside, not waiting to see if the others followed him.

Jensen and Stacks entered warily, and their footsteps echoed in the space within. The Rialto's interior was a magnificent ruin, the decaying art deco designs of the walls, the suspended gallery above and crumbling rows of seats like a snapshot of a decomposing sculpture. Musty, rain-soaked panels hung on the verge of collapse from the high ceiling overhead, and entire sections of the floor had given way into a darkened basement below.

Pritchard picked a path across a makeshift walkway built out of ladders and sheet metal, heading toward the stage where a giant movie screen would once have hung. On the dais up there, Jensen saw bubble tents and flexible plastic walls set up around banks of glowing computer servers.

A strident beeping tone echoed out across the atrium, and Jensen stiffened, instantly recognizing the pre-detonation warning of a mine template. He saw lights blinking in chains around the walkway. Pritchard's security for his bolt hole was a series of kinetic and electromagnetic pulse grenades with proximity detectors.

Before the devices could trigger, Pritchard cleared his throat and called out a password. "*Aerith Lives,*" he said, his voice carrying. The countdown halted and the mines went back to a dormant mode.

"Interesting décor," offered Jensen, surveying the interior. Off to one side, he saw an area that had been cleared of chairs and piled high with heavy plastic carry cases stamped with the Sarif Industries logo. "Let me guess, you borrowed some office supplies before you got fired?"

"I *resigned,*" Pritchard retorted, climbing up to the dais. He paused to check the cables on an electric-engine motorcycle that was charging from a massive battery pack. "I consider all that as my severance package." He waved at the boxes. "Some of it is yours, I think…"

"What?"

He nodded. "From your office at Sarif. It was in storage. I… appropriated it."

Stacks had found a refrigerator and was helping himself to a can of beer. He sat heavily in the front row and drank steadily.

"Make yourself at home, why don't you?" Pritchard's acid reply went unanswered.

Jensen went to the cases, shifting some aside until he

found a couple that bore his old SI employee code. The first was full of files and desk clutter, but the second contained the contents of his personal locker from the company's security ops center. Inside, there was a spare chest armor rig and a case containing his backup pistol. He checked and loaded the compact CA-4 semi-automatic, clipping it into a shoulder holster that sat inconspicuously under his jacket. "Better," he said to himself.

Jensen crossed back to Pritchard's home from home, the sprawling collection of hijacked computer server stacks, digital projector screens and other items of tech whose functions he could only guess at. Cables for power and data were everywhere underfoot, extending like taproots across the raised platform of the dais. One section of the stage was the hacker's living area, with a careworn leather sofa, a portable kitchen from a disaster relief airdrop module and a bubble tent for sleeping.

Pritchard was already back in his 'cockpit', his hands skittering across a backlit keyboard as he worked through a waterfall of incomprehensible code across one of the big screens. "So," he sniffed. "Where do you want to start with this crusade of yours? The sooner you decide, the sooner you can leave."

Any answer Jensen was going to give was cut off by a strangled cry of pain from the front row. Stacks pitched forward out of his chair and crashed to the floor in a twitching heap. Jensen leapt down to him, in time to see the other man crush the beer can in his hand between the trembling fingers of his cyberarm.

The seizure had come out of nowhere, but now it had Stacks in its teeth, he had to ride it out. Another cry of pain escaped his lips and he fought for breath.

Jensen turned him so he wouldn't injure himself, but there was little else he could do but let Stacks endure the attack.

"He's in neuropozyne withdrawal," Pritchard said grimly. "That's a bad reaction. When was his last dose?"

Jensen frowned. "Damn it, Stacks… You gave that girl your last cap, didn't you?" He guessed that the other man had been holding off as long as he could before taking his remaining nu-poz – and now that choice was paying him back.

"I… I… I'm okay…" Stacks bit out the words as the tremors slowly abated. He coughed, spitting blood where he had bitten the inside of his mouth. "Ah, shit. Hurts like razors, brother."

Pritchard dragged a device trailing dozens of colored cables over to them. He fired it up and connected the wires to maintenance sockets in Stacks's shoulder joints. "A lot of red flags here," he explained, after a moment, reading off a small screen. "Ah, half this stuff is meaningless to me… Looks like there could be connector failures across the PEDOT clusters…"

"I'll manage." Stacks forced himself to sit up, but the effort almost made him black out. "I'll… be okay. Just need to rest."

"Is this something to do with what happened to us at the WHO clinic?" Jensen shot Pritchard a questioning look.

The hacker was well aware of Jensen's lack of need for neuropozyne, but his augmentations were still subject to malfunction just like any other piece of complex equipment. He shook his head. "I don't know, and I can't do much with this hardware, Jensen. I don't have the tech or the knowledge to give you a full system overview. I mean, I'm a hacker, not a cyberneticist."

Jensen scowled. "Can't go through any legal channels, we'd be made in a second. What about black market clinics?"

"If you want to turn yourself over to the tender mercies of the local Harvester clan, go right ahead." Pritchard nodded toward Jensen's arm. "You'll wake up as an eyeless torso in a wheelchair with some gangbanger like Cali wearing those augs instead. If you wake up at all."

Jensen fell silent for a moment, thinking it through. A creeping, unpleasant thought formed in his mind. There was more to be concerned about than just Stacks's well-being. His own was also in question.

I was out for months. I have no idea what they did to me during that time. He looked down at his hands. *How do I trust my own tech?*

"What about Sarif?" he asked.

"I told you, he's in the wind—"

"The company, not the man," Jensen added. "The lab facilities in the SI building, they've got all the hardware to run a diagnostic, right? And maybe some stocks of nu-poz as well."

"If it hasn't already been removed or looted!" Pritchard shot back. "Not to mention that the new owners from Hengsha have the towers locked down tight."

"Pritchard, before all this blew up, you and I were responsible for the security of that building. If anyone can get in there, we can."

He knew Frank Pritchard well enough to know that appealing to his hacker vanity, that desire to break the system, would sway him. He could see the decision forming in the other man's mind even as he spoke.

But there was something else pushing Jensen toward this act. More than the desire to help Stacks, more than the cold suspicion that Agent Thorne or someone else in the chain of his enemies might have tampered with him.

The gaps in my memory. The pieces of the past I'm missing. Maybe I can find some of it there.

"It won't be easy," Pritchard was saying. "We'll all need to pitch in."

"Okay," said Stacks. "Not like I got much option."

Jensen nodded. "We'll go back to where it started."

FOUR

In the shadows of the rooftop, a figure leaned forward on the guard rail surrounding the wide helipad and lit the caffeine stick between his lips. In the distance, the twinkling lights of the City of Angels beckoned through a dull haze of smog. He took a long, deep drag and exhaled – then hesitated, hearing boots crunch on gravel.

He smiled dourly without turning around. "Don't lecture me, Raye."

"Do you ever listen when I do, sir?" He turned as his second-in-command strode purposefully across the helipad toward him. Raye Vande's European accent always seemed a little out of place on an otherwise all-American team, but the woman had fitted perfectly into the group from the very start. She was cool, focused and completely by the book – and that was exactly what Christian Jarreau liked about her. The rest of his unit could be a little unruly at times, and it helped him to have someone like Vande as his number two, someone who could play hardball with the regs when the situation required it.

"Can't smoke anywhere in this damn state," he went on, his gruff Louisiana brogue rising to the fore. "Helps me think."

"The squad's assembling downstairs, sir. Techs say we'll have the neural subnet link with Prague in the next ten." She brushed her short-cut blonde hair back as the wind caught it, eyeing him.

"Roger that." He accepted her report with a nod and took another drag.

They were a study in contrasts: while Jarreau and Vande were around the same height, she was slight and athletic where he was broad and square-cut. Jarreau's dark, chiseled face with its hooded eyes habitually wore a thoughtful expression, but for her part Vande always seemed hawkish and wary, as if she was forever waiting for a trap to be sprung. Both of them wore identical tactical rigs, form-fitting gear with a lightweight ballistic armor vest and a standard equipment loadout that would have been familiar to any counter-terror operative around the world. Jarreau's weapon of choice, strapped to his back and safed, was a suppressed Hurricane TMP-18 machine pistol modified to his personal specifications, whereas Vande preferred a pair of twinned semi-auto Silverballer pistols.

Neither of them bore any kind of insignia on their matte black outfits, but there was an arfid chip embedded in the shoulder of their tac gear that would return a data panel if pinged by the correct interrogation signal. That panel would identify them as law enforcement officers in the employ of Interpol, with wide-ranging jurisdiction and a dozen other permissions that would allow them to get their job done. But it was a rare event for any of them to have to flash their badge, even if it was a virtual one. The group they worked for was high-speed, low-drag – Task Force 29, an international counter-terror, intelligence and investigation group created by special United Nations mandate. They were an agile operation that could react quickly without being mired in legal issues or bureaucracy.

Jarreau commanded the Alpha team of TF29's North American unit, and he was good at it. Recruited right out of the US Navy's E-SEAL team program a few months after the Aug Incident, he was a year into his new gig and he liked it just fine. He knew better than anyone the danger that unchecked terrorism, aug-related violence and organized crime could wreak, knew the reasons why a group like TF29 was needed in the world.

When the incident had taken place, he'd almost died from neural shock caused by the Darrow signal... but rather than remove the augmentations that had nearly killed him, he decided to dedicate himself to making sure such things couldn't be used to hurt people again. TF29 seemed like the best way to do that, and when Interpol offered him a squad, he signed on without hesitation.

Vande was augmented as well, but she never talked much about the fire that had taken her hands, and he didn't ask. Vande was like that a lot of the time, most of her under the surface, like the shape of a shark with only the blade of a fin cutting the water to remind you she was around.

They made a good team, along with the hand-picked tier one operatives that Jarreau had personally selected to ride with them. It bothered him that they had only a single field office with a lot of ground to cover in the US and Canada, but then the doctrine of *minimal footprint, maximum effectiveness* was Task Force standard. TF29-NA, as they were officially designated, was frequently split up into its component action teams to deal with ongoing investigations. Right now, the Bravo and Delta teams were respectively investigating a Triad Harvester ring working out of Vancouver and a rogue militia group in the New Mexico badlands.

The big and loud actions, the common crimes, those could be left to the FBI and Homeland Security. What TF29 did was tackle criminality and terrorism that had *global* reach, the kind of thing that threatened thousands of people on multiple continents.

"Who is the contact we'll be talking to in Prague?" Jarreau surrendered to the inevitable and flicked the caffeine stick over the edge of the roof, gesturing for Vande to walk with him back to the stairs.

"Jim Miller, your opposite number from the Central European office." She fell in alongside him.

"Miller?" Jarreau's eyebrows rose. "I've heard of him. He was with the Tactical Assault Group in Australia before the incident. Hell of a marksman, so they say."

"That's the word. And before you ask, I never met him." Vande was from the Netherlands, recruited by the same channels Jarreau had been, but in her case via the Dutch National Constabulary's Special Intervention Service. She'd spent time in TF29's Lyon headquarters before transferring to the States, but Miller was an unknown quantity to her. "We'll find out for sure when we talk to the man."

"Yeah." Jarreau frowned. "Right now, I'd reach out to Pope Theodore himself if I thought it would get us a lead."

Vande snorted. "With all due respect, sir, divine guidance isn't going to get us these creeps. Solid police work and boots on necks, that'll do it."

"The direct approach. I like—" He was going to say more, but a low vibration through his boots cut him off. "Another one?"

The woman paused, as if she were searching for a scent on the air. "Minor earth tremor. Nothing to be worried about. Baby quakes, they happen out here all the time, so I hear."

Jarreau raised an eyebrow. "I like it better where the earth *doesn't* move." He descended into the muggy warmth of the floor below, noting that the empty building's air con system was still inoperable. Once, this 'see-through' would have been a busy office complex, but the ongoing global economic downturn had emptied it. That was fine for Jarreau's team. It meant no snoopers.

He exchanged glances with some of the other squad members as he passed them, getting nods of assent in return. He didn't need to ask them what they were thinking. Like Jarreau, the rest of Alpha team were chafing at the inactivity that had been forced upon them, after dead end upon dead end had kept the unit from achieving their mission goal.

For the past three months, TF29's North American division had been systematically locating, isolating and dismantling the branches of a widespread illegal smuggling network that traded in black market human augmentations. Since the imposition of new laws and multiple registration acts around the world, all offensive aug tech was outlawed for civilian use except by special permission – but that hadn't stopped people trading in surplus left over from before the aug market crashed, homebrew modifications, or worst of all, mil-spec cyberware harvested from unwilling donors.

Jarreau, Vande and the rest of Alpha team were on their toughest assignment yet – tracking a faceless, unknown broker who had somehow managed to stay one step ahead of the task force every step of the way. Whomever this person was, they were facilitating the movement of combat-grade augs out of the United States. Jarreau had made it his mission to see that pipeline shut off, but so far he had failed to do so.

At their last post-operation briefing, one of the other team members had bitterly complained that to outthink them this much, the broker had to be someone with an inside track, someone with Interpol connections. Jarreau said nothing; but privately he had confided to Vande that he was having the same suspicions. Hopefully, Miller and the Prague office had a new lead that could help them break the deadlock.

"Time to take a dive," said Jarreau. He dropped into a molded plastic chair, inclined at an angle beneath a semi-circular articulated frame that resembled a medical x-ray machine. The neural subnet apparatus comprised of heavy blocks of superconducting quantum image detectors that surrounded the user's head in a thick halo, and as he settled in, the device rotated into place.

Vande took another seat beneath a second NSN unit networked to the first, as the technician working the rig double-checked the last few connections and gave Jarreau a thumbs-up.

"Neural connection is good to go, sir," said the tech, tapping at a monitor unit. "Link parity is five by five."

"I never like using this thing," said Vande, with a grimace. "Too much like giving up control."

"Agreed," Jarreau told her. "Know how I deal with it? I pretend I'm going deep into the ocean. Think of it like a swim in the sea."

Vande's face creased in a scowl as the halves of a clamshell scanner rig rotated around her head. "I'm from Holland," she shot back. "We hate the sea and the sea hates us."

"Then just grit your teeth 'til it's over." Jarreau's own rig settled into place and snapped closed.

There was a sharp, brilliant light that seemed to come from behind his eyes, a sudden sense of dislocation from his body as the neural link engaged – and then Jarreau was in another place entirely.

A deliberately nondescript conference room with a large table surrounded by identical chairs – one of which he was sitting in – and walls with a wood-finish patterning. There was a window that looked out on to a repeating loop of some tranquil, nonexistent hillside under a digitally perfect blue sky, and the only other item of note was a representation of the Interpol symbol, which hung in mid-air above the table like a gravity-defying sculpture.

A collection of pixels accreted in the seat next to him, forming into an avatar of Raye Vande. She looked much the same as she did in reality, but with the detail dialed down a little. TF29 didn't have the bandwidth or processing power for total resolution, which had the downside of making everyone in the NSN's virtual space look like a life-sized toy version of themselves. She gave him a nod, and Jarreau looked down at the digital representations of his hands, flexing his pseudo-plastic fingers.

The Interpol logo popped like a bubble, briefly replaced by the word "*Connecting...*" before it disappeared outright and a third person phased into fake solidity across the table from them.

"This is Miller," said the new arrival. "You seeing me okay?"

Jarreau nodded. He introduced himself and Vande, and felt the odd impulse to shake hands. "Appreciate you working with us on this," he began. "And sorry about the time difference. What is it, morning over there?"

"It's four AM in Prague," Vande told him.

"Don't sweat it," Miller replied, with a weary smile. "Office is quiet this time of day. I get more done." He leaned forward, and Jarreau got a good look at the man's avatar. If it was an accurate representation, then Jim Miller appeared to be in his mid-forties, tall in his seat and short-haired, with a weathered aspect to him that even the NSN couldn't entirely erase. Jarreau knew the type; a veteran cop used to doing the job his way. That was something he could work with. "So, let me tell you what we have at our end and we'll go from there." Miller's hands worked at a keypad that the virtual environment hadn't rendered, his fingers dancing in the air. "We've picked up chatter on our side of the Atlantic. Several persons of interest talking about a consignment of mil-spec augmentations coming out of the States in the next week or so. No details on the supplier, but what we *do* have is a confirmed ID on the perps that will be making the pick-up."

Panes of data unfolded in the air between them, showing intercept records, criminal jackets and surveillance images. Jarreau saw shots taken by a long-lensed camera drone of augmented men wearing dusty combat gear, standing on a desert road.

"Mercenaries?" he said immediately. There was a subtle kind of tell that career military had about them, a way of carrying themselves even when they were outside a war zone. The men in the pictures had something else, a cocksure manner that set off Jarreau's instinctive dislike of soldier-of-fortune types.

"Good eye," said Miller, with a nod. "Head creep there goes by the alias 'Sheppard'. His real name is John Trent, but he hasn't used that in a while. He's been on our radar for some time." An icon appeared next to one of the men in the picture, clearly the leader by the way the others deferred to him. "Along with most of his crew, he used to be part of a Strike Team for Belltower Associates."

"A bunch of bulls," offered Vande. "How appropriate."

"After the Rifleman scandal broke, Trent and his boys were among those who went AWOL. From what we can tell, they decided to go into the lucrative world of dealing illegal arms, training terrorists and just about anything violent that turns a profit."

Vande leaned in to get a better look. "Were they at Rifleman Bank?"

Miller shook his head. "But he's no saint. When Belltower downsized and rebranded themselves as Tarvos Security, guys with dirty records like Trent's were the first to bolt. He's quick on the trigger, this one. Ruthless, too. He doesn't care if civilians get caught in the crossfire."

"A real charmer." Jarreau considered Miller's words. When the story about the private military contractor Belltower, and its involvement in running a black site prison in the Pacific called Rifleman Bank, had hit the news feeds, the company's carefully presented reputation went into a nosedive. Questions of ethics, rumors about medical experiments being performed on unlawfully held detainees, all of it swirled around and stuck to Belltower's spit-shined uniform like mud. These days, the company didn't exist anymore – aside from its last vestiges as Tarvos Security – but in its death throes, Belltower had spat out enough trained, augmented triggermen to make a hell of a lot of trouble for the world's law enforcers. *Case in point*, he thought. "Where is this 'Sheppard' and his crew now?"

Miller frowned. "We don't have eyes on them. Same time we got our intercept, they went dark. Best guess? I think they're making a low-key transit into the States, probably via Canada."

Vande shot Jarreau a questioning look, then turned back to Miller. "Do you have any idea what his endgame is, once he has the augs?"

Miller pinched the bridge of his nose. "That is a question that has nothing but a lot of unpleasant answers, Agent Vande. Sheppard's been known to deal with just about anyone. There's a chance he could trade them on to the Jinn smuggling cartel, maybe to his contacts in the African conflict zone. My personal fear is that he sells them to ARC, and then all bets are off."

"I thought the Augmented Rights Coalition were towing the *peaceful resistance* line," said Jarreau. The radical pro-augmentation activist group didn't operate in North America, but he'd seen a security briefing about ARC's growing presence in the European area of operations. They were centered in the Czech Republic, right on Miller's doorstep, so it was no wonder he was wary of them.

"On the surface," Miller told him. "But we're hearing rumors of ARC moving toward a much more militant stance." He spread his hands, and for a moment his avatar shuddered and jumped as parity briefly fell over the NSN's satellite link. "You see now why I don't want those military augs leaving US soil any more than you do."

"This is all good intel," Vande began, "but we'll need more before there's anything actionable. Ideally, we want to net this Sheppard character and his cargo…"

Miller nodded again. "Agreed. And as much as I'd like to be there with you on this, I've got fires to put out here in Prague. But there's one other piece of the puzzle we got from our intercept that you're going to find real helpful. We know where Sheppard and his crew are heading, and my guess is, that's where the exchange will go down."

Jarreau felt a tingle of anticipation. This could be the strongest lead they'd had in months. "Let's hear it."

"You ever been to Detroit?" asked Miller, with a wan smile.

SARIF INDUSTRIES – DETROIT –
UNITED STATES OF AMERICA

The twin pillars of the building rose up into the midnight sky before them, and Jensen traced the shapes of the towers, black and dead against the rain that was falling. For a brief moment, it was like looking up at a giant grave marker, and the harshness of the mental image made him grimace. For all the light that David Sarif's self-styled 'beacon' had cast over the streets of Detroit, it would always be cemented in Jensen's mind as a place that had changed his life in darker ways than he would have wished.

Pritchard nodded toward the main entrance from beneath his hoodie. "Can't get in that way," he said. The first two floors of the building were surrounded by a fence topped with barbed wire, the windows blacked out by metal security grilles retrofitted to the walls. Dim lights moved around behind the panels, back and forth in regular patterns.

"Guards in there?" asked Stacks. His breathing was labored, but he was keeping up.

"Not human ones," Pritchard explained. "Follow me. There's another route inside."

The streets were deserted here. Aside from the metallic rumble of the occasional passing people mover overhead, there was no-one around to see the three of them pick their way toward the locked entrance to the SI building's underground car park.

A massive metal shutter sealed it off from the street level, but one corner of the panel had been dented and stove in. Jensen saw the hulk of a burned-out Motokun cargo truck nearby.

"Some people tried to break in the hard way," said Pritchard, off his look. "They didn't get very far."

Rounding the front of the dead truck, Jensen saw that the grille and the windshield were a mess of bullet holes. Whatever weapon had done the damage was large-caliber and fully automatic. "Cops just let that happen?" he asked.

"They pulled out of the local police precinct after the riots," said the hacker. "These days, the law doesn't come down to this part of the city unless it's in an APC or a gunship."

"So, who did that?" Stacks pointed at the truck.

Pritchard jerked a thumb at the barrier. "The new owners."

On the drop-gate there was a warning sign in Chinese, English and Spanish which made short work of explaining that this site now belonged to Tai Yong Medical Incorporated, and that intruders would face lethal force.

The hacker crouched low and peered into the gap between the floor and the bent door. "A little help?" He looked pointedly at Stacks.

The other man blew out a breath, and with a grunt of exertion, he pulled the bent corner of the door up a little more, enough so Pritchard could squeeze through. Jensen went after him, and Stack followed, shouldering awkwardly through the gap.

Inside, the parking garage was murky and the air held the lingering stink of burned plastics and battery acid. The smart-vision system in Jensen's cyberoptics immediately adjusted for the low-light level, and he watched Pritchard advance gingerly across the concrete cavern. Keeping pace, the three men moved as silently as possible from one support pillar to another. In the far corner of the garage, Jensen saw a blinking crimson light on the exit door leading to the stairwell.

Pritchard had explained his intrusion plan on the way from the Rialto, and Jensen didn't like it. While the hacker made his way to the door to disarm the alarm module in place there – along with the fragmentation mine it would trigger if set off – Jensen's task would be to keep watch for the garage's guardian. He'd already told Stacks to stick with Pritchard, framing it like he wanted the ex-steeplejack to protect the hacker, but more truthfully it was to keep him out of harm's way. Stacks wasn't a fighter, he didn't have the instinct for it, and Jensen was afraid he would get the man killed.

They split apart, and Jensen drew his CA-4, flicking off the safety catch. He pulled back the slide to be sure a round was already in the chamber; there it was, the tip of the bullet glowing with a faint blue halo. The modified rounds were a gift from Pritchard, and instead of a lead head or a hollowpoint, they had a tiny pack of conductive gel and a super-dense capacitor at the tip. On impact, the shots released a small, focused electromagnetic pulse, supposedly powerful enough to give any electronic hardware a headache. If they didn't work as advertised, he wouldn't be around to complain about it.

Stalking around abandoned, dust-covered cars, Jensen moved deeper into the dimness. Off to his right, he heard the rattle and click of tools as Pritchard got to work on disarming the lock.

He stepped past a support pillar and his gaze fell on the perfect, straight edges of a giant cube measuring five meters along each axis. In the shadows, it was black and featureless, but as he watched the surface of the cube trembled. Jensen caught the sound of a muffled curse from the direction of Pritchard and Stacks.

The cube gave off a hydraulic sigh. Then with a flurry of motion, the sides of it folded up and away like some complex puzzle toy. The dormant Box-Guard robot, likely awakened by the hacker's actions, was stirring.

Legs emerged from each corner, along with gun clusters and an articulated neck that ended in a rectangular, cyclopean head. Pin-lamps snapped on, flooding the garage with sodium-bright light – and found Jensen standing before it.

The Box-Guard hesitated a split-second, still getting its bearings as it rebooted, and that was the vital window of action Jensen needed. Aiming the semi-automatic at the robot's head, he put a shot right into its sensor grid. Bright sparks flared, but all that seemed to do was narrow the machine's focus. Its legs stomped as it turned in place to give Jensen its full attention. He heard the whine of servos as the gun pods spun up to power.

"Shit!" He stood his ground long enough to fire a few more shots, but the EMP rounds seemed to do little to slow it.

The Box-Guard made a grinding sound and advanced on him, picking up speed with each stride. Jensen broke into a sprint as it came after him, swerving aside as one of the robot's legs kicked away a Navig subcompact, rolling the car on to its roof. The guns tracked him, swinging back and forth as they coughed out shotgun rounds, but Jensen dodged and wove between the parked vehicles, making it hard for the machine to target him. Belatedly, a recorded message began to play, a soothing female voice speaking in Chinese delivering some kind of demand for a surrender.

When the robot stumbled into a pillar, Jensen realized that the EMP rounds had made some difference, just not enough to deal with the machine outright. Its motions were becoming sluggish and drunken.

He took a breath of dusty air and circled back around a sedan, before launching himself right at the Box-Guard. If he could just place his shots in the right spot…

The robot slammed a leg into the concrete floor with enough force to knock him off-balance and his first round went wide. He fired another, clipping the side of the Box-Guard's menacing head, and that seemed to agitate the machine. If it was having difficulty targeting him with its guns, then the robot's programming told it to use a more direct, *more kinetic* approach instead.

Rearing up, the Box-Guard raised one leg and calculated the exact amount of hydraulic pressure to crush a human body. It loomed over Jensen, clipping its frame on a dangling light strip.

He fired, unloading every bullet remaining in the CA-4's magazine, marching each flashing hit toward a gap in the plating beneath the Box-Guard's head, where its flexible neck connected. Jolts of sparks vomited out from behind its single eye-lens, and the leg descended with a juddering clank, stopping just short of grinding Jensen into the dust. He rolled away as the machine repeated the action over and over, never quite completing it, stuck in some kind of loop.

"Jensen!" Pritchard's nasal shout echoed across the garage. "Quick, get over here before it resets! The door's clear!"

He sprinted over, mantling the hoods of parked cars. Pritchard held on to an inert mine template draped with dozens of connector wires, while Stacks shouldered open the door, revealing the stairwell beyond. "Gotta go, gotta go!"

"Don't wait for me." An idea flashed through Jensen's mind and he snatched the explosive device out of Pritchard's hands, reactivating it as he raced back the way he had come. He ignored their calls to follow, pausing long enough to toss the frag mine under the shuddering Box-Guard before doubling back once again.

Jensen was at the door, wrenching it closed behind him when the robot finally snapped itself out of its temporary malaise – and stamped down, right on top of the mine template. The explosive detonated with a flat, loud crack and the Box-Guard toppled.

"So much for the quiet approach," snapped Pritchard.

Jensen shot him a cold look, and started up the stairs toward the upper level. "Next time, have a better plan."

They emerged through a service door and into the main atrium of the SI building. What hit Jensen first was the smell of stale smoke, an acrid stink that lay heavy in the air all around them. Across the reception area, where once there had been illuminated video-pillars showcasing the achievements of Sarif Industries, there was only a mess of half-dismantled machinery and piles of broken office furniture. Along the walls near the sealed main door there was a wide black stain that reached up to the second level of the atrium. The slick of old soot and melted plastic was like a great burn wound.

"Firebombs," Pritchard said quietly, by way of explanation. "Courtesy of the good people of Detroit. Never mind that the company had nothing to do with the incident." He shook his head. "Idiots. Like trying to burn down a hospital just because someone gets sick."

"P-people get afraid, they need someone to blame…" muttered Stacks. "Ain't no-one's fuh-fault."

Jensen saw splashes of paint over the doors and angry scrawls over the glass – slogans like AUGS OUT and DIE HANZERS! left behind in the aftermath.

He looked away as movement caught his eye. Set out across the atrium, there were stubby, drum-shaped sensor pods endlessly scanning the area with laser rangers. Each had a multi-barreled gun atop them, and they were actively tracking back and forth. The Box-Guard in the parking garage would have sent a warning to all the units on the security network, upping their alert status to full. Above, on the second and third levels, Jensen saw small, wheeled robots wandering in pre-programmed patrol loops, the same kind of armed sentry that had threatened him outside the Chiron Building apartments.

"Typical Tai Yong…" Pritchard crouched in the lee of what used to be the reception desk. "Too cheap to bring in any real security."

"You forgetting that mech downstairs?" said Jensen.

Pritchard ignored him. "They're using SI's own robots, they just reprogrammed them for deterrent duty." He tugged on a zip at his cuff that opened the sleeve of his coat along the length of his forearm, revealing a flexible keyboard and monitor screen clipped to the inside of his wrist. The hacker went to work, his other hand dancing across the panel. "Their protocols are always sloppy. Hengsha's never produced a single decent black hat…"

"What are you doing?" Jensen demanded.

The hacker sighed. "TYM's acquisition team take what they want and abandon-in-place everything else. And they typically don't bother to deep-sweep the main grid for backdoor passwords embedded by, *oh*, let's say, the company's former head of digital security." Pritchard's wrist-keyboard gave an answering beep and he showed a sly grin. "Done. Now those bots will register us as friendlies." He got up and walked out of cover. "You were actually right for once, Jensen. This was easier than I thought it would be."

"Easy for *you*," Jensen muttered.

Pritchard ignored him and approached one of the pods. It momentarily tracked him with a red thread of laser light; then the beam snapped to green and moved on as if he wasn't there.

"Whoa," said Stacks. "Your... buddy, uh, he's real impressed with himself, yeah?"

Jensen nodded. "And then some." He paused, eyeing the other man as he walked awkwardly after the hacker, clearly in pain. "Can you handle this?"

"I... got it." Irritably, Stacks waved him away. He was sweating and his breathing was shallow. "This place, brother, it gives me the damned creeps."

"I hear you," Jensen told him, the honesty of his own response giving him a moment's pause. He offered his hand to Stacks, but the other man refused with a scowl and moved off without him, trying not to draw attention to the tremors going through the fingers at the end of his hulking arms.

Jensen followed, but his own thoughts kept straying as a steady stream of old memories washed over him. He'd come here partly hoping to reconnect with his past, but it wasn't working the way he wanted it to.

Being inside the Sarif building seemed somehow *unreal* to him, the knowledge of the place where he had worked filtered through a lens of uncertainty. He knew the layout of the office complex intimately, but part of him felt as if he had never set foot in there before, as if it were all some kind of abstract illusion.

Jamais vu, he remembered. That was the term for it, the polar opposite of *déjà vu*, the eerie sense of when something intimately familiar felt totally new. His eyes narrowed and he shook off the feeling with a physical shrug. As he did so, he caught sight of a dim corner of the atrium where the remembrance monument had been situated.

Back in 2027, a group of mercenaries known as the Tyrants had struck the company and many lives had been lost. Jensen's was almost counted among them. What at first had seemed like a covert attack by one of Sarif Industries' corporate rivals was revealed as the cover for the multiple kidnappings of several of SI's top scientists. It was only Jensen's dogged investigation of the assault that allowed him to track down the missing in the custody of Hugh Darrow, who had secretly abducted the group to work on his biochip control scheme at the Illuminati's behest. Everyone else had thought they were dead, many laying the blame for that at Jensen's feet – he had been in charge of security that day – and for a long time, a monument had stood to honor their loss… and his failure. But he had always known they were alive.

I always knew she *was still alive*, thought Jensen.

"Why don't you just get it over with and ask the question?" He turned to find Pritchard close by, watching him intently. The other man nodded toward the smoke-blackened monument.

"What happened to… the others?" He frowned, angry at himself for being unable to draw up the words he really wanted to utter. "You said David Sarif went off the grid, but what about the rest?"

"For the most part, the people who worked here were either caught up in the incident or else they scattered to the four winds soon after." Pritchard folded his arms. "I know that Sarif's assistant, Athene… she quit after what happened. Couldn't live with herself being part of the company after all the chaos. She was the first to go. Your security teams were kicked out when Tai Yong bought up the company assets." He paused, thinking. "Malik, the pilot… Last time I saw her she was with you, heading off to Hengsha, so you would know better than me." Pritchard shook his head. "But we both know who you're *really* interested in."

Jensen bit out the name. "Megan Reed."

The hacker gave a nod. "I'll never understand that woman's attachment to you, Jensen. You were never good for her."

There were a hundred different retorts that pushed at Jensen for release, and for a brief moment he hated Pritchard for making him face that cold truth head-on. He must have seen that flash of pure fury in Jensen's eyes, because Pritchard's superior expression slipped for a moment.

"I went halfway around the world for her," Jensen said, at length. "I found out the truth."

And that truth was complex and troubling. Before coming to work at Sarif, they had been lovers, even spoke of settling down together, and although it hadn't worked out, Jensen could not deny that he had still carried some affection for her. Maybe that had been what fueled his search after the Tyrants attacked, at least at first. But in the end, he had discovered that Megan Reed's priorities were very different from his own.

She'd kept secrets from him, sampling his DNA in hopes of isolating his unique super-compatibility, even ensuring he would be offered a job at Sarif Industries to keep him close. And when at last he had confronted her with that, her reaction wasn't what he'd expected. Megan believed she was working in the name of a greater good, and Jensen still wasn't sure if she was right or wrong.

Pritchard's tone shifted. "All I know is that Megan came back to Detroit after Panchaea, and then she vanished. But there have been rumors that she's working for Versalife, maybe in their Hong Kong or San Francisco labs."

"And Versalife is an Illuminati front." Jensen let that sink in. "I don't know what to make of that."

"For what it's worth... I'm sorry," said the hacker.

Jensen took whatever emotional reaction was forming and crushed it before it could coalesce. "It's over and done," he said firmly. "Come on, we've got work to do."

Stacks was waiting for them by the elevator bank, and Pritchard ran another bypass subroutine to call a lift car down from the upper floors. Jensen drew his gun and reloaded it as they began their ascent to the laboratory levels, while Stacks kept to the corner of the elevator, panting hard.

Pritchard eyed the other man and shot Jensen a questioning look, but he said nothing.

"What are the odds this place will have what we need?" Jensen watched the floor number display count up and up. "Didn't you say Tai Yong stripped most of it?"

"Only what was portable, and what their goons could actually get into." Pritchard gave a brief, smug smile. "Someone might have tampered with the key codes on his way out the door..."

"Can... we get out soon?" Stacks breathed. "Too close in here."

There was a hollow *ping* and the elevator halted, the doors parting to reveal darkness beyond them. "We're here," said Jensen.

"Testing and quality control," Pritchard told them. "Main power is off on this floor, but I should be able to get the emergency batteries up and running." He reached into the daypack on his back, retrieving a spherical drone. The hacker gave it a twist and tossed it into the air, where it floated away on micro-rotors. The unit immediately cast out a weak orange glow that spilled over desks, chairs and other equipment, casting strange, jumping shadows.

Jensen stepped out, his pistol raised, with Pritchard right behind him.

Stacks came last, but he made it only a few steps before his trembling iron hands came up to his face and he started screaming.

FIVE

SARIF INDUSTRIES – DETROIT – UNITED STATES OF AMERICA

The sound that came out of the other man's mouth was something tortured and animalistic, a raw cry of pain that cut right through Jensen's skull. Stacks staggered out across the corridor, shaking his head violently and clawing at the air. His heavy cybernetic arms crashed through racks of discarded equipment, smashing them to the ground. The man cast around, swinging back and forth, as if he had been thrown into a pit of horrors that only he could see.

"No, no, no," he cried, tears running down his cheeks. "I'm sorry, I didn't mean it, I didn't do it, oh no, no, please, no…" For a brief moment his wild gaze crossed Jensen's and he saw the panic in Stacks's eyes, the blank lack of recognition, the all-consuming shock and horror. "The blood, all the blood, make it stop, please!"

At Jensen's side, Pritchard was fumbling for a weapon, a Buzzkill stun gun unfolding as he dragged it from a pocket in his hoodie. "Wait!" Jensen pushed him away before the hacker could draw a bead. "Don't shoot!"

"He's lost his mind!" Pritchard shouted back.

"Just back off, damn it!" Jensen gave him another hard shove and deliberately put himself in the line of fire. He advanced on Stacks, hands raised and his eye shields retracted.

"All this blood, the blood," Stacks repeated, muttering the words over and over. "*How*? How did it happen…?"

For a moment, Jensen wasn't sure what he meant, but then he looked down at the floor and the implication of the other man's words clicked. The muddy orange light from Pritchard's little light-drone spilled over the floor of the corridor, where the contents of storage boxes had been upended and scattered. All around there were piles of augmentation components, bits of circuitry and mechanical limbs in a chaotic mess. The light from the drone gave everything a blood-red cast and Jensen felt sickened as his mind suddenly reframed what he was seeing as a vision from some hellish abattoir.

And that was how Stacks was seeing it. He'd stepped from the elevator and straight into a nightmare. Jensen reached up, as gently as he could, and grasped the man's mechanoid forearm, trying to steady him.

It was difficult. Stacks had heavy-gauge augs designed for hauling him up the side of derricks and lifting girders, and if he turned on Jensen, he could rip the other man's cyberarms from their sockets.

"Harrison," he said firmly, deliberately using Stacks's first name to hook his attention. "Listen to me. It's Adam. I want you *to come back*." He worked to keep his voice moderated, just like he had been taught during his police training. "Where you are right now, that's not here. It's not happening, man. *Come back. Talk to me.*" Jensen didn't dare to employ his CASIE implant – the same 'social engineering' device Agent Thorne had tried to use on him back in Alaska was good for reading and influencing the moods of others during direct conversation, but Jensen had no idea how it would react to someone in so extreme a situation. *Gotta do this the old-fashioned way*, he told himself

He held out his other hand. "You're not there," Jensen insisted. "You don't have to be afraid."

"I... I..." Stacks was breathing in short, panting bursts – but slowly that normalized and the hollow distance in his gaze faded away.

Jensen threw a hard glance over his shoulder at Pritchard, who scowled and reluctantly put away his stun gun.

"What the hell was that...?" Stacks slumped against a wall, all the frantic energy suddenly drained from him. "I don't know..."

"I knew it had been a while since your last neuropozyne dose," said Jensen. "But this?"

"I just saw all that and I... I freaked out..." He shuddered. "Lost control."

"Can you keep it together?" said Jensen. "Don't lie to me this time."

Stacks gave a wooden nod. "I'm okay." He very carefully made sure that he wasn't looking down at the severed mechanical limbs. "Thanks..."

Pritchard gave a grunt of disapproval and crossed to a door on the far side of the corridor. "The quicker we do this, the better. I don't want any more surprises."

Jensen surveyed the door. It was a thick barrier of armored glass, secured in place with a magnetic lock, and there were signs around the mechanism of failed attempts to force it open. Beyond it was a small laboratory set up with the kind of gear he recognized from LIMB clinics for maintaining augmentation systems. "Can you get us in there?" he asked the hacker.

"Oh, *please*," said Pritchard, with a scornful glance. He made a sweeping motion with his hand to indicate the locked door and a dozen others along the length of the corridor. "Tai Yong Medical may have stripped Sarif Industries for all its assets but I was under no obligation to make it easy to get to them." Pritchard leaned into a control panel by the door and spoke a string of numbers. A light on the lock switched from dull red to bright green and the door dutifully retracted open.

Stacks was still shaky on his feet, so Jensen helped him inside, guiding him to one of a pair of maintenance cradles in the center of the room. Like old-style dentist's chairs, they reclined back so that automated scanner heads and spider-like service arms could come in and work any fixes – short of invasive surgery – on an augmented person with damaged or malfunctioning tech.

"Take a load off," Jensen told him. "We'll get you fixed up, trust me."

"Yeah…" Stacks nodded wearily. His panicked episode had left him disoriented and weak.

Pritchard pulled Jensen away and spoke to him in low tones. "He needs neuropozyne, that's not in doubt… but what just happened out there? That wasn't withdrawal shock! Your friend there just had a psychotic episode!"

"Thought you said you didn't know anything about cybertech?"

"I know what I saw!" he hissed. "Whatever's wrong with him, the withdrawal is making it worse!"

"So *help* him," Jensen demanded.

Pritchard scowled. "Check in there." The hacker pointed at a sealed compartment on one of the lab's walls.

Another magno-lock held the temperature-controlled cabinet shut, but Jensen didn't wait for Pritchard to open it for him. Extending half the length of the nanoblade in his left forearm, Jensen used the blunt tip of the fractal-edged weapon to cut through the lock and pawed through the contents inside. There were dozens of ampoules of the vital anti-rejection drug in there, but he frowned as he looked over use-by dates on the packets. "These meds are expired…"

"It's all there is," Pritchard insisted. "That or nothing. Unless you want your pal here to get worse?" The hacker had started up the scanner unit, letting it move back and forth over Stacks, but Jensen didn't miss that Pritchard was keeping one hand on the grip of his stun gun in case the man had a sudden relapse.

"Fine." These doses were in liquid form, in disposable injectors, and he popped one out of a bubble pack and pressed it to the carotid artery in Stacks's neck. The other man let out a low gasp as the drug filtered into his system. "That should help… for a while, at least."

Stacks looked up at him. "Thanks, brother. What about you, you need a hit too, right?"

Jensen shook his head. He wasn't about to try and explain how his uncommon genetics made neuropozyne redundant for him. "I'm okay. Don't worry about me."

Pritchard peered at the monitor. "The scanner says

there's structural fatigue in some of his joints. Fluid lubricant reservoirs are almost empty. Should be able to fix that…"

Jensen gave a nod, and moved to the second maintenance cradle. On an impulse, he climbed into it and pulled the unit's control screen around so he could operate it. "Might as well check myself while I'm here," he said.

"There's something wrong with you too?" Pritchard sniffed.

"I was out of it for months," Jensen shot back, dismissing the comment. "Just being thorough." He activated the scan program and sat back; but Pritchard's words cut closer to the truth than he wanted to admit.

It was hard for Jensen to frame the strange disquiet that had been with him ever since he awoke in the clinic. If he had been forced to sum it up in a single word, it would have been *disconnected*. He felt out of synch with the world, and there was a quiet, corrosive fear in the back of his thoughts that something had happened to him during his lost time, something he couldn't grasp.

The scanner did its work, moving over his limbs, projecting a sensor image on the display screen. Jensen's augmentations were all in working order, showing the same outer wear and tear they'd had before he embarked on his mission to the Arctic but no more than that. Strangely, he found himself almost *willing* the scanner to find something amiss, almost as if that would confirm his unrest.

He got his wish. The sensor head stopped suddenly and a text box lined in crimson appeared on the display. *Anomaly Detected*, read the warning.

Jensen shot a look at Pritchard. The hacker had his

full attention still on Stacks, wary for any possible burst of fresh violence.

There was something wrong with Jensen's right cyberarm. He lay it across his lap and triggered the nerve-pulse sequence that opened up the scuffed polycarbonate sheath. Revealed below were alloy bones of spun metals made in zero-gravity factories, surrounded by bunches of coated myomer muscles and hair-thin digital nerve pathways.

And there, where it should not have been, was a foreign object.

Before either of the others could see him do it, Jensen delicately plucked at a thin wafer of plastic lodged in a myomer cluster, pulling it out between thumb and forefinger. It was no larger than a microcircuit, but the shape and design of it told Jensen that it very clearly *did not belong*. It wasn't recognizable as any kind of Sarif-made tech.

He turned it over in his palm and without warning the circuit gave off a weak double pulse of light, like a heartbeat.

A tracker? Without thinking, Jensen's hand closed into a fist and crushed the tiny device into powder, his thoughts racing as the question of who had put it there pushed at him.

"Something the matter?" said Pritchard, seeing the shift in his expression.

"Nothing." The lie was automatic, and he wasn't sure why. Jensen switched off the scanner and stood up. Suddenly, all he wanted was to be away from here, away from all the memories that the building stirred up for him. "We should get moving. Don't want to outstay our welcome."

"Finally, an intelligent suggestion," Pritchard agreed.

But Stacks had his attention elsewhere. "I don't reckon they're gonna let us walk out of here easy..." He nodded in the direction of the open doorway. Jensen turned to see a half-dozen figures crowding out in the corridor, and the concealed chip he had found was suddenly the least of his concerns.

In the spill of white light from the lab, Jensen saw nothing but angry and desperate faces, all of them sunken and hollow with malnourishment and withdrawal. They were street scavengers, the lost and homeless reduced to existing on the ragged fringes of society, just like the girl they had encountered back at the mech-ghetto camp.

Pritchard pulled his stun gun and retreated back. "Jensen!" he hissed. "I told you this was a bad idea."

Two of the scavengers had firearms – a stocky, scarred man and a jittery, thin woman both carrying Widowmaker shotguns that had to have been looted from the Detroit police. The others had an assortment of makeshift clubs or blades.

The first through the door was another woman, whose left arm was a broken mess of damaged aug parts. She brandished a huge combat knife like a short sword in her other hand. "You try anything, you'll regret it," she hissed, but the warning was more desperate than it was threatening.

Her companions with the guns followed her in, while the others loitered cautiously outside. "How'd you get it open?" demanded the scarred man. "You Tarvos? Tai Yong?"

Before anyone could answer, the thin woman licked her lips and drew a bead on Jensen's head. "Let's just smoke these creeps and take the salvage. This ain't gonna be like last time at the Junction, getting cut to pieces by their goddamn army!"

The Junction? The name raised a red flag in Jensen's thoughts, but he didn't have time to consider what it meant. "We don't want any trouble," he said, raising his hands.

"They're here f-for the nu-poz," said Stacks, wavering on the verge of standing up but unwilling to risk the wrath of the scavengers. "Ain't that so?"

"You're gonna give us all you got," said the woman with the ruined arm. It was a bald statement. She put no anger there, only weariness and resignation. "Or you're gonna die for it. Your call."

"We got needy people," said the man with the scars. "Kids, some of 'em. So we ain't got no choice." He raised his shotgun and pointed it toward Pritchard.

Jensen let the moment hang, and then finally he lowered his hands. "No," he said firmly.

"*No?*" echoed the thin woman, her voice rising. "Who the hell do you think you are saying no to us? I had—"

He silenced her with a look. "No-one is getting hurt today. No guns or knives." Jensen gestured at Pritchard. "Put the stunner down. We're not fighting our way out of this."

"You're a second away from being dead, friend," said the other woman. Closer now, and Jensen could see she had twinned cat's-eye cyberoptics. "And everyone here is about as desperate as they come. So you give it up or pay the price."

He studied them. "We're not animals," he said, his voice carrying out to the others in the corridor. "I know it can seem like that now, after what happened to us. Because of how we have to live. But all that came from outside, not from us. We don't have to be the monsters everyone else thinks we are. We don't have to turn on each other just for one last dose of nu-poz." Jensen found the pack of drug ampoules from the cabinet. "Here, take this. It's yours."

The woman's eyes narrowed, and then with a sudden rush of motion, she stabbed her knife into a nearby tabletop and snatched the packet from his outstretched hand. "There's a lot here..." she muttered.

Jensen turned to Pritchard. "The other labs on this floor... are there more neuropozyne stocks in them as well?"

"It's possible," said the hacker.

"Open them up. All of them," Jensen insisted. He looked at the two scavengers with the shotguns. "You hear me? Take as much as you can carry. Meds, repair packs, praxis kits... You say you have people who need aid, so give it to them."

Pritchard frowned, then brought up his wrist-keyboard, working through a series of remote commands. After a moment, Jensen heard the thuds of other magnetic bolts opening in sequence further down the corridor. "Done," said the hacker.

"Just like that?" said the thin woman, distrust heavy in her voice. "You're giving us a goddamn scav jackpot?"

"Yeah," Jensen told her. "Because you need it. Because you're not thugs and murderers."

"Just desperate," said the other woman, shakily taking a shot from one of the syrettes. The tremors that had been running up and down her damaged arm eased away to nothing.

The scarred man let his weapon drop. "Thanks," he began. "I hate this stinkin' place. We scoured it for every damn piece of salvage we could find, then those

Tarvos assholes set the robots shooting everyone who came near…" He called out to the other scavengers, directing them to gather up the vital medicines.

The thin woman finally relented and let her shotgun drop to dangle at her side on a single-point harness. "Goddamn Samaritan, huh?" She helped herself to a handful of syrettes from the pack, eyeing them to make sure it was the real thing and not some sort of trick. After a moment, she took a dose and let out a low moan of relief. "Don't expect nothing else," she snapped at Jensen. "You get to walk outta here, so go."

"One thing before that," he said, halting in front of her. "You said something about the Junction. You mean Milwaukee Junction?"

"Yeah," she said, with a shrug. "The Sarif factory on the edge of the city. We got a whole bunch of us together, went out there. Figured there would be stocks, maybe, or salvage…"

"We needed the pozy bad enough to risk it," said the scarred man. "But they killed a lot of us."

"Who did?" Jensen pressed.

"An army of the sons-of-bitches!" snarled the thin woman. "No-one stuck around to ask them their names, yeah?" She pushed past him and stalked away.

LOCATION UNKNOWN

Lines of light ranged across a fathomless, unending digital void. The endless gulf resembled a virtual of deep space or the immeasurable depths of an abyssal ocean.

This anti-place existed far below the strata of the global data network. High above it, billions of people cross-communicated via a myriad of social media portals, while mega-corporations traded valuable non-linear currencies and untold other waves of information washed back and forth. But here, living in the unseen spaces of forgotten server farms and the ghostly margins of the virtual world, there was still activity. Like the blind chemovores that swarmed around volcanic black smokers at the bottom of polluted seas, a tenacious kind of digital life also clung to existence in data-arid wastelands of the deep web.

Above, a web of faint neon-bright lights pulsed with rays of shimmering code that surged between its threads like electrical pulses bouncing from neuron to neuron in a brain – but down in the dark net there were only the occasional blurred constellations of information, nested geometric constructs of lonely data shrouded by complex security programs that glittered in the utter blackness. Snatches of garbled, lost binary data flashed by, fragments of speech or music too fast to register.

Adrift here was a glassy raft built from lines of redundant, meaningless code, a brief but fragile safe haven for the gathering of a fugitive few. Aboard it, a group of abstract digital avatars faced one another, their identities and voices heavily masked.

A pixilated human form addressed the others. It was a phantom bled of all uniqueness such as gender, race or vocal tonality – but still there was an urgency behind the words it spoke. "Thank you all for coming. I appreciate the risks you are taking by linking to this nexus, but I believe what I have to say will make it worthwhile." No-one replied; it was unprecedented to gather so many of the Collective in one place, even if that wasn't a physical locus. Face-to-face communication was almost unheard of in their world of digital dead-drops and multiple blinds. "I have confirmation," continued the human avatar. "I've traced and double-checked the location. He's resurfaced, after all this time."

Nearby, another of the virtual selves – this one a winged skull that drifted about in quick, darting motions – fixed the human shape with its empty eye sockets. *"That's* why we're here? I've never been convinced by the great stock you put in this man's ability to get things done. Do I need to remind everyone of what happened at Panchaea? How can we know what effect that had on him?"

There were three more avatars waiting motionless on the raft, but none of them volunteered a reply to the skull's brusque question.

"A fair point," allowed the human. "Our predictive model does draw from old data, that's true. But I believe that he's ready to deploy. We'll make certain of it, of course. But it would be foolish of us not to use this opportunity. We've waited a long time for these conditions to come into synchrony. I admit, I thought our window had closed. I'm pleased that is not so."

"And if you're wrong?" demanded the skull. "How can we be sure about him?"

At length, another of the avatars spoke. This one was a glowing light, made to resemble a distant star as viewed through a telescope, and it pulsed with a woman's voice. "Like Janus says, we'll keep a close watch. If it comes to it, I can make sure he stays on the sweet path."

There was a wry sniff from the avatar closest to the human shape, a silvery letter from the Cyrillic alphabet that morphed randomly from one character to another.

"Are you sure you can handle him, little sister?"

The voice behind the star ignored the comment. "You've all seen the intercepts. We need someone who can be proactive, someone outside the group. Our boy's the best choice."

"We are committed," agreed the human shape. "I'll set things in motion."

The last avatar – a featureless cube made of blue crystal – finally spoke. "If he becomes aware he is being manipulated—"

"This isn't manipulation," interrupted the phantom. "We are just showing him the way."

The Cyrillic symbol glittered and shifted shapes. "I doubt he'll see it like that. Not the forgiving type, you know?"

The human avatar paused, glancing up toward the distant glow of the global network. "We've been here too long, our encryption is decaying. They've set seekers after this node."

The cube spun on its axis. "Time to go, then. We all know our assignments. Make contact again through the usual channels." The avatar lost definition and faded away, the word DISCONNECTED flashing briefly across the space where it had stood.

"Roger that," said the star, and followed suit. A moment later, the silver letter winked out, leaving only the human and the winged skull to stare blankly at one another.

"Fifteen seconds to intercept," said the ghostly avatar. "Seekers incoming." Above them, distinctive streaks of color were now visible, dropping toward the glassy platform on spiraling paths. The objects resembled comets, but moved like sharks.

The skull did not seem to notice. "We can't afford to

let the Illuminati have another victory, Janus."

"To them, *every* outcome is a degree of victory. That is why they think they will win." The human shape looked away. "We'll prove them wrong."

The last two virtuals severed their connections and the raft where they had stood broke apart like sand, dissipating back into the endless digital noise of the networks, as if the clandestine meeting had never taken place.

The hunter-killer programs swept in, their dog-smart synthetic intelligence anticipating targets to pursue and subdue. An analogue of disappointment washed over them at finding nothing, and they looped listlessly away.

THE RIALTO – DETROIT – UNITED STATES OF AMERICA

At first the sound in his thoughts was like a rattle of rainfall or the rumble of faraway thunder, but as Jensen rose quickly to wakefulness the noise shifted and changed to the irregular clattering of fingers on a keyboard.

He opened his eyes and righted himself, careful not to disturb Stacks, who was snoring lightly on a folding camp bed across from him inside the yurt-like bubble tent. Jensen watched the other man for a moment. Now and then, Stacks would twitch in the depths of REM sleep, the tiny motors in the joints of his iron fingers giving a faint buzz as they gathered into fists and relaxed over and over again. He wondered where his companion was, down there in his dreamscape. Jensen suspected it was not a good place, and for his part tried to reach for a remnant of whatever dreams he had just left behind.

Jensen came back with nothing. Usually there was the ghost of a memory, the faint tracery of an emotion, but he had nothing to hold on to. It came to him then that he hadn't clearly recalled a single dream since the day he had awakened in Facility 451 – or was it just that his mind didn't want him to carry them into the waking world?

He scowled, shaking off the morose thought, and quietly left the tent. Across the wide stage of the movie theater, the endless tapping continued, and Jensen found Pritchard hunched forward over a keyboard, his expression slack but his eyes totally focused on abstract digital figures on a tall, narrow screen.

He helped himself to some water from a salvaged purification module and approached the hacker, who didn't look up. "Just so you know," Pritchard told Jensen. "There's no maid service here, so clean up after yourself."

He looked around at the sloughed walls and tumbledown surroundings. "I'll keep that in mind."

Pritchard paused to grab a handful of caffeine tablets and tip them into his mouth, crunching them down dry like they were candy. "To keep me alert," he said, by way of explanation.

"Right," said Jensen. "What are you working on? Is that… a game?"

The typing stopped and he closed the program window. "It's a *tactical simulator*," Pritchard corrected. He shot Jensen a look. "So what exactly are you doing here? I understand your white knight thing back in the lab that saved our lives—"

"And it was the right thing to do," he interjected.

Pritchard went on as if he hadn't spoken. "But what do you propose to do next? You came to Detroit because you needed somewhere to lie low, but that's not really your style, is it? Now you're grumbling about picking up where you left off with your crusade against Darrow's mythical cadre... Are you going to move on or are you going to stay here and keep drawing attention? Because I need to know, I need to... modify my situation..."

"You want us to leave?" Jensen folded his arms. "You want things to go back to how they were, with you getting shaken down by gang members and doing petty cyber crime just to keep your head above water?"

"Nothing I do is *petty*," Pritchard shot back.

Jensen hesitated. In truth, he had a lot of questions himself that he couldn't answer – but somehow coming back to Detroit after everything that happened at Panchaea felt like a step toward some kind of *closure*. He had the very real sense of a chapter of his life coming to an end, but he wasn't quite there yet. "Hate to break it to you, Frank, but I don't think lying low is really an option. There's more going on here than just a city falling to pieces. You heard what those scavengers said. Somebody is raking through the ashes of Sarif Industries, and I want to know who and why. These things aren't happening in isolation. There's a connection..."

Pritchard frowned. "I admit, that subject is vexing me as well. So I've been looking into it." He brought up a new display window on the screen. "You're not going to like what I found."

Jensen peered at the data, but the lines of code there meant nothing to him. "Spill it," he demanded.

"You're right that someone is systematically raiding

the Sarif facilities in this city and looting them." He held up a hand. "And no, I'm not just talking about the homeless and the dispossessed searching for some doses of nu-poz. I mean someone organized. As for who they are... That's still unclear."

"The next question is *why*?" Jensen voiced the uncertainty, but he was already assembling the answer for himself.

"Remember back before everything fell apart, that whole situation with the Typhoon augmentation prototype Sarif had designed for the military? You know how valuable he considered it."

Jensen nodded. After recovering from the assault on Sarif Industries that had almost killed him, Jensen had been called back into work early by the company CEO in order to deal with an anti-aug activist group threatening the Milwaukee Junction factory. He remembered very clearly how David Sarif had stressed the importance or saving the Typhoon prototype as well as the workers being held hostage.

Pritchard went on. "The fact is, that wasn't the only military-focus hardware SI was looking at. Nanoblade enhancements, variants on the Typhoon, other implanted weapons... Sarif had a lot of secret projects in development that he didn't share with the rest of us."

"I figured as much," Jensen said grimly. "But that stuff was hypothetical."

The hacker's lip curled. "You know Sarif. You think he'd leave an interesting technical challenge *on paper*? He might not have planned to sell them, but I'm pretty sure he built them... And that's what our mystery men are looking for." He brought up a different data window. "Every Sarif sub-office in the Detroit area has been broken into in the last couple of months, that's why TYM ordered Tarvos to up security at the tower."

"So we know it can't be Tai Yong doing this, then."

"After all the trouble in Hengsha, they have their own problems to deal with back home. If they didn't, they'd be here in force. No, this is someone else." Pritchard shook his head. "The manufacturing plant at Milwaukee Junction has been shut down since the incident, but it's the most likely place where this tech would have ended up. And if our unknowns get hold of these prototypes, then there's no telling where they might resurface. I don't need to tell you, Jensen, these are deadly weapons. In the wrong hands…" He trailed off.

"So we do something about it," Jensen insisted, a sense of new purpose taking hold in him. "A last job for the boss. Cleaning up his mess." He gave a humorless smile. "Just like old times."

But Pritchard was shaking his head. "That's not what I had in mind. I'm not risking my life again – breaking into the tower was enough! I'm preparing an anonymous data packet containing everything I've uncovered; I'm going to drop it on the central servers of the Detroit Police Department and the local FBI field office… Let them deal with this."

"You said it yourself, the DPD barely patrol the city outside of the secured areas. They're not going to risk their necks on an anonymous tip. And by the time the Feds wake up, this will all be over!" Jensen eyed him. "No. I'll go in. You can cover me by remote from here."

"Out of the question!" Pritchard's voice rose. "I told you, I don't have the resources that I used to!"

"I'll make allowances," Jensen said dryly. "Stacks can back me up on the ground."

Pritchard shot a glance in the direction of the

bubble tent. "That's not a smart choice. I don't trust him. You saw how he reacted at the lab, that wasn't a neuropozyne reaction... that was post-traumatic stress!" He lowered his voice. "He's clearly unstable."

"He may be," Jensen agreed. "But the truth is, after the incident we were all damaged in one way or another."

"Touching," Pritchard said with a scowl, "but that sentiment could get you killed."

"The alternative is that we sit back and don't do a damn thing." He gave the hacker a hard look. "That's not gonna happen."

WEST SIDE – DETROIT – UNITED STATES OF AMERICA

The swell of the Detroit River slapped against the side of the long, broad barge, but it sat so low in the water that the motion barely translated through the rust-caked hull. Heavy black tarps formed a tent across the barge's upper deck, a recent addition that covered all that was taking place on board. Concealed along the rows of derelict store yards under the shadow of the Ambassador Bridge, the barge was nondescript and forgettable.

It was exactly what Task Force 29 wanted, a covert location to serve as a temporary base of operations inside the city limits, but Jarreau wasn't comfortable with it. The site had been put together by an advance unit with little time to prepare, and that made the Alpha team commander feel like he was starting the operation on the back foot. It was just one more thing on a long list of details that didn't sit right with him.

The mission brief he had been given on the flight in from Los Angeles was terse to say the least, as if someone high up at Interpol operational command wanted the job done fast, with no questions asked and no opportunity to think too hard about it.

He looked up at the flexing covers as the wind ripped across them, catching sight of the dark, winged shape they obscured. Below in the hull of the barge, elements of a mobile command center and staging area had been set up, where the rest of his squad could gear up and make ready.

He frowned. It wasn't that Christian Jarreau wasn't used to taking orders – he'd been military before he was with Interpol, after all – but there was something direct and cold in the tone of his standing instructions. He couldn't shake the sense that there was more to this operation than he was being told. He wondered if Jim Miller felt the same way; but all NSN conferences were monitored by HQ, so asking that question out in the open would draw attention he wasn't looking for. He pushed the thought away and set himself to concentrating on the work ahead.

Jarreau grabbed a can of self-heating GeeEmGee coffee and carried it over to the makeshift operations area, where a flat map screen displayed an aerial view of the city. He used the can as a marker, placing it on the riverfront where the barge was moored, and leaned over, peering at the grid of streets. Detroit had been a fractured city for decades, but in the past year it had slipped to the ragged edge of lawlessness and near-total collapse. While that meant less in the way of local law enforcement to potentially obstruct their operations, it also meant more unpredictability. Whole sectors of downtown were currently under gang control, and that made finding his marks all the more difficult.

He studied the screen. There were a dozen locations of interest that had already been entered into the mission database as potential sites for the smugglers to meet or store the hardware they were trafficking. Jarreau cast a practiced eye over them, winnowing out the ones that he knew were unlikely, highlighting others that seemed like good leads.

After a while, he reached to a margin band at the edge of the map screen, pulling out a dozen digital 'pages' to fan them out over the table like a hand of cards. The face of Sheppard, the ruthless gunrunner at the top of their hit list, glared back at him. The ex-Belltower mercenary's brutish swagger set Jarreau's teeth on edge. Thugs like this guy considered themselves as apex predators in the clandestine world of black ops. It didn't matter if it was true or not – it only mattered that in any given circumstance Sheppard and his crew were likely to shoot first and damn the collateral damage.

"Boss?" He turned as one of his team came walking in his direction. "Sitrep. I got remotes deployed all around us, sensors and video are up." Seth Chen was nominally Alpha's senior field technician, a former member of the US Coast Guard's cyber-ops force who had traded in shoreside base duties for something more challenging. Short, with olive skin and emerald augmetic eyes, he always seemed too flippant to Jarreau, but the tech had never let him down on a mission, and that granted him a lot of latitude. "No sign that we stirred up any interest coming in. If anything changes…"

"We follow orders and we won't be here long enough to worry about it," Jarreau told him. "Locate, isolate, neutralize. That's the plan."

"Copy that," nodded Chen. "Info-sec and data intrusion tools are coming online as we speak. I'll be in the city data-grid in the next ten." He gestured toward the image of Sheppard and his men, and gave a wry smirk. "There he is. Handsome lad. Looks like a decent citizen, wouldn't you say?"

"Think so? We find the guy, I'll send you in to talk to him. Rest of us'll go for a beer."

"You'd put me in harm's way?" Chen made a mock-sad face. "Really, boss? You realize how many hearts would break if I was hurt in the line of duty?"

Jarreau shrugged. "I guess I wouldn't want to upset your mother."

"Vande would never forgive you," insisted the tech. "You know she's got a thing for me."

"In your dreams," said Jarreau's second-in-command, as she strode out of the shadows. She made a dismissive motion in Chen's direction. "Go on now. The adults are talking."

"Okay, but don't beg, Raye," said the tech, retreating away. "It's embarrassing for both of us."

If Vande found Chen's manner even the slightest bit amusing, she showed absolutely no sign of it. "New intel dump just off the comsat from Director Manderley's office in Lyon," said the woman, placing a data stick on the surface of the map screen. The display immediately interfaced with the stick and new pages of intelligence were dealt out across the panel. Jarreau saw the Interpol sigil atop the first page and frowned as he saw the directive written below. "Mandate for use of lethal force against all targets is authorized and highly recommended," Vande went on, reading the words aloud.

"We're supposed to be a police force, not an

assassination team," Jarreau said grimly. "What happened to *arrest and detain for questioning*?"

Vande paused, processing her answer. "You've seen the files on Sheppard and his associates, sir. They're very dangerous, they will be heavily armed and they don't show restraint. I'd suggest that we start putting together a long-range intervention package. Snipers for an initial strike with a sweep team to deal with any stragglers."

"Shoot on sight?" said Jarreau. "We don't even know for sure who we're dealing with, and HQ has already hung out the red flag. Those orders might neutralize our immediate problem with the smugglers, but it gets us no access to the rest of the network." He shook his head. "I'm not okay with this."

"With respect, sir…" Vande paused again, clearing her throat. "I see where you're coming from, but do you think for one second that Sheppard and his merc friends are going to shy away from gunning down any one of us? We don't know what forces he's already got in play here in Detroit, but I'm willing to bet they're just as dangerous. And they have the defender's advantage."

Jarreau had more to say, but his train of thought was broken by Chen, who came back at a run from his panel on the other side of the cargo bay. "Boss, you need to see this." He had a digital tablet in his hand, and with a flick of his wrist he ported the data across to the map screen. "I got a subroutine running, digging through all the local PD and security webs looking for anything hinky, specifically stuff that fits the profile of our bad guys."

The map and the data pages folded away, and now the screen was showing grainy footage captured from a camera. Jarreau made out the shapes of parked cars and flat concrete walls. "What's this from?"

"Emergency alert exload from a Tarvos Security Box-Guard patrolling a building in the business district," Chen said, his words coming machine-gun fast. "Get this; the building is the former corporate headquarters of Sarif Industries."

"That's on our watch list," said Vande.

Jarreau nodded. "Okay, you've got my attention."

Chen advanced the recording and Jarreau found himself looking at a blurry still of a man with dark hair and an angular face, a gun in his hand frozen in the moment of discharge. "Judging from the robot's telemetry feed, it looks like he was using electromagnetic pulse rounds," said the tech. "Those kind of bullets are not what some ragged-ass street scavenger could afford."

"He moves like he's trained," offered Vande. "The face is a new one, what I can see of it…"

"Not one of Sheppard's guys?" said Chen.

"That we know of," Vande corrected.

The video playback spun on, the point of view slewing around wildly as the Box-Guard tried to terminate the intruder without success. Then finally the man was fully in the frame again, throwing an object toward the machine. A moment later, there was a flash of detonation and the recording went dark.

"I saw something in the background," said Jarreau.

"Sure did." Chen nodded, and spooled back along the video's timeline. "Here and here." He excerpted more stills, these showing two muddy, shadowed figures. One was partly lit by the glow of a portable screen, and the other was stocky with hulking, oversized shoulders.

"Augmentations," Jarreau said, almost to himself. "Maybe military or industrial models. Can we get a facial recognition match on any of these jokers?"

"It'll take me a while," admitted the tech. "There's not a lot to go on. But if I can assemble a three-d model, we might be able to run them through the usual databases."

Vande leaned forward and tapped the image of the man with the gun. "Concentrate on this guy."

Chen shot Jarreau a questioning look, but the team commander confirmed her order with a nod. "On top of that, I want you to run a hard target search on Sarif Industries and whatever holdings they have in the city. If this is connected to our boy Sheppard's deal…" He trailed off. His gut instinct told him there was something there; the break-in seemed like too much of a coincidence not to have some link to the smuggling network. "We need to know about it," he concluded.

Chen accepted his orders with a nod, and walked away. Jarreau looked up and found Vande watching him. "Armed and dangerous," she repeated, tapping the image again. "Like I said."

S I X

MILWAUKEE JUNCTION – DETROIT –
UNITED STATES OF AMERICA

Jensen crouched behind the burned-out husk of a cargo truck and surveyed the flanks of the four-story factory building across the way. If anything, it was in a worse state than the Sarif Industries tower, with not a single exterior window unbroken or a meter of the exterior that wasn't covered with hateful anti-aug graffiti. Thick concrete jersey barriers had been dropped into place around it to fence off the facility, and expandable metal blockades covered all the doors and access panels across the side of the factory he could see. Getting in wasn't going to be easy, Jensen reflected.

"I've got the blueprints for the building up in front of me..." Pritchard's voice issued out over his infolink. "There's an annex off to the west, do you see it? A two-story compound, a warehouse."

Jensen found the slab-sided building. "Got it." There was movement around the base of the annex, but he could only get a partial view through the scattered wreckage and debris across the open area between his hiding place and the building.

"When the stock market crashed and SI shares tanked, the last thing the board of directors did was order all the hardware off the production line. There was a plan to sell it to Kusanagi. Liquidate the assets for cash to hold off the death spiral they were in. But it never happened. Kusanagi were bought out by Tai Yong and the deal collapsed. Whatever is left in that building is the last of Sarif Industries' augmentations, still waiting for TYM to come in and strip them to the bare metal."

"Then the prototypes will be there," said Jensen quietly. "If Tai Yong knew they existed, they would have emptied it already."

"No doubt," Pritchard replied.

A figure moved, low and quick off to Jensen's left, and his hand tensed around his pistol. He didn't want to fire a weapon unless he had no other option. Without a sound suppressor, any gunshot would carry across the factory compound and then all bets were off.

The shadow resolved into Stacks, his high shoulders arched forward as he dashed from cover to cover. Jensen relaxed a little as the big man skidded to a halt beside him. "Hey," he began, breathing hard. He jerked a talon-like finger at a half-collapsed building behind them. "I got up there like you asked, put down that camera thing." His head bobbed. He was sweaty and tense. "Okay?"

Jensen nodded. "Good. Pritchard, you copy that? Remote camera is online."

"I have it," said the hacker. *"Position isn't optimal but it'll have to do. Scanning the annex exterior now…"*

With all network access to the manufacturing plant's internal security system cut off, they had been forced to figure out a work-around. Pritchard supplied Jensen with a couple of 'sticky' wireless micro-cameras – one of which was clipped to the front of his body armor – that could be placed in any location and monitored remotely.

"What did you see up there?" said Jensen.

Stacks showed him a grave face. "A lot of guys, man." He pointed. "Far side is all lit up. Gotta couple of trucks there, as well, looks like they crashed 'em through the gates. Loading up stuff."

Jensen had explained the situation to Stacks back at the Rialto. The mil-spec augs, the threat they posed, all of it. The other man hadn't hesitated to offer his help, even though Jensen could tell he was way out of his element, and scared by the danger they were in. That Stacks was still willing to back up Jensen spoke for the man's character.

"I was right," said Jensen. "They're moving the hardware out of here."

"*Looks like,*" Pritchard added. "*I have a visual now.*" He paused. "*It seems that 'army' we were warned about are old friends.*"

"A whole bunch of gang-bangers out there," Stacks was saying. "Same colors as those creeps who were giving your buddy shit."

"The MCBs?" Jensen considered this new information. "They're moving up from exterminating rival gangs to dealing in stolen tech. That's a big step."

"*Confirmed. Jensen, watch yourself. I see two men taking up a position across from you. They're armed.*"

He fell silent at Pritchard's warning and motioned for Stacks to do the same. Moving slowly, Jensen peered out from behind the ruined truck and found the pair. He saw the telltale yellow bandanas and loose-fit jackets favored by the Motor City Bangers, and noted that both of the men carried Hurricane machine pistols on straps over their shoulders. They shared a joke over something and one of them pulled a conical drug vial from his pocket, jamming it into his neck for a quick shot while the other lit a cigarette. Their body language reflected only boredom, not alertness – but the two of them were between Jensen and the only way into the annex that was in shadow. Attempting entry by any other route would be dangerous in the extreme.

After a minute or so, it became clear the two MCBs were in no hurry to leave. *"You're going to have to deal with them,"* noted Pritchard.

"I figured that," Jensen muttered.

Stacks gave him a sideways look and tapped a metal finger to his temple. "Snakey giving you trouble?"

"Tell him not to call me that," snapped Pritchard.

Jensen nodded. "Stay here. I'll go take care of the guards."

Stacks looked doubtful. "Nothing but open ground over there. They'll see you soon as you step out."

"I don't think so." Jensen stood up and holstered his pistol, before calling up a nerve-impulse pattern to interface with another of his implants. It was energy-hungry and he'd been reluctant to use it until now, but after the scan at SI showed his augs were still in good working order, he was willing to chance it. "Now you see me…"

Jensen trigged his thermoptical camouflage and light bent around him, turning his shape into a shimmering, hollow outline. Stacks jerked back in shock, as if he'd seen a ghost.

"Now you don't," concluded Jensen, and slipped away.

* * *

He moved slowly and carefully, making sure he did as little as possible to disrupt the pattern field, aware of the ever-present energy drain on his bio-cell batteries. Each wary step brought him closer to the two MCBs and the muzzles of their machine pistols. If they made him, he'd be cut down before he could react.

"You don't know a damn thing," the smoker was telling his compatriot, waving the cigarette in the air between the fingers of a gold-plated cyberarm. "That ain't how it happened. Folks didn't go crazy because of no germs, fool. The incident was all down to the gov'ment!"

The other ganger bounced on the balls of his feet, the pistons in his augmetic legs hissing with each motion. "What makes you the one who knows?" His speech was slightly slurred, and Jensen recognized the effects of a zee dose. The artificial neurochemical was a potent street drug that was popular among Detroit's criminal underclass. The other MCB snapped his mouth open and shut. "Millions of people wind up dead? That ain't just the government, man. Too big for that." He shook his head vigorously. "Those cog-hatin', natch-lovin' Purity First assholes did it! Them and that Humanity Front, pretending they's all decent and shit, but they was in it together, they made a killer virus! Sent everybody loco, is what it did." He flexed his arms. "Heard it from a guy who used to work at LIMB, man. That's stone cold truth."

Jensen crept closer, moving to keep himself out of their fields of view. He was almost in range.

The smoker cleared his throat and spat into the weeds sprouting through the damaged tarmac at his feet. "Nope. Let me tell *you* what's real. The Man, he want to keep us down 'cos of this!" He curled his metal-clad fingers into a defiant fist. "The Man kisses up to those corporate sons-of-bitches and they mess with the pozy! That's how they did it, yeah? *Con-tam-in-ate-ed*." He sounded out the word for extra emphasis. "They knew it was a bad batch, but they still wanted their paper. And now they get to come down hard on all us cogs, pretend like it was our fault!" He spat again. "Hey! You listening to me?"

The other ganger was looking away, staring into nothing. "Reckon I saw something moving, is all."

"You crazy," snorted the smoker, taking another long drag.

"He's really not," said Jensen, decloaking between the pair of them. Both the MCBs reacted with shouts of alarm and went fumbling for their guns, but neither of them were fast enough to avoid Jensen's reflex-boosted attack as he struck out and grabbed them by their necks. With a single, lighting-fast move, he yanked them off-balance and cracked their skulls against one another with enough force to knock them both unconscious. He released his grip and let them slump into a heap among the overgrowth.

Stacks burst out of cover and sprinted to his side. "That is some neat trick," he said. "I know you said back at 451 that you was some kinda cop, but level with me. Is that *all* you is?"

"I'm someone trying to do right," he told him. "That's what matters." Jensen gathered up the machine pistols and ammo clips from the two fallen gangers and Stacks followed him to the sealed doorway.

The expandable metal barrier blocking the entrance had a magnetic lock holding it closed, and Jensen took a second to consider how he was going to deal with it.

Stacks shook his head and pushed him aside. "Allow me." The ex-steeplejack reached down, and with a spin of his wrist, he wrenched the lock mechanism out of the frame. "Easy…"

Despite Stacks's wary grin, Jensen still saw the tremors in his artificial hand. "I need you focused," he told him. "Okay?"

"No… no problem," Stacks breathed. "I'm just a little new to this breaking and entering stuff, is all."

"Stay close and watch my back." He handed the other man one of the machine pistols. Stacks took it like it was poisonous. "Don't use it unless you have to."

"You can… count on that."

Jensen put his shoulder to the barrier and forced it open. Passing through, they emerged on a raised platform above a sunken loading bay. It ran the full length of the building, vanishing into darkness and shadows. But a few hundred meters away, there was a knot of activity illuminated by the lights Stacks had seen from the rooftops.

"Tread careful," Jensen whispered, and then set off in a crouched walk, panning his gaze from side to side. The smart vision implant in his skull parsed the environment around him, projecting a sensor grid overlay on to his optical display, highlighting movement and potential targets. There were a lot of gangers down there, some of them milling around with weapons at the ready, others working in a ragged line as they carried plastic containers out from deeper in the warehouse annex.

Jensen halted in the lee of a support pillar and watched as two men hefted a long box into the back of a six-wheeler cargo truck. The familiar stylized seraph's wing logo of Sarif Industries was visible on the side of the crate.

"*Ishtar-model leg augmentations,*" said Pritchard; for a moment, Jensen had forgotten that the hacker was seeing more or less exactly what he did. "*At least, that's what the barcode on the box says. In reality, it could be anything in there.*"

"That's not mech limbs," said Jensen, as he caught sight of another MCB ganger approaching, pushing a wheeled barrow with an open crate atop it. He saw the recognizable honeycomb pattern of Typhoon modules inside, wrapped in plastic packing sheets. Distributed around the torso and limbs of an implantee, they could project a series of directed-blast explosive spheres, effectively turning the user into a human cluster bomb.

Another ganger stepped in the way and Jensen saw a face he knew – the one called Cali, who had tried to shake down Pritchard for protection. "There's your buddy with the attitude problem," he said quietly, watching as a bull-necked man wearing a reversed baseball cap came striding over to interrupt Cali's conversation.

"This guy looks like... like he's in charge," muttered Stacks from nearby.

Jensen nodded in agreement. The new arrival had implanted eye shields, gold mirrors that were thick and round like antique coins. He sneered as he spoke harshly to Cali, revealing more gold worked into his teeth. One arm was artificial, plated with a fake skin-tone sheath and lines of white chaser lights beneath the polymer epidermis. The rest of the MCBs gave him a respectful berth as he jabbed a finger at the air. In his other hand he was holding a digital tablet.

"*Magnet,*" said Pritchard. "*The top dog of the Motor*

City Bangers, in the very unpleasant flesh."

As he watched, Jensen saw Magnet aim a kick at the wheels of the barrow and he caught a snatch of swearing as the gang leader berated the younger member. The MCB pushing the barrow left it behind and sprinted back off into the storage racks, while Magnet turned his attention fully on Cali. He pointed at some of the crates and shook his head, instead jabbing his finger at others that hadn't yet been loaded.

"He's got himself a shopping list," Jensen thought aloud.

"That's not all," added Pritchard. *"I'm reading another encrypted signal in your area, tagged on an infolink channel. Someone is speaking to Magnet directly through a mastoid com implant, just as I'm talking to you."*

That confirmed the suspicion that had been forming in Jensen's thoughts since the start. While the MCBs clearly had ambition beyond their station as just a street gang, it didn't track that a group like them would be players in the theft and sale of prohibited human augmentation technology. "Whoever is on the other end of that infolink conversation is the one holding Magnet's leash," he said. "Pritchard, can you back-trace the signal, find out where it's coming from?"

The hacker's reply was predictably terse. *"What do you think I'm doing?"*

"Hey," whispered Stacks. "A lot of trouble waitin' to happen down there, Jensen." His tone began to rise, taking on a fearful edge. "You mind telling me how we're gonna puh-put all this hardware outta action, without getting lead-lined? *Huh*?"

"Keep it together," Jensen said firmly. "There's a way. But it's a little showier than what I'd hoped for..." He paused, scanning the warehouse. The scavenger had been right, there *was* an army of them down there. Far too many for two men to take on directly. "Pritchard, check the blueprints. I need you to find me an access shaft down to the sub-basement. The main utilities conduit."

"Working on it…" A moment later, an icon blinked into existence on Jensen's retinal display. *"Waypoint uploaded. That'll take you to it."* He paused. *"I see what's down there, so I think I know what you're planning. And it's idiotic."*

"Didn't ask your opinion," he retorted.

"What?" Stacks shot him a nervous look.

"Follow me," Jensen told the other man. "I'm gonna need that muscle of yours."

In the end, it took both of them to force open the doors to the service shaft that dropped down into the darkness. Jensen pushed through the gap and found a ladder that allowed him to descend quickly and quietly. Stacks followed, grimly moving down one rung at a time, hand over hand.

There was little light, but his smart vision mode got past that problem, the Eye-Know optics rendering the area in a grid of geometric shapes that he could navigate easily. He glanced over his shoulder. "Still with me?"

"I gotta choice?" grumbled Stacks. He followed as Jensen moved on, but he was flinching at every echo of noise from above them, every knock and thud of the pipes that lined the sub-basement floor.

Jensen quickly found what he was looking for. Set into the pipes were a series of smaller branching conduits and a regulator mechanism studded with valves. He tested one experimentally. The wheel atop the valve moved a fraction and then stuck.

"I need you to throw this open," he told Stacks. "All the way. Can you do that?"

The other man peered through the dimness at the regulator, seeing the warning plate bolted to the pipe that specifically said *not* to do what Jensen was asking. "Are you c-crazy? This here's a gas main. If there's anything still flowing through it—"

"There is." Jensen cut him off, tapping on an old-style gauge that had a needle gently twitching in the lower ranges of its dial. "Not full on, but enough."

"Oh, man." Stacks raised his hands to his face, clasping it between his spindly augmented fingers. "You wanna cause a leak, blow this place to hell? How you gonna do that?"

Jensen reached into a pocket on his tactical vest and produced a flexible rectangular pack filled with a blue gel. "This is a remote-detonated explosive. We plant it, get the hell out and then…" He spread his hands.

"That'll bring the whole building down on the heads of those idiots upstairs."

Jensen nodded. "That's the idea."

Stacks's hands were trembling, so he knotted them together. "And you're okay with that?"

Jensen's jaw hardened. "You want to go up there and ask them real nice to put those augs back where they found them?" He frowned. "If you've got another way to stop them walking out of here with that tech, let's hear it."

"I… I guess not." Stacks gave a doleful nod. "All right then. Step back, let me do it." Clasping the valve wheel, he gave a deep grunt and turned it. Stacks's aug arms juddered as he applied more force to the action, and then suddenly the valve failed catastrophically. The wheel snapped off in his hands, taking part of the mechanism with it.

Jensen immediately caught the stink of gas from the fractured pipe, and he tossed the explosive pack down next to it. "Okay, we gotta book, now!"

But they were only a few steps away from the maintenance shaft when voices echoed down to them from the upper floor. Jensen pushed Stacks back to the wall as a flashlight beam stabbed downward, followed by a gob of thick spittle as someone spat down into the gloom and laughed.

"Pritchard, our way out is compromised," whispered Jensen. "Need an alternative, now."

"Hey, whatssat down there?" called a voice from above.

As he pulled Stacks away, Pritchard's voice sounded through Jensen's bone-induction transceiver. *"According to the building plans, five meters to your right is a crawlway that should take you up to an access channel underneath one of the materials recycling bays."*

"Copy that." The acrid taste of the gas was gathering at the back of his throat. "Stacks, this way."

"I hope you... know what you're doing, man." Stacks coughed and fell in step with him.

Later, Jensen would reflect on the thought that *here* was where everything started to fall apart.

Yanking open the vent concealing the other shaft, he didn't waste any time climbing up and through. As Jensen ascended back toward ground level, he felt the crawlway shake and creak as Stacks forced his way up behind him. It was a tight fit for both of them, and the other man's thick cyberlimbs scraped along the inside of the metal walls. He thought he heard Stacks muttering under his breath, like he was talking to someone only he could hear. Pritchard's warning about stability echoed in Jensen's thoughts.

His shoulder made contact with a gridded metal plate and he forced it up and open, rising with a gasp as he emerged in the gloom of the recycling bay. Jensen gave an involuntary shudder as his lungs filled with cold air. The chamber had a damp, refrigerated chill, and he could hear fluid dripping on to a tiled floor. In the dim light that crept in around double doors at either end of the room, Jensen made out strange rectangular shapes hanging from suspended rails. He brushed one with his hand; it was flexible plastic, with something bulky but supple contained within.

Behind him, Stacks came climbing out of the crawlway, shivering and nervous. "I... I gotta get out of here."

"No argument there." Jensen took two steps and heard the dull buzz of a motion sensor as it brought the room's lighting out of rest mode and up to full brightness. With a sudden shock of bright white, the whole of the recycling bay was revealed around them.

Jensen's first sense was of a meat locker. Hundreds of meter-long packets dangled all around them, and in each one was a human limb, bathed in an inert liquid sealant. Not organic limbs, of course. The riot of skin colors – from normal human shades to ink-dark and metallic emerald, from candy-apple crimson to zebra stripes – belied their origins. Each packet was marked with a red stamp bearing the Sarif Industries logo, showing that the cybernetics had failed at some critical juncture of testing and been sent down here with intent to be dismantled and recycled.

In that brief moment, Jensen turned back to see the expression on Stacks's face and he could only imagine the lens of horror through which the other man saw the room.

"Wait!" Jensen reached out for him, desperately trying to forestall any fear-fueled reaction Stacks would have. But he was already too late. It was the moment in the lab all over again, but this time the animal terror in the other's man's eyes would not abate so easily.

Stacks cried out in utter shock, swinging his massive machine-arms around, recoiling from the severed limbs hanging all around him. Panicking, he raked and clawed at the grotesque orchard of synthetic legs and arms, his boots splashing across puddles of the milky preservative liquid where it had congealed like watery resin. He began screaming, and the sound rebounded off the tiled walls. It was the bellowing of a man pushed beyond dread into the worst fear he could imagine.

"Why did you bring me here?" he screamed. "Why are you showing me this?"

"I didn't know!" Jensen went for him, reaching out in a vain attempt to grab the ex-steeplejack, but his heavy rust-red metal limbs knocked him aside, the glancing blow blasting the wind out of his lungs. Each mad sweep of Stacks's grinding, piston-hissing arms tore down dozens of packets, the useless augs tumbling to the floor and cracking apart.

"*What did you do to me*?" Stacks bellowed. "Why did you make me do this? Who are you? *Who are you*?" He shrieked the words, eyes wide but with no recognition in them. Jensen realized too late that Pritchard had been right; whatever had triggered in Stacks at the Sarif lab had not just been due to his neuropozyne withdrawal. It went far deeper than that. The man was damaged inside, tormented by personal demons that went way beyond anything else.

"Stop!" Jensen shouted back at him, desperate to snap him out of his mania. "Stacks, this isn't what you think!"

"I couldn't stop myself! I couldn't stop couldn't stop *stop stop STOP...*" Stacks's cries became thunderous and his metallic fingers raked across his face, drawing runnels of blood as they gouged his cheeks.

Jensen tried again to grab him, and this time a thick steel elbow joint cracked him squarely in the sternum. The impact rattled his teeth in his head and Jensen tasted blood as he stumbled back, barely keeping his footing.

Then there were shouts from the corridor beyond the chamber, and the heavy doors crashed open as three MCB gangers burst in, each one brandishing a weapon.

Stacks wheeled around and howled, spittle foaming on his lips, his claw-hands snapping at nothing.

The gang members did not hesitate. Their guns barked and Jensen instinctively threw himself to the ground as a salvo of shotgun blasts and 10mm rounds ripped through the air, carving into the other man. Stacks lurched forward, blood jetting from his wounds, and crushed the head of the nearest MCB between the fingers of one mechanical hand. Another he sent careening into a wall with a vicious backhand blow, before the pain signals from his body finally reached his brain and he crashed to the ground.

The third ganger broke out of his shock at the sudden violence of Stacks's assault, and raised his shotgun toward the fallen man's head – but Jensen made sure he never pulled the trigger. Leaping up from where he had fallen, he extended his arm-blade as he moved and ran the MCB through with the blunt tip. As the ganger fell, Jensen stumbled toward his fellow fugitive.

Stacks stared into nothing, trembling with shock. Each breath from his mouth came in a wet, rattling gasp and his clothes were awash with blood. Even with the protective vest Pritchard had found for him, Stacks had been shot at so close a range that the Kevlar weave could not stop the hollowpoint rounds and solid slugs from tearing him apart.

"Ah hell…" Jensen reached for him. "Stacks, no…"

"I'm… killed." He forced out the words with a low gurgle of blood. His eyes found Jensen, tried to focus. "How… did this happen to us, brother?" He shook, racked with agonized sobs. "Look what… they did!"

"*Good grief…*" Over the infolink, Pritchard made a retching sound as the portable camera on Jensen's webbing caught sight of the damage to the man.

Out in the corridor, he could hear the rush of more footsteps as other MCBs were drawn by the crash of gunfire. He pulled up the Hurricane machine pistol, aiming it toward the open door.

Jensen's throat tightened as he searched for something to say, some platitude to ease the horrible moment, but there was nothing that didn't seem empty or trite. In his time as a beat cop, Jensen had seen more than his share of gunshot victims, and he didn't need a paramedic to tell him that Harrison Stacker would be dead in minutes, if not less.

"I'm sorry." The words came from nowhere. Stacks nodded at him; it seemed to be enough.

A blood-flecked, clawed hand clasped Jensen's shoulder. "You were right back there, in the lab," he wheezed. "We can't be animals. We have to be better... but I couldn't stop. Couldn't stop myself, Adam. Oh, god forgive me, I did it. *I did it.*"

A sickly chill passed through Jensen. "What did you do?" He sensed the answer that was coming, but he couldn't stop himself from asking.

"Killed." It took a massive effort for Stacks to force the word out of his lips. This was his confession, and he had to voice it. "I never told anyone... when that damned... signal came." His metal hand scraped across the wet floor, almost of its own free will. "My family..." He shuddered, and coughed up a gush of fluid. "When it was over, all that was left were the pieces... of them..."

The blood. The severed limbs. Suddenly it all made a horrible kind of sense. What could it have been like, to be a good man and then lose yourself in a torrent of madness? To awake and find all you loved destroyed, torn to shreds by your own hands?

Jensen silently cursed Hugh Darrow and his masters in the Illuminati's inner circle for the lives they had trampled in the search for their lofty, high ideals.

Stacks gasped with pain and snatched at Jensen's armor vest, grabbing the firing key for the remote detonator. "I got this," he choked. "You go. You go, brother, you stop it. *You stop it all!*" The gang members were close, just seconds away.

"I will," he said, with a grim nod. Jensen rose up, catching the stink of the leaking gas in his nostrils. He broke into a sprint back across the chamber, shoving his way through the dangling racks. There was yelling and gunshots behind him as a few of the more daring MCBs ventured into the room, searching for targets.

He didn't see if Stacks triggered the detonator

deliberately, or if it was some random nerve impulse that contracted his mechanical hand, but there was a sudden hammer of noise and fire at his back that pushed him up and off his feet, straight into the other doors at the far end of the recycling bay.

Jensen came through them like a cannonball, his eye shields snapping shut to protect him from the blast as he spun through the air. A fat plume of orange fire and black smoke followed him into the area past the bay, emerging across from a loading dock laden with empty polymer crates that scattered under the force of the explosion.

The world spun madly around him and Jensen collided with a storage rack that broke apart beneath him. The shrill ringing of the concussion echoed through his ears. Even with the aural augmentations in his skull, for long seconds all Jensen could hear was a high-pitched tone and a broken, random buzzing that made his jawbone itch.

As he hauled himself up, ignoring the sharp flares of pain across his body, the buzzing resolved itself into Pritchard's voice. *"Jensen? Jensen, respond! I lost all the cameras, I don't have any visuals…"*

"Still here," he grunted. "Stacks… He took another way out."

"Oh." The bleak import of Jensen's words hung in the air. *"All right. You need to get moving. Red flags are springing up all across the utility grid in that area, the fire from that explosion is only going to spread…"* He paused, and Jensen took the moment to get his bearings.

As Pritchard noted, the fire from the ruptured gas main was quickly taking hold, and the MCBs in the loading area had lost all sense of purpose other than self-preservation. Jensen caught sight of Cali, shouting at another of the gangers to get the last of their spoils on to the trucks, rather than abandon them to the flames.

"*Something else,*" said the hacker. "*More coded com broadcasts in your area. But its military-grade encryption, I can't co-opt it.*"

"Same as before?"

"*I can't tell…*"

He shook his head. "Never mind," said Jensen, moving out of cover. He watched as Cali sprinted across the loading dock, finding Magnet with a shotgun in his hand and a murderous expression on his face. "I'm not done here yet."

In the chaos from the explosion and the growing inferno, Jensen's presence was now of less importance to the MCBs than securing their bounty before the warehouse came apart. As he sprinted along a walkway, Jensen heard the crash of breaking glass and the groan of damaged girders. Time was not on his side, but he couldn't risk getting out of the area without being *sure* – sure that these military prototypes were not getting out into the world, sure that whoever was behind it was going to pay the price. And that person had to be the voice that was talking to the gang leader, Magnet. He had the next link in the chain.

Flecks of Stacks's blood dotted Jensen's armor and his face, and a hard-burning rage was rising in his chest. In that moment, he needed someone to hold responsible, someone he could *punish* for the wasteful death of an ordinary man who had gone in harm's way because he believed in Jensen's crusade. *It won't be for nothing*, he told himself, making a silent vow. *I will stop this*.

He had only a split-second to make his choice, and Jensen did it without pause. He vaulted a safety rail and came down with the machine pistol at the ready.

"You!" he shouted at the thug with the gold optics. "You're coming with me!"

Magnet swore violently as he saw Jensen emerge out of the smoke, and he shoved Cali toward him. "Man, who the fuck is this guy? Waste him!" As Cali drew his gun, Magnet sprinted away, more than happy to let his lieutenant deal with the troublesome intruder.

"You gonna pay for what you did, you son-of-a—" Jensen didn't let Cali get the rest of the words out, instead firing a burst of bullets down in a low arc that shredded the ganger's all-too-organic ankles and shins. Cali went down in a howling heap, his augmented arms clawing at the bloody ruins of his legs.

Jensen came in and kicked Cali's gun away into the smoke, before letting off another spray of rounds into the wheels of the nearest truck. He aimed the Hurricane's muzzle at Cali's head as he loaded a fresh ammo magazine. "Where's Magnet going? Who's behind all this? *Answer me!*"

Cali whined in agony. "Offices upstairs or some shit, hadda get somethin'… The rest, I don't know! Who gives a damn?"

Jensen looked away. "Reckon you can make it to safety if you start crawling right now," he growled, as nearby part of the roof crumpled and fell inward. "Or maybe not. Your call."

As Cali scrambled desperately toward the open loading gates, Jensen peered up into the thickening smoke. He felt the flutter in his chest as his rebreather kicked in, the implant acting like a micro-lung air reservoir. It wouldn't last forever, but he guessed Magnet wasn't going to stick around. "Pritchard, gimme a waypoint. I need to find the offices."

"You should be leaving, not going upstairs," came the irritable reply, as a marker icon popped into view on the heads-up display projected directly on to Jensen's cyberoptics.

"Just find me that way out," he snapped, and broke into a run.

He caught Magnet inside a corner office where the door had been kicked off its hinges. The gang leader was tearing the base of a desktop computer from its mount, in the process of stuffing it into a backpack. His shotgun was lying nearby, and he lunged for it, the awkward mass of the pack pulling him off balance.

Jensen fired high, bracketing Magnet with a full-auto burst. The sound merged with the clanging of the warehouse's fire alarm. He wanted the gang leader alive, to find out what he knew, but Magnet didn't flinch from the gunshots.

The MCB snatched at the Widowmaker and let off three chugging blasts in quick succession, firing wild to put Jensen off-balance. It had the desired effect, and he was forced to duck back out into the corridor.

Magnet cocked back his heavy cyberlimb, activating a piston accelerator in the forearm that turned it into a fist-sized battering ram. With a massive crash, he punched clear through the nearest wall and threw himself through the gap into the adjoining office.

Jensen ran after him down the corridor, as Magnet repeated the action over and over. The two men exchanged fire through windows and open doors as they ran, shot and bullets cutting through the smoky air. Belatedly, the damaged fire suppression system activated and sprinklers in the ceiling came on, instantly drenching everything in a hissing downpour.

"The only way out is past me," Jensen shouted. "Toss your gun and you can still walk out of here!"

Magnet's answer was another salvo of shotgun blasts that chewed great divots out of the walls around Jensen. He broke cover and kicked open an access door that led to the roof, vanishing through it before Jensen could draw a bead.

"Where the hell is he going?" Jensen muttered.

Pritchard's voice buzzed in his head. *"Something's going on out there. I'm reading disruptions in what's left of the local data grid… This isn't the MCBs, Jensen, there's another hacker…"*

He didn't have time to acknowledge the message. Every moment he hesitated, Magnet would extend his chance to escape and the truth about what was happening in Detroit would be lost. Jensen steeled himself and kicked open the access door, ready to duck back inside if Magnet was lying in wait. But instead, he saw the gang leader running along an elevated catwalk toward the rear of the warehouse, where a sky bridge connected it to the rest of the manufacturing plant. *His escape route.*

If Magnet made it across and down into the back alleys of Milwaukee Junction, he was as good as gone. Ignoring the plumes of smoke rising up from the skylights, and the dangerous creaking of the fracturing roof, Jensen let the Hurricane drop on its sling and sprinted after Magnet, the synthetic muscles in his augmented legs reconfiguring into sprint mode for maximum speed across the short, straight-line distance.

He was on the gang leader in a heartbeat, kicking off a guide rail to propel him up and then back down. Magnet whirled, firing as he moved, and a hot gush of exhaust gas seared Jensen's face as the blast narrowly missed taking his head off. He landed a powerful blow on Magnet's shoulder where his aug arm connected to his torso, and the shock of impact knocked them both apart again.

Jensen recovered faster, reacting with reflex-boosted instinct, and slapped away Magnet's weapon. The Widowmaker spun over the guide rail and skidded away across the sloped rooftop. The gang leader staggered back, triggering the heavy-punch piston again, cocking it to throw a strike at Jensen's head – but his opponent's arm bent back on itself in a move that no human limb could have made, snatching at the grip of the dangling machine pistol.

The Hurricane came up to aim at Magnet's broad chest and Jensen blew out a breath. "End of the line," he snarled. "I want to know who is running you."

"Man, screw you," Magnet retorted. "No-one runs the Bangers but me!"

"*Jensen…*" Pritchard's voice carried a distinct note of fear. "*They've got the trucks moving… They're clearing out!*"

He ignored the hacker for the moment, concentrating on his improvised interrogation "Who told you to get the augs? Where are you taking them?"

"Goodwill," spat the ganger.

Jensen shook his head and he went for a different approach. "Try again. You're just punks with big mouths and poor impulse control. You're not smart enough to shift gear like this on your own… Or are they playing you? Did the man in charge tell you what it's *really* worth?"

His ploy worked, and for a moment a flicker of doubt crossed Magnet's face. "Ain't no *man* in charge, asshole…" He straightened. "Shoot me, if you gonna do it."

"*Jensen!*" This time Pritchard's shout couldn't be ignored. "*Listen to me! You've got company!*"

From out of nowhere, a thunderous downdraft blasted across the roof, spinning the plumes of smoke into vortices, and both men staggered beneath the blasts of hot exhaust fumes. Jensen reacted without thinking, looking up just as a blazing spotlight snapped on, drenching the surrounding area in white light and hard-edged shadows. The anti-glare coating of his eye shields lessened the effect, but it was still dazzling. He made out the shape of a bulky, drum-shaped VTOL suspended on four tilt-thrusters at the end of stubby winglets, turning slowly against the night sky.

Magnet saw the opportunity and made use of Jensen's distraction, scrambling to his feet, up and over the rail. Jensen saw him move and went after him, skidding across the corrugated metal of the roof – but the gang leader was already out of his reach.

Without hesitating, Magnet threw himself off the ledge and into a three-story fall straight toward the tarmac below. The fall would have left anyone else shattered and broken, but an instant after the gang leader dropped away, a glowing sphere of electromagnetic force flashed into existence around him and slowed his descent enough to let him hit the ground and survive. Like Jensen, the MCB's augmentations included an Icarus implant, a technology originally developed for military use to assist in high-altitude low-opening parachute jumps. Magnet was right at the edge of the aug's operational envelope and he landed badly, but still well enough to stagger away. Jensen swore as one of the six-wheeler trucks he had seen in the loading bay slewed around to pick up the gang leader.

But before he could react to that, the lights from the heavy VTOL overhead shifted around him as the aircraft moved and a cluster of drifting, wavering crimson dots appeared on his chest and throat. The VTOL dropped until it was level with the roof, and he saw that it was a cargo-carrier model, the central section a square metal container with sliding panels open to the air. Figures rendered into black shadows by the backwash of the spotlight were aiming angular weapons in his direction.

He hesitated, his finger on the Hurricane's trigger but the weapon's muzzle aiming at the roof beneath his feet. Jensen knew that if he moved, a dozen guns would cut him down in an instant. The fact that the new arrivals hadn't immediately opened fire made him suspect there was more going on than he knew.

Three figures in black leapt from the VTOL's crew bay to the rooftop, and they came into the light with flechette rifles raised, the muzzles of the FR-27s and their laser sights all tracking together. The closest to him was a blonde woman with an athlete's build and sharp European features, and as she stepped forward, she cocked her head and subvocalized something. She was talking on another infolink channel. Jensen remembered Pritchard's earlier warning.

For a long second, it seemed like the woman was going to execute him then and there, but then her expression shifted into something like weary resignation. "*Police*! Lose the gun!" She shouted the words so he could hear her over the constant rumble of the VTOL thrusters. "Put up your hands, unless you want to stay here and burn to death!"

They carried themselves like professionals, Jensen

noted. This crew were way past the random, thuggish threat of Magnet and the MCBs – and so they were a lot more dangerous.

Jensen nodded, as if he was going to comply, but in his mind the exact reverse was his intention. He peered at the roof beneath his feet, using the micro-miniature t-wave lenses in his smart-vision optics to see through the thin metal to the gantries and floors below. "Pritchard," he muttered, his words drowned out by the engine noise. "I got a situation here."

"*I know. I was the one who told you, remember?*" The hacker's nasal sneer made his jaw itch. "*I'm going to distract them. There's a sewer tunnel under the southwest corner of the building. How you get from where you are to there, I can't help you with.*"

"Last chance!" shouted the woman. The red thread of the targeting lasers lifted to dance across his eye shields.

In the next second, an ear-splitting shriek of feedback crashed over the infolink and Jensen cried out in pain. It was as if someone had jammed a spike into his skull, and he staggered with the force of it – but so did the woman and her companions, and the effect must have been felt by the VTOL pilot as well, as the spotlight suddenly blurred away as the aircraft rolled to the left before abruptly course-correcting itself.

Jensen gritted his teeth and unloaded a full clip of bullets from the Hurricane into the roof, cutting an arc through the corrugated metal. Already weakened, it gave way like a trap door and he fell into a haze of hot, choking smoke.

Gunshots followed him into the raging fire, but Jensen was already gone, vanishing into the flames.

SEVEN

THE RIALTO – DETROIT –
UNITED STATES OF AMERICA

Jensen kept to the shadows, slipping from one pool of darkness to another, pausing every few moments to listen carefully for any ambient sound. Once in a while, he glanced up, wary of the sudden appearance of a black shadow high over the alleyway; but nothing came.

Whatever the identity of the strike team he'd encountered at the Sarif factory – Jensen put little stock in their claim to be 'police' – they were clearly a professional crew, and every step of the way along his escape from Milwaukee Junction, he had been looking over his shoulder for them. He wanted to believe that he was out of their grasp, but it was two hours now since Jensen had last had radio contact with Pritchard and he suspected the worst.

The hacker had been right about the sewer access beneath the building, but to reach it meant a run through an inferno. The shabby surplus jacket Jensen had been wearing since Alaska had burned off his back, and without his rebreather implant and smart-vision optics he would never have made it through the thick, choking smoke filling the warehouse annex. Wading through the waist-deep filth of the sewer pipe was practically a relief, and by the time he crawled out of a manhole a kilometer away, Jensen was on the verge of collapse. His bio-cells were at a low ebb, his lungs felt like they had been filled with metal shavings, and every step was an effort.

But one look over his shoulder at the glow of the fires told him he had to keep going. Such destruction would have to bring the DPD in to investigate, and he needed to be far away when they finally arrived. He felt a knife of guilt twist in his gut over Stacks and the brutal fate that befell him. *The man's death is on me*, he thought grimly. *I took him into harm's way and he wasn't up to it. Pritchard was right. I should've listened.*

On his way back to the derelict cinema, Jensen picked over his reasons again and again. He wanted badly to strike at the people who had robbed him of so much, to lash out at the shadowy cabal manipulating events from on high… and with his mind set on that, he hadn't stopped to consider if Harrison Stacker was really ready to stand with him. Now a deeply troubled, damaged soul was dead and any chance he might have had at redemption was gone with him.

A bleak question gathered in Jensen's thoughts. Pritchard had been an irritating, arrogant ass for as long as he had known him, but by the same token he had always been brutally honest with Jensen. There were few people, he reflected, that he could truthfully say that about. And if Pritchard had been right about Stacks, was he right about this road that Jensen had started down? *My crusade, he called it…*

"Where the hell do I go from here…?" Jensen

said the words aloud, looking across the alley to the back entrance of the old building. But no answer was forthcoming. He could see the metal security door hanging open in the gloom, and his fingers gripped the butt of the Hurricane machine pistol hanging at his side. Was Pritchard in there, collapsed over his keyboard with a bullet hole between his eyes? Had Jensen's single-minded need for retribution cost the life of someone else tonight?

There was only one way to find out. He couldn't chance the energy drain of using the cloak; this would have to be a direct approach.

The Hurricane's magazine was half full. Jensen extended the gun's wire-frame stock and pulled it to his shoulder, moving low and fast to the door. He circled the entrance, peering into the semi-darkness within, then slipped inside.

The random clutter of the interior worked in his favor, meaning that no shooter with a high vantage would be able to get a clear sight-line and shoot him as soon as he entered – but it also meant that Jensen couldn't gauge what kind of threat might be waiting for him. His cyberoptics cycled through vision modes, looking for the telltale threads of an invisible ultraviolet targeting laser or the bloom of heat from a concealed gunman. He saw nothing.

Although most of the movie theater looked like the aftermath of a bomb explosion as a matter of course, Jensen saw no signs that Pritchard's remote mines had been triggered. That meant that whoever had opened the door and taken the hacker off the air was capable and dangerous. He thought about the black-clad woman on the roof and her unit. They certainly fit that profile.

Moving around a heap of rubble that had fallen from the ceiling, Jensen caught sight of the stage. Nothing had been upset, everything was untouched. He made out a motionless figure sitting in a chair, back-lit by the glow of a monitor screen – thin, angular, with an unkempt ponytail hanging over his shoulder.

For a long second, Jensen thought Pritchard was dead, but then the hacker gave a low sigh and looked off to his right, where shadows fell thick and deep. "How long do you expect me to sit here?" he asked.

"Clearly, until you learn the meaning of *stay there and don't say a goddamn word*." The terse reply had a Hispanic lilt to it, and presently a woman in a baggy civilian pilot's jumpsuit emerged from the darkness. A heavy Diamondback revolver dangled at the end of one of her hands, and she crossed toward Pritchard, her manner lazy but her eyes alert. Her hair was short in a mix of cornrows and a semi-military cut, revealing a lengthy augmentation scar running from just above her left brow in an arc that ended behind her ear. She wore the mark like a badge of honor, but the woman's gear and her swagger didn't chime with the team Jensen had run into at the manufacturing plant. He had the immediate sense that he was looking at a brand new player here, someone with an agenda of their own.

Jensen took aim with the Hurricane, considering his options. The range wasn't good, and he had a fair chance of clipping Pritchard with a stray round if he let off a burst of fire. He held his finger away from the trigger as the woman suddenly halted, casting a look in his general direction.

"He's here," she said to the air. "Huh. Took long enough." The revolver rose to aim toward Pritchard's head. "Come on up, *esé*. We're all friends here."

Jensen took a step forward into the spill of light from the stage and he saw Pritchard shift in his chair. "Want to tell me what's going on here, Frank?" He ignored the woman, even as he kept the gun on her. It wasn't just the three of them in the building, he was certain of it.

"They came in right after I lost the infolink," said the hacker, confirming his suspicion. "Jammed the signal and shut me down at gunpoint."

"Lose the weapon," said the woman, nodding toward Jensen. "Let's be civil, yeah?"

"You first, *chica*," he shot back. "And tell your pal to quit the cloak-and-dagger routine. It's been a long day and I'm not in the mood."

"Jensen," said a voice from nearby, dragging his name out into a languid, reproachful Irish drawl. "And here you used to be such an affable fella." Until that moment hidden from view, a man got up from one of the slumped chairs in the front row and turned to face him, spreading his hands in a gesture of conciliation. He had short hair over familiar, deliberately average features that were marred by circular scar-lines indicating subdermal implants and neural augmentations.

"Huh." Jensen lowered the machine pistol, but not the whole way. Of all the people he might have encountered in this moment, the last face he expected to see belonged to a man he'd crossed paths with half a world away, on a deep water platform in the middle of the South China Sea. "Hello, Quinn... or do you have a new identity this time?"

"Garvin Quinn is as good a name as any," he replied, with a wan smile. Then his expression shifted, becoming wolfish, and when he spoke again his accent was pure Muscovite Russian. "It's been a while. Surprised to see me, *bratán*?"

WEST SIDE – DETROIT – UNITED STATES OF AMERICA

Vande followed Jarreau through an open hatch in the barge's bow, into a compartment that Alpha team had been using as a temporary gear store. He tore his tac vest off his shoulder and threw it hard on the table in the center of the room.

Out of sight of the rest of the team, the big man allowed himself to swear, grinding out a curse word between his teeth, before turning to look back at her. "That deployment was a damned mess! What the hell happened out there?"

She swallowed hard. "Sir, I take full responsibility for this. It was my call, I made the judgment to order Mendel to go for the high ingress instead of a ground landing."

Sol Mendel was the unit's VTOL pilot, a taciturn former Marine Corps aviator who said little but always got the team where they needed to go. Jarreau had been in the co-pilot's seat right next to him as the flyer pivoted over the roof of the burning warehouse. At the time he hadn't second-guessed Vande's command – he never did – but that was because she usually produced results. *Usually*.

Not this time, though. The mark had got the drop on them, escaping through a collapsing roof that they barely got clear of.

Jarreau slowly shook his head. "No. The buck stops

with me, Raye. You're my two-I-C, so your orders are my orders. I'll have to explain it to Manderley."

"You don't need to cover for me, sir," she insisted. Vande frowned. "The facts are: I played a gamble and it blew up in my face. I'm sorry, I screwed the op and we all know it."

He eyed her. "So tell me why."

She took a breath. "I saw him up there. The guy with the pistol from the Tarvos robot's video. I had a choice to make – drop us down and deploy or go for the arrest. I picked the wrong option."

"You're absolutely sure it was him?"

Vande nodded. "No doubt in my mind." She tapped a slender metallic finger on her temple. "I've already uploaded the contents of my optic buffer to Chen's search matrix, and the others who were out with me on the roof are doing the same right now. It was the same shooter, believe it."

"If we'd caught him that might have counted for something," said Jarreau, scowling. "As it is, we're back to square one."

Chen's initial searches of the Detroit city grid had thrown up the locked-down Sarif Industries manufacturing plant as the most likely target of interest, but it was pure bad luck that brought the Task Force 29 unit there right in the middle of what looked like an exchange gone wrong. The team had tracked two vehicles escaping into the city before they vanished into backstreets where no traffic cameras were still functional, so those leads were coming up short. The gunman with the augs had willingly dropped into a raging fire to get away from them, but Vande suspected that he hadn't perished there. The look she'd seen in his eyes... it was smart, not suicidal.

"He already had an out," she said aloud. Jarreau raised a questioning eyebrow at that. "We saw another runner as we came in, remember? Maybe both of them had escape routes set up. Whatever we interrupted, those two weren't about to die because of it."

"Chen's monitoring the DPD tactical feed and he has data snoopers placed on their central precinct intranet, so we'll know what their emergency response crews pull out of there." Jarreau shook his head again. "But I'll tell you right now, that'll be shit. No-one in this city is going to put any effort into investigating a fire in a Sarif factory. Wounds from the Aug Incident are still raw around here."

"They're raw everywhere," said Vande. She had ordered two of Alpha team's operatives to shadow the Detroit cops at the site, but they hadn't reported in yet. After a moment, she decided to venture an opinion. "Sir, I have an idea about what's going on here. The fire, the trucks… These people are tying up loose ends. They burn the building so there's no evidence, they take their hardware and hide it somewhere else in the city… It's the most likely explanation I can see, and it fits the facts."

"I'm not so sure about that," Jarreau shot back. He sighed. "Next time, Raye, think twice. You have a tendency to get bore-sighted on something, to the detriment of everything else. It's your only failing."

"I—" she started in on an explanation, but a loud clatter at the hatch took her attention.

Chen leaned in through the door, a smirk on his face. "You can shower me with praise later. This day may not have been a total waste of time after all, boss…" he told Jarreau. "I just got done with the first-pass compilation on the images from the team's optic buffers and the footage from the Box-Guard. Ran it through the matrix and we got us a match, right out of the gate."

"You ID'd the man on the roof?" said Vande. "Already?"

"Impressed?" The tech nodded. "His name is Adam Jensen… and according to the database, he's been stone cold dead for over a year."

THE RIALTO – DETROIT – UNITED STATES OF AMERICA

"You *know* these people?" snapped Pritchard, affronted by the idea. "Why am I not surprised?"

Jensen nodded toward Quinn. "Him, yeah." He looked toward the Latino woman with the pistol. "Her, not so much."

"The young lady with the large sidearm is Alex Vega," said Quinn. "I suppose you could say she's my… driver."

Vega rolled her eyes, slipping the revolver back into a holster on her thigh. "I'm a pilot, I'm not your damn *driver*. But I will be the kicker of your ass if you keep that up."

"Fiery too," Quinn grinned, back in the Irish brogue again. "And she's certainly capable. Alex is a lot more than just a talented flyer."

"Also," said the woman. "Just once, do you think you can pick an accent and stick with it?"

Quinn slipped into the rough-edged Russian manner and chuckled. "Where would be the fun in that?"

"You're a long way from Rifleman Bank Station." Jensen studied the other man carefully. "Last time we talked, you were about to blow the whistle on Belltower's dirty little black site."

"We did exactly that. And you were searching for a woman you cared for, along with some hard truth…" Quinn cocked his head. "But looking at you now, I would hazard a guess you didn't really find either of those things."

Jensen's lips thinned. "I got all the answers I needed," he said, after a moment.

During his investigation into the conspiracy behind Hugh Darrow and the Illuminati, Jensen had found himself on a floating prison complex where the Belltower PMC was illegally confining hundreds of innocent people, all of them abducted from cities around the world. It was one part of 'the Hyron Project', a grotesque research and development program to use human beings as part of a bio-organic computing system.

Quinn had been there, at first presenting himself as the base's opportunistic black marketeer – but that had just been the first of the masks he wore. At the end of it, Jensen tore Rifleman Bank's horrific secrets wide open, and Quinn showed his real face – or something close to it. He revealed he was working toward the same thing as Jensen, to sabotage the plans of the Illuminati and disrupt their schemes at every turn. Or so it seemed. That seemed like a long time ago now, with all the revelations and greater tragedy that had come afterward.

"You never did tell me who you're working for," Jensen went on.

"It's complicated," said Quinn, with a sigh. "But the important thing to know is that we have common goals."

The enemy of my enemy is my friend. Jensen recalled

the old proverb, turning it over in his mind. *But that doesn't make him someone I trust.*

"Panchaea," said the woman, changing tack. "We heard that was you. Sent it all to the bottom, huh? How'd you get out?"

"People keep asking me that. I wish I knew." Jensen eyed her. "What's your part in this? You here to make sure Quinn keeps his lies straight?"

"Something like that." She shrugged. "Me, I'm just another lost soul like you and your hacker pal here, who wound up in the wrong place at the wrong time and had to make some tough choices."

"Wait… I know who you are. You're with *Juggernaut*," Pritchard said slowly, understanding creeping over his features. "Janus runs you."

"Nobody *runs* us," snapped Quinn. "The Juggernaut Collective doesn't work that way. We're a collaborative effort working together to oppose the same forces." He glanced at Jensen. "The same people who have been trying to destroy you, Adam."

"Oh, good grief." Pritchard's face twisted in a sneer. "I thought this was someone with an axe to grind here to bury it in your head, but that's not it at all." He glanced at Jensen. "Don't you get it? They're here because they want to *recruit* us!"

"Actually, just him," Vega corrected. "Not you. We got enough hackers."

Pritchard's expression became thunderous at the implied slight. "What, those Go-Five idiots from Korea and that script kiddie D-Bar?" He snorted. "How did they work out for you?" He stood up. "Jensen, these people are not on anyone's side but their own! They're hooked up to every conspiracy theorist fringe group from the secessionist militia to the UFO abductees. All directed by some faceless ghost-hacker called Janus whom no-one has ever seen in meat space. They're cyberterrorists and anarchists. Their only interest is in causing chaos and disorder!"

"There's some truth in there," admitted Quinn. "But mostly you're quoting the lies spread by our mutual adversary."

Pritchard's tone turned cold. "I know Janus's sort. You pretend to be white hats, but really you just want to watch the world burn."

"I could stand to burn down some of it, yeah," said Vega, an edge of venom in her reply. "The parts where all the rich bastards live behind their sky-high walls and fuck with the rest of us."

"Clearly, your friend Pritchard has some trust issues," Quinn told Jensen. "And perhaps a bruised ego into the bargain? If I'm honest, I don't care. I just came here to talk to you, on behalf of Janus."

"Is that so?" Jensen's hand hadn't left the grip of the machine pistol. "You told me once that we were all pawns... is that what you are right now?"

Quinn's jaw hardened, but Vega answered for him. "Janus has an offer. And we came a long way to find you, so the least you could do is hear us out."

"No, the *least* he could do is let you leave without shooting you!" Pritchard snapped.

"This isn't a good time," said Jensen. "I got my own issues to deal with right now."

"Yes, we've been monitoring the police frequencies. Some sort of local trouble, is it?" At length, Quinn let out another sigh. "Okay, all right. Cards on the table, *bratán*. The fact of the matter is, we need your help."

"Why should either of us give a damn?" snorted Pritchard.

"Because the Collective can give Jensen what he wants," said Vega. "A way to reach those creeps hiding in their ivory towers, and drag them kicking and screaming into the light." Her eyes flashed as she looked toward him. "Interested?"

"Keep talking," said Jensen.

WEST SIDE – DETROIT – UNITED STATES OF AMERICA

Vande watched Jarreau's expression harden as he peered at the array of data panels Chen had dealt out across the table screen. She knew that look by now; outwardly, he seemed impassive, unresponsive, but inside he was running a fine-tuned tactical mind over all the intelligence being put before them.

"So, what do we have on this man?" she asked.

"A whole lot of goodies," said Chen, his head bobbing as he spoke. "Turns out that Mr. Jensen is a local... just a city boy, born and raised in South Detroit. And get this, he was a cop. That's where I sourced most of this data, it's sitting there in a secure file on the DPD's personnel database."

"Give us the high points," ordered Jarreau.

Chen took a breath and began. "Adam Jensen, born March of ninety-three, grew up in a blue-collar neighborhood, a B-average student with no youthful indiscretions of any note, later graduated with a Criminal Justice Bachelor's from the University of Phoenix and enrolled with the Detroit Police Department at age twenty-one." He tapped a still image of a young man in a dark dress uniform, a white-gloved hand raised in salute. Vande recognized the same face she'd seen on the rooftop, minus the beard, the lines of experience and the augmented eyes. "Graduated in the top ten percent of his Academy class. In 2018, he joins the DPD's SWAT division and finds his niche, rises up the ranks until he's leader of Team Two… but then it all goes to shit."

Chen slid other images across the panel so Jarreau and Vande could see them clearly. The first one that caught her eye was of a front page from *The Detroit Chronicle* bearing the lurid headline MASSACRE IN MEXICANTOWN; the others were what looked like transcript documentation from closed-session interviews. Jensen figured prominently in them, so it appeared.

"There was a shooting," Vande read aloud. "It says here Jensen's SWAT unit were called in to neutralize a dangerous augmented individual… and when the time came to commit, he refused to take the kill-shot."

"Yeah," said Chen. "They stood him down on the spot, but someone else *did* pull that trigger and the whole thing led to the Mex-Town locals kicking off in demonstrations, confrontations with the cops and finally full-on rioting."

"The target was a fifteen-year-old boy," Jarreau said grimly.

"Whatever the circumstances," said the tech as he went on, "by the time it was all over, Jensen's career was in the toilet. Reading between the lines, I reckon there's more to it that didn't go into the official report… But anyhow, they threw him under the bus after the unrest, so he quit. Six months later, he's head-hunted by the CEO of Sarif Industries for a new gig as their director of physical security." Chen paused. "Then, the info we have gets hazier. There are reports that Sarif gets attacked soon after by what appears to be a mercenary hit squad intent on wiping out their top scientists…"

"Most likely a rival corporation attempting to sabotage Sarif's research," suggested Vande. "*Unscheduled external contract termination*, they call it."

Chen nodded in agreement. "Jensen is almost killed in the process, but he clearly had a real good medical plan, 'cos a few months later he's back at work sporting a whole bunch of shiny new augs, with Sarif footing the bill. Once again, he turns up on the DPD's radar when the company forces the cops to stand down, so Jensen can deal with a gang of idiots from Purity First who took over a Sarif production facility. Wanna guess which one?"

Vande's eyes narrowed. "The manufacturing plant that got torched?"

"*Exactly*. Give the lady a gold star." The tech swiped through more of the virtual documents. "That building was familiar turf to him. In fact, this whole city is his home territory, so that's gonna be a problem when catching him."

"Not necessarily," Vande insisted. "We can use that to our advantage. Being on home ground will make him complacent, and he may drop his guard…"

"What happened after that?" said Jarreau, pulling them back on to the narrative of events. "Chen, you said the records show him as deceased."

"More accurately, *missing-presumed-dead*," said the other man. "Jensen is mentioned again in a police report about him confronting one William Taggart at a Humanity Front rally at the convention center, and then he fades away."

"Taggart…" Vande turned over the name. The man had been the public face of the world's largest anti-augmentation group, touring the globe with lectures and book signings. But like many others, Taggart had gone missing in the madness of 2027, in an event that some believed he had a major hand in making happen. "We've all heard the stories about how his Humanity Front were connected to the incident," she went on.

"None of that has been proven," Jarreau said firmly.

"But the Front *were* connected to the violent anti-aug radicals in Purity First," she insisted. "I doubt very much that Jensen was a fan of either."

Chen took a long breath. "Whatever his intentions were, that's the last piece of viable intel we have on the guy. Jensen goes off the grid, then the Aug Incident hits and suddenly everybody is dealing with that." He indicated a post-recovery image of the man, his face marked by the black commas of implants around his eyes. "Jensen had forty to fifty percent of his body replaced with augmentations, so there's no way he would have come through the incident without being affected, right? Anyhow, the next time his name rises to the top, it's attached to a formal declaration of his may-be-a-corpse status."

Vande nodded to herself. In the nightmare of the incident, a lot of augmented people had died of shock or been killed in the throes of it. Years later, there were still many families with unanswered questions and missing people who had never been found. But the tragedy had also given opportunities to the more calculating.

She voiced a thought. "Jensen wouldn't be the first person to use a major disaster like the incident as a way to disappear. All he had to do was let the world go on thinking he was dead, and he'd have a free pass…"

"For what?" Jarreau shot her a look. "If he wanted

to remain a ghost, why come back to the one city in the world where he's the most known? It doesn't track."

"Because the reward must be worth it," she retorted. "We can assume Jensen is pro-aug, enough that he picked a fight with the most well-known anti-aug spokesman on the planet... It's not much of leap to suggest he could have been radicalized."

"You think our boy is involved with those ARC activists over in Europe?" Chen considered the possibility. "Yeah... I could see it."

"You've got nothing to prove that, just circumstantial evidence," said Jarreau.

Vande held his gaze. "The point is moot, sir. It doesn't matter how Jensen connects to ARC or Sheppard and his mercs. He's clearly armed, dangerous and capable." She ticked off each word on a finger.

Jarreau was silent for a long time, before he turned to Chen. "Seth. Dig deeper. If Jensen went dark, we should find out why. Where was he? Who was he with? He worked with a lot of people at Sarif and in the Detroit police force. Look for someone that he might reach out to." He dismissed the tech with a nod. "Get on it."

"Copy that," said Chen, as he walked away.

Then the team leader's hard gaze was on Vande again. "Raye, listen to me. I know it's tempting to put all your energy on this one guy because of that screw-up at the plant," he told her. "But just make sure you're not reaching too far. We don't know why Jensen was there. Until we do, I'm not going to hang him *in absentia*. Clear?"

"Clear," Vande replied, tensing as she spoke. "So let's put him in a cage, give it a shake and find out what's really going on."

THE RIALTO – DETROIT – UNITED STATES OF AMERICA

"I admit, there were a lot of things I kept from you at Rifleman Bank," said Quinn. He dropped into the depths of the worn-out leather sofa across from Pritchard's makeshift living area.

Jensen leaned against a support pillar, cleaning off the accumulated film of dirt, cordite and dried blood that still coated his combat gear. He made sure he kept Quinn and Vega where he could see them both at the same time. "I'm shocked," Jensen said, deadpan. "What are you lying about this time?"

Quinn smiled thinly. "I deserve that. But I'm on the level now."

"That right?" Jensen eyed him. "Then tell me your real name."

That got him a shake of the head. "I said *on the level*, not *stupid*." Quinn leaned forward. "Your man Frank, he's right. The Juggernaut Collective wants you on side. You were already known to Janus before your unscheduled stop at Rifleman Bank, and what you did there… Well, consider it a successful audition."

"That's how he works," offered Vega. "Janus looks for like-minded people, people whose lives have been screwed by the Illuminati. He brings us together, gives us common cause."

"That what happened to you?"

The woman grimaced. "Let's just say that without Janus and a mutual friend, I would have wound up floating face-down in Panama Bay with my throat slit."

"So Janus is a man, then?" said Pritchard, catching Vega's use of the pronoun.

She shrugged. "Maybe. That's how he presents. But

it doesn't matter to me what Janus is. He gets results, that's what is important."

"You did a lot of damage on your own, Jensen," said Quinn, picking up the conversation again. "Think of what you could accomplish with some real resources behind you. Janus is connected, worldwide, and that means the Juggernaut Collective has eyes and ears everywhere."

"*Almost* everywhere," corrected Vega, glancing back at Jensen. "We tried to secure evidence from the Panchaea site but that was a bust. You're probably the only one who really knows what was going on down there. I've seen the data on you, man. You got skills. We need someone like you to get into the Illuminati's power structure."

"They know his face," said Pritchard, folding his arms over his chest. "Well, some of them might…"

"They think he's dead," Quinn countered. "Look, it's a simple enough equation. You work with Juggernaut and do what I reckon you're planning on doing anyway – fuck up the enemy wherever you find them, eh? But the difference is, Janus can get you access to the intelligence you need to make that happen." He made a show of looking around. "With all due respect to Frank here, I don't think he's going to be able to give you the same depth of help as we can."

Pritchard made a low, growling noise in his throat. "That's the deal? Jensen, are you really going to pledge allegiance to a faceless ghost who may not even be an actual human being? Are you going to put your confidence in *this* man?" He stabbed a finger at Quinn.

"He makes a good point," said Jensen. "I never heard of this Juggernaut Collective before now. For all I know you could be another front for the Illuminati…"

Vega turned her head and spat. "Juggernaut didn't end up on the National Security Agency watch list for nothing. We brought down Belltower, smashed a viral weapons plant in Syria, did for Zapphire Biotech and that whole thing with the contaminated riezene…" She paused, thinking through her next words. "You wanna know why *I* signed on, Jensen? Because it gets me some payback."

"There's a real opportunity here to expose and destroy our mutual enemy," insisted Quinn. "But to do that, we need to work together. Every dictator in history knows that the best way to keep the little people down and suppress revolution is by making sure that the disaffected can't *connect*." He meshed his fingers together in a lattice. "Alone, individuals can only make a small dent. But a collective…" Quinn let the sentence hang – then abruptly he stood, brushing imaginary dust from his fingertips. "Listen, *bratán*, you don't have to give me an answer right now. Take some time." He walked away, patting Jensen on the shoulder. "Just consider what we've discussed."

Jensen watched him go, his gaze meeting Vega's on the way. She gave him a wry smile.

"I'll think about it," he heard himself say.

EUROPEAN AIR TRANSIT CORRIDOR –
GENEVA – SWITZERLAND

The strong and sweet black tea began to tilt toward the shallow cup's gold-rimmed edge, and Elizabeth DuClare's eyes flicked up from the encrypted data tablet holding her attention. Weak light through the oval windows of her private jet shifted across the interior wall of the opulent cabin as the aircraft started its final inbound leg, on course to descend into Geneva International.

The trip had been swift, not following the more circuitous route that a common civil flight might have made, but cutting directly over zones of disputed airspace that other aircraft would have been prohibited to transit. That made no difference to her. Those in positions of power knew whom the jet belonged to, and they knew what kind of retribution would befall them if there was so much as a momentary delay to the flight passing through their area. She rode inside a shell of power that was soft and ever-present on the surface, but steely and inviolate beneath. And this was as it should be.

DuClare frowned, taking a purse-lipped sip of the tea before straightening the elegant scarf around her neck. An expensive brand from London, the garment also served a dual purpose of masking her identity – woven into the threads of the innocuous-looking cloth was a frequency-flattening material that made it nigh-impossible for digital cameras to get a coherent image of her face.

Her eyes dropped to the tablet again, as she tapped the screen to lock away the reports she had been reviewing on her flight back from Naples. There were so many issues that required her attention.

In her leading position at the World Health Organization, the everyday and the mundane tasks of programs for the sick and needy were dealt with by lackeys. Her work was far more important, concentrating on the clandestine, the places where the WHO's operations dovetailed with the Council of Five's plans. She considered the reports of work in progress from the retroviral vector team in Kiev and the various Helix-designation genetics labs and their many initiatives. DuClare made a mental note to check in on the status of the D-Project, as once more her bio-programmers were tardy with their latest summary.

She was reaching for her seatbelt when the jet's engine note suddenly changed, shifting to a keening whine as the aircraft lifted its nose above the horizon and angled into a sharp turn. The landing had been aborted, and they were climbing again.

DuClare stabbed an intercom button on the arm of her chair with one perfectly manicured fingernail. "Pilot. What's going on?"

"Orders, ma'am." The reply came immediately from a speaker on the desk before her chair. *"We've been told to divert into a waiting pattern."*

"Orders from whom?" she demanded. The jet's identity transponder carried permissions equivalent to that of any head of state, effectively giving it carte blanche to land whenever and however it wanted. DuClare shot a look out of the window but saw nothing amiss. The very idea that someone could divert her flight, even for a moment, was ridiculous.

"Stand by for incoming communication," said the pilot, and from above, a holographic projector hidden in one of the crystal light fittings came alive, sketching a human figure in glowing laser lines.

As a virtual representation of a face took shape, she knew immediately whose orders had superseded hers. In the end, it could have been no-one else.

"Elizabeth. Apologies, my dear, but something has come up and this seemed the most expedient method of contacting you." His digitally rendered voice echoing across the distance, the synthetic version of Lucius DeBeers stood

before her, unaffected by the turning motion of the jet pulling everything slightly to the starboard.

She gave a demure smile. "Of course." The subtle message here, that Lucius had overruled her standing orders at a whim, was not lost on DuClare.

"You'll just circle for a bit," he said. *"Up here, the signal compression is better and we can talk in real-time."* Lucius's avatar gestured toward her. *"About what we spoke of at the hotel? It seems our adversary is moving assets into play in North America. Something is afoot."*

"Where? This is the first I've heard of it."

He nodded. *"Just so. I've kept it from all the others, for reasons of… confidence, you understand? This remains between you and me for the moment."*

"Of course." His desire for secrecy also explained this unscheduled conversation. On the ground, there was always the chance of unwanted ears listening in.

"Janus has sent people to Detroit, Michigan. I don't know why as yet, but there's other activity in that city that concerns me and their presence there cannot be coincidental."

She frowned. "I'm afraid I don't follow you, Lucius."

"There's more. News has reached me from our asset embedded at Interpol. It appears that operatives from the Task Force 29 counter-terrorist team have located a target of particular interest. They've been searching for information on Adam Jensen."

DuClare's lips thinned, finally shifting into a cold smile. "He went home? How very like him to do something so… *human*." DuClare had reluctantly taken responsibility for the loss of Jensen after the man escaped from a WHO clinic under her nominal control. It had been the job of her people to monitor him after his recovery, and that failure had caused her to lose face with Lucius. But now Jensen had resurfaced, and there was a chance that she could regain control of the situation. "Not for the first time, I must admit, I wonder if things would have been better if we had simply left him in the sea after Panchaea…"

"*There's truth in that,*" offered DeBeers, "*but after everything that has been invested in our next phase, we have to take a firm hand here. This needs to be handled decisively.*"

She leaned back in the chair, thinking of plans operating within plans, of layers of intent and scheming that went deep and far. Her cold amusement returned once more. "Perhaps there is an element of fate to it. All the pawns, gathering in the same part of the board, each unaware of what guides them."

DeBeers chuckled. "*I quite like that analogy. You have a flair for a poetic turn of phrase, dear Beth.*" He paused, considering. "*We're going to press the situation forward, I think. See what the roll of the dice offers up.*"

"And what about potential risk to *our* assets in the city?"

"*Oh, you let me take care of that. In the meantime, revisit your initial plans. This may even work in our favor.*" The hologram gave a slight bow. "*Until next time.*"

With a flicker of color, the lasers vanished and DuClare was alone in the cabin once again. She heard the engines shift pitch and felt the jet returning to its original flight path.

Her hand moved back to her data tablet and called up the contents of a secured file. "Open search mode," she told the device. "Show me all files pertaining to data string 'White Helix Lab', subset project name 'Black Light'. Begin."

A myriad of pages began to build across the screen, one after another.

EIGHT

From the roof of the derelict building, the steady fall of
the rain seemed to throw a shimmering curtain over the
entire city – but the amber glow and the parades of neon
lights that Jensen had come to take for granted were no
longer present. The skyline that was as familiar to him
as the lines of his own face had been changed while he
was gone, and now it was filled with the black ghosts of
dark, abandoned towers and low flickers from fires in
the lawless districts.

Other cities around the world had been hit hard by
the shock of the Aug Incident, but standing up here,
seeing it all so clearly, Jensen realized that Detroit had
taken the crippling hit harder than most, like a boxer
past their prime. The city had gone down to the mat,
and now the count was dropping away toward zero.

Before, with the augmentation industry on the rise,
there had been a chance for Motor City to rise out of
the economic mire that had trapped it during the late
twentieth century. The incident had cut that dream off

at the knees, and now Detroit was backsliding into the abyss, dragging everyone who lived there along with it.

Jensen took a slow breath of the wet air, and turned up the collar of the worn long coat he'd found at the bottom of the crates from his old office. He patted the inside pocket and found a pack of smokes, still half full. He cupped his hand over the nozzle of his lighter and lit a cigarette, drawing in deeply, as the metallic rattle of distant rotor blades reached him.

He looked in the direction of the noise – there, off over Forest Park, Jensen made out the shape of a beetle-shaped police helicopter circling some kind of disturbance on the ground. Spotlights stabbed down out of the sky, and Jensen saw a flicker of yellow tracer reach back up toward the chopper, the crackle of gunfire arriving a moment later. The helo lurched away and vanished into the low cloud.

Footsteps clanked up the fire escape and Jensen heard Pritchard curse under his breath. "What are you doing?" demanded the hacker. "There's a good reason no-one comes up here." The other man picked his way across the creaking roof until he stood beside Jensen at the lintel. "You do understand this building is condemned? Put a foot wrong and you'll go straight through the ceiling!"

"I needed some air," Jensen told him.

"Oh. Right." Jensen's distant tone registered with Pritchard and he took a moment to frame his next words. "Look… I'm sorry about your friend."

He shook his head. "You were right, he wasn't stable." Jensen took another draw. "I guess I didn't want to see it. Thought I could help him…"

"You can't rescue everyone," Pritchard said, after a

DEUS EX

moment. "If anybody should know that by now, it's you."

"Still keep trying, though…" Jensen went on. "More fool me."

The hacker studied him. "You look strung out," he said. "When was the last time you got more than a couple of hours' sleep?" He nodded at the lit cigarette. "Those won't help. It's a filthy habit."

"Says the guy who mainlines caffeine tablets…" Jensen's expression became a scowl. "I've slept enough."

It was hard for him to put it into words; that sense of dreamless darkness that waited for him whenever he closed his eyes. Try as he might, Jensen couldn't hold on to anything his resting mind brought forward, and it frustrated him. He could sense the shape of it but never grasp it, like he was a blind man feeling around the edges of objects that he would never be able to see. They might have been memories, they might have been nightmares, but all he was left with were the empty vessels of failed recollection. The content gone, with only the ghost of the thing left to imprint on his waking thoughts. Every time he awoke, it was the same feeling, an identical moment of dislocation and wrongness – his mind briefly filled with an uncanny black light that seemed to invade him and blot out everything else.

Frustration churned inside Jensen's chest, and at length he looked away from the bleak cityscape and the ceaseless downpour. "We need to maintain our focus," he told Pritchard. "Stacks is gone and there's nothing we can do to call that back. But we can still do something about the people responsible for his death."

"Magnet?"

"For starters." Jensen gave a nod. "But the MCBs

are just the next link in the chain."

"There's someone holding the leash of those gang-bangers, that's a certainty," said the hacker. "Remember those infolink signals I detected? Along with the line from me to you, there were two other distinct encrypted communications nets up and running while you were at the manufacturing plant. One was talking to Magnet, the other to that strike team in the VTOL."

"So we know they weren't connected…"

Pritchard shook his head and pulled his jacket closer against the drizzle. "It doesn't look that way. Totally different operating frequencies, different triangulation. At a guess, I'd say Magnet's contact was somewhere to the east of the city, but those gunmen were talking to a satellite downlink." He jerked a thumb at the sky.

"Which more or less confirms they're a professional crew," said Jensen. "That could mean government, private military contractor, intelligence agency…"

"I've already put out some feelers," Pritchard noted. "Whoever they are, someone will recognize their profile."

"Good." Jensen took a last draw on the cigarette, and then ground it beneath the heel of his boot. "What else have you got? I know you didn't come up here because you were worried about my well-being."

"There is something more," Pritchard admitted. "The break-ins at the different Sarif Industries sites around the city, and then what you said about the MCBs having a 'shopping list'… it got me thinking about what kind of information they have to have. I mean, on the surface these look like smash-and-grab raids, but when you step back and look at the big picture, there's a pattern." He spread his hands. "Draw it down to one basic question – how did they know what to look for?"

"We got that. Someone wants what Sarif had. The missing prototypes."

"More!" Pritchard went on. "Don't you get it? They'd need information that only someone on the inside would have."

"There is no 'inside' anymore," said Jensen, following his reasoning. "Everyone at Sarif Industries was kicked out after Tai Yong's hostile takeover."

The hacker nodded. "But as I ably proved, there are still security protocols in place that Tai Yong haven't purged yet. So I dug into the police reports from the first couple of raids and I found a common denominator. Each time, there was evidence that outer security doors were opened with no signs of forced entry."

"You're saying the MCBs had a *key*?"

"At the start, yes, until the system caught up and shut them out with a global lockdown, so they had to tackle the last few the hard way. And here's the thing, that backdoor I left in the SI mainframe? After our two guests left last night, I accessed it to check the entry logs for the dates of those first couple of raids. The data was still there – those idiots in the DPD hadn't even bothered to check it!"

"Give me the name," he told Pritchard. If someone had been using their key card to assist the MCBs in their thefts, then the entry logs would have recorded their identity.

Pritchard sighed. "*Adam Jensen.*"

"What?"

"It's *your* key card that was logged both times, Jensen. That's why I was reluctant to tell you about this. It's another dead end, not a viable lead… Someone must have gained access to your office in the weeks after the incident and stolen the pass so they could use it later." He paused, thinking back. "There were plenty of opportunities. Things were a mess at Sarif. Anyone could have grabbed the pass."

Jensen took that in, running the scenario in his mind. "Makes sense. Somebody made a smart play…"

Pritchard saw the change in his expression. "Do you actually know who took it?"

"I've got a few ideas." Jensen strode away from the edge of the rooftop, making for the stairwell. "And I know where to start looking."

"Wait," Pritchard called after him, and he hesitated. "Before you take off on another quest to go beat information out of someone, there's something else we have to talk about. Specifically, the *Juggernaut* in the room."

"You've made it clear what you think about Janus and his group," said Jensen. "I get it. But I haven't agreed to anything yet."

"You're going to!" Pritchard shook his head. "I know how you think! Did you forget who was sitting on your shoulder in Hengsha, Omega Ranch and Montreal? I may not have been in the field with you, but I saw enough."

"So what?"

"Janus is manipulating you!" insisted the other man. "Offering you exactly what you want so you'll cross over."

"You may be right," Jensen admitted. "But that cuts both ways. I don't have to trust these people to get what I need from them."

Pritchard gave a snort. "I know you're going to go ahead and do whatever you want to, but just remember," he said. "I was right about Stacks… and I'm right about this."

CASS CORRIDOR – DETROIT – UNITED STATES OF AMERICA

A nondescript green-gray door in the middle of faded brick frontage was all the face that Spector's Tavern presented to the world. It sat in a side street just off Cass Avenue and it had the weathered, dogged air of a place that had lived defiantly through every attempt at gentrification, redevelopment and the failure thereof. Twenty years ago, the surrounding area had been on its way to becoming trendy; now it was as drab as it had been in the Great Depression, but Spector's remained unchanged. Hard-edged and bloody-minded, like the locals who drank there, the aging dive bar remained a fixture in the neighborhood that fires, riots and gang warfare hadn't managed to dislodge.

Inside, the place wasn't any more inviting than its exterior. Dim lighting and a perpetually smoky atmosphere hid the aging décor, with most of the illumination coming from lamps over the pool tables in the back and the glow spilling from a projector screen on the far wall.

A hockey game was in its final moments on the big screen, as the Red Wings fought across the ice to pull back a tie from what was otherwise going to be a narrow defeat. Spector's didn't so much draw a crowd as it did have a crew of stubborn regulars, but still there was a collective expression of annoyance from them as the game clock hit zero and the equalizing shot didn't materialize.

A broad-faced man in a faded brown jacket cursed under his breath and turned around on his stool to find the tall, bull-necked bartender offering him a wireless reader device. "Ah, shit, Jake. You can't even let it sink in before you want me to pay up?"

"Losing a bet is losing a bet," said the man behind the bar, his eyes hard and unfriendly. "Boss said you're not good for credit anymore, Henry."

"Your boss can blow me," he retorted. "I got money. I'll pay, then screw you!" Henry leaned forward and angrily pressed his thumb to the reader. A moment later, there was an answering beep and he was fifty credits poorer as the stake vanished from his bank balance. "I'll take another drink while you're at it," he demanded.

Jake obliged, blankly pouring another two fingers of bourbon into his glass.

Henry raised the drink in a sarcastic salute to the hockey team. "You guys have sucked ever since you moved to Canada! Up yours too!" The liquor burned pleasantly on the way down, and he turned his back on the screen once again, his mind already thinking about the next wager he was going to make.

"Henry Kellman..." The voice was all gravel, and it came from close at hand. "Didn't you quit drinking?"

Henry twisted on the stool to see who was talking to him and he started answering before his brain caught up to what he was seeing. "Yeah, well, I *un*quit, so go mind your own business—" He froze; he was looking at a ghost. "Holy shit. *Mr. Jensen.*"

How the man had walked into Spector's, how he had made his way to the stool next to Henry's, all without him noticing until right now, those questions flared and faded in his thoughts before he could utter them.

Jensen gave a slow nod. "Back from the dead. *Again.* Guess I'm making a habit of it."

Henry put down the glass before the sudden

shaking in his fingers made him spill the contents. He blinked, trying to make sense of what was going on. "Wait, they said you'd been killed in all that crazy shit that went down…" He caught sight of Jensen's black polycarbonate hands as the other man signaled Jake for a drink of his own. "Oh man. *Oh man…*" He forced himself to stop talking, in case he said something he would regret. Regrouping, Henry forced a brittle smile. "I'm real glad that wasn't true. I guess we're all in the same boat now, right? Shit out of luck?" He gave a weak laugh.

Jake had a bottle of Tango Foxtrot black-label whiskey in his hand, but he hesitated before pouring a shot for Jensen. "This place isn't a hanzer joint," he said firmly. "Maybe you wanna go drink somewhere else."

"I really don't," said Jensen, ice forming on the words.

"Hey!" Henry tapped a thick finger on the countertop. "This guy, he's okay! He used to be my chief when I worked security over at Sarif, I'll vouch for him!"

Jake's vacant expression didn't shift, but eventually he poured out a drink for Jensen and walked away, never once taking his eyes off the man.

"Don't blame him, he don't have a lot of what you might call 'social skills,' Mr. Jensen," Henry went on. "So. Uh. You're back in Detroit? How's that going for you?" He shifted uncomfortably on the top of his stool. Half of him wanted to get up and make his excuses as quickly as possible, and the other desperately wanted to know what the hell Adam Jensen was doing in town.

"It's a work in progress, Henry," Jensen replied, taking a sip of the whiskey. "You're not an easy man to find. I had to do a lot of asking around."

"You were looking for me?" Henry gradually started to slide himself off the stool.

"Your apartment was closed up."

"Yeah…" he admitted. "I had to move out. I mean, after the incident and all, it's not like I was an aug or nothing, but it was tough times… I ended up in a flophouse 'cos that's all I can afford." Henry paused, and a churn of old anger rose briefly in his gut. "Shit, man, they just fired the whole damn lot of us! No severance pay, no call-back, no help… Everybody on the security team, out of a job overnight! And after all we did to keep that place from getting torn apart during the riots…" He shook his head, and took a pull from his bourbon to steady himself. "That sweet kid Cindy on the front desk, she could… *would* have died that night if we hadn't been there." The drink helped him focus, and when he looked back at Jensen it was with a brief surge of defiance. "Those sons-of-bitches on the company board screwed us over, plain and simple. Sold Sarif to the Chinese, just washed their hands of us… And you too, looks like."

Jensen nodded to himself, as if something was making sense to him. "So you've got to take whatever work you can get, right?" He nodded toward the screen on the wall. "Earn some money to make your bets."

"Yeah." Henry couldn't stop himself from shooting a look toward the clock above the bar and then toward the doorway. He had somewhere else to be.

Jensen knocked back the rest of his whiskey. "Why don't you tell me about the pass card, Henry? Who took it from my office?" His tone was flat, without inflection. "Was it you?"

"I don't know what you mean—" Henry started to

rise off his seat, but then the arm lying across Jensen's lap suddenly grew a black, meter-long sword blade that extended out to hover over Henry's thigh.

"Stick around," Jensen told him. "Finish your drink. We're not done catching up."

Henry gingerly settled back on to the stool and placed his shaking hands around his bourbon. "Look, Mr. Jensen… you gotta know how hard it was here after the incident. Everything falling apart, no-one with any damn answers about what was gonna happen next. You weren't here, Sarif was AWOL, and that dickhead up in digital security was no help to any of us on the guard detail…"

Jensen cocked his head, as if he was listening to a voice that only he could hear. "Go on."

"So when the word came down I was out, I took advantage, yeah. Figured I'd hold on to it, could be worth something… What the hell else was I gonna do?" He paused, the reality of it settling on him. Henry thought that the part of him that was ashamed by his conduct had died off, but it was still in there. "No-one else was looking out for us," he added. The justification seemed pathetic.

"*Us*?" Jensen seized on the word. "Who else?"

Inwardly, Henry cursed. That single slip had been enough, and Jensen had caught it immediately. He looked at the clock again. Now he was late, and that made things worse.

"You waiting for something, Henry?" Jensen had seen his nervous glances. "Anyone I know?" The other man turned and faced him with a cold, measuring stare. "I know *you*. You used to work for me, remember? I know you're not the only one in on this."

"Hey, that's not how it is…"

Jensen slowly shook his head. "There's a reason I came looking for you first. It's because you're the weak link. Don't get me wrong, you did your job at Sarif just fine, but you're a follower… you always have been. It's why I always gave you the soft jobs." He paused to let that sink in. "So tell me who wanted the pass card. Who put you up to it?"

Hearing it stated in such flat, blunt terms pulled all the resistance out of Henry like an exhaled breath. *Who the hell am I fooling?* he asked himself. *I'm just a washed-up mall cop out of his league.*

Henry polished off the last licks of his bourbon. "This comes back to me, I'm in the shit," he muttered. "Wilder's changed a lot since he went off the chain…"

"Don Wilder?" Jensen took that in. "Huh. Figures it would be him. Always thought he was too good for the job."

That got a nod from Henry. Wilder had been security pit boss on the day shift at the main Sarif Industries office, and while the guy had the instincts of a hawk, he had the manners of a hyena. The rumor around the locker room was that before working at Sarif, he'd quit a job with the Illinois Department of Corrections just ahead of an investigation that would have seen him fired – but that was all hearsay. Henry had never liked the man, and had always been intimidated by him. Now that truth lodged itself in his thoughts, he found himself talking. "It was Don's idea. I mean, we were both on the outs and we knew that there was no more money coming from Sarif. And with everything else that was going down, we had nothing in the tank. 'No lifeline,' he said."

Both of them knew about the high-security storage areas in all the Sarif Industries facilities, and while neither man had direct access, they guessed that the content would have to be valuable. And to be honest, Henry had liked the idea of giving David Sarif the finger for leaving his employees to twist in the wind.

"You knew my pass card would get you into those places," said Jensen, laying it out. "How'd you get around the voice code?"

"Don said he knew someone who could deal with that. Said she had the tech and everything." He shook his head. "I never met her. Just got paid up front. A finder's fee."

"You owed anything?"

Henry shook his head again, afraid to lie out loud. There was still some money coming his way, the last of the cash Don had promised after the thefts were done.

Jensen leaned closer, and his voice dropped to a low register. "Do you have any idea what you opened up for him?"

"I dunno, Don said it was a stock of nu-poz. I didn't question it!"

"Weapons," Jensen replied. "You helped him get his hands on military-grade hardware."

"Oh no." Henry felt the blood drain from his face. He'd always suspected it could be something like that, but he'd never had the guts to look too hard at things. "You gotta believe me—"

The sharp chime of a vu-phone cut Henry off before he could say anymore, and by reflex he pulled the device from his pocket. The number was unlisted, but he immediately knew who it was. Jensen must have seen the answer on his face, because he reached out and plucked the phone from his hand, triggering the call.

"*Where the fuck are you at?*" said the familiar voice through the phone's speaker, all snarls and arrogance.

"You were supposed to be here ten minutes ago. You keeping me waiting, asshole?"

Henry managed a lame reply. "Sorry, Don... Something, ah, came up."

"What did I tell you about names on the phone, stupid?" There was a spitting noise, and when Wilder's voice returned his tone was sly. *"Ah, don't worry about it. I sent someone to bring you your cut. It's all good."* Then the line went dead.

"What did he mean by that?" Henry began, looking to Jensen.

But the other man had stood up, stepping away from the bar, his hand slipping into the pocket of his long coat. Henry spun around to see what had alerted Jensen, and there in the tavern's open doorway were three men in yellow-gold gang colors, all of them grinning, their pupils dark with drug-effect dilation.

"It's payday," said one of them, bringing up a drum-fed machine pistol with a wicked, hungry sneer playing across his lips.

Jensen hadn't expected to cross paths with the gang-banger called Cali again, but there he was, large as life and twice as ugly, clearly doped up beyond all reason with whatever cocktail of drugs was the choice of the MCBs. It was the only way the man could still be standing. A day or so before, when they faced off at the manufacturing plant, Jensen had left Cali with ruined legs and figured that would be the last he'd see of him. He hadn't reckoned on the enthusiasm the Motor City Bangers had for elective cybernetic augmentation.

Cali was wearing torn, bloodstained cut-offs that revealed his newest enhancements. From the knees down, both his shattered legs had been replaced by shiny, gold-plated augs that ended in skeletal, claw-like feet. They matched the designs of Cali's twin cyberarms, and he was grinning like he'd been reborn, his weak flesh replaced with glittering metal.

He came stiffly through the door of the tavern, followed by a gangly kid with a pump-action MAO shotgun and a third ganger carrying a giant, heavy-caliber pistol that was far too big for his skinny frame. All the MCBs drew down as one, and Jensen knew this was not a robbery, not a show of force, but an execution squad.

Jensen shoved Henry away, down toward the bar, launching himself in the other direction as he tore his pistol from the holster beneath his coat. Lightning-fast, Jensen fired three rounds as he dove, and at least one shot clipped the kid with a big semi-automatic. But Cali and the shotgunner were already firing, filling the air inside the bar with hot, screaming lead, and Jensen took multiple hits across his shoulder and upper arm that slammed him off course. Jensen spun and fell across tables and chairs, crashing to the floor among a rain of broken glasses and spilled beer. Pain shocked through the muscle-machine interface in his bones, the ripple effect of the impact over the polycarbonate implants like a kick in the chest. He took a wheezing breath, tasted blood.

"I know you!" Cali was whooping and laughing as he sprayed rounds from the machine pistol across the room, cutting down the other drinkers who were too slow to take cover or flee through the fire exit.

Behind the bar, Jake perished as a shotgun blast blew him back into a rack of liquor bottles. He toppled out of sight in silence, his sightless eyes looking at nothing. The gunman who had ended him hunted for Henry Kellman, who was scrambling desperately across the floor between the legs of the bar stools. The MAO barked again and Jensen saw Henry go down in a bloody heap.

"Done, man, let's jet!" shouted the punk with the shotgun.

"No!" bellowed Cali, as his weapon ran dry. He ejected the drum mag and let it clatter to the floor, jamming a new load into the ammo port. "Where's that hairy-faced fucker? I'm gonna smoke him!"

It registered distantly with Jensen that he wasn't actually the one the MCBs had come to kill, but Cali had no intention of leaving without taking his scalp as a bonus. Jensen lurched forward, coming back to his feet underneath a circular table bolted to the floor. Ripping the table's central support free, he took it up with him like a battering ram and slammed it into Cali before the ganger could finish reloading. Without stopping, Jensen used the broken table to flatten the shooter against the wall and knock him down. Cali's gun went spinning away, and Jensen pivoted before the second thug with the shotgun could track to him. Blind-firing once again, he hit the other gang member and sent him staggering away, out on to the street. The kid with the big pistol had already fled without firing a shot.

Jensen went to Henry, who lay face-down in a puddle of blood and cheap Scotch. "Kellman!" he snapped, turning him over. "Can you hear me?"

He was wasting his breath. A ragged gouge cut by a close-range shotgun blast had torn away the right side of Henry's head, killing him instantly. Whatever he had known about Don Wilder's part in the break-ins was lost – *Murdered to keep him silent*, Jensen thought.

It didn't matter that Spector's Tavern was way outside MCB turf, or that a shooting here might have some serious gangland blowback. Magnet's crew were only interested in making sure Kellman never talked.

Beside his body, Henry's vu-phone was smashed beyond recovery. That meant Jensen's immediate sources of information had now narrowed to just one. Rising to his feet, he strode back to where Cali was struggling to extract himself from a mess of broken chairs and splintered wood. He tried to talk, but Jensen punched him hard enough to knock the ganger to the edge of unconsciousness. Then, grabbing one of Cali's brand-new metal-clad ankles, Jensen dragged him across the ruined bar and out through the fire exit, into the dimly lit alleyway beyond.

Cali came to, moaning and coughing, trying and failing to sit up. That was the thing about recent augmentees with new limbs, they instinctively thought the tech would work just the same as their old organic arms or legs, that they would be able to start walking normally from the moment they got off the operating table. Jensen knew from long, bitter experience that it didn't work that way. No amount of painkillers could change the fact that it hurt like hell and it took months of physical rehab just to learn how to move again. That the ganger had come out looking to make trouble instead of healing up spoke volumes about his bravado and stupidity.

"Fuh…" Cali managed, trying to assemble a curse. "Fuh… yooo."

Jensen holstered his pistol and listened for the sounds of sirens. Cass Corridor was on the edges of the zones still patrolled by the embattled Detroit

Police Department, so there was a chance the cops were on their way. "Pritchard? Monitor the DPD alert frequencies. Warn me if they get close."

"*Will do,*" said the hacker over the infolink. "*I'm also running down anything I can on the whereabouts of one Donald Wilder, ex-employee of Sarif Industries…*" Pritchard had listened in on the whole conversation with poor Henry, but Jensen suspected that Wilder would not be easy to locate. He was too smart to leave a clear trail, and that meant using other means to find him.

Jensen put a boot on Cali's chest and pressed down, making the gang member choke. "You like the metal, huh?" he asked, nodding toward the signature gold limbs. "I wonder how you're gonna do without it."

With a flash of motion, Jensen extended the nanoblade in his forearm and sliced cleanly through the mechanical core of Cali's right shoulder. In a gush of white processing fluid, the aug broke off and rolled away, the fingers clutching at air. Without pausing, he moved, putting his boot on Cali's other shoulder. The ganger cried out as Jensen took Cali's left arm and bent it back the wrong way at the elbow joint. He gave it a savage twist and the bearing gave way.

Jensen tossed the ruined mechanical limb down the alley, then went to work on Cali's new legs. He stamped through the left knee joint, severing vital myomer muscle feed lines, finally dropping into a crouch and extending the blade again. It made short work of the other leg, and at length Jensen took a step back. Lying there, limbless and powerless, Cali rocked back and forth, screaming at the top of his lungs.

"Where's Wilder?" Jensen demanded. "Tell me now. Otherwise, I'll leave you here for the cops, the local meatheads... or whatever finds you first. Understand?"

Predictably, Cali's responses followed a path from threats to refusals to insults, then back to dire warnings of retribution from the MCBs. It was only when Jensen put the nanoblade at the gang member's throat that he started to bargain and plead with him. And eventually, as the skirl of a police siren sounded close by, he came up with the name of a street across the city in the Ravendale district.

"*Got a possible location,*" said Pritchard, refining his search with the new information. "*An apartment complex, with a residence there registered in the name of Wilder's ex-wife.*"

"Copy that." Jensen turned his back on Cali and strode away, ignoring the man's renewed cries for help.

"*You're just going to leave him there?*"

"He'll get the same chance they gave Stacks," said Jensen, and he kept on walking.

RAVENDALE – DETROIT –
UNITED STATES OF AMERICA

It was almost possible to believe that the Aug Incident hadn't taken place here. On the surface, everything in this neighborhood seemed in order – no homeless and dispossessed crowding every shadowed alleyway, no darkened buildings without life or power. As Jensen walked quickly, his collar turned up, he allowed himself a moment to look around and take it in.

Ravendale had been the site of massive urban renewal in the 2020s, and the corporations that had taken control of it then had never let go. Jensen saw bright holographic signage promising safety and prosperity beneath the company banners. Tai Yong Medical's abstract logo was everywhere, and he wondered if there was any part of this protected enclave that the Chinese conglomerate didn't own to some degree. He grimaced, wondering how David Sarif would have felt seeing his old business rivals with such a foothold in 'his city'. For his part, Jensen knew that whatever sense of security Tai Yong projected was false. Beyond the edges of the Ravendale district and the other protected zones, the rest of Detroit was barely hanging on. The city was on the verge of turning feral, and if that happened there would be no stopping its self-destruction.

He shook off the thought as he approached the apartment block where Wilder's bolt hole was located. A sculpted rectangle of glass and steel, it climbed twelve floors into the night sky, glowing with soft amber illumination.

Pritchard had already scouted the location via cyberspace, conducting a virtual recon of the building that didn't show up any good methods of entry. Jensen resolved to tackle the security quickly and directly. It was imperative for him to reach Wilder's apartment on the eighth floor without triggering any alarms – Jensen knew that the man would have an escape plan, and that he would flee at the first sign of danger. The element of surprise was Jensen's only advantage.

A pair of ubiquitous Big Bro security cameras were set in the ceiling of the lobby, constantly scanning back and forth across the room for any signs of intruders. Jensen hesitated behind a low planter and watched the sweep patterns for a few moments, waiting for the brief moment when the cameras slipped out of synch with one another. Chancing the use of his cloaking aug would be too risky – the lobby was long and he'd need to be fast, risking disruption of the invisibility effect. Timing was the key.

Jensen blink-set a countdown clock in the corner of his optic display, and when the numbers began falling, he bolted from his cover. Without missing a step, he ran to a spot beneath the first of the cameras just as it swept back toward him. Another count of three more seconds before it moved away again, and Jensen sprinted the rest of the distance, barely making it into the corridor beyond as the second monitor looked his way. The camera caught a glimpse of black coat-tail, but he was in.

"What was that?" A voice, tired and bored, issued out from a security room across the hall. Jensen heard the sound of a chair scraping on the floor as someone stood up, and he was at the door as it opened inward.

He saw a thickset man in a rumpled security uniform through the widening gap, but didn't give him time to react. Jensen slammed the heel of his hand on the door, forcing it back to hit the unwitting guard in the face.

The man stumbled back, shouting out. "Hey, you can't be in here…" Belatedly, he caught up to what he was looking at and his hand dove at a holstered stun gun.

But Jensen was ready and he was faster. He pushed in, snaking his arm around the guard's throat, tightening the hold in a matter of heartbeats. The man tried to say more, but all that emerged from his lips was a dry gasp.

Jensen carefully applied more pressure to the sleeper hold, feeling the resistance ebb out of the guard. Too tight for too long, and he could kill this guy; too loose and he risked him breaking free. "Don't fight it," Jensen told him.

The stun gun clattered to the floor and at last the guard went slack. Jensen lowered the unconscious man into a chair, kicking the door closed as he did so.

Next to a TV running the Picus News channel, a bank of monitors showed points of view from all the Big Bro cameras on every floor of the apartment block, and Jensen spotted the shadows of small, drum-shaped security bots rolling back and forth on trike wheels. Acting quickly, he brought up a systems display and a brief smile crossed his lips. The guard had left the console logged on to the security mainframe, immediately getting Jensen past the first line of digital resistance.

He cast a wary eye over the network display, and set to work running a quick-and-dirty intrusion of the system. Jensen wasn't in the same league as career hackers like Frank Pritchard, but he knew enough to brute-force his way through a data net. Bouncing an intercept from the input/output port, he guided a cursor to an API node, then through a redundant directory, edging closer to the vital registry he was targeting with every step.

He was two nodes away when the system's diagnostic subroutine triggered, redlining the intrusion. The computer began a rapid back-trace, closing the gate on Jensen as he swiftly ran out of room to maneuver. Failure would mean every alarm in the building going off, and the end of his clandestine entry.

Jensen pushed on, taking the risk. At last, he connected to the registry and triggered a capture function. As the program co-opted the command data, the seeker trace enveloped it – one percentage climbing, another falling, with success going to whichever executed first. Jensen's hands left the keyboard and he got ready to run; but then the registry flashed green and the network warning fell silent. In the next second he was looking at command authorities for the cameras and the patrolling robots, and with a few deft keystrokes he ordered the systems to ignore him.

Jensen blew out a breath and leaned back. On the Picus News feed, he saw the permanently friendly smile of anchorwoman Eliza Cassan as she covered the day's headlines. She looked the same as she had when he confronted her in Montreal, only to learn that Cassan was no more human than the intelligent network running this apartment building. Was she the same Eliza he had spoken to, the secret AI with all its questions and uncertainties? Or was that just another model, a freshly rebooted upload of the same software forced back into the same patterns as its original? The thought came too close for comfort to Jensen's own circumstances, and he dismissed the question, returning to the mission of the moment.

He found a resident index and discovered Wilder's ex-wife listed there as a current owner-occupier, despite the fact she had been killed in the Aug Incident over eighteen months ago.

Apartment 8-12, noted Jensen. *One of the Executive Suites. Where does an out-of-work security guard get the cash for a place like that?*

He rode the elevator to the seventh floor. The apartment directly below Wilder's was locked and vacant, but a high air vent allowed Jensen to gain entry without forcing the door. He crossed the echoing, empty room, noting that the apartment could easily have swallowed the entire footprint of his old place in the Chiron Building.

Jensen slipped out on to the balcony, and leapt up from a standing start to grab the edge of the floor above him. Working slowly and in near silence, he swung his body up, his augmented arms taking the weight, until he could hook his leg over the other balcony and pull himself up. Jensen heard the micro-motors in his damaged shoulder complain, and ignored it.

A conversation was taking place inside Apartment 8-12 – or, to be more accurate, an *argument*. Don Wilder's raised voice cut across another reply filtered through the buzz of a video feed.

"For cryin' out loud! You're such a tough guy but you got nothing but excuses to give!" Jensen crouched on the balcony, peering into the sullen lighting of the room beyond. Wilder was pacing back and forth in front of a wall screen, gesturing with a shiny black cyberarm that he hadn't possessed during his time at Sarif Industries. In his other hand he had a stranglehold on a half-empty bottle of Red Bear stout.

On the screen, Jensen could make out the broad, dark face of the leader of the Motor City Bangers. Magnet was sneering. "*Man, who the fuck you think you are? Don't talk to me like you is in charge here.*"

"You think *you* are?" Wilder shot back. "Your chumps have a simple job to do and they can't even handle that. Kill a man or two. It's not that hard to understand."

"*MCB don't work for you, asshole,*" said Magnet. "*This? It's a whatever, a courtesy call. I got her the computer like she wanted, so that's all good. As for you? Out.*" He gave Wilder the finger and cut the line.

The other man swore violently and took a long, angry swig of beer. "I am having the worst goddamn day!" he said to the air.

"You're just getting started," said Jensen, stepping into the room with a pistol in his hand.

NINE

There was a flash of emotion over Don Wilder's face, a micro-expression that anyone other than Jensen might have missed. *Fear*. Despite the blank, glassy gaze of his twinned cyberoptic implants, the shock of seeing his former boss right there in the spot he doubtless thought was his safe place was clear.

But then it was gone and Wilder's expression became one of careless false humor. "Well, damn. Jensen, here you are. Come in, then. Take a load off." He waggled the beer in his hand. "Can I get you a cold one?"

"Put down the bottle and keep your hands where I can see them," Jensen replied, keeping his semi-automatic leveled in Wilder's general direction.

The man shrugged and obliged, unconsciously flexing the black plastic cyberarm as he did so. The action reminded Jensen of how he'd behaved after first getting his aug limbs. Like the optics, Wilder's replacement arm was new, and if Jensen was right, their make was Sarif Industries.

"When did you get that arm and the eyes?" said Jensen. Considering how human augmentation technology was being heavily regulated since the incident, the fact that he'd come across two people in the space of a few hours with brand new mech augs couldn't be an accident. "Take it off the top for yourself?"

"You like 'em?" Wilder flexed the arm in a bodybuilder pose, stepping slowly around the table in the middle of the room. "Better than yours, I reckon." He paused. "How'd you find me? I mean, I paid off some hacker punk to trash the SI employee database, erase the ID files of everyone on the security detail... make it look like it all got lost in the incident, y'know?"

"You forgot that I know your face," Jensen told him. He moved slightly, keeping a good distance between them. "Did you really think you were going to get away with this?"

"I don't know what you mean," Wilder said, with a shrug. "Look, if you ain't gonna put that gun away, then I suggest you leave. Last I heard you went missing up north. I don't know what happened to you there but it's nothing to do with me... You don't want me to call the cops, do you?"

"Sure. You can tell them how you had Henry Kellman murdered to keep him quiet," Jensen spoke over him. "Or was it just that you wanted to keep the rest of his money for yourself?"

Wilder paused, rocking on the balls of his feet. Finally, he let his hands drop. "You know, I heard a rumor you were back in Detroit but I thought it was bullshit. Stupid me, huh?" His tone turned mocking. "Adam Jensen, the bullet-proof man. David Sarif's attack dog." He sniggered. "Gotta say, you're looking a little worse for wear."

Jensen ignored the comment. "The hardware that you helped the MCBs to steal. You're going to tell me where it is, right now."

Gradually, Wilder let the false good humor slide off his face. "Or what? You're gonna shoot me in cold blood? I don't think so—"

"Don't test me." Jensen aimed the compact CA-4 pistol directly at the other man's head and cocked the hammer. "It's been a long day and I'm a little short on patience."

Wilder backed away a step, his hands coming up again. He almost stumbled over a low armchair. "Okay! Shit!" He swallowed hard. "Look, Kellman, that was something that had to happen, he was a drunk and he couldn't be trusted… You know that. You know he had no guts."

"Explain it to me," Jensen growled.

"You weren't here, you didn't have to live through all the aftermath." The other man let out a heavy sigh, bitterness and anger clouding his next words. "Kellman got the pass card, yeah, so we took advantage. Believe me, there were more than enough interested parties. They came to *us*."

"Who did?"

"I'm not telling you that. More than my life is worth." Wilder shook his head. "Anyhow, I don't care about her name, just the color of her money. But there's connections there, man, like you wouldn't believe." He fluttered his aug hand in the air. "Up *way* high."

"I can imagine," Jensen prompted. "Keep going."

The other man shrugged. "Be realistic. You're just one guy with an overdeveloped hero complex. You're not gonna stop these people from getting what they want, you or those spec ops assholes from Task Force 29…"

"Task Force?" He seized on the name, understanding immediately. "You mean the crew at the manufacturing plant?"

A derisive snort escaped Wilder's mouth. "See? You don't even know who the players are! You got no idea what you're messing with." He shook his head. "Bad enough I got those pricks from Interpol sniffing around, but now here you are busting in like the Lone Ranger! Don't you know to leave well enough alone, Jensen? The deal's already been done. This time tomorrow, the hardware is going to be somewhere over the Atlantic, halfway to who-gives-a-shit. This is my endgame, man. Time to cash out and retire."

"Those are military weapon prototypes we're talking about," insisted Jensen. "Dangerous black market hardware. Did you even consider for one second how many lives they could destroy?"

Wilder rolled his eyes as he circled the table. "Oh, spare me the bleeding heart routine. How many guys have *you* put down? How many deaths are *you* responsible for?" Jensen stood his ground, his aim never faltering. "What, you don't think that the rest of the security detail knew?" Wilder shook his head. "You're no angel. You're no better than me."

There was a truth in the other man's words that cut deeper than Jensen expected, and his lips thinned into a hard line. Wilder saw it and knew he had touched a raw nerve.

"You know, for a second there I actually considered cutting you in," he continued. "But you'd never have gone for it. You ain't honest enough to admit who you really are." He smiled coldly. "In a way, you're just like poor old Henry. Hollow inside. All that shit about the Mexicantown shoot back in the day, and what happened with that stuck-up witch Reed...? I heard about it all." Wilder pointed at him with the fingers of his cybernetic hand. "You let it rule you, Jensen. It made you *weak*."

Then in an instant, the action like a magic trick, Wilder's hand snapped backward at a 180-degree angle and the forearm behind it bifurcated, revealing the narrow mouth of a pulsed energy projector hidden inside the mechanism.

Even as Jensen's finger squeezed the trigger of his pistol, the kinetic wave from the pulse projector blasted outward with the force of a chained hurricane. Hit squarely by the shock effect, he was catapulted back through a glass partition and into an anteroom.

Momentarily dazed by the assault, Jensen tried to shake off the blurring of his vision as a strident, high-pitched beeping reached his ears. He rolled to one side, catching sight of a mine template fixed to the bottom of another low-slung armchair, the blue glow of a Pulsar electromag charge in the discharge slot.

"Stay down," sneered Wilder, just as the powerful EMP lit off and Jensen was wracked with pain. Lightning-like sparks crackled all over his augmentations, making him shake and convulse uncontrollably. His limbs became dead metal, unresponsive and immobile.

Jensen tried to lean up and failed, his sight filled with jagged sheets of false color and error messages as his augs spun through one failed reboot cycle after another.

He saw Wilder approaching, his cyberarm reshaping itself as it reset. "Cool toy, huh? When I saw it, I just had to get me one." He bent to scoop up Jensen's gun from where it had fallen. "But it's non-lethal, though, just like that EMP. What a shame." Wilder checked to make sure there was a round in the pistol's chamber. "Thanks for leaving that key card behind, man. That made me rich! The buyer, she gave me a vox synth to spoof the locks…" He paused, pressing a small metallic disk to his throat. "*That opened a lot of doors.*" An artificial emulation of Jensen's own voice echoed through the room. "Clever, huh?" Wilder toyed with the device. "Of course, you ruined it all by actually blundering into everything, but I'm gonna deal with that right now."

Jensen put all the effort he could muster into moving his right arm toward a jagged shard of glass lying just out of reach of his fingers, but nothing happened.

Wilder cocked his head and mumbled words too soft to register; the man was using an infolink's subvocal pick-up to talk to someone else. *The buyer*, Jensen guessed.

The conversation didn't stay hushed for very long. "What?" snapped Wilder. "Are you kidding me?" he asked to the air, gesturing with the pistol. "I got him right here. One shot and—" Wilder winced as a voice that Jensen couldn't hear cut him off. "Fine. But I want a bonus for my trouble! He knows me and that complicates things." He nodded again and let the gun drop. "Okay."

"Trouble with… the boss?" Jensen forced out the words.

"She must like you," Wilder spat, grabbing a telephone handset off a nearby shelf. "Whatever." He dialed 911 and then he pressed the voice-shifter to his neck again. "*Yeah. Police.*" Jensen heard his own voice once more, the strange disconnection of it making his head swim. The throbbing pain from the aug implants in his skull meant it was hard to concentrate. *"I want to turn myself in. My name is Adam Jensen. I hurt a bunch of people at Spector's Tavern. I've got a gun."* Then Wilder hung up and tossed the pistol into the shadows. "That ought to do it. Unlike in the rest of this town, the cops around here will actually come looking."

Jensen shifted slightly, the first tingles of feeling returning to his fingertips; but Wilder was standing over him.

"Lights out," he grinned, and his boot came down with pain and darkness close behind.

WEST SIDE – DETROIT – UNITED STATES OF AMERICA

When awareness returned, it wasn't gradual or easy.

Jensen snapped awake, as if a switch had been tripped inside his head, and his first breath of air came back with the taste of rust and damp.

He was lying on a folding cot in a wide metal compartment, which was otherwise empty except for a skeletal chair and a wireless remote camera unit fixed to the discolored wall with a blob of epoxy glue. Jensen righted himself, staring at a sealed hatchway that was the only way in or out. His new circumstances had the unpleasant ring of the familiar about them. Waking up in a cell was nothing new to Jensen, and it never boded well.

He looked around. If this was police holding, then the Detroit PD were even worse off than he thought. He was missing his weapon, the contents of his pockets, his coat and tactical gear, and there was an unpleasant buzzing sound in the air that made his teeth itch.

"Terrific." Jensen scowled as he located the source of the sound. "This again." Clamped around his arm was a metallic bracelet that was the twin to the one that had been fitted to him at Facility 451. It made his augs feel leaden and heavy, as if they were moving in slow motion. He tested his infolink for a carrier signal, but got nothing back but white noise.

The latches around the hatch clanked open in sequence and the door creaked open. Jensen half-expected to see Agent Thorne or Dr. Rafiq step through, but his first sight was of a different, but still familiar woman.

The operative from the roof, the one with the short blonde hair, came into the cabin followed by a big, dark-skinned guy with shoulders broad enough to fill the doorway. Jensen caught a glimpse of others moving around in the area beyond the hatch, seeing equipment and monitor screens before it was shut again.

Both of them were wearing the same matte black combat outfits he'd seen earlier. There was nothing to indicate what they were or who they worked for. All Jensen had was the name that Wilder had dropped during their confrontation.

He had nothing to lose, so he decided to throw it out there. "Tell me something. Does the Detroit Police Department know that Interpol are working on their turf?"

The big guy snorted, but said nothing, inclining his head in a way that gave the woman permission to speak. *So he's in charge and she's the number two.* Jensen filed that away for later consideration.

"You should be glad we picked you up before they did." There was that European accent again, which chimed with the Interpol connection. "The police have a BOLO out for you in connection with that shootout across town. And then there's the matter of a Federal alert, something to do with a situation in Alaska."

"It's not how it looks," Jensen offered.

"It rarely is," rumbled the man, and Jensen picked out a southern twang to his words. He produced a pocket secretary and set the device into playback mode. An audio file of Wilder's faked emergency call sounded out across the compartment. "Of course, that ain't you," said the big man. "Our techs saw through it. But the locals wouldn't have known any better. So you want to explain why someone left you to take the fall?"

Jensen eyed them. "Remind me of what laws it is you're breaking by holding me here? What due process you're ignoring? Or is that just how Task Force 29 operates?" He was fishing for a response, and it worked.

The woman stepped closer, looming over him. "You want to talk about your rights? I think you gave up any claim on legal protection when you threw in with smugglers and killers. You don't get to run this time, Mr. Jensen. Yes, we know who you are, and we know who you're working with."

"Is that so?" It was a bad sign that they had his name, but he didn't let it show. "And who is that, exactly?"

She leaned in. "Here's what I think happened. I think you and your friends from Sarif Industries decided to make bank by putting mil-spec weapons on the underground aug market, but you didn't reckon on them double-crossing you. Now you're out in the cold and you've got nothing to show for it."

"We know your access code was used," said the man. "And when the DPD picked up Kellman's body, it wasn't hard to piece together the rest."

Jensen gave a snort. "Except you're looking at it all wrong. I wasn't in on this deal. I'm trying to *stop* it."

"Like a good policeman?" said the woman. She shot the other man a wary glance. "But you haven't been that for a long time, Jensen. Funny thing… we found your police record easily enough, but your employee files from Sarif Industries are all corrupted. I wonder how that happened?"

"You know these guys?" The man held up the pocket secretary so Jensen could see it and tabbed through a series of pictures, watching him closely for any reaction. The shots were of unfamiliar faces, men in combat gear whose profile suggested they were mercenaries.

Jensen shook his head. "Never seen them before," he replied truthfully.

That wasn't the response that the woman wanted, and her expression soured. "Who is running this transaction?" she demanded. "Give us a name and we'll cut you a deal. We don't want some burnout ex-cop like you. We want the people with the money."

The corner of his lip quirked up at the insult. "And what would you do with that name? Report in to your bosses? Or go put a bullet between someone's eyes?"

"We'd bring them down," said the big man, and Jensen sensed that he meant every word of it. "That's what we do. You could say our unit has a… a broad remit." He paused, then reached for the chair resting by the far wall, planting it backwards in front of Jensen so he could sit and look him in the eye. "I read your file. I reckon I get you well enough. Cop with a code, right? Someone with principles." He gestured around. "Only you're in the real world, and it don't have much room for that kinda thing."

A silent communication passed between the two Interpol operatives, and at length the woman stepped back, folding her arms across her chest. She continued to watch Jensen like a hawk.

"You said you were trying to stop the aug deal," continued the man. "So are we. You tell us what you know, that may still happen."

Jensen frowned. "And what happens to the hardware?"

"It'll be destroyed," said the woman. "The kind of tech your boss Sarif was tinkering with is too dangerous to leave lying around. Too many mercs, terrorists and criminals in the world want to get their hands on gear like that."

The momentary silence that fell in the wake of her words stretched into seconds as Jensen weighed his options. Whatever happened, he was going to have to take a risk if he wanted to get out of this makeshift prison cell. One way or another, he would find out what this Task Force 29's true motives were once they had what they wanted from him.

He nodded toward the hatch, in the direction of the activity he'd seen beyond it. "I'll tell you this. Time's running out to stop these people." Jensen thought back to what Wilder had said in the apartment. *This time tomorrow, the hardware is going to be somewhere over the Atlantic.* "Those augs are being flown out of Detroit, and it's going to happen in the next ten or twelve hours. If you really want to stop them from getting into the wild, then you need to be doing something about it right now."

A low, humorless smile crossed the other man's face. "Let me guess. You got an idea about how we can do that, right?"

Jensen nodded again. "I know who's involved. I know their faces. You don't. So why don't we cut all the bullshit and start acting like professionals?"

A chuckle escaped the big man, and he glanced at the woman. "I think I like this guy."

YUKON HOTEL – DETROIT – UNITED STATES OF AMERICA

Wilder ignored the acid looks he got from the natch residents of the Yukon as he strode across the expensively minimalist lobby toward the elevator bank. Decorated largely in crushed black velvet and gray brushed steel, the structure of the original building showed through in artfully random patches of raw brick, but for the most part the interior was achingly post-modern. Security was cleverly worked into the ornamental panels and sculptures dotted around the space, from the thick bullet-proof glass doors to the low kennels hiding dormant patrol bots. The Yukon had always been a place for rich snobs with a high degree of paranoia, and ever since the Aug Incident it had come into its own. Many of those people with money – but not quite enough to quit the protected inner enclaves of Detroit – called it home.

A large man in a black suit with the craggy, broken nose of a career boxer stepped up to discreetly block Wilder's path before he could reach for the elevator's call button. The guard had barely raised his hand when he halted, blankly cocking his head in that way that those with active infolinks always did. Their eyes met, and the other man stepped aside. "Go on up, sir," he added. "You're expected."

Wilder sneered and entered the elevator. There were no buttons or floor indicators on the inside. Once the door shut, he was whisked up the side of the Yukon and delivered to where he was expected to be.

She had a modest suite on the twenty-second floor that shared the same abstract geometric décor as the lobby. All the windows were fully polarized to obsidian black, and in the central room of the suite the only items that appeared to belong to her were an armored briefcase containing a portable computer, what Wilder guessed was an encrypted communications rig and a commercial-grade portable hard drive, the kind from an ordinary office desktop. Those, and a black-anodized Mustang Arms pistol sporting a targeting laser and integral silencer.

Wilder's own weapon, a thick-framed revolver resting in a paddle holster in the small of his back, seemed like an anchor, causing drag with every step he took. On the way over, he'd taken a cocktail of zee and nu-poz, hoping that the drug combination would keep his edge sharp; but he found it hard to stop himself continually making and relaxing a fist with his cyberarm.

She had her rust-colored hair up in a precise cluster, and if anything it made her look even paler than she had when Wilder had first met her. Back then, he'd made a lame joke about her having a misspent youth as a goth chick, and the withering glance the comment had got him stopped Wilder from even thinking about speaking out of turn in her presence ever again.

She was busy making herself a cup of herbal tea. "Why are you here?" she asked, in the way a teacher would disparage a particularly dim pupil. "We established a protocol, and you were told to stick to it."

"Yeah, well," he began, holding his nerve. "Things change. I'm gonna have to cut short our association here and now. We're done."

"Are we?" She carefully poured boiling water on to a teabag and the aroma of strawberries filled the room.

Wilder nodded, looking around again. Jensen's surprise appearance in Detroit had been the one complication that he hadn't planned for, but now with him left out for police custody and Kellman dealt with, Wilder had no more reason to remain in the city. There had always been a risk that one of those MCB punks might have been able to put the spotlight on him, but that wasn't anything he couldn't handle... However, Adam Jensen was another story. Wilder's former boss had the potential to cause some serious blowback, and the baffling order to let him live complicated matters immeasurably.

He laid that all out for her while she made her tea, all the while acting like she wasn't listening to a word of it. "I mean, I don't get it. Why the hell didn't you just let me ice the son-of-a-bitch?"

She favored him with a brief look for the first time since he had entered the suite. "I have instructions. If Jensen has to be killed, it won't be down to you to pull the trigger." The way she said it showed she wasn't happy about the order either.

He snorted and glanced away. His optics caught sight of a series of nested video displays on the screen of the portable computer. They looked like security camera feeds, and he saw shots of large warehouses with broad frontage, wide open expanses of tarmac and big shadows moving behind bright spotlights.

"Okay, fine. Whatever you say." Wilder shook his head. "I don't give a fuck. But as of now, I am out.

Pay me and color me gone."

"All right." She put down the cup. "A finish to our cooperation, then. I'll be honest with you, in terms of usefulness, you've been mediocre at best."

"What?" Wilder bristled at her tone. "To hell with you," he retorted.

She went on as if he hadn't spoken. "You complicated matters needlessly by interfering with the gang members and their tasks, not to mention the murder of Kellman. Why not just pay him and be done with it?" Wilder didn't get time to reply. "You've made a number of mistakes, and served largely to remind me why it is I don't often use local talent. Understand this: if you hadn't granted access to what my employer required to facilitate this transfer, you never would have been part of the operation."

His cheeks darkened as his anger rose. "Y-you don't get to talk to me like that! I made this happen! Now give me my damn money!" Wilder's hand slipped toward the paddle holster and the butt of the revolver.

But then she moved so fast that even with his new, high-acuity optic implants, the woman was a blur of black material, pale skin and red hair – and she suddenly had that silenced pistol in her hand pointed right at him.

"Hey, wait…" His tone became one of pleading. "Fine, forget the cash. You keep it, Thorne."

She shook her head slightly. "Don't say my name." The pistol jerked in her grip, discharging a single caseless bullet with a chug of noise.

The round hit Wilder in the chest, just below his heart. It penetrated his lungs and broke apart into thousands of frangible needles, kinetic energy immediately translating into a murderous shock effect. The bullet was designed never to exit the body, removing the untidy issue of ragged exit wounds, blood spatter and all the other mess that shooting someone at close range usually left behind.

Wilder staggered back and collapsed to the floor, dying with a gasp as he lay slumped against the edge of an ornate couch. Pink foam collected around his mouth and nostrils.

Jenna Thorne put down the gun and tapped a string of numbers into the encrypted comm unit. A moment later she heard the line open and the gruff voice of the gang leader, Magnet.

"Yeah?" In the background, the whine of jet engines faded into the distance.

"This is a warning. Wilder may have compromised the operation. You need to be aware."

She heard Magnet spit. *"That asshole. Gotta be messing with everything… Don't worry. MCBs got this. Anyone comes around… they get smoked."*

"See to it. The pick-up is on its way." She cut the line before Magnet could reply, then entered another code. Thorne's gaze fell to study Wilder's slack face and sightless eyes as she waited for a link. She would need to deal with his remains before leaving the hotel.

The second call connected, whispering through a myriad of digital masking subroutines, blind servers and redirects. "Thorne," she said aloud, knowing that the word would be deconstructed by smart scanner programs clever enough to parse her voice as clearly as if it were a fingerprint.

Circumstances have changed, she went on, mouthing the words without sound, knowing that her masters were listening to her silent, subvocalized speech. *I advise we move the secondary contingency plan to active status and prepare to execute.*

WEST SIDE – DETROIT – UNITED STATES OF AMERICA

An hour later, the hatch clanked open again and the blonde woman stood in the doorway, beckoning Jensen with one hand. "Come on," she told him.

He got up and followed her out into the compartment beyond. He'd pieced together that they were on some kind of boat, and when he looked up and saw the distant arches of the bridge through a rent in the tarp roof, he knew where they were. "Smart place for an FOB," he offered. "No-one comes down to the docks these days." When the woman didn't acknowledge his words, Jensen tried a different tack. "You don't think much of me, do you?"

"Vande don't think much of anybody," said an olive-skinned man as he walked past them. "It's not personal."

"Shut up, Chen," she told him.

Jensen watched the guy cross the room to where the rest of the Task Force team were assembling. It was a familiar setup. A few techies were working keyboards, prepping comm channels and scanning through the city data grid, and by their sides, a small squad of hard-faced men and women made ready their weapons and told bad jokes, burning off any pre-mission adrenaline.

The blonde – Vande – brought him to her commander as he climbed out of a folding chair, pushing aside a clamshell VR helmet rig on an extending arm. They exchanged weighty looks again, and Jensen understood that these two had the kind of highly synchronized behavior patterns that could only be earned through shared combat experience.

"So if we're introducing ourselves," he began, "the name's Jarreau. I'm what passes for in charge of this band of reprobates. Vande here, she's my red right hand."

"I thought Interpol were all admin and investigation," said Jensen. "Since when have they had covert mobile strike teams?"

"The Aug Incident changed a lot of things," said Vande, by way of explanation.

"We track, locate and neutralize criminals and terrorist groups," added Jarreau. "It's that simple."

"I doubt it," Jensen replied. "So what happens now?" He nodded toward the team, unconsciously reaching for the inhibitor bracelet around his forearm.

"You'll be pleased to know that the folks who write my paychecks agreed with the intel you gave us. Turns out, there happens to be a certain cargo lifter coming into Wayne County Airport from across the Canadian border tonight, and its flight plan is what you might call sketchy." He glanced at Vande. "It's a good probable for Sheppard and his crew."

"That'd be the connection picking up the stolen augs?" said Jensen.

"Affirmative." Jarreau nodded. "So, you're gonna liaise with Chen over there, keep an eye on the screens and sing out the moment you spot a face you recognize, got it? We tie this all up with a neat little bow tonight, and then everyone goes their separate ways."

Jensen shook his head. "That won't work. I can't do this by remote, I need to be on site."

"Not going to happen," Vande said immediately.

"No?" Jensen fixed her with a steady gaze. "You're not new to this and by the looks of your people over there, no-one on this tub is a day-player. So you tell me: in a high-tempo operation, every moment is vital, right? Do you really want to chance me missing something important because I'm getting it second-hand through someone else's optics?"

Vande glared back at him. "You seem to think we're operating as equals here, Jensen. But you're in our custody. You're not part of our team."

"And how well has *your team* been doing so far?"

The woman opened her mouth to retort, but Jarreau interceded. "Okay, enough. Jensen makes a good point. Make a space for him on the bird, he's coming with us."

Vande shot an *are you kidding me* look at her commander, but he gave nothing back. "Your call, boss," she said, after a moment.

"All right." Jarreau pointed toward the tech Jensen saw earlier. "I assume you'll want your tac kit back? Chen will fix you up."

"Do I get a weapon?" Jensen held up the arm with the inhibitor bracelet. "And what about this?"

Jarreau smiled. "I'm not stupid, Jensen. Consider yourself an observer, not a participant." He walked off toward the gathered team.

The steel index finger of Vande's right hand prodded Jensen squarely in the chest and she lowered her voice so only he could hear her. "He's taken a shine to you. That's a rare failing on his part, one that I don't share."

"And yet you seem so warm and friendly." Jensen's deadpan reply didn't land.

"You get in the way out there, do something I don't like, look at me funny... I'll make you regret it. All I care about is getting that tech off the grid. You don't matter to me, clear?" Vande stalked away before he could offer a reply.

WAYNE COUNTY AIRPORT – DETROIT – UNITED STATES OF AMERICA

Magnet's gold eye shields glittered in the dimness of the vast hangar, and he ran his flesh-and-blood hand over his shorn scalp, sweating a little despite the cool of the night. He stalked past the rest of his boys, all of them alert, a lot of them chemically so, every man with a shottie or an assault rifle. This was the last step of the job he'd got the Motor City Bangers involved in, and the gang's top dog wasn't about to let it come apart at the end. This had become a personal thing, and his boys needed to see him bring it home.

They'd already lost good soldiers to this shit, some dead and some in jail. Cali's arrest was the one that cut him the most; his little cousin, the one he'd looked out for all this time, the bastard had rolled the moment five-oh threw him in a cell. Magnet was all kinds of angry with him, with goddamn Wilder and that other asshole who'd been messing with the plan. It was getting in the way of what he wanted, which was the cold hard cash that red-headed witch was promising.

The past year had been a bonanza for the MCBs, starting with the end of their arch rivals in Derelict Row and growing by the month as they took control of more and more of the unpatrolled precincts of the city. But Magnet was smart enough to know that they were in danger of getting spread too thin. He needed money to solidify his hold on the outer wards of Detroit, money for guns and new recruits… and this deal would provide it, as long as all those motherfuckers kept their distance.

"Yo, Mag." Mano, a lanky Hispanic banger from Mexicantown, came toward him, cradling a vintage AK-74. "It's time, boss. I think I seen 'em coming."

"Oh yeah?" Magnet followed him back to the hangar's massive doors, which sat open just wide enough for a man to fit through.

He paused on the threshold, glancing back into the dim interior. In the middle of the open space, an irregularly shaped cargo container sat on an electric jack, waiting to be picked up. Inside, the unit was packed with almost the entire haul of gear the MCBs had stolen from the Sarif Industries sites around the city – minus a few choice pieces taken by Wilder and a couple of Magnet's lieutenants. The gang leader just saw it as dollar signs. The sooner he was shot of the hot augs, the better.

Stepping out into the night air, his nose wrinkled at the ever-present stink of jet fuel, and Magnet followed Mano's raised arm to where the other man was pointing. There, out over the top of the distant North Terminal complex, was a cluster of indicator lights dropping toward the far runway. A black shape like a manta ray moved against the low cloud. He sneered at it.

"That them?" asked Mano.

Magnet didn't answer, turning back into the hangar. "Eyes up," he shouted. "Get these doors open. We be done with this shit soon, boys."

* * *

The Task Force VTOL landed firmly on the helipad across from the de-icing pans where the big airliners were sprayed down in the winter months. The hatches on the side dropped open and Jensen was the last out, letting Jarreau's people deploy in quick, careful order.

He glanced around, taking in the territory. It was a smart move on the part of the smugglers, making the trade in the middle of an active civilian airport. They were bound to be watching the terminal buildings by remote for any sign of an increased police presence, and the fact that there were four active runways operating out of the area meant that aerial drones and flyers like the VTOL couldn't loiter without being spotted.

The Task Force aircraft had got past that hurdle by using some kind of electroactive pigment on the fuselage, which shifted the VTOL's usual matte black coloration to the nondescript yellow and white livery of an XNG Shipping transport. Parked out on the edge of the airport apron, they were down as close as they dared get to the hangar where the MCBs were congregating.

"Move out," hissed Jarreau, and the squad broke into two groups, each slipping across the runway in the pools of darkness between the landing lights. Jensen kept in step with the team he'd been reluctantly assigned to. Leading from the front, Vande made a habit of checking to make sure he was still following them every minute or so.

Vande's group gathered in the shadow of some parked service vehicles, surveying the hangar from the western approach. There were no lookouts Jensen could see, but every entrance to that side of the building was padlocked shut.

"We go loud on the doors, that's two, maybe four

seconds we lose," said one of the other operatives. "Not good."

Vande nodded, unhappy with the evaluation. "We'll have to cryo the locks before we breach." She picked out two of the team and pointed toward the doors. Jensen watched them scuttle across and set to work with small liquid nitrogen aerosols on the door mechanisms.

"Copy," Vande said quietly, reacting to something unheard that Jarreau had transmitted over her infolink. As well as forcing Jensen to wear the inhibitor and denying him a gun, the Task Force had also cut him out of the communications loop.

"Hey." The operative who had spoken before nudged Jensen with his elbow and placed a lowlight scope in his hand. "By the main doors. See them?"

Jensen raised the monocular to his eye and saw two figures standing outside the hangar. He glimpsed a flash of gold-plated teeth and eyes like bright coins. "Yeah, I got it. One on the left, that's Magnet, leader of the MCBs. If he's here, he's brought his troops."

Vande cocked her head. "One, this is Two. Observer confirms, Target Bravo is on site." She listened to something, then nodded to herself. "Roger that. Go on your signal."

The sound of engines reached Jensen's ears and he glanced up the runway. A large, smooth-sided form was rolling toward the hangar, strobing lights spilling from its flanks. Slowly, the hangar doors began to roll open.

The 'manta ray' Magnet had glimpsed earlier was more like some kind of whale when seen close up. The hull of the cargo jet was a blended shape, the thick wings tapering out of a bloated body that sprouted tail fins and a pair of massive ducted engines, which continued to spin and idle as the craft pivoted and backed halfway into the hangar.

He couldn't see a cockpit. The front of the plane was flat and featureless except for all kinds of chunky antennae that gave it a whiskered look. But someone had to be in there, he reckoned. This load was too important to be left to machines to handle.

There was a clatter of metal on metal, and spindly latches along the belly of the cargo plane snapped open and unfolded. With a low whine of hydraulics, an entire mid-section of the jet detached and sagged on to a vacant jack rig with a dull boom. The robot jack rolled it away, and Magnet saw that the disconnected unit was exactly the same dimensions as the waiting container his boys had filled.

He couldn't resist taking a look inside the plane, and Magnet swaggered across the hangar to peer into the opened fuselage. Three mercs armed with flechette rifles and cold gazes stared back out at him, their guns at the ready. One of them saw the gang leader and hoisted his rifle with a shit-eating grin. "Well, howdy," he offered. "Who the hell might you be?"

"Could ask you the same, man," Magnet sniffed. "You working for her too, huh?"

The merc shook his head. "Nah. We're more like… independent contractors, you feel me?"

"Sheppard," said one of the other men. "We here to load up or we here to chat? Come on, man, tick-tock."

"Fair point," said the merc, and looked back toward Magnet. "You got something for us, bro?"

"Whatever," said the ganger, and he stepped away, throwing a loose wave at his men. One of them hit a switch, and the self-seeking jack shifted the full container into the space vacated by the old one.

Jensen used the monocular to sweep the area, but there was no sign of any other faces he recognized. He'd expected Don Wilder to be here for the close out, but the ex-security guard was conspicuous by his absence. That made him a loose end that would need to be tied off – if Jensen got the opportunity. It was equally likely that someone else had already done that job for him.

He still wasn't a hundred percent sold on Jarreau's story about Task Force 29 and what they were here for, but for now their goals aligned and that was all Jensen could be certain of.

Vande spoke quietly, relaying new orders. "Surveillance confirms we have detected a positive voice trace for Target Alpha. Repeat, Target Alpha is on site. This is a green light."

Bravo was Magnet, listed by Interpol as a second-tier objective and a 'warrant of opportunity,' but Alpha was the mercenary smuggler known as Sheppard, a prime scalp that Jarreau's unit were itching to take. Jensen felt the tension crackle in the air as the two teams stiffened like runners on the starting blocks.

Vande looked at the operative who had spoken earlier. "You. Hold here, watch him." She pointed at Jensen. "He doesn't move from this spot, copy?"

"Copy," said the other man.

"I can help," Jensen told her.

"I don't care." Vande made a striking motion with the blade of her hand, and as one the rest of her team burst into motion, loping toward the hangar. He watched them vanish inside.

A few seconds later, Jensen heard the chug of a suppressed weapon – and then from out of nowhere came the metallic screaming of a heavy-caliber autocannon, the vicious thudding crack of anti-material rounds blasting everything in sight.

He saw the sudden flash of ragged holes appearing in the thin walls of the hangar building as wildfire bullets sliced through them and hummed through the air around them. Jensen dove to the asphalt behind the wheel well of a runway tug, but his guardian wasn't quick enough. Heavy rounds designed to tear open armored vehicles cut into the luckless operative in gouts of bright blood, and he crashed to the ground.

Inside the hangar, all hell was breaking loose, and above the noise the shriek of engines rose high as the cargo plane began to roll back out on to the runway.

TEN

Vande followed the point man through the door into the
hangar, kicking away the brittle, super-chilled fragments
of the lock mechanism where they lay shattered on the
ground. The team filed silently into the gloomy interior,
directing left and right with jerks of the head and swift,
sharp hand gestures.

She had her twinned semi-automatics out and at
the ready, the long suppressors attached, the muzzles
doubling the length of the silver pistols. Slipping
behind a stack of oil drums, Vande chanced a quick
look out across the hangar proper.

Clamps along the center of the idling jet were in
the process of grasping a cargo module, drawing
it up and into place beneath the fuselage. In a few
moments, the aircraft would be ready to depart, and
she guessed that Sheppard's pilot would be unlikely
to wait around for permission from air traffic control
if the shooting started. She looked over her shoulder
and nodded at the woman coming up behind her.

"Lund," she whispered, "prep the charge."

"Copy." Lund was a muscular Texan woman with bright eyes and an auburn buzz cut, and her primary role was as the squad's anti-vehicle specialist. She carried a powerful mine template in her backpack with an overcharged EMP unit that had enough jolt to shut down a main battle tank. The plan was to get her close enough to knock out the cargo plane's electronics before it could escape.

But even as Lund set the charge's mechanism, Vande had the creeping, sixth-sense feeling that something was wrong. Long, hard-won field experience and raw gut instinct went a long way, and both were gnawing at her.

Despite surveillance getting a positive detection of Sheppard's voiceprint inside the hangar, she saw no sign of the mercenary or any of his crew outside the aircraft. There were only the Detroit gangers, who milled around, on edge with their fingers on their triggers.

"*Go, go, go!*" Jarreau's voice whispered in her ear and Vande launched forward as he spoke the last word, seeing other figures in black emerging from behind cover on the far side of the jet, moving to surround the criminals.

The gang members reacted with shock and fury, bringing up their guns as one.

"Police! Drop your weapons!" Vande shouted, instantly aiming at the first two targets in front of her. She let the aiming enhancer in her cyberoptics kick in, allowing it to lock on to both threats at the same time with no loss of accuracy.

The MCB ganger to her right turned an auto-shotgun her way, his finger tightening on the trigger. "Ah, go fu—"

Vande cut him off mid-speech with a single round that went through his left eye and blew out the back of his skull.

"Guns down or you die!" She heard Jarreau bellow the command to anyone who didn't take Vande's demonstration to heart, but his voice was drowned out as the cargo jet's engines began to rev up.

Lund broke cover and sprinted for the flank of the big aircraft, dragging the EMP with her; she never got there.

A hatch behind the blunt nose of the jet clanked open and a ring of black gun muzzles emerged – a multi-barreled autocannon, already whining as it spun up to firing speed.

With a deep, tearing sound like sustained thunder, the cannon opened up on Lund and savagely cut her down. Brilliant streaks of crimson tracer lanced across the hangar's interior, shredding anything in their path, blasting through the building's sheet metal walls as if they were paper. The gun's automatic tracking didn't differentiate between Task Force members or MCBs – if it was moving, it was a target.

Other guns opened up in the melee as the gang members fired at every threat around them, and Vande's colleagues defended themselves in kind. Suddenly the air inside the hangar was thick with cordite and hot metal.

She hurled herself back into the cover of the oil drums just as the cannon tracked her way, spraying heavy jacketed rounds at her heels that splintered the concrete floor. In just a few seconds, the entire operation had gone off the rails, and there was nothing she could do to stop it.

The cargo jet rocked forward on its fat wheels and

rolled out into the darkness, the thrust from its engines adding a screaming gale to the unfolding chaos.

Jensen dragged the fallen man out of the line of fire, his hands gripping a tac vest that was already soaked through with blood. The Interpol agent was twitching, going into shock as spurts of fluid vented from his horrific wounds. No matter what kind of medical Sentinel implants the man had, he was going to bleed out in moments.

Ignoring the gunfire and howling engines from across the way, Jensen grabbed for the operative's first aid pack and emptied out the contents on the tarmac. He grabbed a morphine syrette and shot the drug load into the man's neck, then tossed it away, in favor of a thick injector bulb filled with a bio-foam compound. In a few seconds, the injector clogged the brutal wounds, buying the man the precious time he would need to survive.

The agent's eyes fogged as he looked up at Jensen, before the pain dragged him away into unconsciousness.

Strobing lights washed over the pair of them and Jensen looked up, seeing the wings of the big cargo hauler sweep around as it pivoted on to the taxiway. The autocannon had fallen silent, but there was still a ferocious firefight in progress inside the hangar. Whatever hornet's nest the TF29 squads had stepped into, they were caught there.

Jensen rocked on his heels, still feeling the leaden drag of the inhibitor on his augmentations. He couldn't try the stun gun trick he used back in Alaska again; instead he went back to the bloodied, unconscious

Interpol agent, searching for and finding the same cryo-spray aerosol the man's teammates had used to break the hangar's locks. Acting quickly, Jensen pressed the nozzle to the casing of the inhibitor bracelet and let a jet of super-cooled liquid nitrogen coat the metal. He flinched as the pain sensors in his augmented arm went off, knowing that he risked doing serious damage to the myomer muscles beneath the polycarbonate skin – but Vande had neglected to leave behind a key and Jensen had no other options.

After a moment, Jensen straightened, and struck his arm against the roll bar of a service jeep parked close by. The inhibitor's power lights went out and it cracked in two. Shaking it off, he felt the surge of fresh input as all his augmentations began to cycle back to full operability. Reboot icons crowded the edge of his vision as the systems reactivated one by one. He shook his head to dismiss them. There wasn't time for a steady, cautious restart.

The jet was receding with every passing moment as it headed toward takeoff position at the far end of the runway. On foot he would never catch it in time – and even though Jensen was now making this up as he went along, he followed his first impulse to climb into the parked service jeep and tear open the ignition cylinder. Twisting the ragged ends of the starter wires together, he stamped on the accelerator and the open-topped 4x4 lurched forward into a skidding start. Jensen hauled the jeep around in a turn so tight it almost put it on two wheels, and aimed it away from the hangar toward the retreating lights of the cargo jet.

* * *

Magnet was shouting and swearing at the mercs in the plane as they powered away and left the Motor City Bangers to be cut down by the force of so-called cops that had ghosted in from out of nowhere. Emptying his own gun at the men in black, he watched a dozen of his crew take hits that ended them, some from the new arrivals and more from the crazy blind-fire from the big cannon on the jet. That died off when the plane pulled away, but by then the firefight had well and truly erupted, and it wouldn't end until one side was destroyed.

But who lived and who died among the MCBs was the last thing on Magnet's mind in that moment. Right then and there, he didn't care about any of them, he just wanted someone to vent his towering rage on. He wanted to make someone pay for the double-cross.

Staggering to the hangar doors, he saw the flash of headlights as a 4x4 revved up and kicked into gear, swerving across the asphalt to follow the jet.

Behind the wheel was a face that was burned into his memory – that bastard from the warehouse, the one who had tried to take him down on the roof. If there was a more fitting target for Magnet's anger, he couldn't think of it.

The gang leader threw away his empty weapon and broke into a run, his augs powering up as he triggered the illegal modification in his cybernetic arm. Magnet surged forward, reaching out with his gold-plated cyberarm.

Jensen saw movement from the corner of his eye as he hit the runway; then in the next second a human figure collided with the front of the jeep, and he almost lost control of the vehicle.

Clinging to the hood as they sped away from the hangar, the leader of the MCBs showed Jensen a feral snarl full of gold-plated teeth. His hand was fixed to the metal with buzzing electromagnetic pads on the palm, and belatedly Jensen realized how it was that 'Magnet' had become the criminal's nickname.

He roared and his other fist came through the windshield, showering Jensen in pieces of glass. "I seen you!" Magnet shouted, dragging himself closer. "You gonna pay for messing with me!"

Jensen threw the jeep into a quick series of right-left-right swerves that sent them back and forth across the width of the runway, but Magnet wasn't so easily dislodged. He slid his cybernetic hand off the hood and lurched at Jensen, snagging the frame of the broken windshield, rising up to swing a kick toward the other man's head.

Jensen ducked, sensing a familiar tingle in his mastoid bone as his infolink belatedly rebooted. A heartbeat later, and he heard a voice echo through his skull.

"*So you're not dead,*" began Pritchard. "*Tracking you... at the airport? What's going on, Jensen, you've been offline for hours—*"

"Busy," Jensen bit out the word as Magnet came at him, silencing the distraction. It was a risk taking one hand off the wheel at this speed, but there was no other way he could defend himself. Magnet landed a punch that lit fireworks behind his eyes and hauled back for a follow-up, but this time Jensen was ready and he blocked the blow by enveloping the gang leader's flesh-and-blood fist in the artificial fingers of his polycarbonate hand. He gave Magnet's arm a brutal twist, breaking the other man's wrist.

Howling with pain, Magnet threw himself at Jensen in a desperate, wild attack as they closed in on the turning circle at the end of the runway. Up ahead, the cargo jet was coming about to line up for its departure run.

Jensen punched forward to meet Magnet's assault, his arm blade extending as he landed the blow. The fractal-edged blade pierced the gang leader's chest and throat, the shock slamming him back. Jensen stamped on the brakes and Magnet flew off the hood, ripping away the windshield frame still held in his augmented grip.

The dazzling glow of the cargo jet's running lights flashed brightly as the aircraft's engines rose in pitch once more, and with a rush of motion it came hurtling back up the runway toward the jeep. Jensen slammed the vehicle into gear and hauled it around, sliding away to the grassy border strip as the jet thundered past. Lying across the center of the runway, Magnet's body disappeared under the central wheels of the aircraft and was crushed against the asphalt.

The jeep roared as Jensen threw it into high gear and raced after the jet. He had only moments to try and match pace with it. Once the cargo plane's engines were cycled up to full thrust, nothing would stop it from climbing into the air.

"Pritchard!" he shouted, reopening the infolink as he guided the jeep into the jet's turbulent slipstream.

"Oh, now you want my help with something?" snorted the hacker. *"I'm in the airport monitors right now, I see you. What exactly do you think you're doing?"*

"Stop this thing!" he snapped. "Shut down the jet!"

"In the next twenty seconds? It's tempest-hardened, EMP-shielded. I can't hack that remotely with the gear at my disposal..."

The jeep's wheels screeched as it bounced over the runway, and Jensen spotted the hatch on the prow reopen as the mercs on board rolled out the autocannon. Bright flares of tracer fire cut back toward him, a lucky shot cracking off the headlights.

"How do I stop it?"

Pritchard came back immediately. *"The cargo pod! There's an emergency ejection control on the flank, if you could reach it…"*

Jensen spotted the black-and-yellow striped panel next to a series of handholds and locking points. It was close – but he would only get one shot at this.

Pushing the jeep as fast as it could go, he yanked the steering wheel to the right and cut under the cargo jet's tail as the aircraft began to pull away. He didn't allow himself to think of the speed or the insane risk of what he was doing, and instead Jensen lost himself in the pitch and moment of the act.

The jeep bumped the side of the jet and lost traction. A front tire split and the vehicle flipped into a roll – but by then Jensen had leapt the gap and slammed into the side of the cargo pod. Wishing he'd chosen the same mods to his cyberlimbs as Magnet, he hung on grimly as the jet crossed the takeoff threshold and the nose undercarriage began to lift away from the ground.

With all the force he could muster, Jensen punched the emergency release panel, ripping right through the mechanism. He tore out whatever circuitry he found inside, hoping that it would be enough. The screaming wind tore at him, the force of it trying to tear him free of the fuselage. Dimly, he sensed the heavily-laden aircraft clawing its way off the ground as it came in sight of the end of the lengthy runway.

Then there were a series of loud bangs, gunshot-sharp, as the clamps holding the cargo module in place abruptly released. The pod detached as the jet lifted and Jensen went with it. Suddenly relieved of its extra weight and mass, the cargo plane shot upward at a steep angle, its engines shrieking as the pilot struggled to regain control of it before it tipped into a lethal stall.

The pod dropped like a brick, falling twenty meters back to earth to land in the crash pan of dense sand beyond the end of the runway. Jensen let go as it went down, trusting his Icarus implant to stop him from being broken apart.

There was a blur of gold fire, a numbing series of painful shocks as he hit and caught air again, before – mercifully – everything went dark.

The next thing he remembered was someone slapping him across the face, and Jensen blinked back to awareness, unsteady and disoriented.

"There, see? He's not dead." Vande peered at him with an unreadable expression on her face, while at her side Jarreau stood watching Jensen under hooded eyes, his bulky night-vision goggles perched high up on his forehead.

Jensen was sitting up in the back of an ambulance, and the air inside the vehicle stank of blood and chemicals. Crammed in there with him on the other gurneys were three more members of Task Force 29, all of them with injuries of varying severity. A pale-faced paramedic worked silently on the agents, with a look on his face that said he was petrified by what was going on.

Jensen stiffened and got up, pushing past the others

as he stepped out of the vehicle. There were warning indicators blinking in the corner of his vision, but his augs were still in working order, and he suddenly felt the driving need for a breath of fresh air.

"I told you to stay put," Vande said to his back.

"Yeah." Jensen shrugged. "You're welcome, by the way."

He looked around. There were regular cops and emergency crews all around, most of them glaring at the Task Force agents in an angry stand-off as Jarreau's operatives forcibly kept them away from the fallen cargo module. As he watched, the squad's big quad-engine cargo carrier VTOL came down from the sky on plumes of thrust, extruding thick cables from its belly, each one ending in a magnetic grapple plate. A pair of agents gathered them up and set to work clamping them to the cargo pod so it could be lifted off.

"You were almost killed chasing down that plane," said Jarreau. "What the hell was going through your mind, man?"

"Adapt and react." Jensen shrugged, searching his pockets for a cigarette and his lighter. "I get bore-sighted on things," he admitted. "Focus on a target to the exclusion of everything else. It's not one of my better qualities."

Jarreau shot Vande a wry look. "I know someone like that."

"You can't smoke here," Vande insisted. "There's fuel—"

"So sue me." He lit up and took a long drag. It helped.

Jarreau showed his teeth in a wide smile. "You gotta be fearless or stupid, Jensen. Still, we got a result and that's better than nothing at all."

"What about Sheppard and the jet?"

"Gone," said Vande. "He's no fool. When they lost the pod thanks to you, Sheppard's crew cut their losses and fled for the Canadian border. There's still a chance we might be able to catch them before they leave the country…" She trailed off, her grim tone showing how unlikely she thought that outcome was.

The VTOL took the weight of the cargo module, and with a whine of engines, it hauled it off the ground and into the air. Moving with ponderous slowness, the flyer carried the damaged pod away toward the east. Jensen took an involuntary step after it. "Where's that going?"

"Headquarters in Lyon pulled some strings, called in a transporter rig from the Army," Jarreau explained. "Mendel's gonna drop it off. They'll ferry it to a military base, and everything in that pod will be decommissioned and melted down for scrap." His grin faded. "Shit. Headquarters will call this a win, but it don't feel like one." He nodded toward a line of body bags lying on the runway near the hangar, where MCB and Task Force dead lay side by side. "We paid for it."

Jensen nodded. He knew full well how that felt, and he could see the need in the eyes of the two agents to get after the men responsible for the deaths of their comrades. But all too often payback had to take a backseat to the needs of the mission at hand. "So what happens now?"

"We're packing up," said Vande. "The barge crew are clearing out as we speak. I'm going to escort those damned augs personally, right into the furnace if I have to." He heard the venom in her tone. "I am so done with this bloody city."

"As for you… there's about a dozen different state and federal charges you could be arrested for," Jarreau told Jensen, "but I got enough paperwork as it is. So let's say we're all on the side of the angels and call it even here."

Vande turned to walk away, then hesitated. "Franklin, the man I left with you... You saved his life back there when you could have just cut and run. That's something." Then she strode away, back toward the rest of the team.

"That's the closest you're going to get to a compliment from her," noted Jarreau.

"And all I had to do was nearly kill myself." Jensen took another draw on his cigarette. "How is Interpol gonna deal with all this?"

"I got a badge that says 'Read This and Weep' on it. I've done this before. We'll piss off a lot of locals, but by tomorrow we'll be nothing but a bad memory. Don't worry, we'll keep your name out of it."

"Sorry about your men," Jensen offered. "I know how it is."

"Yeah, I read your jacket. You got the experience..." Jarreau nodded toward the runway, changing the subject. "And clearly, you have the skills. If you're interested, Task Force 29 is always hiring."

In spite of himself, Jensen gave a low chuckle. "Are you actually offering me a job?"

"We need people who can... *adapt and react*."

An odd impulse Jensen couldn't quite explain pushed at him to respond, but he fought it down. After a moment, he shook his head. "I'm still figuring some things out," he added, and he realized there was more truth in those words than he expected.

Jarreau accepted that with a nod. "Your call, man. My advice? You'd best get outta here before one of your old DPD buddies recognizes you. I'm guessing they won't look the other way." The agent shouldered his rifle and set off after Vande.

Jensen ground out his cigarette on the asphalt and found his way toward the shadows.

Thorne sat back in the passenger seat of the rented Navig sedan and brushed a stray thread of hair out of her eyes. A cold sense of satisfaction welled up inside her. She had been proven right. From the start, her evaluation of this operation had been correct and now the dead lying on an airport runway proved it. Still, it was ashes in her mouth, just another reminder that her superiors would never truly respect the skills she brought to the game.

The inset screens displayed on her laptop monitor showed the exact opposite of what had been planned for. Instead of a quiet exfiltration from the city, a massed gun battle had drawn the attention of the police force, civilians and the media. And now the materials that she had been tasked to secure were in the hands of a group that Thorne had no direct control over. From most points of view, the operation would have been considered a failure.

But there were degrees of misfortune, levels of random chance that her masters were willing to accept – even encourage. What looked like chaos to an outsider was actually the end result of careful manipulation. Management, for want of a better word. It was, after all, the greatest skill Thorne's masters possessed. To control the uncontrollable, to influence and guide the elements that appeared impossible to govern.

And now her recommendation – for the deployment of a covert operational unit rather than the use of local proxies – would play out. It had taken wasteful effort to reach this point, however, and she despised that.

Too many plans working within other plans, she told herself. *All those old fools and their schemes.* They never saw it from down here on the ground, and she knew they wouldn't care even if they did. Her masters delighted in reminding their agents that they took the long view – but that was easy to do when one was looking down at the world from an ivory tower. For those who did their dirty work, it was often difficult to see anything beyond the immediate situation.

She glanced across the upper level of the parking garage where she had sequestered herself, looking across the freeway to the airport buildings clustered around the runways. Sirens reached her as more police units came racing toward the area, and she paused, thinking about her exit route. The Interpol team's VTOL had passed over just a few moments before, and already its path was logged, considered and its final destination predicted.

She sifted through digital footage stolen from the airport's multiple monitors. It had been difficult to remain in the network and stay undetected after things started to fall apart. At one point, she noted that there was a *second* intruder in the system, and Thorne had been forced to cloak her virtual presence with a shrouding subroutine to make certain she wasn't discovered.

She quickly found what she was looking for. Images of the action on the runway, caught through a window by a distant security camera inside the main passenger terminal. The footage was grainy and difficult to read, but there were a couple of moments where the monitor had captured the impression of a man's face behind the wheel of a speeding vehicle.

Leaning in, she studied the face for a long time, considering the lines of it blurred by pace, the dark shields over the eyes, the determined aspect.

"What makes you special?" The question slipped out of her, spoken aloud before she realized it. Frowning at herself, Thorne closed the lid of the laptop computer and turned away, reaching up to punch in a code on the encrypted transceiver module sitting on the dashboard.

As the device went through the process of making a connection, her gaze turned inward. By now, the scouring programs she had left in the Yukon Hotel's security net had done their jobs. Aside from one inconvenient corpse, there would be no evidence that she had ever stayed there.

The transceiver beeped and she told it her name. Momentarily, a silky male voice made itself known. "*As was predicted, the smuggler failed to extract the materials. Our optimal result did not occur.*" The words seemed to come from all around her, but she knew that was merely an artifact of her implanted communications link. "*Your assignment to facilitate the transfer remains incomplete.*"

She resisted the urge to tell her masters that this was the very outcome she had warned them about. "The chance of a successful extraction was only thirty percent, but I am confident I can still secure the materials, if that remains the primary objective," she stated. "For the record, there were added complications. Another active vector entered the scenario, the fugitive Adam—"

A sigh sounded across the distance, cutting her off. "*That is not your concern. Naturally, there are multiple vectors in action at your current nexus. You are not the only asset in play.*"

She frowned at that, but said nothing. *More games*, she told herself. Her next words were tight and emotionless. "I await instructions." If they were treating her like an automaton, she would behave like one.

"*The secondary option you suggested has been approved by the Council. Additional operatives have been deployed to Detroit and they will arrive within the hour. Rendezvous with them at Location Gamma and take field command of the group.*" The voice in her head paused, taking a breath. "*There is no more margin for error. If transfer of the Sarif materials cannot be achieved, our plans in Europe will be impeded, and we will be forced to seek alternative options. That is unacceptable. Are we clear?*"

"Clear," Thorne repeated. "I'll report in when it's done."

DOWNTOWN – DETROIT –
UNITED STATES OF AMERICA

Jensen found a seat at the back of the augs-only carriage on the MiTrain Express from the airport, and did his best to fade into the background as it sped back into the city. With his collar turned up and his head down, he was just another passenger.

At this time of night, the train was half empty. His only companions were a group of dirty, work-worn laborers heading home after a late shift at one of the deconstruction yards out in Dearborn. Jensen could see the smoky, ill-lit site from his window, a vast scar in the landscape that went for miles. Dozens of city blocks out there had been lost to fire and chaos during the Aug Incident, and now the area was being systematically razed by one of the big conglomerates – FiveLine or Santeau, he wasn't sure which – so they could move in and remake it as they saw fit. The irony that the augmented were the only ones who were willing to work in the dangerous conditions out there seemed lost on the rest of the world. Dust, thick and gray, covered the visibility jackets and hoodies worn by the workers, and Jensen listened with half an ear as they griped amongst themselves about their poor pay and the low quality of the company-mandated neuropozyne doses they were given.

With the dust on them, the workers seemed like washed-out charcoal sketches of real people, faded and ghostly things. In their eyes he saw the fate that the city was sharing with them. Augs like him were being ground down, slowly and carefully being erased from the world. He imagined that there would be little place for people like them in whatever would come next. Jensen dwelled on thoughts of what the future would bring and he didn't like what he saw there.

A low buzz sounded through the bone of his jaw and his teeth clenched in response. "*Jensen, it's me,*" said Pritchard. "*I've found something you need to be aware of.*"

He straightened, pushing away the fatigue that was pressing down on him. "Let's hear it," he told the hacker.

"*A red flag went up on one of the search strings I left in the Police Department's data net. Our former colleague Donald Wilder was named in an incident report that went live a few minutes ago.*"

Jensen frowned. After Wilder had shot him and left him to be arrested, any hope of finding the former security guard had vanished along with the man. But had Wilder really been arrogant enough to stay in the city, rather than take the opportunity to make tracks? Pritchard's next words answered that question.

"*He's quite dead, according to the police officers who found him in a hotel bathroom uptown. The statement from the evidence tech who logged the report says he was shot and killed no more than an hour after I lost contact with you in Ravendale.*"

"What hotel?"

"*The Yukon. Far too exclusive for someone like Wilder.*"

He nodded in agreement. "Anything in the report about leads?"

"*There's the rub. Apparently the Yukon's booking records and security monitors suffered some kind of breakdown...*" Pritchard's acid tone made it obvious how little he believed that explanation. "*Long story short, there's nothing there. I took the liberty of taking a pass over their network myself to make sure they weren't hiding anything, but it's been scrubbed. A very professional job, I might add.*"

"Somebody is tying up all the loose ends," Jensen said quietly, voicing his thoughts. "Kellman's dead, the MCBs are out of the picture... and now Wilder turns up a corpse." He paused, thinking it through. "This is standard Illuminati operating procedure. When something doesn't go how they want it to, they sanitize everything and fade away."

"*Indeed,*" agreed Pritchard. "*I'm looking at the file on Wilder's remains right now. His body is in an ambulance heading to Medical Center, but not for the morgue. Somewhere along the line, it was flagged as 'infectious material'. His corpse is going to go straight into the furnace.*"

"What?" Jensen's thoughts raced. If the people in the shadows wanted Wilder's body destroyed, that could mean that even in death, he carried some information of value. Jensen remembered the new augmentations he had been sporting, the pulse-gun arm and the high-spec optics. An industrial furnace would reduce them to molten slag. "Where's the ambulance now?"

"*On Fort Street heading east. A couple of miles from where you are…*" There was a pause as the hacker suddenly caught on. "*Wait. I can get into the traffic grid… I could reroute it, maybe for a brief detour…*"

Jensen vaulted up from his seat as the train pulled into the crossover station at Cobo Center. "Bring it to me," he snapped, getting angry shouts as he barged through the workers clustered by the doors and sprinted across the platform.

"What the hell is wrong with these signals?" Ignoring the atonal chorus of horns sounding from the cars lined up behind him before the crossroads, the driver leaned forward and looked up at the traffic lights hanging over the street. They remained resolutely stuck on red, just as they had for the last two minutes, and showed no signs of shifting.

The other paramedic sitting across from him in the ambulance's cab gave an airy shrug. "First that 'Road Closed' sign pops up outta nowhere, then this?" She looked away. "I dunno, at this rate we ain't ever getting to the end of our shift."

A sedan pulled out from the queue behind them, rolled past and jumped the lights, clearly unwilling to keep waiting. The driver got a slew of invective from the woman in the sedan, and then it was gone – but movement caught his eye as a man in a dark long coat stepped purposefully off the curb and came right up to the side door.

Before the driver could react, the door was wrenched

open and the man in the coat raised his arm. A black blade grew out of his knuckles. "Out," he said simply.

"Oh shit!" The driver threw up his hands and scrambled out of the vehicle, his shift partner doing the same. "Look, man, just take the rig, okay? We don't want any trouble—"

The man with the blade didn't wait to listen to his words. He leapt into the seat vacated by the driver and stepped on the gas, peeling out in a screech of tires.

Overhead, the traffic lights obediently changed to allow him to proceed.

"A right, then your second left," Pritchard was saying. *"That'll take you into an underground car park. You'll be out of the way there, no-one should bother you."*

Jensen worked the ambulance's big steering wheel, pulling it around until he saw the yawning mouth of the garage. The vehicle barely fit through the entrance, a burst of sparks and broken plastic coming from the rooftop emergency lights as he threaded the needle and brought it to a lurching halt.

"How long until they track the lo-jack in this thing?" he asked.

"Ten, fifteen minutes at the most. Don't delay."

"Yeah." Jensen squeezed through the gap in the back of the cab and climbed into the rear compartment of the ambulance.

A sealed body bag, detailed with a bright yellow biohazard strip, lay strapped to a folding gurney. He found a plastic panel on the outside of the bag noting that one *Wilder, Donald F. (CisMale/B Neg)* was inside, along with a warning tab indicating the man's corpse was contaminated with Strain 5 of Neo-SARS, a particularly virulent version of the respiratory disease. But unless Wilder had contracted the exotic virus in the last few hours, that was more likely something that had been added to his death record to keep the curious from taking too close a look at him.

Nevertheless, Jensen hesitated. "You *sure* he's clean, Pritchard?"

"Don't be dramatic, Jensen. He died of a gunshot wound to the throat. There's no virus in there."

"Easy for you to say. You're halfway across the city." Jensen extended a short length of nanoblade from his arm and used it to slice open the seal on the body bag. He peeled back the plastic and found Wilder's bloodless face staring up at him, a vacant look of pain and confusion still etched there.

The entry wound was right where Pritchard said it would be. Discoloration and shape told Jensen that it had been a close-range shot, but not near enough to leave powder burns. Acting quickly, he patted down the dead man, but found no clues. Everything Wilder had been carrying on him was gone.

Jensen checked the dead man's cyberarm, but nothing about it seemed off. He scowled and sat back, looking the body up and down, searching for something that didn't belong. He met Wilder's dead gaze and a thought occurred to him. "His eyes…"

Leaning in, he peered at the twin Sarif Industries cybernetic implants. Both the glassy orbs were intact and undamaged. The last thing they had seen was the person who took Wilder's life.

"Read me the serial code on the iris ring!" said Pritchard, becoming animated. Jensen did as he was asked, and the hacker gave a snort of approval. *"Those are the 'Atid' models,"* he explained quickly. *"Named after an angel of*

memory. And that explains why someone wants Wilder's body destroyed."

"The data buffers in the cyberoptics..." Jensen guessed what the hacker was thinking. "They'll still have imagery stored in there from earlier in the day. We just need to access it..." He cast around, looking for something to use to remove the eyes.

"There's a way to do that," Pritchard said warily. *"I can talk you through it from here... but it's a little unpleasant."*

Jensen caught sight of his face, and his own optical implants, in the reflection of a mirrored panel. "I see," he said.

If removing the artificial eye from Wilder's right orbital socket with a scalpel and a pair of forceps was a painstaking task, doing the same to himself in reverse without cutting open his face was one of the more testing things Jensen had ever had to do.

He willed himself to ignore the queasy sensations churning in his gut as he pulled on his implant until the self-seeking optic nerve connectors detached, and he went partially blind.

Jensen called on the same careful skills he had cultivated building model clocks during the months he had been in recovery, after the attack at SI that nearly killed him. It helped to think of this action in the same way, of pieces coming together in uniform order.

Wilder's cybereye shared the same universal jacks as Jensen's, and he cautiously inserted it into the gaping socket, taking care not introduce any blood or dirt along with it. With a moist, unpleasant click, the dead man's eye snapped home and half of Jensen's vision became a fuzzy blur of start-up displays.

"*Did it work?*" said Pritchard. "*Are you seeing anything? An Atid eye will be compatible with your neural hub. You should be able to go through the menus and navigate to the memory buffer.*"

"Getting there," said Jensen. The sickly feelings faded away as his body quickly accepted the new eye, and he soon found the subroutine Pritchard referred to. The buffer was still intact, and Jensen drew it up into *replay* mode.

It was disorienting for his brain to parse two different visual inputs at once – one from his real-time view of the interior of the ambulance and the other from Wilder's recent past – but he managed.

Jensen blink-clicked the buffer, spooling down the time index into the recent past. He rocked back slightly as he suddenly saw himself standing in front of a glass panel, a gun in hand. He watched his lips silently mouth the words 'keep going' as the moment unfolded. "Too early," he said aloud. "Gonna run it ahead."

Jensen forced the replay to run on fast-forward, becoming a blur of motion. He glimpsed himself taking the pulse-gun hit; then Wilder's point of view sliding around as he left the apartment in Ravendale; the interior of a bot-cab; the lobby of an expensive hotel—

Switching back to normal speed, Jensen began a ride as a passenger through Wilder's meeting at the Yukon Hotel. His breath caught in his throat as Wilder's gaze met that of the person he had come to meet.

"*Thorne?*" It was absolutely the same woman that had interrogated him at the WHO facility in Alaska. That distinctive pale skin, henna-red hair and an air of haughty coldness that set him on edge, even second-hand.

If Jensen has to be killed, it won't be down to you to pull the trigger. He read her lips, and the chill in him deepened. The old talent – learned back in his time at SWAT for use when staring down sniper scopes at dangerous perps – came easily to the fore. Jensen tried to imagine Wilder's poorly pitched bravado rebounding off Thorne's icy, calculating exterior, and his thoughts churned as he tried to guess at what chain of events had brought the woman to Detroit. Had she come to find him? Or was there more to her presence in the city?

Then the gun appeared in Thorne's hand and she fired the shot that ended Wilder, as blankly as someone might turn out a light. It was so sudden, and so horribly immediate that Jensen physically recoiled at the moment the recorded bullet struck home. A heart-rate display in the corner of playback showed a final flurry of peaks and then went flat; but the optic feed didn't end. The tiny bio-energy cells in the implants were half-charged, more than enough to keep running and record what went on in front of Wilder's dead eyes.

Jensen watched Thorne move in and out of view. She activated an encrypted communications unit, and he caught snatches of her speaking again; *Wilder may have compromised the operation.*

He was still wondering who had been on the other end of the line when Thorne made a second call. *Move the secondary contingency plan to active status and prepare to execute,* she said, and everything about the woman's body language told Jensen she was talking to the people holding her chain. He could see it in her every motion and gesture, defiance warring with ingrained obedience.

What Thorne said next was as clear as if she were standing right in front of him. *We need to be prepared for the hangar transfer to fail,* mouthed the woman. *I have a contingency in place if the Task Force take possession of the cargo. Confirm the deployment of a kill squad. We can hit them on the train and leave no survivors.*

ELEVEN

As he emerged from the alleyway and on to the street, Jensen saw a fast, bat-winged shape moving at rooftop level. The police drone had its strobes flashing red and blue, and the complex scanner head slung under its narrow fuselage was turning this way and that, gathering up sensor data on the area.

It was coming his way, following the digital scent of the ambulance's lo-jack transponder, and he couldn't afford to be seen by it. The Detroit police force knew too much about him for Jensen just to slip past the drone unnoticed. If it captured his face, it would draw heat from real human cops in short order.

He turned sharply into the first lit doorway that he came to – a 24-hour branch of Lucky Dot, the Chinese-owned convenience store chain that had popped up on every city street corner like a plastic and neon fungus.

The door clacked shut behind him just as the drone thrummed past. From the corner of his eye, Jensen saw the machine pivot on its ducted rotors and rise up to take an eagle-eye view of the area. He'd have to kill time until it moved on.

"Hi there, welcome to Lucky Dot!" The canned, pre-programmed greeting spun out of a cartoonish robot cat mounted behind the cluttered counter of the long, narrow store. Set on a rail that let it move back and forth, it had a fat torso, two chubby telescopic arms and a video screen for a head. Modeled on the company's mascot, it resembled a giant child's toy – but like most of the chain's robot shopkeepers, it was grimy, cracked and covered with graffiti. "How can I help?" Its chirpy voice was generated by a limited artificial intelligence subroutine, but Jensen knew that there would be an actual human operator watching through its eyes – and those of a dozen others in a dozen other stores – from some office cubicle half a world away in Guangzhou.

He waved the machine away and made a beeline for an automated coffee vendor on the far wall, punching in a request for a beverage. The only thing that was not out of order was Lan Ri RealTaste Synthetic CoffeEsque, and he grimly ordered a cup, deliberately keeping his back to the store's surveillance cameras.

Jensen rubbed his face as he waited. The skin around his right eye was tender and bruised from being twisted and pulled, and although he had replaced his own cyberoptic once again, it felt gritty and uncomfortable. The aug eye he'd stolen from Wilder's corpse was rolling loose in his pocket.

He listened to the fake coffee brewing, blotting out the constant background twitter of the Lucky Dot jingle music playing from hidden speakers. His mind was going around and around on what he had seen through Wilder's eyes.

"*Jensen…*" Pritchard's voice buzzed through his

infolink. *"I suppose it would be a waste of time for me to tell you to do what I told you to do at the start."*

"Drop off the grid and go dark..." He subvocalized the words so the server robot wouldn't pick them up. *"Way too late for that now."*

Maybe Thorne was with Homeland Security, just like she'd said. But Jensen's instincts to be wary of her had been right, and now he knew for certain that she had other, more sinister masters. The same people who had engineered the events that nearly killed him, that took his life and turned it inside out.

"The ramifications of this reach a long way," said Pritchard. *"You see that, right?"*

"Yeah." He couldn't help but wonder, how much did the shadowy cabal of the Illuminati know about his missing time between the destruction of Panchaea and his awakening at Facility 451? Was he like Thorne in all this, some sort of piece in their endless games? Was he being guided and never knowing it? Each question begat more of the same, branching off into threads of unknowns that would strangle him if he tried to grasp them all at once.

Instead, he took a breath and silenced the chaos in his thoughts. "I need to focus on what is in front of me," Jensen said, half to himself. "Deal with what I *can* deal with... and handle the rest as I go." The coffee machine ejected a cup of something mud-colored and tasteless. He took it and walked slowly back toward the front of the store, looking for any sign of the police drone.

"That's not the smartest approach," Pritchard replied. *"But when did that ever stop you?"*

The hacker laid out the facts: it was very possible that the people running Thorne and the smuggling network the TF29 team was trying to dismantle had planned for this series of events from the beginning. And more so, Thorne's specific mention of a train – which had to be the military transport Jarreau had mentioned – meant that they had inside knowledge of Interpol's plans. Did Jarreau and Vande have any idea that they had a mole in their organization? There was no way to contact the Task Force unit to warn them.

"*I'm searching all rail routes and databases in the area, but nothing is coming up,*" he concluded. "*If this is being done, Interpol have concealed it very well.*"

"We can't just stand by and let Jarreau's people ride into an ambush!" Jensen's temper flared, and he said the words aloud without thinking about it.

The robot behind the counter seemed to react to his outburst and it juddered on its hydraulic mount. "How can I how can I how can I?" The synthetic voice became distorted and growly, and the machine's arms jerked into peculiar positions.

Suddenly the video screen blanked out and rebooted itself. When the picture resolved, it was a grainy and poorly lit image from a small handheld camera. Jensen picked out what looked like the interior of a van, and resting up against a metal panel with a smirk playing on his lips was Garvin Quinn.

"Hello, lads," he began, speaking through the robot's vocoder. "Nice night for a stroll, eh?"

Jensen froze. "How'd you know where to find me?"

"Francis is going to get upset when I answer that."

Pritchard made a snarling noise that made Jensen's infolink implant twitch, but he went on before the hacker could reply. "Cut the bullshit, Quinn. Now is not the time."

Quinn's tone shifted. "Aye, you're right at that." He

gave an apologetic nod. "Long story short, Vega and I planted surveillance devices in your man's hideout back there."

"*I know*," Pritchard shot back. "*I found them and destroyed them!*"

"Well, you missed one. Because we wanted you to," Quinn went on. "Okay, so the Juggernaut Collective have been listening in on most all of your chats over the last day or so. Don't take it the wrong way, we were looking out for you."

"Didn't seem like that to me," Jensen said coldly. "Did your pal Janus enjoy the show?"

"You continue to impress, Adam," Quinn said, his cocky grin returning for a moment. "Look, you can stand there all night sipping shitty coffee or we can cut to the chase. Bruised egos aside, you're at a dead end, so I'm breaking protocol because Juggernaut can *help* you."

"*How are you going to do that*?" demanded Pritchard.

"We know where the military train is and what route it's taking across the state. And of course, I've got the lovely Alex here and her jump jet at my disposal. Do I have to draw you a picture?"

Jensen frowned. "How does Janus know about the train?"

"How does Janus know about anything?" Quinn shot back. "I told you before, he's connected *everywhere*." He paused, moderating his tone. "Consider this a demonstration of intent. Establishing Juggernaut's *bona fides*, as it were. I know you don't trust us, and you've got no reason to. So let us do this for you. Let us show you we're on the same side by getting you where you need to go, eh? We're already in the air. Closer than you think."

"*This is a bad idea*," said Pritchard. "*This could be a setup!*"

"Time to find out," Quinn replied. "What's it going to be?"

Jensen tossed the cup in the trash and glared at the screen. "How fast can you get me the VTOL?"

Quinn grinned again. "How fast can you get to the roof?"

LAKE MONTCALM – MICHIGAN – UNITED STATES OF AMERICA

The group of six made their way down the embankment to the railbed in silence, quick and sure-footed, spilling out into a circle as their boots crunched on the gravel between the concrete sleepers. Thorne emerged from the middle of the group and paused, flipping up the visor that covered her face so she could taste the air. Like most of the group, she wore a non-reflective helmet with integral low-light scopes, and a matching bodysuit of signature-dampening meta-materials. Her weapons and equipment hung off her chest in a cross-rig, and she ran her gloved fingers over the safety latch holding her Zenith semi-auto pistol in place. She turned to face eastward and glimpsed the faint glow of the city in the far distance, the weak amber light of it reflecting off the bottom of low clouds.

One of the others detached from the group and came to the closest of the rails, on the line that threaded west out of Detroit toward the state line and beyond. He sank into a crouch, and she heard the faint whine of micro-motors in his joints. The largest of them in build and bulk, he was almost a full-body prosthesis cyborg and what flesh there was of him seemed more like a coating applied to a steel sculpture than the true matter of the man. In particular, his organic face hung on a hairless chromed head like a mask, inset with two bulky crimson optic implants that gave him a permanently doleful expression.

Thorne knew little about him, other than rumors that the man had been patched together with experimental augmentations and vat-grown bio-mech limbs after surviving the detonation of a truck bomb. All she cared about was that he was as capable as he looked. Others had chosen these operatives to assist her, based on algorithms and predictive models that Thorne would never be privy to. Each was augmented to a lesser or greater extent, many with exotic modifications that she had never seen before. But that mattered little in the situation before her; all that was required of Thorne was to marshal them to complete the objective.

He placed a hybrid flesh-metal hand on the rail and was still. "It is coming," he said. His words were precise, clipped and heavily accented. "We should prepare."

"You heard him," Thorne told the others. "Take your places." She indicated three of the operatives. "Team One, board in the crew car behind the locomotive. Team Two, we'll board the rearmost car and sweep forward."

The others all gave nods of agreement and set to work double-checking their gear. A slender, athletic man with recurved cyberlimbs dropped the bulky backpack he had been carrying and handed out the contents to the group – each of them were given a disk-shaped device with a pair of grips on one surface, a glittering metallic nanofluid on the other. "Test," he called, when all the units had been distributed.

As one, the group twisted the grips and red

indicators on the disks turned blue.

"Deploy," ordered Thorne. On the breeze, she could hear the fast-approaching rush of an engine, and at her feet the rails were starting to vibrate. Each of the nine operatives found their assigned positions along the straightaway before them, each dropping down to lie on their backs with the disk devices resting across their chests, like offerings to the night sky. "Activate timers," she called, snapping her visor shut as the rumble of the oncoming train rose to a roar.

There was a brief flash of white as the headlight on the engine swept across her, but the wavelength-deadening material of Thorne's suit blended her body shape into the shadows. She tensed against every rational sense that told her to flee from the oncoming train, for fear it would crush her beneath its spinning steel bogies – and then it was thundering over her, a black wall of noise a few centimeters from the brow of her visor.

Thorne closed her eyes and let it happen. She felt the electromagnetic disk in her hand go active and held on tight as it automatically triggered and drew her up off the ground, and into the spaces on the underside of the train's trailing carriage. The shock of the impact resonated through her limbs, but she hung on regardless. After a moment, Thorne dared to turn her head slightly and catch a glimpse of the railbed blurring past right below her.

Five green lights flickered on in her visor's display; they were all aboard. Somewhere to her right, she saw a bright flare of laser light as a beam cutter began to slice through the floor of the carriage above her head.

* * *

Vande looked up as Chen entered the rear cargo wagon, swaying slightly with the motion of the train. She nodded toward the door he had just come through, leading to the center-most car where the load they were guarding was held. "How many times are you going to check those crates? We still have a long way ahead of us."

"And miles to go before we sleep," Chen added, with a faint smile. "I can't help it, I'm on the spectrum. Just indulge my mildly obsessive-compulsive impulses and leave it at that."

She frowned. Now they were clear of Detroit's city limits, the train would not stop again until it reached their destination, a military decommissioning center in the Dakotas where the US Army disposed of their more dangerous hardware. Vande had already applied a no-sleep drug patch to her arm and she intended to remain alert and awake – but after everything that had happened during this investigation and the chaos of the firefight at the airport, fatigue was making her patience run thin. Chen's good-natured banter chafed on her, and what he thought was endearing, she found irritating. Vande got up and toyed with the idea of moving to where the other members of her team were situated, in the forward cargo carriage two cars closer to the engine at the head of the train.

She tapped a spot behind her right ear, manually activating her infolink. "All call signs, report in." Chen, the other agent in her car and the three up front all did as ordered, drawing a nod from her. "Solid copy. All right, from this point we are going to clear protocol. Check in every hour, alert calls only, otherwise maintain radio silence. Base, you get that?"

Jarreau's voice echoed distantly in her head. *"Roger*

that, mobile team. We're tracking you from here. Safe journey."

Vande nodded again and cut the signal. Jarreau was about to go into a virtual meeting with Manderley and the directors in Lyon via the NSN, largely to answer for the disruption caused in Detroit and the heat Interpol was going to draw because of it. She didn't envy him. Vande had never liked dealing with the upper echelons of command, even in her time as a regular cop. She was better in proactive situations, in the field, in the action. She'd joined Task Force 29 because she thought they could provide that for her, but lately...

"So, anyone got a deck of cards?" said Chen. "I forgot to bring an e-book."

She eyed the tech. "I think I may have to shoot you to shut you up," Vande told him, her tone suddenly ice-cold and utterly serious.

AIR TRANSIT CORRIDOR – MICHIGAN – UNITED STATES OF AMERICA

Jensen stared across the VTOL's enclosed cabin at Quinn, watching the other man scrutinize a handheld repeater screen. Over his shoulder, a narrow hatchway revealed the cramped virtual cockpit beyond, where Jensen could see Alex Vega's hands in constant motion as she guided the aircraft over the dark countryside. They were flying low, nap-of-the-earth, skimming treetops and following the line of the terrain to stay off local ATC radar.

Vega was humming absently to herself, lost in the work of piloting. *She's good*, Jensen thought, *military or merc trained, I'll bet.*

Being in an aircraft like this, heading into an unknown situation – it was an old, familiar state of affairs for him. He closed his eyes and for a moment he was in a different time, a different place.

"Got the train on my scope," Vega said, breaking off from her tune to look over her shoulder. "Five minutes out, fellas." She flipped a switch and the cabin interior lighting switched to dim crimson tones – not that Jensen's augmented eyes needed time to become night-adapted.

For a moment, Jensen expected to see Faridah Malik's face looking back at him from the cockpit, and he frowned. As competent as Vega appeared to be, it would have put him at ease to have somebody he had complete trust in on the stick. As Sarif Industries' senior pilot, Malik had been there to get Jensen into and out of a lot of dangerous situations in the past, and her absence here and now was keenly felt. He let out a sigh. Thoughts of tracking down Malik's whereabouts threatened to split his focus and he shut that away, returning to Quinn.

"How deep has Juggernaut been on this thing with the illegal augs?" he asked. "And for how long?"

The other man gave a shrug. "I'm not in charge, Jensen. I don't set the targets and the missions. We're a *collective*, remember? The clue's in the name. Juggernaut is a gathering of people who operate in concert. Decisions get made by the whole, not by one person."

"Not even Janus?"

He smiled thinly. "Janus brings a lot to the table, for sure. Valuable intel, access that the rest of us can only dream of… So maybe his voice carries a little more weight, but at the end of the day we strive toward a shared goal."

"Destroying the Illuminati."

Quinn nodded. "That's the big one. A work in progress, you might rightly say. Maybe a chess game would be a better analogy..." He paused, considering his own words. "They move, we counter them. We blockade, disrupt and generally mess with their shit in every way possible." He chuckled. "And we do it pretty well. Their organization is old and big and hidebound, it reacts like a bloody supertanker trying to make a turn. *Sloooow*." He sounded out the word. "Despite the name, Juggernaut is more agile, and we're always there to get in their way. See, they think they have inevitability on their side, that they're the irresistible force. But the Collective is the immovable object."

"Cute speech," said Jensen, as the VTOL bounced through a patch of clear-air turbulence. "Practice it much?"

"Little bit," Quinn admitted. "Did you like it?"

"Still waiting for you to answer my first damn question," he shot back. Jensen looked away, using the time to take inventory of the gear he was carrying. He checked the actions on the Hurricane machine pistol and the Zenith semi-automatic Quinn had supplied him with, counting spare magazines by touch in the pouches on his tactical rig.

"You've had the pleasure of Task Force 29's company," said the other man. "They're a special operations unit under the aegis of Interpol, or so their mission statement goes. Working internationally to stamp out terrorism and crime in the wake of the incident." He made air quotes with his fingers. "*Good cops dealing with bad things*."

"All that I know."

Quinn's smile turned sly. "But what if I told you

the Juggernaut Collective believes that TF29 are tied to the activities of the Illuminati? Most likely through co-opted assets distributed through Interpol and the active Task Force units around the world."

Jensen shook his head. "If that's true, why are Jarreau and his people working so hard to bring down this smuggling network? Supplying combat augmentations to terror groups has the stink of those shadowy bastards all over it."

That got him another shrug. "Janus says there are factions within the Illuminati. Opposed elements working to different agendas."

"Janus says?" repeated Jensen. "You ever wonder how he knows that?"

"All the time. But I trust him." Quinn's cocky manner faded, and Jensen got the sense the man was recalling a buried personal truth that would never be revealed. "And that's all I'm going to say about that."

Jensen wondered what burden Janus had lifted to get Quinn to become a loyal part of Juggernaut, filing the thought away for later consideration.

The other man went on. "I know you used to be police, so you think you get where TF29 are coming from... only you *don't*." Quinn gestured. "Lift up your head and look away from the moment, Jensen. The Task Force was formed to fight a surge in criminal and terrorist activity, and so on... But those circumstances have only come to a head *because* of the Aug Incident! The Task Force is a direct result of a situation the Illuminati *invented*! You know this, you were there, for crying out loud..." He became more animated as he warmed to the subject. "It's the thin end of the wedge, *bratán*. Today, the Task Force is a bunch of small units scattered around the world, doing the tough jobs so decent folks can sleep soundly in their beds... but tomorrow? They'll grow into an army with soldiers in every city and every nation. Answerable to no government, acting without oversight, all to keep us safe from the specter of techno-terror. The Illuminati manufactured the reason for the Task Force so they could sow the seeds of a New World Order military."

Anyone who hadn't lived through what Adam Jensen had experienced, anyone who hadn't seen what he had seen, might have dismissed Quinn's words out of hand as tinfoil-hat levels of conspiracy theory. But for Jensen, there was a troubling sense of the *possible* in it all. He sat back against the inside of the VTOL's cabin. "Let's say Janus is right. That Task Force 29 is being manipulated by an insider. What do you want to do about it?"

"Go in there and root around," offered Vega, who had been listening to the conversation from the start. "Juggernaut wants a face that fits, get it? Only none of us on the roster meet the bill."

"Alex puts it better than I could," said Quinn. "We want to penetrate TF29's organization and find proof positive that the group has been compromised."

"And then we'll burn it to the ground," added Vega.

US ARMY RAIL TRANSPORT 995 – MICHIGAN – UNITED STATES OF AMERICA

The first inkling the team at the front of the train had that something was wrong was a clanking noise from the deck beneath their feet. Agent Doe was a First Nation ex-patriot with a high black topknot and a suite of advanced neural implants, and she slipped off the crate she had been sitting on and crouched low to the floor. "You hear that?" she asked the others.

Away at the top end of the cargo wagon, where a connecting door led to a crew car behind the locomotive leading the train, the noise sounded again and Doe drew her sidearm.

"You want me to call it in?" said one of her colleagues. "Vande will be pissed if we break comm protocol for nothing."

"If it's nothing," said the woman, striding down the length of the long car. She reached the door and slammed the heel of her hand on the panel that would open it.

The metal door slid aside, and standing directly behind it was a shadow with dark, light-absorbing skin. In its hand was a wide, diamond-shaped push dagger that shot out and hit Doe in the throat and chest a half-dozen times before she could cry out. Gushing blood, the agent stumbled forward, her gun clattering away. Her killer grabbed her before she could fall, spinning her around as another hand came up with a large-frame Steiner-Bisley semi-automatic in it. The heavy pistol was doubled in length by a fat sound suppressor on the end of the barrel.

Pulling Doe close as a human shield, her killer advanced into the cargo wagon followed by two more featureless black-clad figures, each of them like pieces of the night given form and will. Other guns came up as Doe's teammates drew down, but shots were already in the air. Subsonic armor-piercing .45 caliber rounds hit the Task Force agents in perfect double-tap groupings.

When they fell, Doe's killer allowed her to collapse as well, and he stood aside as his comrades moved up, watching them pause to shoot the other two agents in the head, to be certain they would not rise again.

The killer tapped a key on the palm of his glove, sending three clicks of static over an encrypted channel.

"Forward car is secure," Thorne subvocalized, watching as the last of her squad climbed up through the ragged hole in the floor and into the trailing carriage of the train. "Three kills."

"Half of them terminated already," said the hulking cyborg, in a manner that might have been disappointment. "I will neutralize the remainder."

The members of the military train's duty crew – two engineers and two soldiers – were already lying dead in a heap at the far end of the compartment. Silenced shots and close-quarter kills had seen an end to them in short order.

"This isn't a game," Thorne told him, looking up to stare the machine-man in the face. "We're not here for you to score points."

The lenses of his glassy eyes shifted slightly to focus on her. "Stay out of my way," he warned, and advanced to the forward door. It slid open before the cyborg, revealing a line of two flatbed wagons between the rear car and the next cargo carriage. The sharp-sided shapes of denuded, wingless aircraft fuselages sat across the flatbeds beneath the flapping tarpaulin covers and heavy hawsers that held them in place. The cyborg set off, moving ahead without looking back.

The tall, thin operative with the sword-blade legs shot Thorne a look. "Don't sweat it. The German gets twitchy if he can't get his hands dirty," he said, raising his voice over the rush of wind through the open door.

She nodded at the dead men. "What do you call that?"

"Just warming up," he noted, and set off after the cyborg.

"We're here," called Vega, as she pulled the VTOL into a hard turn. "I got the bird in whisper mode so we're ghosting… But I think I saw movement out on one of the flatbeds, so watch it…"

Quinn peered through a porthole in the door at his side. "Don't take any chances, little sister. Get us up to the engine at the front and hold her steady." He turned to Jensen. "Your show now."

Jensen gave a determined nod. "Pritchard," he muttered, triggering his infolink. "I'm going in. You read me?"

What came back was a scratchy, hissing tide of interference. Jensen picked out a few words from the hacker, something about 'jamming' and 'disconnection' before Pritchard's faint voice sank entirely beneath the crashing waves of static. It seemed that he would be doing this alone.

"*Udači*," said Quinn, reaching for the hatch's release switch. "Come out of this alive, and I'm sure we'll talk some more."

The hatch retracted and a roaring gale flooded the compartment. Jensen snapped off the safety belt across his lap and went to the edge. Speeding along less than a meter below the belly of the VTOL was the top of the military train's olive drab locomotive, a wide line of exhaust grilles and metal plating. Aside from a few running lights, the engine was totally dark. It had no human driver, controlled instead by a robot brain that saw through the night with infra-red and radar senses.

Jensen watched the rocking motions of the VTOL and the locomotive, timing the moment to the last possible second; then he was away, dropping the distance to land in a three-point fall on the midline of the engine. He found a grab bar on the hull and gripped it tightly before wind shear could tear into him.

The black-on-black VTOL whispered away, the hatch sliding shut until it was nearly invisible. Jensen watched it dip below a tree line and then it was gone.

Using the grab bar and others that followed a line astern, Jensen moved hand-over-hand toward the rear of the engine. He counted seven more wagons beyond – a crew car, three cargo wagons, a pair of flatbeds and a tail-end caboose. From his vantage point, nothing seemed awry, but the jamming of communications and the fact that the VTOL's low pass hadn't immediately drawn someone's attention did not bode well.

Quinn's words echoed in his thoughts. Exactly how Thorne and the Task Force fitted into this byzantine chess game wasn't immediately clear to Jensen, but what he did know for sure was that the stolen Sarif tech was too dangerous to be allowed to get out into the world. The only goal that mattered to him right now was making sure those mil-spec augs were destroyed. The rest of it he would figure out along the way.

The tech was David Sarif's secret legacy, and somehow Adam Jensen had taken on the mantle of responsibility for it. *So be it*, he thought, recalling his words to Pritchard. *One last job for the boss.*

There was a skylight in the roof of the next car along. Jensen hopped the gap from the engine and got the vent open as a low bridge loomed up out of the night. He dropped through and into the crew car a split-second before it whooshed overhead, red indicator lights across its length lighting up the air.

Drawing his pistol, Jensen advanced up the length of the wagon. Air was rushing through the train car, but not from the open skylight. He searched around and came across a ragged wound in the floor. A rough oval slice was missing from the deck, and through it Jensen saw a blur of dark ground whipping past. Discarded next to the damage was a laser tool and a heavy battery pack. He dropped into a crouch and tapped the edge of the hole. The metal was still hot to the touch.

A dull thud sounded from the rear of the wagon, and Jensen's head snapped up. He raised the Zenith and advanced, closing in on the source of the noise. There was little illumination in the crew car, and oddly cast shadows fell everywhere, but he could see no places for anyone to be hiding.

Ahead was the door that led to the first of the cargo wagons. Jensen lowered his gun slightly and started forward again. It was exactly what his attacker was waiting for.

From the corner of his vision, Jensen saw a hazy orange shimmer as light warped and bent around an invisible form. He spun as the cloak of twisted radiance fell away from the helmeted figure in black, getting a momentary glimpse of four magenta-hued lowlight lenses set in a featureless blank mask.

The thermoptical camouflage dissipated and the figure threw itself at Jensen, a bright dagger snapping into place across the knuckles of their hand like a switchblade. Acting on pure reflex, he brought up his arms to block the stabbing motion and turn it aside. Artificial arms clashed with a dull clatter of polycarbonate and Jensen's hand jerked. He let off a shot into the ceiling, the report of the pistol lost in the noise of the train as it thundered through a tunnel.

Darkness descended, lit only by pulses of light from passing warning lamps as they flashed by. In the strobing, staccato glow, Jensen and his attacker twisted and fought in dangerously close quarters. The wide dagger blade hummed as it cut through the air toward his throat time and time again. With each swing, Jensen tried to extend away, but there was nowhere to retreat to. Instead he went on the offensive, bringing down the butt of the pistol on the brow of the helmet. He smashed one of the quad-eyes and the attacker flinched; Jensen guessed they were neural-jacked straight into the overlapping mech-optics, and although there would be no pain effect, it was hard for anyone to have their eye – real or not – crushed and not shrink from it, even for a moment.

He saw the opening and took it, landing a maximum-force punch in his opponent's throat, the impact shocking through the armored ruff around their neck. That wide blade came at him again, but he parried it and shoved his attacker off-balance.

The figure in black shot out a hand and tried to pull him close, grabbing at his tactical rig, looking for a gap between the armor plates to put the tip of the dagger. Jensen kept up momentum, knowing that to lose it would be to end this mission before it had barely started. They stumbled together in a ragged shuffle and crashed into the connecting door. The hatch slid open behind them and the fighters swung around into the next carriage.

Jensen had barely a quarter-second to grasp a

snapshot of the interior – bodies and blood on the floor, another pair of black-suited assassins at the far end of the rail car among racks of crates and boxes – before his opponent reared up and butted him across the bridge of his nose with the helmet. Pain ripped across his face and one of his eye shields grew a jagged crack.

The other attackers reacted, one dropping into cover, the other releasing a burst of automatic fire from a silenced SMG. Caseless rounds whined and sparked off the racks along the walls, and Jensen used the distraction to knock his close-quarter attacker away, finally gaining the distance he needed. Jensen fired and the figure in black dropped to the deck.

The others came storming toward him, firing as they went. A hail of bullets tore up the interior of the cargo wagon, ricochets shrieking as they bounced off bins of scrapped equipment and other hardware on its way to be melted down.

Jensen put his shoulder to one of the racks and gave it a hard shove, dislodging a metal basket of splintered ceramic armor inserts. It landed with a crash on the deck, upending its contents, and he went with it, using it as momentary cover before launching himself at the other two attackers. He had to close the distance to them, use the confines of the cargo wagon's narrow width to stop them raking him with more bursts of gunfire.

They were shoulder to shoulder as he dove at them, blocking his advance. Jensen swept up and threw forward his arms, as if he were about to punch both men at once – but instead he deployed the nanoblades hidden in his aug arms at maximum extent, and followed all the way through with a stabbing attack. The blunt edges of the monomolecular weapons skipped off hard polymer chest plates and found purchase in the seams of the Kevlar bodysuits beneath. Any cries of pain they gave were lost, trapped behind their soundproof helmets, and they collapsed atop one another, rapidly bleeding out.

Grim-faced, Jensen stepped back and studied his bleak work, spotting the bodies of three of Jarreau's operatives who had died where they fell. In death, there seemed little difference between the two sides of the fight. Each were darkly clad, fearsome but efficiently anonymous in aspect.

Proxy soldiers, he thought, recalling something David Sarif had once said to him, a lifetime ago. *All run by faces in the shadows*. The thought sat badly with Jensen, and inevitably a question rose that he had no answer for. A question that had been playing on his mind since his reawakening.

Who is running me?

TWELVE

Vande gave Chen the same look she always did – as if he
was something that she'd scraped off the bottom of her
boot – and she walked away down the cargo wagon. "I'm
going to go check on the other team," she told the tech.

"Missing you already," he said. Chen couldn't help
it, the ironic comment came automatically. He heard
Kastillo, the other TF29 agent in the carriage, give a
low snigger.

"You know every time you talk to Vande like that,
you're just annoying her a little bit more," he noted.
"Knock it off, before she strangles you in your sleep."

"Can I help it if I have a crush on our second-in-
command?"

Kastillo rolled his eyes. "You know everyone else
just thinks you have no idea when to shut up, right?"

"It's part of my charm," Chen insisted.

"No, it's not—" began Kastillo, but he never got
to finish his sentence. Without warning, the hatch
leading from the rear end of the cargo wagon suddenly

distorted in its frame as a massive impact slammed into it from the outside.

Chen and Kastillo went for their weapons by reflex, just as the hatch broke free of its mountings and was torn away. Ducking to stride through the low entrance came a massive augmented man, with unblinking crimson eyes glaring out of a dead, immobile face. Other figures were advancing up behind the invader across the flatbed cars beyond, but Chen only registered them as fleeting glimpses of shadow.

He raised his revolver and fired, just as Kastillo pulled his FR-27 flechette rifle to hip height and did the same.

The cyborg moved fast for his size, heavy footfalls clanging against the deck of the train car as he deliberately crashed through a support rack, sending containers spinning to the floor. Chen was sure he landed a round in the intruder's chest, but it might have been a feather for all the effect it had. "Contact, contact!" he shouted, activating his infolink. "We've been boarded!" Static hissed back at him.

Kastillo was closer to the intruder, and he tried to put shots into the hulking cyborg's head, but the rounds went wide. Then their attacker was on the agent, ripping the rifle out of his grip and smashing it to pieces against the wall. With his other hammer-sized fist, he slammed Kastillo back against a window, the toughened glass breaking with the force of the impact. Blood streaming from his nostrils, the agent reeled, dazed and disoriented by the powerful blow.

Chen couldn't see Vande; was she still in the carriage with them? He had no time to look around for her, as the cyborg turned his attention in the tech's direction, flexing his thick fingers as he stormed toward him.

The revolver bucked in Chen's grip as he loosed off more shots that did as little to halt the intruder's advance as the first one had. Whatever dermal armor the attacker had implanted in him was as tough as tank plate.

"*Trottel*," snarled the cyborg from the side of his mouth. The word was foreign to Chen, but he could tell by the almost-sneer on that dead-eyed face that it was one of contempt. There was a black-and-steel blur as a fist came out of nowhere and the cyborg punched Chen so hard he left the deck and flew back with the force of impact.

The tech felt his ribs shatter, and the searing pain as jagged spars of broken bone pierced his lung. Tumbling to the floor, agony washed over Chen as he tried to drag himself away, back toward the next car. "Vande!" he cried. "I need some help here!"

The mech glowered at him, then turned away, stalking back to where Kastillo was slumped semi-conscious against the wall. Other intruders in black anti-scan oversuits were filing in through the entrance.

The cyborg's hand opened wider than it should have, fingers extending to envelope Kastillo's face. Then it tightened, crushing the bones in his skull with deliberate, exacting slowness.

How did they make it on board without any of us knowing? Chen forced himself not to surrender to fear, trying desperately to grasp the sudden shift in events. *How did they find us?* The tech tasted blood in his mouth as a cold wash of dread reached deep into him. *This is a setup! We were sold out…*

Then Chen felt a hand on his shoulder, and looked up to see Vande standing over him with a silver pistol in her hand. "This isn't going to end well," she said.

* * *

The third car down from the locomotive was dead center of the train, and by Jensen's reckoning, the most secure place to load the cargo of proscribed augmentations. He shouldered open the door at the forward end of the carriage and saw the stacks of familiar black hard case containers, the same ones he'd seen at the manufacturing plant in Milwaukee Junction. Each was held in place by magnetic locking clamps that would keep the cargo secure until it reached its destination.

The Sarif Industries logo was on every one of them, a mute testament to David Sarif's endless desire to tinker with human enhancement technology. Jensen wondered about what had motivated the man. Sarif had always been an enigma, determined to chart his own course, outwardly a man with ethics, a genius with principles... Or had that all been for show? Jensen never once doubted that his former employer *believed* that he was doing what was right – but it seemed less important to Sarif what others thought of his intentions. His vision of an improved humanity, of a world where people could determine their own evolution, had been seductive in its own way... until you looked down into the gritty details and started asking the hard questions. If you could make a person run faster, think quicker, live longer, it wasn't difficult to make them more dangerous as well.

And David Sarif was not the kind of man who would put aside a compelling technological idea just because it could have applications for war as well as peace. Jensen hesitated, looking down at the mechanical hands that had taken the place of the flesh-and-blood ones shattered two years earlier. He had never been given the choice, the chance to decide if he wanted to remain a flawed and broken human or become augmented with systems that had not only remade him, but forged him into a walking weapon. Not for the first time, a bitter kernel of resentment toward his ex-boss burned in his chest.

Jensen moved on; it would never be the time or the place to dwell on that. The moment of clarity he so badly wanted was still beyond him, still out of reach.

The hatch at the far end of the cargo wagon hissed open on its hydraulics and he snapped back to the moment, bringing the Hurricane TMP-18 to his shoulder in a firing stance. Jensen heard the low-pitched thud of a Shok-Tac stun grenade detonating, then the wild clatter of bullets bouncing off metal. Before the door was fully open, he saw two people come rushing through the gap, wreaths of cordite smoke gathering in with them.

In front was one of the operatives he'd seen before at the TF29 staging post on the barge, the field technician with the cocky smirk. The man wasn't smirking now. Pale and bleeding, he was moving in great pain. Shoving him through the gap in the door was Jarreau's cold-eyed second-in-command, the blonde woman he called Vande. She had a gun in her hand and a clinical, determined look on her face.

Vande hit the control to close the door again before Jensen could make out who was coming after them, and then she barked a command at the tech. "Get it done!"

"I…" The tech – *Chen, that was his name* – coughed wetly and spat blood. "Ah shit, I don't think I can—"

Vande came to him and poked him in the face with her silver-plated semi-automatic, cutting him off in mid-speech. "I gave you an order! Do it now or I will put you down before they get the chance!"

Chen nodded weakly, staggering away to a control panel on the wall, dragging an override module from a pouch on his bloodstained gear vest.

Jensen took a breath. *What the hell is happening here?* Every other Task Force agent he had seen on the train up until this moment was dead, and his fear that he had arrived too late to warn Jarreau's people seemed to have been borne out – but now here was the team leader's second, threatening one of her own men at gunpoint.

His thoughts raced. From the moment Vande had entered the cell on the barge, Jensen had been wary of the Interpol agent. At first he thought it was natural animosity spinning out of their first encounter on the roof of the Sarif manufacturing plant, but now he was wondering if there was more to it. Whereas Jarreau had been willing to give Jensen the benefit of the doubt, Vande had made no secret of the fact she disliked him on sight, and pressed for his arrest. He never got the sense it was a *good cop, bad cop* thing. Vande's contempt was the real deal.

But was it something *other* than a gut feeling on her part? Did she really know what he represented, what he'd done?

The replay Jensen had seen in Wilder's memory buffer confirmed without question that TF29 had been penetrated by the Illuminati, and he knew how they worked. The shadowy cabal wouldn't just have people at the highest levels, they would place their agents on the ground as well. *They'll have a traitor in the room.*

He stepped out from behind the racks of black crates, holding the machine pistol on Vande. "Nobody move."

The woman saw him and spun around, drawing a second pistol by reflex. Vande's eyes widened as she recognized Jensen's face. "*Verdomme...*" The momentary surprise switched to annoyance and she pivoted, one gun aiming toward Jensen, the other in the direction of Chen and the door. "How are you here?" Vande demanded. "You're a part of this? I should have known!"

"Guns down!" he snapped.

Vande swore at him and shook her head, the air of wintry calm she had shown back in Detroit evaporating into real anger. Her gaze flicked to the technician. "*Chen!* Do it! Access the lockdown, *now!*"

"No!" Jensen took a step toward Chen, but Vande blocked his way.

Still holding one of the guns on him, she fixed Jensen with a hard glare. "Don't test me. Come any closer and I will ruin that pretty head of yours."

Chen coughed again and then the device in his hand let out a loud chime. "Got... it..." He wheezed and spat. "Activating..."

Jensen expected to see the mag-locks holding the SI crates release, but instead Chen's actions activated a different system. Armored metal slats dropped down over the windows and restraint clamps clunked into place around the access hatches at either end of the cargo wagon. Vande hadn't ordered the tech to open the containers; she'd ordered him to seal them inside the train car.

Chen's labored breathing was coming in ragged, panting heaves and he dragged himself across to the far side of the compartment. He almost collapsed atop a low crate beneath one of the shuttered windows, giving Jensen a bleary-eyed look. "This guy?" he gasped. "You don't have... a ticket for this trip."

Heavy blows echoed on the other side of the sealed

hatchway, quickly followed by gunshots ringing off the metal door. Then there was silence, and Vande dared to take a step toward it, listening intently. "They'll be through as soon as they figure out how to bust in here without blowing the train off the track." Her guns remained steady.

"I took out a team in the front carriages," began Jensen. "They had a laser cutting rig. Odds are your friends on the other side of that hatch will have one as well."

"My *what*?" Vande's eyes narrowed. "You appear out of thin air with a weapon in our faces and you're implying I'm in on this attack?" She grimaced. "I have shot people for lesser insults than that."

"It's true." Chen gave a weak nod. "I've seen it."

"I came here to warn you," said Jensen. "After what happened at the airport, I uncovered a new lead… a woman called Jenna Thorne. Know the name?" He subtly activated his CASIE implant, using the aug's built-in lie detector to monitor the two TF29 agents for any sign of recognition. The software registered nothing. "She's Homeland Security, but that's just a cover. My guess is she's working for the people bankrolling the smuggling network that TF29 have been chasing. They want this hardware, and after you guys stopped them airlifting it out of Detroit… they're taking a more proactive approach to recovering it."

Vande risked a glance over her shoulder. "This Thorne… she's one of them?" A thin wisp of white smoke curled from one of the lockdown clamps around the hatch, and the metal began to turn red-black with heat. "You were right. They're burning their way in."

"Yeah." Jensen made a judgment call and let the Hurricane's muzzle drop. Had he been wrong about the Interpol agent? Wherever Vande stood in this situation, he would find out for certain in a few minutes. "So I guess we're in this together."

To his surprise, the TF29 agent lowered her pistols and set about reloading them. "Our comms are being jammed. We've already missed a check-in, so Jarreau will have someone on the way to find out why… but they won't reach us in time to make a difference. If you really are here to help, Jensen, I hope that means you were smart enough to bring some back-up."

He shook his head. "Just me. But there's an aircraft on station nearby; if I can reach them, I might be able to get us out—"

"And let this be stolen again?" Vande gestured at the crates. "No. These intruders are professionals – we retreat now and they win. They'll have a pick-up already dialed in, count on that. And after all the blood we shed to get this junk, I'm not about to just hand it over."

"What about him?" Jensen nodded at Chen, who grew paler by the moment. "He needs medical attention."

The tech managed a weak grin. "I can't l-leave Raye when she so desperately needs me."

"You're an idiot," Vande told him.

Chen's opportunity to reply was lost in the next second. The only warning was a brief clattering of metal on metal from across the side of the train car, close to where the tech was slumped. He reacted in alarm, but far too slowly to make any difference to what happened next.

A ball of fire tore through one of the shutters and the reinforced glass behind it, filling the front section of the cargo wagon with a brief torrent of heat and shrapnel. The blast – most likely from a remote-detonated explosive pack – ripped across Chen like a blowtorch, searing flesh to ash and bone to blackened ruins. He was dead before his body struck the deck.

A flurry of bullets followed as the shadow of a hulking shape appeared outside the great tear ripped in the side of the carriage, firing blindly into the interior. Vande was down, knocked aside by the backwash of the detonation, but Jensen was far enough away to hold his ground, and he let off three-round bursts, out through the ragged hole and into the howling darkness flashing past beyond it. He hit something, because the shooting stopped, although Jensen knew the respite would be only momentary. Over the scream of the wind, he could hear the sizzle and buzz of the metal latches around the sealed door melting into slag.

Two-front attack. They're splitting our focus. It was an assault tactic right out of any counter-siege operations manual – and with that thought, Jensen suddenly realized what would come next. He surged forward, reaching out to pull Vande to her feet and away. "Get back from there!"

A trio of black-and-yellow cylinders little larger than a man's fist came spinning into the cargo wagon through the blown-out window, and clattered across the deck. Ingrained reaction made Jensen turn his face away, shouting wordlessly to equalize the pressure inside his body as the concussive charges went off in rapid succession.

He lost long, precious seconds to the shock effect, struggling to pull back from the sickening disorientation that washed over him. The flash suppressor lenses in Jensen's optic implants kept him from being blinded, but there was little he could do about the deafening whine from the stun blasts.

That he and Vande were alive was the only luck they had. Thorne's killers could have tossed fragmentation grenades in after the shaped charge and turned them both into bloody rags, but clearly the intruders were not willing to risk any damage to the cargo.

Jensen stumbled, trying to shake off the stark jolt of sound and light, and grabbed Vande, hauling her up from where she had fallen. The TF29 agent was blinking, reeling, and two streams of blood trickled from her nostrils where the overpressure had hit her hard. She lurched into Jensen, unsteady on the continually oscillating deck of the moving train. He caught an expression of surprise as Vande's gaze raked over his shoulder and behind him. She called out his name as a warning, but he only saw her mouth the word, his ears still ringing.

The laser burner had done its job and the hatch was grinding open in fits and starts. Jensen fumbled for his gun as the monstrous black shadow he had glimpsed outside the train car now filled the hatchway.

The big cyborg was a full-frame design, the class of augmented human that was known in military and law enforcement circles as an 'ogre.' Like the mythological beast they were named after, ogres were strong, tough-skinned and very hard to put down. Outside of national armed forces and certain sanctioned corporate military contractors, an ogre's very existence was illegal. The United Nations classed them not as people, but as lethal weapons.

In it came, carelessly ripping through the frame of the hatch. Jensen missed the chance to fire off a burst from the Hurricane, but by the looks of the multiple entry wounds across the big aug's torso, anything smaller than a heavy-caliber bullet wasn't likely to do more than piss this guy off.

Jensen had been up against this kind of enemy before, but not in such close quarters, and not with another combatant in the kill box. He saw the hint of an icy sneer on the face of the intruder, and then a hammer blow came down, the force of it separating him from Vande with a single swipe. Jensen hit the deck and collided with a rack of storage crates, the painful ringing in his head gaining a fresh chorus of tolling bells. He glimpsed other black-suited attackers following the big cyborg into the compartment.

Vande tried again to get to her feet of her own accord, but the ogre put her down with an off-hand shove that threw the woman into a heap next to Jensen. Somewhere along the way, she had lost her twinned pistols, and Jensen saw his Hurricane lying just out of reach. Any thought he might have had of diving for it faded when one of the other intruders picked it up and pitched the gun away through the ruined window.

The lithe figure in black pulled back a form-fitting hood and a rush of henna-red hair tumbled out, framing a pale, unpleasantly memorable face. "I'm sorry I made you wait, Mr. Jensen," said Thorne, her voice rendered dull and flat as the tinnitus effect began to wane. "But we caught up again eventually."

"Long way from Alaska," he managed. "Not far enough for me."

"It would be a lie to say your appearance here is a surprise," Thorne went on. "You have the singular ability to turn up exactly where you are most unwanted." She frowned, as if considering something. "Perhaps that is what interests them about you."

"Who would that be?" Jensen came up, dragging himself to a standing position.

Thorne ignored his question, turning to another member of the black ops team – a man with sculpted blades that replaced his lower legs – and pointed toward the panel that Chen had reprogrammed minutes earlier. "Can you take control of the train's systems from there?"

The other operative nodded. "It's only military encryption. I'll take ownership of the network and then I can release the sealed hatches and cargo locks, re-task the locomotive…"

"I didn't ask for a commentary," Thorne spoke over him. "Do your job." The hacker set to work, and she turned back to the cyborg. "Interpol will have reinforcements here in less than fifteen minutes. We need to be ready to take their VTOL when they arrive. Terminate the crew, but we must have the aircraft intact, are we clear?" The ogre acknowledged the order with a solemn nod, but said nothing.

"Huh." Jensen gave a dry chuckle. "That's how you're getting the augs away, on TF29's own VTOL. Smart. Because you knew they'd come running the moment the guard team on the train went off the air."

"It is an efficient use of available resources," Thorne replied. Behind her, the other operative did something with the panel and a tone sounded as the crate latches released in sequence. She nodded at that, and spared Jensen a withering look. "You, however… I consider surplus to requirements." She raised her gun and aimed it at a point directly between his eyes.

"Those were not the orders." The ogre broke his silence, a hard Germanic accent coloring his tone. "You are exceeding your authority."

"It seems like a lot of people don't like you." Vande eyed Jensen and took a shuddering breath. "They want... you alive? Or some maybe not so much..."

"Hell if I know," Jensen snarled, his anger rising sharply. "Shoot me or don't, Thorne. I'm through playing by the Illuminati's rules!" He tensed, ready for whatever would come next. *I'm not going down without taking these creeps with me.*

Thorne didn't seem to be listening to any of them. She went on, speaking as if she were voicing her thoughts aloud. "The questions persist. What makes Adam Jensen different from the others who were fished out of the Arctic Ocean on that day? Why was he there? Who sent him?" Her dark eyes narrowed. "Think, Jensen. Ask yourself, what *really* drove you? What was the true, undeniable reason you went to Panchaea?" Thorne pulled back the hammer on her pistol, measuring out the moment. "And why didn't you drown out there?"

There was hate in the words, and he couldn't fathom why. Had there been some fragment of his memory that he had lost after the incident, something that Thorne was part of? Or had she known something about him all along, just as he had suspected on their first meeting? Some secret truth that even he wasn't aware of?

"You tell me," he said.

"You'll never know," said Thorne, with calculated cruelty and the briefest hint of a smile playing on her bloodless lips. Her finger tightened on the trigger.

"She talks too much," Vande spat, and with a sudden blur of movement, the Task Force agent sprang off her heels.

The next few moments happened so fast, they were

barely distinct events, each threading into the other; Vande barreled straight into Thorne, landing a hard cross on the woman that sent her spinning, the big cyborg snatching at her and missing; Thorne struck out with her gun and the revolver went off with a crashing discharge; Vande tumbled away, colliding with Jensen as he moved to grab her.

Blood grew in a great bloom across Vande's belly, but she was showing her teeth in a savage grin. In her hand, she held the flat, slab-like shape of a Pulsar electromag grenade, torn from Thorne's belt as the two women had briefly exchanged blows. She mashed down on the trigger pad and hurled it at the feet of the ogre.

Jensen acted on instinct, curling an arm beneath Vande's and dragging her back and away toward the rear of the train car. He heard the EMP grenade detonate on an impact fuse, felt the buzzing crackle at the edge of the pulse flash as they threw themselves away from the area of effect. His vision blurred like a poorly tuned video signal, but the moment was fleeting as they stumbled out of range and through the hatch at the forward end of the carriage.

He let Vande fall, ignoring her cry of pain as she went down, and he bodily dragged the open hatch shut behind them. The magnetic locking mechanism thudded home, but he knew it would be no barrier to Thorne and her team now that their hacker had access to the train's systems.

He went for the brute force option. Jensen deployed a blade from his right arm and slashed open the lock control pad in a shower of sparks. Without pausing, he reached up and cut off the head of the security camera over the doorway, blinding it.

"I... am..." Vande forced out the words. "Surrounded... by fucking idiots." He looked back at her and saw the Task Force agent clutching at her gut, her gloved hands wet with her own blood. "So much so... I've caught *stupidity* off them." She glared up at him. "Why else would I have done something like that? Tell me!"

"You saved my life," he said simply.

"Was it worth it?" Vande spat back. She caught sight of the bodies of the rest of her team, the ones in the forward car who had been the first to be executed. "Shit. *Verdomme* shit. Seth's gone, he was the last one... This is a stinking mess, Jensen."

"I'll get you out of here," he insisted, pointing to the roof of the train car. "There's a skylight up there, I'll signal the pilot who brought me in—"

"*I told you no!*" she thundered. "Americans, you always think you know the only way to do things... *No!*" Vande pulled herself into a sitting position, and fumbled for a tiny .454 derringer pistol concealed in an ankle holster. "Listen to me," she insisted. "Those bastards do not get this train, understand? *They do not.*" Her eyes lost focus for a second, and Jensen knew she was looking at something projected on to her retinal heads-up display. "This train will cross... cross the state line in about eight minutes, and when it does, there's a curve... It will slow down." She shook her head. "Speed it up. *Faster.*"

He nodded as he realized what Vande was asking him to do. "The train takes the turn too fast and it'll go off the rails. Be torn apart."

"And all that tech they want so... so badly will go up in flames," she said with venom, glaring at the hatch they had come through. "Go do it. Manual override is in the engine's cab." Jensen opened his mouth to protest, but she swore at him again, her expression hostile. "Please don't give me... some mawkish speech now. Don't pretend we are friends just because the same bunch of assholes shot at us..."

"You want to die here?" he snarled.

"*No!*" she shouted back at him, slumped against the wall, clutching the derringer like it was a talisman. "But who says I get a vote?" Vande shook her head. "So get up there and *kill this fucking train!*"

"They've destroyed the door controls on the other side." Thorne's hacker scowled at the portable monitor mounted on his armored wrist-guard. "I'll get the laser, we'll just cut through again."

"Do it. And in the meantime..." she said, with a sniff. Thorne looked across to the cyborg. "*You.* Do what you are best at. Find Jensen and the woman, kill them both. That's a direct order."

"It is contrary to what we were told—" began the cyborg, but Thorne silenced him with a savage throat-cutting gesture.

"Are you going to disobey me?" she said, as hard and cold as ice.

"No," he replied, after a moment. The dead-eyed expression on his face never shifted. "But you will be held responsible." He walked away, flexing his thick fingers experimentally.

"How do you expect him to get through there?" said the other operative.

"By the direct route."

The hulking cyborg approached the torn-open

hatchway at the rear of the cargo wagon and reached up, hands clutching at broken fragments of metal. With a grind of pistons, he hauled himself off the deck and on to the roof of the speeding train.

The locomotive's cab was a sparse affair, a repeater console mounted in one corner of the compartment next to a tall server module behind steel access plates. The module controlled the train, sensing the motion and mass of the wagons behind it, managing their speed in real time as it sped down the rails at breakneck pace. On a display screen mounted beneath an armored window slit, a digital display showed a dozen virtual gauges and above them a rolling map. On the latter, the railroad ahead was visible as a narrow line growing into a steep curve that was coming closer by the minute.

Jensen looked around and found a set of emergency manual controls, a redundant system placed there in the rare event that a human driver would need to take over. The manual system was locked beneath a thick plastic shield that resisted his attempts to lever it open. Instead, he cracked it with the butt of an FR-27 flechette rifle he had found on the deck in the crew car, and the plastic fractured. In a few moments he had the controls exposed. There was a dead man's switch, a speed governor, and a bunch of other dials and switches that he didn't recognize.

He rammed the throttle bar forward to the highest setting and felt the train lurch as the engine put on a burst of acceleration. Red alert lights flashed, warning him to ease off on the power, but Jensen ignored them. He would have to jam the controls so the speed could not be reduced.

If in doubt, he told himself, *break it.* Jensen found the manual switches for the emergency brakes and fired a burst of rounds into the panel. More alarms sounded as he turned back to the main controls, ready to repeat the action.

But then the sliding hatch on the side of the cab squealed open on poorly oiled runners and a huge arm made of steel and corpse-pale flesh came through the gap, grabbing at him. The thunderous, constant bellow of the engine filled the compartment on a gale of damp air as Thorne's pet cyborg squeezed in through the narrow hatchway. Arms swinging wildly, the ogre connected with Jensen's shoulder and even the glancing blow was enough to make the motors in his cyberlimb stutter.

If it had been difficult to battle an opponent in the confines of the narrow train cars, then here in the locomotive's cab it was like fighting inside a phone booth. There was no room to maneuver, and the long assault rifle in Jensen's hand was exactly the wrong kind of weapon to use. He tried to bring it around, firing wildly into the ceiling, letting clusters of razor-sharp flechette rounds whicker and keen off the inside of the metal cab – but the big cyborg was too close, trying to back him into a corner.

"*Ach*," muttered the ogre, as if he was disappointed with something, and he swatted Jensen away toward the rear of the compartment.

The blow kicked the air out of Jensen's lungs and shook the teeth in his head, pitching him up off his feet and into a support frame. Agony erupted down Jensen's spine and he belatedly realized that he had lost his grip on the rifle.

Burning through the pain, reacting more than

thinking, Jensen shot off his feet and dove back at his opponent, deploying his nanoblades as he went. One snapped forward from across his knuckles, the other back from his elbow, and he pivoted in the tight space. Against an unarmored target – or even one with a standard Kevlar rig – Jensen's slashing attack would have been deadly. But to his dismay, the tips of the blades skipped off the smooth ceramic-metallic plates that covered the ogre's broad torso. Sparks flew and the monomolecular edges left scored lines across the armor without cutting any deeper.

"My turn," rumbled the cyborg, and he backhanded Jensen into the control server. He lost an eye shield and for one dizzying moment, the power of the blow forced his optics into a rapid reboot, blinding him for a few milliseconds.

The ogre reached for Jensen as if he was going to embrace him, the mechanisms in his giant hands snapping open, widening so they could envelop his skull and crush it.

Again, Jensen did the opposite of what his opponent would expect. Rather than try to block the attack, he mirrored it. He grabbed at the cyborg's smooth metal skull and dug in his fingers; the brief flash of shock on the ogre's dead-flesh face told him he had wrong-footed the killer.

He pushed his thumbs into the center of the wide crimson lenses that covered the ogre's eye sockets, and one of the dull plastic disks cracked under the pressure. The cyborg clawed at Jensen, trying to drag him off – but now he had purchase on his opponent's right-side optic, and with a violent wrenching motion, he tore it out.

The ogre let out a low, sustained moan that carried

over the rumble of the train, as the augmented eye dragged with it hair-thin lines of cabling and synthetic optic nerves. Bright blood and milky processor fluids drooled from the ruined socket.

For a brief second, fate allowed Jensen the fantasy that he had hobbled the ogre – only a second, though. "I see you," hissed the cyborg, swallowing the pain.

The return punch was like a thunderbolt, and Jensen took the full force of it across his chest. He heard the brittle fracturing of his tactical rig's polymer armor plates, he felt the sickly jolts of pain as his ribs cracked, all of it whirling around as the ogre's angry blow threw him across the short span of the cab once again. Before he could react, the cyborg grabbed his ankle and pulled hard, pitching Jensen up off the deck and into the wall before letting him drop again.

His body felt like it was full of knives, stabbing and clawing at the inside of his torso. Icons from Jensen's Sentinel implant flashed orange and red at the edges of his blurred vision, as the device went into overdrive and struggled to keep him from blacking out. His arm scraped across the floor and fell on something – the butt of the flechette rifle.

Jensen snatched it up and slid back against the rear of the cab, putting as much distance as he could between himself and the big cyborg. He raised the rifle, the muzzle wavering as the damaged servos in his arm struggled to hold it steady.

"That won't be enough to stop me from killing you," the ogre said matter-of-factly. "It will take something better than you to end me."

Jensen's lip twisted in a sneer. "Not aiming at you, asshole." He squeezed the trigger and the rest of the FR-27's ammo magazine discharged in a sustained snarl of gunfire, ripping across the train's manual control panel and destroying it.

The locomotive shook beneath them and Jensen heard the screeching of metal far below as the spinning wheels bit into the curvature of the approaching track. A shudder ran down the length of the entire train and the cab rocked alarmingly. The cyborg looked around, taking in the damage. "You have turned this machine into a runaway. Foolish."

"You think so?" Jensen got to his feet, letting the spent rifle drop. "The way I see it, you got one choice, big man." He let his nanoblades extend. "I just turned your mission into a zero sum game. Time to exercise a little logic. Either we die together when this thing crashes, or—"

The ogre didn't wait for him to finish. As cleanly as if he were stepping off at a station, the cyborg walked to the cab's open hatch and dropped into the dark. Jensen rushed to the hatchway and looked out after him. He caught sight of a thickset shape picking itself up from the weeds along the railroad cutting, receding away and then lost in the night.

Beneath his feet, Jensen saw more flashes of bright orange sparks jetting from the bogies as the train's braking system malfunctioned. The wind ripped the breath from his mouth and he cast a look ahead. In the distance, he could make out the vague silver lines of the railroad and their steepening curve. Beyond them was lost, decayed scrubland. At this speed, there could only be a few minutes until the locomotive left the rails and dragged all the wagons along with it.

Jensen tightened his damaged armor plates, flinching at a jolt of new pain, and started back down the train.

THIRTEEN

The lurching motion almost threw Thorne off her feet, and she turned back to glower over her shoulder. "What was that?"

The tech-operative paused with the glowing laser cutter in one hand, and peered at the virtual screen on his wrist-guard, his eyes widening. "Ah. This is non-optimal."

"Explain."

"The locomotive's control systems have just gone into critical mode." He stabbed experimentally at a few buttons. "No. The control interface is unresponsive. It's no longer answering direct commands."

"And yet we've just picked up speed." She pushed past him to the hatch that Jensen had sealed shut, eyeing the streak of blood on the floor around the doorjamb. "Who made that happen?"

"Who do you think?" The operative nodded at the door. "Looks like the monster they gave us hasn't done his job."

Thorne's temper frayed at his sarcastic tone and she pointed at the hatch. "Get it open! Now!"

The panel shifted open a few inches. "Almost got it," said the operative.

She steeled herself. If by some fluke Jensen had been able to find a way to defeat the German, then, as with so many things, Thorne would have to do the job herself. That brought a cruel smile to her face. Her masters wanted the ex-cop to keep breathing, for reasons she could not comprehend; and given how tired she had become of their gnomic, contradictory and overly elaborate orders, Thorne felt a special kind of thrill at the idea of deliberately killing Jensen. She liked the taste of that defiance.

"Once I get past this," the operative was saying, as the laser melted through the locking rods, "I can get up to the locomotive and burn the couplings. If we're lucky, that'll slow us down..." The door juddered and retracted with a sudden crunch of metal on metal. The cargo wagon revealed beyond was a disordered mess of dead bodies and fallen crates.

Thorne saw a puddle of fresh blood on the deck just inside the hatchway. "Wait..."

But the other operative had already stepped through. He was barely inside the next train car when Thorne saw movement from the shadows and a white-knuckled hand jammed a compact disposable derringer into the flexible ballistic cloth around the operative's throat. There was a flat bang of discharge and the little holdout gun blasted the man's neck into a ruin of meat and bone. He spun toward the deck.

A second – and final – shot from the derringer droned out toward Thorne as Vande pushed away from where she had been hiding in the lee of the hatchway, and let gravity drag her down, firing as she went. The heavy-caliber bullet went wide, humming past Thorne's head to bury itself uselessly in the wall.

Her smile returned and she stalked forward, shaking out her arms like she was warming up for an exercise routine. Vande was on the floor, cursing at Thorne in Dutch with the empty disposable still smoking in her grip. A lot of the TF29 agent was already spilled across the deck of the rocking train car, and the pallor of her face showed how close she was to death. Thorne decided to hasten that inevitability.

Flexing the muscles in her arms in a predetermined pattern sent nerve impulses to a dozen hardened nubs of myomer implanted down the outside of her arms. From slits in the surface of her skin emerged curved barbs made of a synthetic diamond analogue, each one of the razor-edged spurs whispering through the material of her sleeves until her arms resembled the stem of a rose.

Vande tried to back away, but her wounded body betrayed her and she failed to find the energy she needed to do it.

Thorne picked her way closer, moving with the swaying motion of the floor, and grabbed a handful of the Interpol agent's short hair. "You've failed. That's the last thing you will ever know." She raised her arm to strike.

"*Thorne!*" Jensen shouted her name from the hatchway at the far end of the train car, listing as he came through from the engine cab. "*No!*"

Her lip curled in contempt. As if he could stop her with a word. Thorne swept down in a wide arc that let the spurs on her arm cross the bare throat of the woman on her knees, opening Vande's neck in a jet of crimson.

She kicked the agent away as she died, watching the shock in her eyes harden into glassy emptiness.

Thorne looked up, her gaze locking with Jensen's, and the raw fury on his face was perfect. It was the most honest emotional reaction she had seen from him since the moment they had met in Facility 451.

"You sick witch..." he growled. Blunt-headed swords slid from hidden slots on his hands, twitching with barely caged violence.

"No, just easily bored," she corrected, shaking her head. "Where's the German? I refuse to believe you are capable of killing him..."

"He abandoned you." Jensen bit out the words. "Figures. The Illuminati have never been big on loyalty, right? Everyone is *disposable* to them."

By pure chance, in his rage Jensen hit on a blunt truth and Thorne's post-kill smile melted off her face. "You're an impediment. A nuisance, too stupid to die. You're no-one's hero, Jensen. Why do you keep acting like you *matter*?" Her voice rose and she shouted the words at him, but they were directed as much at herself as at him. "You're just a crude, ignorant tool, do you understand?"

He had no gun. The empty flechette rifle had been abandoned in the engine cab and the next closest firearm to him was lying on the deck, down at the far end of the train car. To use the nanoblades, he'd need to be close in – but he saw those glistening thorns that the woman had grown, saw how she had dispatched Vande, and Jensen knew that she would kill him before he could kill her. He was wounded and he didn't have the speed.

Vande. His gaze tried to stray to the dead agent.

He'd been wrong about her, wrong to suspect that she was a turncoat. And now she'd paid the highest price to prove her loyalty to the Task Force and its goals. The callous, almost *amused* way in which Thorne had ended her ground on Jensen and it was all he could do to keep his rage in check.

Thorne was still snarling at him. She jabbed a finger in his direction as a violent shudder shook the deck of the train car. "You think anything you've done will make a difference? *Do you think that* anyone *who opposes them makes a difference*?" She barked out a cold, sneering laugh. "You're only alive because of the blood in your veins! If it wasn't for that, you'd be decaying at the bottom of the ocean."

He stiffened. She was talking about his unique gene markers, the super-compatibility effect that Megan Reed had discovered and kept from him for so long. *And if Thorne knows that about me, who else does?*

"You've lost," he growled, silencing the questions in his mind. "I'm taking your prize off the board. We're gonna end this here and now." The carriage's wheels shrieked as the curve finally began to bite, and the deck tilted, loose items slipping away toward the apex of the turn.

"Good." Thorne's pale face split in a wide smile, her lips reddening. "That's how I want it." She exploded into motion, nerve-jacked and neuro-accelerated reflexes boosted to their maximum potential, her muscle implants forced to the red line.

Jensen sprinted down the car to meet her, boots clanging on the deck as he closed the distance. Time slowed as fresh adrenaline flooded his veins.

* * *

He had one chance to take down his opponent; a wicked, twin-blade slashing strike as they passed one another, like two ancient samurai on a dueling field going for that singular, perfect cut. But Jensen had been beaten to within an inch of his life, he had a throat full of blood-laced phlegm, who knew how many busted ribs and the tiny motors in his augs were slipping gears with each movement.

Thorne was at full strength, she was agile and ruthless, and she would kill him.

The game had to change.

His implanted bio-cells had just enough charge for one final offensive option, and a moment short of their paths crossing in the middle of the train car, Jensen suddenly retracted his nanoblades and went down on one knee, ducking his head and swinging up his arms like he was about to take to the air.

Across the upper surface of his torso and his limbs, micro-miniature ejector ports snapped open as one and expelled a storm of tiny spherical explosive charges. Each one no larger than a ball bearing, they spun out from Jensen, putting him at the core of a detonation that briefly turned him into a human cluster munition. When David Sarif created this augmentation weapon, he named it the *Typhoon* – and it was a deadly storm.

Flaming arcs of concussive fire spread like Icarus's burning wings and ripped apart the interior of the train car. Too close to stop her headlong rush into the blast radius, Thorne took the force of the detonation wave and the discharge tore into her.

Jensen rose, and against all odds, he realized she was still alive. Broken, fluid sounds emerged from Thorne's throat, forming into words. "This... means... nothing. This is... not the war. Not even... a skirmish.

A *distraction*." Her eyes stared blankly into nothing and her last breath was spent mocking him. "They... still win..."

Thorne's voice stilled, her ruined body slumped into an untidy, smoking heap. Dying here, this was retribution for every pitiless murder she had committed – but it didn't seem like it was *enough*.

Jensen pitched back as the cargo wagon groaned and pulled away from the outer rails, the angle of the tilting deck growing steeper. In a few seconds, the whole train would follow it into ruin and fire.

He sprinted toward the broken skylight hatch where he had first boarded and hauled himself back through it, ignoring the pain down his chest and stomach. Every movement was like acid burning him from the inside out.

On the roof of the train car, his vision was distorted by driving rain and screaming wind. He couldn't clearly see the ground streaking past on either side of him at nearly two hundred miles per hour, he could only feel the fatigue clawing at him, trying to pull his hand free of the grab bar he was clinging to. His power cells were almost drained, his landing system implant useless to him. If he fell, he would be dashed to pieces.

Metal screamed and Jensen felt everything around him give a monumental shudder. This was it; the train was crashing.

He let go, and against all reason he ran, allowing the wind and the rain to push at his back. Light, stark and blinding, came from out of the sky, suddenly surrounding him in a halo of whiteness. He heard a woman shouting his name, saw the shimmer of cables swinging into arm's reach. Behind him, the locomotive left the rails and there was a crashing, tearing discord as loud as the world ending.

Jensen leapt into space without thinking, without hesitation, without fear.

SOUTH OF GRANGER – INDIANA – UNITED STATES OF AMERICA

The VTOL thundered low along the line of the railroad, cresting a shallow rise in a howl of engine noise.

In the cockpit, Sol Mendel leaned forward against his flight restraints and gave a low mutter. "Dear god…"

Jarreau stood behind him, wedged in the open hatchway between the cabin and the rear crew compartment. Both men saw the destruction laid out before them, projected on to the inside of the aircraft's virtual canopy. Where the rail line bent into a shallow curve there was a mess of metal wreckage and dozens of smoldering fires scattered all about it. Jarreau saw a wide, ugly scar cut across the ground at an angle to the rails, a deep gouge in the earth that ended in the burning mass of the train's locomotive.

From behind him, one of the Task Force techs was sending out calls over the unit's encrypted radio channels, entreating anyone still alive down there to respond. No replies were forthcoming.

"I'll orbit around," Mendel said grimly, snapping on twin spotlights that stabbed down from the VTOL nose to sweep back and forth across the crash site.

"You said you saw something on the scope as we closed in…" said Jarreau, glancing at the local radar scope. "Another aircraft?"

Mendel shook his head. "Not sure. It was just a transient, there and gone again." He sighed. "Probably a ghost echo."

"Give me a thermographic overlay," ordered Jarreau, and the pilot complied, tapping a key that turned the image on the canopy into a patchwork of heat-color. Hot white blooms surrounded the fires and a dull orange trail marked the final path the crashing train had taken. He scanned the landscape, looking for any signs of life.

And he found one. "There!" Jarreau stabbed a finger at a human-shaped blob moving slowly across the image.

Mendel drew that sector of the image closer and revealed the body heat of a man, his torso glowing orange but his arms and legs the cold blue of machines.

"Put us down, now!" Jarreau snapped, grabbing his weapon and turning to the rest of his team. "Squad, deploy!"

Panels dropped open along the side of the VTOL as it settled on to the ground with a bump, and Jarreau was the first one out on to the wet, muddy earth.

Jensen staggered toward the Task Force aircraft, raising his hands to show he was unarmed. Each step was slow and unsteady. The damage to his augmented legs was severe but not enough to disable him.

Figures in the familiar black combat oversuits of TF29 spilled out of the VTOL, brandishing assault rifles in his direction. At the head of them was Jarreau, and there was a bleak expression on the team leader's hard face. "Jensen..." he began, his lips thinning. "What happened out here?"

"Vande's dead," he told him, cutting straight to the worst of it. "Chen, the others… they're all gone."

"*Fuck*." Jarreau barked out an order to the rest of his squad. "Spread out! Check for bodies, double-time! The locals will be here as soon as they get their asses in gear, and I want us gone by then…"

"I'm sorry," added Jensen. "You people were set up. There was a woman, her name was Thorne…" He hesitated. He had to be careful what he said here. There was no telling what Jarreau knew or who else might be monitoring them. "She was working for the people behind your smuggling network."

But to his surprise, Jarreau raised his hand to stop him. "Yeah, we know. That goddamn bloodbath at the airport was just a sideshow. They sent a team to intercept the train and take the black market augs en route."

"You know?" echoed Jensen.

"This person Thorne was here, then?" asked Jarreau. "After all this, tell me she didn't get away with the hardware."

Jensen shook his head, and jerked a thumb toward the burning remains of the cargo wagons. "Destroyed, every last crate. And Thorne along with them." He took a breath, grimacing at the oily smoke filling the air. He told Jarreau about Pritchard's lead, the images he pulled from Wilder's cyberoptic, and the desperate race he had run to reach the train and warn Vande. "How do you know about Thorne, and the hijack?"

"I know because something I've been suspecting for months was proven right, Jensen," said the other man. His expression turned stony. "Since the first moment we were on this smuggling network, they've been two steps ahead of us at every turn. At first I thought it was because they were good, but the longer it went on, the more I started wondering if we'd sprung a leak…"

Jensen resisted the urge to tell Jarreau that the footage he had seen of Thorne's conversation pointed to the same damning conclusion – that the Task Force had been penetrated by a double-agent. "Someone at Interpol?"

Jarreau shook his head. "Closer to home." He gestured at the wreckage. "Vande sold us out."

"*What*?" Jarreau's words came as a sudden shock. After what the woman had done on board the train, there was no doubt in Jensen's mind that Raye Vande was anything but an Illuminati mole. Any suspicions he had held about her had been brushed away. Before he could voice that, Jarreau went on.

"During the tear-down and exfil from Detroit, one of the techs found something on her panel… A secret, compartmentalized data drive." He shook his head in sadness and disbelief. "All our mission ops, all our intel on the network, every bit of it was in there. Along with data trails showing regular uploads to a dark net server array in Brazil. They timed out to all of our ops over the last three months."

"That… that can't be right." Jensen tried to find the words. "It has to be a misdirection."

"No." Jarreau shook his head again. "I didn't want to believe it. But the drive was biometrically encoded to Vande alone. Interpol's data intercept team in Lyon are looking into it as we speak. There's evidence of some kind of Swiss bank account…" He trailed off, scowling. "She was the leak, Jensen. We worked side by side for months, right in the thick… and I never saw it."

Because she wasn't the one. The denial tore silently through Jensen's thoughts. *It's a setup, just like everything else.*

This was another Illuminati shell game, their eternal ploy of misdirection and obfuscation. Layers of lies, one atop another. It made perfect sense: had Jensen never been there to interfere with Thorne's plan, her team would have made off with the stolen Sarif augs and left Interpol to sift through the corpses they left behind. Vande had been chosen to be the scapegoat, and with her dead at Thorne's hand there would be nothing to prove that she was innocent – only Jensen's instinct, and that would never be enough.

He could see grief and bitterness warring across Jarreau's face. The Task Force commander badly needed it not to be true, but the evidence in front of him was ironclad. *Of course it is*, Jensen told himself. *They don't make mistakes.*

Vande's framing was a perfect fit, even if the attempt to steal back the mil-spec augmentations had failed. If Jensen spoke up now, if he challenged that version of events, there was no way to know what the outcome would be. There was only one fact that could not be denied. The double-agent operating inside Interpol and Task Force 29, perhaps even directly under Jarreau's command, was *still in place*. Everything Quinn and the Juggernaut hackers suspected about the unit was being proven right.

One of the other TF29 operatives jogged across the broken scrub to Jarreau's side. "Sir," she began, "I can confirm the loss of the train crew and all on-board call signs. And Jensen was right about the intruders, we counted five tangos here. We took quick scans and DNA samples as best we could, but we're not going to be able to recover the dead, not before local heat get here. Mendel says police chatter is going crazy, they've got units on the way right now."

Jarreau gave a solemn nod. "Copy that. What about the cargo?"

"Burned to shit," said the woman. "The fire's slagged everything." She looked away. "Goddamn it. This whole op was for nothing."

"Jarreau…" Jensen moved to speak, but the big man shook his head.

"Take thermite charges, smoke all the remains," the other man told the operative. "We don't need anyone knowing we were out here."

"On it." The woman broke into a jog, racing back to the idling VTOL.

Jarreau eyed him. "You look like you need a lift. Those legs are gonna give out on you if you walk another klick. And Interpol's gonna want a full debrief." He made a beckoning gesture, his other hand patting an inert inhibitor bracelet clipped to his belt. "Is that gonna be a problem for us?" The choice being offered was clear and unequivocal.

"No problem," said Jensen.

"Good." Jarreau turned away and started back toward the parked aircraft. "That'll give us time to talk."

Jensen shot a look up into the sky, in the direction that Vega had taken her VTOL after dropping him off. Quinn had wanted to spirit him away and leave the Task Force ignorant that Jensen had ever been involved. But that didn't sit right with him… and now there were new questions rising that Jensen was determined to find answers for.

His gaze dropped to the shattered remains of the train, and he saw flares of bright white light as Jarreau's team used their thermite charges to turn the corpses of their comrades into untraceable cinders.

Those men and women deserved better than this, thought Jensen. *Instead they died in the crossfire because of some elaborate scheme run by a bunch of elitist sociopaths.* "That's enough," he said aloud, a cold and iron-hard certainty solidifying in him. He set off after Jarreau, a new determination in his dark eyes.

CENTRAL STATION – DETROIT – UNITED STATES OF AMERICA

"You really think he'll actually come?" said Vega, pulling her collar closer about her neck and glancing around.

The rain falling on the streets and buildings seemed to go on forever, coating everything with a slick sheen that did little to wash away the dirt and decay of the city. She didn't like this place. The air was too cold, the streets too narrow. Detroit felt like it was dying by inches all around her, and she wanted to be away from it.

Quinn's expression shifted from blank neutrality to a false smile. "He called us, love. Not the other way around. He'll be here."

She shook her head. "I know you think you know this guy, but I'm telling you now. Don't mess with him. If you're anything other than straight with Jensen, this isn't going to work."

"We all have our secrets to keep," Quinn said, the smile fixed and brittle. "Even him. And frankly, I don't think Janus is going to take no for an answer…"

The station doors parted and a figure in a dark coat emerged. He spotted them off to the side of the entranceway, and approached. "We'll find out soon enough," said Vega. She noted a stiffness in Jensen's gait as he came closer.

Quinn saw it too. "You all right there? Those Interpol lads fix you up?"

"Something like that," said Jensen. "New servos. Still breaking them in."

"It's the least they could do, given what you risked to help them," Vega added. "But if I were you, I'd check anything they put in you for trackers."

"Already done." Jensen eyed her. "Thanks to Janus, I know what to look for. I won't make the same mistake again."

"Just looking out for our friends," Quinn insisted. He glanced at Vega. "Alex, keep an eye out while the menfolk talk, will you?"

She shot him a frosty glare. "Whatever."

Quinn led Jensen out of the rain, under a corroded awning across a shuttered storefront. Vega turned away from them, but her augmented hearing meant she still caught every word of their conversation.

"So," began Quinn. "Those nasty little augs your ex-boss cooked up are all gone. I guess we call that a success, do we?"

"A dozen people died," Jensen retorted. "So no, we don't."

"Sure, sure." Quinn back-pedaled. "But take what victory you can from it. And remember that Juggernaut were happy to be of assistance."

"So now I owe you one."

"I wasn't going to bring it up so quickly, but since you mention it… yes." Vega heard the smile in Quinn's voice. "Janus is a real believer in *quid pro quo*."

"We've got that in common, then." Vega expected Jensen to show the same wary attitude he had exhibited back in the old movie theater when they first met, so what he said next came as something of a shock. "I'll do it. I'll work with the Juggernaut Collective."

"Oh." Quinn's reaction showed that he had thought the same thing as Vega. He recovered quickly. "Good. Smart choice, Adam." Quinn forced a chuckle. "We don't have a secret handshake or anything, but you won't regret—"

"I already do," he broke in. "But I've gone as far as I can, and like it or not, I need a new edge. You people are it."

Vega turned to see Jensen walking away and she couldn't stop herself from calling out to him. "Hey. Wait…"

He met her gaze. "Ask me."

"What brought you around? Before you didn't want anything to do with us, now you're signing on just like that." She snapped her fingers. "What changed?"

"*I have,*" he said, with grim conviction. "I reached my limit. I've had enough of the Illuminati. The disregard they have for everyone who isn't one of them." He shook his head. "Harrison Stacker. Henry Kellman. Raye Vande. Vasili Sevchenko. Netanya Keitner…" Every name Jensen uttered seemed to weigh down on him. "And thousands more. Dead, because of them. I've had enough of watching people pay the price for some superior bastard's idea of what makes the world work."

Vega gave a slow nod. Every word he said resonated with her own motivations for becoming part of the Collective. "Welcome to the party," she told him.

Jensen turned up his collar and glared out into the rain. "One last thing," he said, not looking at either of them. "If you cross me… if Janus lies… we are done."

Vega watched him vanish into the sheeting downpour and frowned. "He means it," she said.

"Of course he does," said Quinn. "That's why he's the one we need."

MONTBRILLANT TOWER – GENEVA – SWITZERLAND

The high-pitched tone brought DuClare from the perfect repose of a deep sleep and dragged her up into wakefulness. She rolled over on her wide bed, pulling a snarl of ivory silk sheets with her, blinking owlishly. The black hands of the antique ormolu clock on the far wall were at four and two.

Resting atop a table across the room, the high-end custom vu-phone she habitually carried was glowing brightly atop the charging plate where she had left it, pulsing different colors with each melodic chime of its alarm.

DuClare frowned. She had turned the device off before retiring alone to her apartments that night, and left strict instructions that she not be disturbed. Exiting the bed in an angry fashion, she pulled on a kimono and stalked to the table. Her fingertips were about to touch the device when the bedroom windows suddenly flickered. She turned, alarmed, to see the synthetic-laced glass shimmer as pixels gathered into an image on its surface. Like most of the panes in her rooms, the windows could double as screens or mirrors depending on the commands given to the apartment's pet AI, but they only responded to spoken orders and then, only ones given by DuClare herself. The vu-phone fell silent as the incoming communication linked from it to the window-screens.

Then her sleep-slowed thoughts caught up with her

and she remembered what had happened on the jet a few days earlier. DuClare folded her arms and tried to keep a sour expression from her face, as once again Lucius DeBeers projected himself into her personal space without seeking permission.

"Lucius," she began, before he could speak. "It's very late here. What is so important that it couldn't wait until morning?"

Visible across the glass, with the glittering lights of the city laid out behind him, DeBeers resembled a stern portrait of the man come to life, but still trapped in two dimensions. That was the illusion, though. He was a world away from her, and once more he was demonstrating that there was no space she inhabited where he could not enter, night or day.

"The work doesn't run to your schedule, Elizabeth." His tone was cold and clipped, the usual warmth of his manner turned surly. *"Perhaps if you were more aware of that, this situation would be less problematic."*

DuClare guessed that he knew full well she had no idea what he was referring to. It was another tactic to put her off her mark. "If this is about the D-Project—"

"No," he snapped. *"The situation in Detroit. I am only now learning the full scope of this. Actions on the ground have been totally disrupted. It is a mess, Elizabeth. An utter mess."*

"What have we lost?" She hated asking the question, hated looking to him for information. It made her seem weak, which was exactly what DeBeers wanted.

In short order, he gave her a clipped précis of the failure in Michigan. Valuable assets dead. The target package lost, presumed destroyed. Worse still, these events would have a knock-on effect that would damage activities in Europe. Materials needed to achieve certain ends would now be unavailable.

"*This forces us to source new resources from alternate suppliers,*" he concluded. "*That disrupts our timeline.*"

"We'll manage," she said, affecting a tone she hoped would mollify him. "I'll accelerate our other plans to compensate."

DeBeers sniffed. "*I have my doubts.*"

DuClare paused, once more pushed off-balance by his words. "We talked about this, Lucius," she said firmly. "Commitments have been made…"

"*On a great many fronts,*" he broke in. "*And yet there are failures like this.*"

Slowly, her deferential manner eroded. Did he expect her to accept the blame for something barely within her control? It was impossible to account for every single variable. DeBeers knew that better than any of them.

She felt a moment of clarity snap into place. The relationship they had shared, the private conversations, had he done it all just to draw her in and fake a closer confidence? To position her as a receptacle for any failed actions on his part? *How dare he!* If so, then Lucius DeBeers was vainer than DuClare had given him credit for.

"*More errors of judgment like this will not be tolerated,*" he concluded. "*From anyone. You realize that?*"

The threat hung in the air. She nodded. "Perfectly. I'll see to it," promised DuClare, and before he could say any more, she went to the vu-phone and silenced it.

The image of DeBeers vanished from the windows and with a jolt of sudden anger, she picked up the device and threw it violently across the room. It struck the antique clock and both shattered into pieces.

Awake now, propelled by her irritation, she strode to her study and activated her tablet computer with a swipe of her finger. The White Helix files she had been studying were patiently waiting for her, each one labeled individually under a sub-code that connected it to a particular individual. "Open file designation: Black Light," she told it.

On the screen, a dead man's face looked back up at her.

LOCATION UNKNOWN

Random clusters of dead code and forgotten information came closer, falling into rough orbit around one another until some final point of critical mass was exceeded, and abruptly they merged into a kind of island in the open void of deep data-space.

Three avatars coalesced one by one, standing atop the temporary patchwork of the synthetic landscape, each looped in via the lines of a neural subnet linkage. The connections were vague, temporary things written to live only brief lives in the virtual world. It was important to the Collective's continued existence that no trails be left, out in meat space or equally here in the unreal, for their constant foe to latch on to.

"I am monitoring," said the cube of azure crystal. It turned gently on one apex, catching the reflected light of the myriad data trains running high above them. "We need to be quick. One gathering was risky enough… two only invites danger."

"So talk, then." The words came from the only human-like simulacrum in the data-space, the artfully neutral avatar as featureless as ever.

"Where's our fella with the deep pockets?" The sardonic comment emerged from the slowly transforming silver icon that drifted between them. Letters grew from one into another, spelling out nonsense words in Cyrillic.

"He's otherwise engaged," said the cube. "What do you have to tell us?"

"Jensen has agreed to join us," said the metallic symbol. "I honestly had my doubts, but what do I know?"

"You should have believed me," said the human.

"Fine," came the reply. "That's a ten-spot I owe you."

"This is good news." The cube's flat, mechanical voice robbed the statement of any potency. "With Jensen in play, we can increase the tempo of our operations. We can redeploy Saxon and Kelso, and some of the others."

"One step at a time," warned the human avatar. "The Collective is at a critical juncture. The last thing we should do is overreach."

"So which way do we push our new recruit?" said the icon.

The human figure cocked its head. "This is the start of the next phase in our war," insisted the avatar. "But we still have far to go. The heart of the enemy's infiltration of this so-called Task Force is in Eastern Europe. We need to target the unit operating in Prague to root it out at the source."

The cube's rotations slowed. "Who is in command there?"

"This man." A pane of information grew out of the darkness surrounding them, showing stolen fragments of a personnel file. "James Miller. We'll need to determine if he is corrupt, or merely the unwitting tool of others."

The silver icon flickered and changed again. "We'll need to get our boy out there, then. How do we do that?"

"With care." The human avatar gave a ghostly nod. "I believe Adam Jensen is our best option in this scenario. I see how he thinks. I *understand* him." The figure paused. "Now we have him in the fold, he will help us bring down the Illuminati... or he will perish in the attempt."

THE RIALTO – DETROIT –
UNITED STATES OF AMERICA

Jensen watched Pritchard roll the server rig off the stage and into the back of a minivan. Packed in with all the other hardware from his hideout, it barely fit, and the battered vehicle sank low on its shocks as he slammed the rear doors shut.

"You sure that thing will run?" he said, as the hacker came around the front.

"I'm abandoning the building," Pritchard told him. "Even if I have to push this myself." He shook his head. "You would think that the MCBs losing most of their gun hands would be a good thing for the areas outside the police-patrolled zones... but instead it's just stirred up a different kind of anarchy. As hard as it is to believe, Magnet and his goons imposed a violent sort of order. Now every block in Downtown is picking a fight with the next."

"Where are you gonna go?"

Pritchard eyed him. "I've got other places in Detroit. Better that you don't know where, Jensen."

"You have no idea, do you?"

He gave a rueful nod. "I have no idea." He reached into his jacket and produced a pocket secretary, offering the slim digital pad to Jensen. "Here. You should have this."

Jensen took the device, turning it over in his hands. "A farewell gift?" he said dryly. "Francis, I'm touched."

Pritchard scowled back at him. "As I've come to realize how utterly unreasonable you can be, I know there's no point trying to convince you to steer clear of Juggernaut." He pointed at the pad. "So this is all I can do to stop you from getting killed too quickly. On that device is all the data I've gathered over the past two years about everything that we have experienced – the Aug Incident, Sarif, Humanity Front, the conspiracy, all of it. Everything from the day those mercenaries broke into Sarif Industries until right now. If you're determined to throw your life away on this crusade, there may be something in there that can help you."

"Thanks, Pritchard," he said, and this time he meant it.

"Don't get maudlin," sneered the hacker. "I'm not doing this because we are friends. I'm doing it because I believe if anyone can hurt the people behind these acts, it's you. I just don't think you'll live to tell the tale." He shook his head, as if he were considering a puzzle that had no solution. "You're a lot of things, Jensen, but you're not an idiot. Think for a second, and be honest. Why are you *really* determined to do this?"

The answer came to him without pause. "Because someone has to take a stand. And like I told you before, I don't have anything left to lose." He stuffed the digital pad in his pocket. "I do nothing, and I'm complicit in it, you get that? That's how they've got this far. Because too many people looked the other way."

"They? The *Illuminati*?" Pritchard couldn't say the word without sneering.

"What they call themselves isn't important. It never was." Jensen shook his head. "The only thing that matters is that we have to *stop them*. Fight them right to the bloody, bitter end. If not, then one day we wake up and we're living in their future instead of ours."

"You make it sound like the end of the world," said Pritchard.

"Not yet," Jensen told him, as he walked away, "but you can see it from here."

ACKNOWLEDGMENTS

First off, my thanks must go to Mary DeMarle and Rayna Anderson for our collaboration in creating the original version of Adam Jensen's 'missing time' narrative, which this novel draws from. Along with Mary and Rayna, much appreciation is also due to the rest of my colleagues at Eidos Montréal on the *Deus Ex: Mankind Divided* team – among them Jean-Francois Dugas, Jonathan Jacques-Belletête, Jason Dozois, Rees Savidis, Taras Stasiuk, Mark Cecere, Leanne C. Taylor, Jeffery Campbell, Daniel Dick, André Vu, David Anfossi, and many more.

Thanks to my editors Alice Nightingale, Natalie Laverick and Hayley Shepherd at Titan Books for their patience and enthusiasm.

And of course, thank you to the creators of the original *Deus Ex* games – Warren Spector, Harvey Smith, Sheldon Pacotti, Austin Grossman, Chris Todd and the Ion Storm team – for inventing this dynamic fictional future.

ABOUT THE AUTHOR

James Swallow is a writer on *Deus Ex: Mankind Divided* – the latest incarnation of the blockbuster *Deus Ex* videogame series – and was nominated for a BAFTA award for his work on *Deus Ex: Human Revolution*.

He is a *New York Times* bestseller and the author of over forty books, including *Deus Ex: Icarus Effect* and *Deus Ex: Fallen Angel*, *Nomad*, the Scribe award winner *Day of the Vipers*, *The Poisoned Chalice*, *Nemesis*, *The Flight of the Eisenstein*, *Jade Dragon*, The Sundowners series of steampunk Westerns, *The Butterfly Effect* and fiction from the worlds of *24*, *Star Trek*, *Warhammer 40,000*, *Doctor Who*, *Stargate* and *Judge Dredd*.

Swallow's other credits include the critically acclaimed non-fiction work *Dark Eye: The Films of David Fincher*, scriptwriting for *Star Trek Voyager*, videogames and audio dramas.

He lives in London, and is currently working on his next book.